ALCHEMY

a story of perfect murder

CHRIS JAMES

The science is dark ~
too dark for mere mortals.
But alas, it works ~

L. Da Vinci 1507

Be warned thou prying eye
  These formulae thou dost espy
Only those who dare ferment
  Each and every experiment
Shall find the door and turn the key
  To mankind's dream: Immortality

The Trial: Day 2

London, December, 1894

By the time my carriage arrived at the Central Criminal Court in Old Bailey, I doubted that I, an unescorted young lady, could navigate my way unaided through the squalid mob outside. Pie sellers and prostitutes were enjoying a grand trade amid touts offering front row seats and wagers on the outcome of what was to become the trial of the century.

With the assistance of an overweight brute wielding a horsewhip, I ran a gauntlet of urchins and beggars on either side of the stairs, losing a silk kerchief, though gaining an assortment of spittle and minor stains to my outer clothing, none of which I cared for.

Approaching the crowded public gallery, I feared I would be forced to stand throughout the whole proceedings. However, the grateful usher to whom my maid had slipped a half-crown the previous day, duly appeared, bowed and escorted me to my reserved seat, centre front. I did wonder if another half-crown might have quietened those about me or, at least, removed the stench. I was grateful that my maid, who suffered similarly during the tedium of legal arguments and jurors being sworn in the previous day, had thoughtfully provided a pomander of violets. Proceedings were soon underway and I became fully engaged.

As two burly jailers dragged the prisoner up from the cells and shackled him in the dock I was unsure if this was indeed *my* man – the man to whom I owed so much. Eyes buried deep in his battered face, his ragged apparel was no better than that worn by those cursing and spitting about me. I had doubts I was attending the right trial.

The clerk below called for order and insisted that everybody stood, but the mob around me continued to barrage the prisoner with abuse. It wasn't long before someone down there finally brought those up here to order. Hammering his gavel the judge, skeletal to a point of concern, made himself perfectly understood.

'Any more, the lot o' you'll be thrown out. You hear?'

As the charges were read out, all became clear. Jacob Silver, aged just twenty-four, charged with five counts of murder and one of grave robbing, needed me now more than ever – and none was more ready than I to proclaim his innocence.

Well, that was my state of mind at the beginning of the trial, anyway.

Bewigged prosecutor, Mr Percy Ponsonby, QC, I learned later from reports in *The Times*, was aged fifty-five and nicknamed *the showman*. Tall and distinguished, he was not about to disappoint. Defence counsel, Mr Eustace Ecclestone, on the other hand, appeared to sag by comparison and was described in the same paper as *a run-of-the-mill barrister who happened to be passing at the time*. From the look of his attire, they might have added: *and much in need of the money*. I feared the odds were not in my sweetheart's favour.

Standing in front of a long table covered with a white sheet, Mr Ponsonby faced the jury, whose necks strained to determine what props he was about to produce in that day's performance. Grabbing a huge butcher's knife, from which an exhibit label hung, its blade covered with congealed blood, he stabbed the sheet and whipped it away. As it floated to the floor like a cloud, the jurors were mesmerised by what had been concealed.

'He painted beautiful women,' Mr Ponsonby began, studying the jurors' faces. They stared at four framed portraits of young ladies posing provocatively on the same chaise longue. A fifth frame had yet to be uncovered. In front of each portrait stood a smaller object, concealed under another sheet.

Mr Ponsonby walked along the line of portraits, pointing solemnly at each girl with his vulgar knife. 'Polly, Nora, Letty,' he said, pausing at the next, 'and Rebecca, her portrait unfinished, painted moments before her very last breath.'

Dead on cue, those bereaved close by me squealed and groaned, murmuring the deceased's names before fainting and being carried off. They made a remarkable recovery at the top of the stairs, I observed, as their palms were greased by a smart gentleman in a top hat.

Mr Ponsonby flipped off the last portrait's cover. 'And finally, Rebecca's sister – Emily. His lover. Took her own life to save him pain.'

A hundred gasps filled the court. Emily, looked very young and quite exquisite in a billowing white top. Old men in the gallery stood and stared in awe at Emily's beauty, their caps in their hands and tears in their eyes.

Emily posed on the same chaise longue and in addition to a Louis XIV chair, I noticed an open window had been introduced behind her, her hair flowing gloriously in the wind. Using my opera glasses, I saw that out through the window Jacob had painted fine detail of ornate gardens laid around a fountain. And there was something quite shocking. In the trees beyond, a poacher or gamekeeper, judging by the brace of pheasants hanging from his belt, had hold of a naked lady, the lady's identity conveniently concealed by the undergrowth.

In my eyes, Emily's was far more than a painting, it was a story, but I doubted Mr Ponsonby would tell it. After the reverend, behind me, grabbed my glasses and focused them on what I had discovered, all was soon made public, the gallery awash with tittle-tattle.

'And *this* is what I shall prove beyond any shadow of a doubt, this *monster*,' yelled Mr Ponsonby, jabbing the knife at the accused, 'this *murderer*, did to our children!'

Racing along the table, he flicked off the covers in front of the first four portraits, revealing a row of glass jars.

Pickled inside, each girl's severed head.

So, this *was what all the fuss was about.*

Juror number four promptly fainted and tumbled to the floor followed by number six. Other jurors retched, slamming handkerchiefs and sleeves up to their mouths. Women in the gallery swooned, along with the reverend too late to loosen his collar. I turned away from the jars a moment, and was intrigued to see others willingly accept a coin or two to give way for bolder spectators to indulge in the grandstand view. Below, the judge insisted Mr Ponsonby wait until everyone had composed themselves.

The pot in front of Emily's portrait remained covered until Mr Ponsonby, confident he had regained everybody's attention, performed his grand finale.

'These four women,' he said, pointing to the first four jars, 'were sacrificed to save his one true love, Emily.' Mr Ponsonby pointed to Emily's magnificent portrait. 'And this...' he continued, his knife flicking off the sheet covering the last jar, 'is how far he got with her resurrection.'

A stampede quickly emptied the entire gallery.

I remained steadfast, but the sight of poor Emily's rotting and gangrenous head with maggots wriggling in every orifice did have me wishing I was in some other place.

Oh, my darling! Just what have you been up to?

Mr Ponsonby went on for another hour explaining how he would prove my poor Jacob was guilty as charged of killing four of the women, and murdering Police Constable Albert Everett.

He then called uniformed Police Sergeant Frank Beck as his first witness. Constantly referring to his notes, moustached Sergeant Beck, a softly-spoken man of about forty, presented his evidence confidently like an officer familiar with heinous crime.

'I went to his home where I found him surrounded by a mob of women after his blood. He asked to be taken into protective custody and was taken to Charing Cross police station,' Sergeant Beck began.

'So you hadn't told him why you had gone to see him. Once at the police station, what were his first words?'

Beck read out loud from his notes: ' "The professor. We were working on something. He needed– He's slaughtered my poor girls. We must find him, stop him!" '

'You pressed him further on what they were working on?'

'I did, sir. He said: "You wouldn't understand. It's science. Medieval science. A book he gave me: *Alchemy*." '

'Now, his address at Victoria Embankment, sergeant. Was this the first time you had been called there?'

'No, sir. Although it was a long time before, in December, 1885, to be precise. The accused was fifteen at the time.'

'And what was found on that occasion, sergeant?'

'A body, sir.'

Chapter 1

London, June, 1885

It was my fifteenth birthday, the seventeenth of June. I couldn't wait to get home and show Papa my latest drawing. My teacher wanted to buy it, but, as I told her, I would need to speak to Papa first.

It was almost dark as I ran along the Embankment and seeing the gas lamp flickering down in the basement, I knew Papa would be preparing medicines for the evening trade.

'Papa! Papa! I've sold my first picture!'

As I hopped up onto the bench beside him, Papa laughed. 'There! A professional now. And will I have to pay to see it?'

'I wouldn't let her have it, Papa, not until you'd seen it. Here.' I pulled the drawing from my satchel. Papa's face lit up, but then it always did. 'Is it good, Papa? Will I be famous?'

'Bootiful,' he said. 'Absolutely bootiful. Your best yet, Jacob. Go show your mother, then come and help me down here for a while. Need to finish early tonight. It's someone's birthday, I'm told.'

Papa was an apothecary, like his father and two generations before him. My great grandfather, Hirschel Silberstein, was a Prussian and had fought at Waterloo alongside the Iron Duke, Wellington, as a senior medical officer. Hirschel brought his small Jewish family to London, settling in the East End near Aldgate where he set up shop. But continuing with his profession as an apothecary was more difficult than he envisaged. As a form of trade protection from the unworthy or unqualified, the livery companies of the City of London, known as the *Worshipful Companies* or *Societies*, forbade membership by any non-Christian, or more exactly, anyone failing to take their Christian Oath, until 1830.

'Blow their licensing,' Hirschel declared, ' We'll just trade quietly, unofficially.'

Attending appreciative hard-up patients quietly and cheaply, he was the most qualified quack of his day, Papa often reminded me. Some of Papa's remedies still used today were prepared exactly as concocted by Hirschel and *did the job better than most,* prescribing doctors would begrudgingly admit after their English medicines failed.

The Jewishness of my family wore thin after Hirschel passed, leaving a wife and two sons: Jacob, my grandfather, and his brother, Abel. Both had children, and pregnant wives.

'If a simple oath is all that stands in the way of making a proper living, we're better off taking the damn thing, rather than go to jail – and the rabbi be damned,' Grandpapa Jacob told them all. So take it they did.

As punishment, attendance at the Aldgate synagogue was denied them for decades. But the Worshipful Society of Apothecaries welcomed them with open arms. In retaliation, the now successful Silberstein clan, fearless of the fire and brimstone threatened by the rabbi, adopted the more acceptable surname of Silver.

Mother was Catholic, and since Papa, a generation later, was included as part of that gang of reprobates who denied their faith, he argued that their marriage would really give the synagogue something to complain about. It was only when I was born that Papa decided he should repair bridges and made a generous donation to the synagogue's repairs appeal that the local rabbi welcomed them back into the fold, Mama adopting the Jewish faith, though half-heartedly. Alas, this threw more grief my way, circumcision not least, as well as learning and continually reciting the Old Testament, then the mitzvoth, and now I was fifteen, the Talmud, for which I held much dread. Reading and writing Hebrew was deemed compulsory.

Our home, and the business conducted within it – under it to be precise – sat on the Victoria Embankment facing the River Thames at Blackfriars. The property boasted two stories of living accommodation above the shop, as well as a small parlour behind it, and an attic with a huge skylight under a flat roof, a natural place for an artist's studio. The business consisted of all the ground floor and the laboratory basement. It was near enough for city folk and those employed in London's largest markets and on the river, and within easy reach of the Inns of Court. Papa treated all customers the same; judges waited their turn behind pimps and prostitutes – *ladies of the night,* as Papa called them – and on more than one occasion embarrassment had been caused by one's recognition of the other, from other places of business, no doubt. Customers were served by way of a hatch at a side door ever since the shop had been robbed by French sailors, released after Napoleon's defeat some seventy years before, the story goes. The front of the shop facing the street was still boarded up. The mighty River Thames was just across the street.

That night, I had recited nineteen Latin, Russian, Polish and Greek verb conjugations to Papa's satisfaction by the time we were on to our last order in the smoke and fumes down there. And then came a loud knock at the front door, which only salesmen or private visitors used.

'If they're selling, send them away,' Papa said. 'If it's Mrs Greenstein for more sugar, tell her we're out and to try the rabbi.'

I ran upstairs and opened the door to an elderly, cloaked man carrying a silver-handled walking stick and a large, wrapped package. A top hat cast shadows over his face, revealing only a large wrinkly nose. He touched the brim of his hat.

'Jacob Silver the artist, I presume?' I nodded, flattered that my fame had spread so soon. 'I've come to see the apothecary,' he said and pushed his way inside. He walked with a stoop, leaning on his stick.

'Someone to see you, Papa,' I said, entering the laboratory where Papa was bent over double, coughing in a thick yellow smog.

'Well, ask who it is. I'm in the middle of dispens—'

'Too much sodium I fear, Mr Silver!' our visitor exclaimed, stepping inside the laboratory. Painfully thin, with a yellowed, cadaverous face and bony hands, his eyes appeared almost black in the gaslight down there. He had pure white, fluffy mutton-chop sideburns that stretched down into a scraggly white beard. 'From the Institute, sir. A delivery.' He offered me the package but Papa intervened, grabbing it and turning it this way and that before shoving it back to our visitor.

'They give nought away. I've no money,' Papa growled.

'For the boy's birthday. Without cost, catch or encumbrance, sir,' he insisted, pushing the parcel back to Papa.

Papa turned it upside down suspiciously.

'But they ask that you cover my delivery expenses.'

Papa thrust the package back to him. 'Knew there was a catch.'

'No catch, sir. A mere gesture of appreciation.'

Such a large package! I prayed it would stay and thought I could help negotiations by tendering the earnings from my drawing.

'Will a tanner cover it, sir?'

'A tanner indeed. Thank you, my boy,' and finally, the package rested with me. 'May it inspire your imagination,' he said, pocketing my sixpence before wiping his wet nose on the back of his hand.

Papa grunted his displeasure. 'Show our visitor out. Open it later.'

I took the old man back up to the front door where I asked, 'And who should I be thanking, sir?' but he seemed not to hear and walked off into the night.

It would be a year before I met him again.

After dinner, I blew out the candles on my birthday cake and unwrapped some oranges, a new school satchel and the usual, shiny, freshly-minted silver sixpence from my Aunt Alice. Then, at last, I was allowed to leave the table and set about ripping the brown paper off the gift from the Institute.

It was an ancient tome, its flaking title etched in gold on the weather-beaten leather cover: *Alchemy*.

'Why they'd send anything here after forty years...' Papa said as I curled up in a chair by the fire with the book. 'There's a catch. You'll see.'

A self-portrait drawing by Leonardo da Vinci lay loose inside the front cover. It appeared to be original – and had me mesmerised. The old master had long been my hero; my bedroom walls a testament to my admiration for him.

'He's talking to it,' Mama said. 'Having a conversation with a book, indeed. We done the right thing letting him have it, d'you think, Stanley?'

But Papa, hovering over my shoulder as I turned the pages, was equally smitten by the illustrations of witches and demons at work.

The following day I had a further treat in store, my first visit to the National Gallery. As we climbed the steps outside, Papa pointed to the bronze lions guarding the fountains in Trafalgar Square.

'My father brought me here on *my* fifteenth birthday, the day they installed those lions. And a very special painting was on loan here before being taken to the Louvre, in Paris and exhibited there.'

I was fascinated by the huge canvasses on display as Papa led me inside and into a large hall where a crowd jostled around one particular painting, all others completely ignored.

'Is it the same painting, Papa?' I asked, pointing to a sign hanging from the ceiling.

'On loan from The Louvre – Paris'.

'We'll have to wait and see, Jacob. I'm just as excited as you are,'

Papa said, holding a small bunch of cornflowers he had purchased from a vendor on the steps.

I questioned why people would wait for anything so long and it seemed an age before we finally got to the front. And then I knew why.

'Tell me what you see, what you feel,' Papa said, smiling at my gaping mouth.

'I see the greatest painting of all time. By the greatest artist and scientist of all time. My master. My inspiration. I feel... I feel drawn to it. Like I'm part of it – it's part of me. I *have* to touch it! I *must*.'

Papa laughed, his hand firmly on my shoulder.

'You can't. It's a priceless treas–'

But I wriggled free and ducked under the rope barrier. I reached out, my fingers lightly touching the crackled varnish. Oblivious to the groans and gasps from the crowd, I was in a different place; the revered artist's world, his kingdom. I trembled as something coursed through my whole being, and my hands and legs shook. The room about me turned dark with just a bright light emanating from the painting, drawing me in. I couldn't breathe, my throat constricted. Her smile pulled me ever closer. As I touched her face, a bolt shot through my whole body.

She had me at her mercy.

'You, boy!'

I heard it, but it came from outside that world. Suddenly, a sharp pain in my right ear. Twisting. Pulling me, dragging me back to my papa.

'Stay behind the barrier,' clearer now as the room illuminated once again. Papa spoke to the uniformed guard while I caught my breath.

'She spoke to me, Papa.'

'Jacob, what has got into you, boy? You'll have us thrown out!'

'She spoke to me, Papa. Did you hear her?'

'Mona Lisa hasn't spoken to anybody for nigh on four hundred years.' He dragged me over to a bench, sat me down hard. 'Stay there while I go and apologise. Move an inch and they'll come and lock you up.'

The crowd gawping at me was almost as large as that gawping at the Mona Lisa behind them. I pulled a sketch pad from my satchel and some crayons, hoping they'd disappear. I always sketched quickly. As my hand flashed across the page most of the gawpers had made their way behind me to look at what I was drawing.

I found it amusing as whispers rustled through the small crowd until those whispering inched closer and began to block my light. A young lady carrying a blue-and-white-striped parasol sidled up to me.

'Could I have it when it's done, young sir? I'll pay you.'

She was of rare beauty and not being accustomed to speaking to young ladies I was quite taken aback, too nervous to speak. She took a coin out of her purse, held it up to me.

'Would a half-crown cover it?'

I stopped sketching and looked up into her lovely smiling face – just as she screamed. A wench in tattered clothes had her by her golden hair and wrestled her to the floor.

'Out've it, you hag!' the wench screamed, pulling her away from me across the tiled floor before snatching the girl's half-crown, leaping over her, and squatting at my feet. She promptly ripped open her bodice, baring her breast. Ignoring my embarrassment, she grabbed my hand and thrust in on to her dark nipple, then pressed the stolen half-crown between my fingers. 'Paint me, boy! Make me immortal!' she yelled, breaking into raucous laughter.

A half-dozen women turned and fled, dragging their children along with them. The men seemed to find her performance intriguing and laughed along with her.

I feigned concentration with the drawing in progress, taking an occasional glimpse at the young lady with the parasol as she was helped to her feet and straightened her clothes. Fortunately, the wench lost interest and moved off with two grinning soldiers, leaving room for others to see my work.

'Talented boy you have, sir,' a gentleman said to my papa. When I stood to greet Papa, holding up the painting, my private audience broke into applause. Papa seemed to put my disgrace aside and suggested I took a bow. No sooner than I did so and people thrust coins at me, begging me to sell them my sketch.

'Miss!' I called out to the parasol as it made its way out. I caught up with her, tore the picture from my sketch pad and presented it to her with a bow. 'I'd like you to have this.'

The smile she gave me as she looked directly into my eyes was worth a hundred times more than anything offered thus far.

'The Mona Lisa,' she said. 'My very own copy. Thank you. I shall treasure it.'

'My sincere apologies,' I began, offering back her half-crown, 'for the way–'

She shook her head, gave me another beautiful smile. 'No, no. You earned it. It's a fair exchange. Besides, this may be worth far more when you're famous.' She turned to walk away, then looked back, 'You'll most probably be used to women fighting over you by then.'

And with that she was gone.

Papa took me through numerous other rooms in the gallery and it was as we stood in front of the giant masterpiece, William Sadler's *Battle of Waterloo*, that I learned the purpose of the blue cornflowers Papa had purchased. Papa nodded to the uniformed guard we had confronted earlier and handed me the small bunch of flowers. The guard lifted the satin rope barrier, and stood smartly to attention.

'You may enter, Master Silver,' the guard snapped, talking to a spot on the wall way above my head.

'In the front, attending the wounded soldier in Prussian blue, Captain Herschil Silberstein. Your great grandfather,' Papa said quietly, a tear in his eye. 'The wounded man, his brother Abel. The last man to die at Waterloo, on the eighteenth of June, 1815.' Tears welled in Papa's eyes. I was humbled. After Papa explained the cornflower was the national flower of Prussia I took the posy and laid it beneath the painting, bowed solemnly and returned beyond the barrier. The guard stood proudly to attention and saluted the painting, before replacing the satin rope. I had never seen Papa in such sorrow.

'We can always come back another day, Papa. You will see them again.'

But that was not to be.

This, the seventieth anniversary, would be his final day of remembrance of Great Uncle Abel and Napoleon's defeat.

Outside on the gallery steps the boisterous wench managed one last taunt exposing her bare thigh to me and ensuring I noted the absence of any drawers. But it was the far prettier young woman walking away with her parasol who held my attention – an aura about her head positively glowing.

'What did you feel when you touched the Mona Lisa?' Papa asked. 'You seemed to come over all funny.'

'Dizzy. Something seemed to dive down inside me, choke me. I can't explain. Did the lights go out? I was in a tunnel.'

As we walked on past the fountains Papa added, 'Some believe they used trickery, you know. Da Vinci, Michelangelo and Isaac Newton, all messed with alchemy. Newton said that the gravitational pull their works possessed was far greater than anything he measured in the universe. It's like they concocted potions to draw people to their paintings.'

'Sorcery?'

'Some such wizardry. Take Da Vinci, that crowd in there. Made himself immortal through his art. Did he find a way to provoke people's emotions, perhaps, mix them with the paint?'

'Put something in jars, Papa?'

'Might have. Imagine bottling that? Sell like hot cakes over our counter.' He laughed. 'Tuppence to cry. A tanner to smile.'

'And what price happiness, Papa?'

He hugged me, kissed my head. 'Priceless, son. Priceless.'

A last glance over my shoulder and there was the striped parasol heading off around a corner.

'What emotion is it when you look at someone and you can't look away; seeing them makes you feel all warm inside?'

'Best ask your mother,' he said, laughing.

'Could I do what the old masters did?'

'I doubt you'd ever need to, Jacob. People everywhere will desire your paintings. Never forget that.'

'I meant bottle emotions. Could I do it?'

A hackney carriage pulled up, the horse all skin and bone, and we climbed aboard. As it pulled away, 'If anyone could, you would surely be the one, Jacob,' Papa said, laughing.

'Then I will. And I won't give up till I perfect it. I'll start with a giggle. That'll be worth a bob or two.'

It was only a couple of days after that wonderful birthday that my life changed for ever – and I would dwell in a black hole, from which I feared climbing out of might take an eternity.

I had gone to my room early, content to sketch from the Da Vinci posters Papa brought back from the gallery. A little after midnight, mother shook me and urged me follow her with her lantern into their bedroom. Papa was struggling for breath, his forehead burning up. I sent Mama for the doctor and dashed downstairs, returning with a stethoscope, applying it all over his chest and back. Congestion was very apparent and unaware of when the doctor would appear I applied hot towels to Papa's chest, bringing him some relief. Mother returned but only with instructions from the doctor who had declined a personal attendance. It must have been four in the morning when, after everything the doctor had recommended failed to improve his breathing, I decided to consult *Alchemy*, searching through the numerous languages for a solution. I quickly made up a concoction and together we sat Papa up and poured it into him. Assuming my Latin was sufficient, *Alchemy* claimed it would *clear the stuffed pipes in many an organ*. And so it did. Within minutes Papa was chatting and laughing and thanking us for saving his life. It was a wonderful experience and I went back to bed satisfied that, with my wonderful book, I had within my grasp the makings of magical cures for every illness under the sun.

Tragically, I soon learned this was not to be.

At eight, as Mama was attending to the first customers banging on our door for prescriptions, I found poor Papa in bed in a far worse condition than the night before. I called out to Mama who came rushing up the stairs. Papa pulled me close, whispered in my ear.

'It's over, Jacob. My–'

'No, Papa. You'll get better. I'll make you better. I'll pray for you.'

He ignored me, his voice just a faint whisper. 'Find the secret. Make yourself... immort–'

'I will, Papa, I promise. Stay a while longer. Just a while.' His eyes remained still and glazed. I held up a sixpence. 'A tanner for one last smile, Papa.' I placed it on his lips but Mama shook her head solemnly and brushed his eyes closed.

We both stared at him, tears rolling off both our faces. The knocking downstairs rose to a crescendo by the time Mama pried my hands free from Papa's.

'How we going to manage now, Jacob?'

I cried myself to sleep for two nights after losing dear Papa, but our very survival took my mind off grief. I had overhead Mama dismissing the housekeeper and imagined that was one of the sacrifices needed now the breadwinner was no longer with us. But it was some time later when I realised the housekeeper's removal was part of a grand plan – and the removal of witnesses.

A neighbour's child was sent with a note to my school claiming I needed some time off to recover – from our recent loss, I presumed. I then had the task of hanging a notice on the front gate informing customers *The apothecary is indisposed, and* – more mysteriously – *will return shortly.*

At the back of the laboratory mother had me clear a space where we set down a tin bath retrieved from the garden shed. Then I was instructed to meet the wholesaler's dray out the front and help him unload fifteen carboys, large glass bottles of formaldehyde, standing them next to the tin bath.

Exhausted after unloading, I sat down to catch my breath in the downstairs parlour. That was when I heard the thump, thump, thump, coming from the stairs. Looking up from the bottom of the stairs I could not believe my eyes.

'You'd better give me a hand, Jacob. Might drop him else.'

Mama was dragging and bumping poor Papa's deathly-white body down the stairs. Believing the intention was a pauper's burial, and the price of transportation perhaps out of our reach, I duly assisted. But instead of turning right at the bottom of the stairs and passing out through the front door, we went straight on – and all the way to the laboratory in the basement.

Being assured all would be explained later, I helped strip Papa's body, lift him into the tin bath, and pour in the formaldehyde with an equal measure of water. Finally, a heavy canvas sheet was pulled over the top, giving poor Papa a modicum of dignity.

The explanation was forthcoming after I had cried myself completely dry and was in no state to argue.

'We continue dispensing. Anyone asks, Papa's unwell. Who's ever going to know? Once you get your sustificates, you can carry on in your father's footsteps.'

Warned it was this way or the workhouse, I concurred and took up studying the apothecary's bible, the pharmacopeia, until all hours. I was also enrolled for classes once a week at Apothecaries Hall, for almost six months. Those *sustificates*, as Mama called them, did seem a long way off.

Having imagined a three-month initiation would enable me to cope with only minor ailments it did come as quite a bolt from the blue when, only four days after Papa's demise, Mama insisted we open for *business as usual.*

Passing me Papa's apron, she gave me a couple of prescriptions to prepare and, before I had deciphered the handwriting on those, she went off and attended to frenzied knocking at the serving hatch. Word travelled fast. Before lunch I had two dozen remedies on the boil with only a fifty per cent expectation that those were in fact the remedies prescribed.

One particular doctor's writing left too many unknowns and I was forced to ask Mama for advice on what to do next.

'Can't go and ask the doctor, Jacob, your father knew everything he prescribed. He'd know something was up.' It wasn't long before Mama recalled an old apothecary's rhyme. 'Papa used to sing it to you, remember?'

I didn't.

'Line up the likely remedies, then eliminate.' She started off, 'Eeny meeny, topsy turvy.'

It flooded back to me. 'Take some... No. Take these pills to stop the scurvy.' We finished it together.

'If he hollers let him rest, take a powder to digest.'

Although we laughed and danced round the laboratory with a few more renditions until only one medicine remained, I felt I had to spoil her gaiety.

'But it wasn't serious, Mama. Papa only sang it to cheer me.'

'Can be as serious as we need it to be,' she said sternly.

And so it was. Customers flocked to our door, despite our dubious professionalism. New customers, too. It was a while before I realised I had not been accounting for bottles and overheads in pricing the items we dispensed. Not wishing to worry Mama, I simply increased the prices to ensure the next lot were fully paid for – business slacking off sufficiently so that at least I could return to school and attend Apothecaries Hall to study for the examination. But I rarely got to bed before midnight.

It was six months before Mama asked me to try on a fake moustache she'd made from cat hair and gelatine and go sit my first examinations. I couldn't summon the courage to tell her the moustache fell off until after she opened the results.

'Your first sustificate,' she said, hugging me. 'I'm so proud of you.'

But her pride was short-lived.

A veiled Mrs Blenkensop, head-to-toe in black and beside herself with grief, was brought into the parlour where she showed Mama medicines that had apparently failed. I could hear Mama comforting the woman, offering condolences and then saw her glaring at the labels before showing Mrs B out.

'Two drops a day. Not two spoonfuls! You killed the poor bugger!' Mama yelled at me, standing in the doorway with her hands on her hips.

I felt awful and my eyes welled with tears for poor Mr Blenkensop. Mother soon comforted me, but only after she destroyed the offending label.

'To be expected, I s'pose. Can't make a soufflé without breaking a few eggs.'

My confidence renewed, I returned to the bench and compiled concoctions with gusto – checking every label three times over from that day on.

It was only a day or two after that incident that the rabbi called, seeking a donation from Papa, his yapping Jack Russell straining on a leash. He complained to me that Papa had not attended the synagogue of late, while Mama went off upstairs.

'We've been so busy,' I said, making excuses for Papa. Nothing was more truthful.

So grateful was he for the five shillings Mama produced, *from the man upstairs* she told him, that the rabbi dropped the leash and the dog darted off through the laboratory. Pursuing the dog, the rabbi discovered him worrying a canvas sheet in the back. And that was when he found the lost sheep from his flock, submerged in the tin bath. Papa resembled a bleached prune.

Despite my protesting Mama's innocence and being prepared to face the consequences myself, the police would not listen, claiming they had a full confession. Mama claimed she had prepared every prescription herself; a temporary measure until I was fully qualified. She was in tears the whole time she appeared in the dock, the public gallery full of customers of ours hurling abuse.

'Swing the cow,' one bereaved woman shouted.

'Murdered me ma!' yelled a docker I'd often served.

'Poison the bitch, like she did our gel,' a mother shouted.

The judge called for order. The clerk bade the jailers make the accused stand.

'Ethel Agnes Silver, you have been found guilty of eight charges of manslaughter. Claiming your husband died only the day before was preposterous and you have shown no remorse. You are evil, madam, and caused many a premature death. You'll go to prison for the rest of your natural life.'

Apparently, it was only because *malice aforethought* could not be proven, that Mama escaped the death penalty.

I remained alone at home for a few weeks until my teacher, Mrs Seagal, came calling, concerned by my absence from school. Seeing my condition, she sent word to my Aunt Alice. I don't recall a lot of what happened afterwards, except that I was confined to bed and instructions were given that no outsiders were to call. During the contagious stage, every bone in my body felt like it had been put through a mangle.

Six months passed before the pain subsided and some sort of normality returned. I couldn't wait to return to school.

'Jacob needs your help now, children,' Mrs Seagal told them. 'Who would like to sit next to him?'

I could tell from the look on their faces that not one of them would volunteer for fear of catching whatever it was that had deformed my legs and knees so. How my friends had changed in those few months. It broke my heart. As I staggered out into the schoolyard later, a novice on my clanking leg irons, the ridicule and abuse was too much to bear and I begged to stay inside and study rather than play with my peers. I owed much to Mrs Seagal. She forwent morning and afternoon breaks to provide me with additional personal tuition that served to keep my mind off my infliction. After school, she escorted me to the British Library where, she claimed, everything she had been unable to answer, from my intense questioning, would be explained in every detail. Papa had enrolled me at the library the day I was born.

But when left to my own resources, my iron legs and knees so ravaged by polio set me wondering if the girl with the blue-and-white parasol would fight over me now.

Chapter 2

Northamptonshire, 1886-1888

Greenwold Hall, amid five thousand acres just to the east of the Spencer's Althorp estates, was once home to a mysterious French aristocrat who was gifted the magnificent house by Cromwell after betraying and handing over King Charles I who had sought refuge with him. In appreciation of the hospitality granted by the English, upon the Frenchman's demise the house was bequeathed to the state *to benefit youth education*. A secret elite order won possession for a peppercorn rent, converting the house into a college to educate their offspring and opened enrolment to anyone with the ability to pay their extortionate fees. It would be later forced upon them to offer a scholarship, limited to one place each year. Females were deemed unfit for consideration, regardless of fees or bribes offered.

Headmaster Harold Fellows stood in front of his board of governors one winter's evening in early 1886 dreading the task before him; persuading this group of aged men and one woman, all of upper class, that what had been good for Greenwold for almost two hundred years was not good enough now. His hawk-like demeanour that commanded instant obedience from every boy attending this college for the privileged counted little with the governors. Many a headmaster attempting to change their ways in the past had simply been replaced, including the one who presented a cast-iron case for Queen Victoria's niece to be taught there.

But Fellows stuck to his principles.

'It's not a case of take them or leave them. It's quite clear.' He held up the letter from the county authorities that had caused so much concern. 'Admit *one* less-privileged child every year or we lose our charitable status, and pay higher taxes.'

'We took one. I remember. Cost us the earth,' objected an octogenarian near the front.

'Barely came up to the mark,' yelled another.

'*We* choose our pupils, not the government,' the elderly woman whined.

'But we've no choice in the matter, unless you agree to forego the tax allowances,' Fellows continued, causing many a groan.

'We took two last Christmas,' a clergyman threw in.

'Because we took none the year before, Reverend,' Fellows pointed out. 'I have—' He waited until the dissenters quietened, then tried again. 'There's one boy, particularly bright...'

'Special is he?' from a long grey beard at the back.

'Well, yes. He *is* special.' Fellows held up a list. 'Highest score on the scholarship list, and by a substantial margin.' That held their attention. 'Highest in English, mathematics, geography, biology and science; fluent in six languages including Latin and classical Greek, and a brilliant artist, according to his teacher.'

'That's all very well, Fellows,' from the front now, 'but what breeding does he have? Who's his father?'

'Far more important,' a colonel with a waxed moustache agreed.

Fellows waited for the chants of *hear, hear* to diminish.

'Gentlemen, please! This is someone able to shine. The boy could be a credit to us. Someone we should be proud to shape in the Greenwold mould.'

'But is he a man of God, a Christian? The place might go to ruin if we carry on like this,' the clergyman again.

Louder *hear, hears* to that.

'The boy—' Fellows stopped, turned to the cleric. 'Is that so important, Reverend? We have a Hindu. And doing very well, I might add.'

'But the son of a Raj, for heaven's sake. Highly acceptable,' the colonel offered.

'I would remind you that our benefactor didn't have too good a reputation so far as God was concerned. The boy is—' Fellows hesitated, unsure they were ready for this. 'The boy is—'

'Spit it out, man!' the colonel demanded.

'Devil got your tongue, Fellows?' from the reverend.

'The boy is...' Fellows looked around the room. 'Jewish.'

'He's *what*?' they yelled in unison.

In torrential rain a carriage turned into the extensive grounds and four sweating horses pulled-up in front of the historic oak doors. The solitary passenger disembarked.

'Jacob Silver, sir.'

Outside the open doors, Jacob stood in the porch; dripping wet, a sodden satchel sloshing at his hip and his leg braces vibrating noisily as he shivered.

Lofty Housemaster Williams, aghast at the new boy's appearance, summoned two boys of Jacob's age and barked orders without so much as look at the new arrival.

'He's in your dorm, Muxlow. Show him around, clean him up and feed him. He learns the rules before lights out, reports to me at nine tomorrow sharp.' Williams left them to it.

A pug-nosed, spotty-faced boy, standing a good foot taller than Jacob, stood menacingly close to him.

'I'm Bateman. You call me sir.'

Jacob held out his hand. Sneering, Bateman ignored it.

'I'm Jacob. Jacob Silver. Pleased to–'

'You're *yid* here. Geddit? Baggage?'

Jacob nodded to the satchel hanging from his shoulder.

'No, your stuff, idiot. You'll be living here, remember?'

Embarrassed, Jacob touched the satchel again, nodded.

Muxlow, a much smaller and friendlier boy smothered in freckles, shook Jacob's hand. 'Hello, Jake. I'm Muxlow. Let me help you.' He grabbed Jacob's satchel. 'Ignore Bateman, he's an arsehole.'

Jacob laughed.

Bully Bateman grabbed Muxlow around the neck and the smaller boy began to tremble.

'Another word, poop-face–'

Thwack! A leg brace in Bateman's crotch. He yelled as he toppled over. Jacob steadied himself on the now grinning Muxlow.

'We'll be great friends, Jake. Come on.' Muxlow led him upstairs, Bateman still rolling on the floor groaning, his hands between his legs.

At breakfast Jacob ate alone in a corner but could feel a hundred pairs of eyes drilling into him from the other boys, all silent and rigidly sitting up straight. A master prowled covertly with a cane.

Thwack! As it dealt with elbows on tables.

Jacob held his knife and fork left-handed.

Thwack! The cane smashed across his knuckles. Jacob winced in agony as the tip of the cane guided the cutlery into the correct hands. Hand swollen, Jacob struggled to eat as Bateman sniggered behind him, urging others to ridicule him.

Housemaster Williams took a book from hundreds lining his office, opened it and passed it to Jacob. 'Aloud,' he ordered.

Jacob studied the page, stammered and stuttered, until...

'They said you knew Greek,' the teacher said.

Jacob went to a shelf, pulled out a book, then two others. Opening a book entitled: *Ancient Greek* and with its script in Cyrillic, Jacob recited lyrically in English.

' "I don't need a friend who changes when I change and who nods when I nod. My shadow does that so much better." ' He turned a page. ' "Youth is the best time to be rich," ' and choked, ' "and the best time to be poor." ' Opening a second book entitled: *Hebrew Philosophy* at a random page printed in Hebrew: ' "The commandment *thou shalt not kill*, confirms we are descended from generations of murderers—" '

'You read Yiddish?' interrupted the housemaster.

'Hebrew, to be exact, sir.'

'You practise your faith?'

'Since my father died, sir, and *this...*' Jacob looked down at his leg irons, 'I'm finding it difficult to believe in any god.'

'We don't have the facilities here. You would have to find a synagogue nearby, if there is such a thing.'

'My mother was Catholic. I'd like to explore that further, if I may?'

'There are many Catholics here. Muxlow's Catholic. I'm sure they'll make you feel most welcome. Do you have any other languages?' his tutor asked.

'Six, sir.'

Jacob Silver was a star pupil, as far as the tutors were concerned. Unfortunately, the crippled *poor* boy in their midst only highlighted the inadequacies of most other pupils who had always felt that their titles and family wealth meant they never had to try very hard to succeed. The sons of warmongers and the aristocracy, feeling humiliated by young Silver, found their parents more supportive in arranging for the boy's removal rather than attempt an academic battle they would only lose. Threats of removing their darlings and the consequential loss of income, had the school agree to Master Silver receiving private tutorship together with sworn assurances that their boys' performances would not be compared to his.

Jacob's separation did spare him the ridicule and often physical abuse he had received from his peers when entering or leaving classes, reducing it only to occasions when their paths crossed, in the bath house or on the way to the dormitories or dining hall. That wasn't often enough for Bateman, who organised night raids on

Jacob's dormitory, when anything of any importance was stolen or damaged and anyone in the way throttled. Fortunately, Jacob's one treasure, *Alchemy*, remained unharmed, being well concealed beneath his mattress.

Lying awake from a particularly severe beating after being ambushed by Bateman's boys in the middle of the night, Jacob went in search of his one and only ally, Muxlow. Finding his friend stripped, gagged and tied to a tree in the grounds, Jacob vowed the culprits would pay, but Muxlow's subsequent pneumonia and delirium wiped their names from his memory, he told Jacob. The truth was that the boy feared for his life and could name every boy who laid into him. The two never spoke of the lack of supervision, and the convenient absence of the duty master during often outrageous disturbances. Their fathers were neither lords nor leaders, and ordinary Tommy Muxlow and Jacob Silver accepted this was their lot, that the pain would get easier once their bodies grew accustomed to it or when the bullies finally left the college.

Jacob sat on the edge of Muxlow's bed in the sickbay, sketching. When he'd finished he showed his friend the caricature he'd made of Bateman. Muxlow was cheered. He loved the finishing touch and Jacob left him with it before going back to the dormitory.

Neither of them noticed little Rachman, a timid boy who looked no older than twelve or so but was in fact their age, and a follower of Bateman. Rachman appeared at sleeping Muxlow's bedside soon after Jacob left and found the drawing of Bateman. After laughing at it, he put it in his pocket, certain it would earn him more respect from Bateman, after he'd shown it to him. It then struck Rachman that Muxlow would be beaten harder, as a consequence. The timid boy couldn't stomach that and so kept the drawing hidden. It was to have a profound effect on the little man and he kept it for years, never dreaming it would become evidence in a murder trial.

Muxlow lost many a night's sleep concerned that the missing drawing might get back to Bateman.

Back in the dormitory, Jacob, too, was about to have a profound experience, *his* affecting the rest of his life.

In the early hours, Jacob awoke and saw an elderly cloaked figure hovering over his open book: *Alchemy*, with a lantern. Standing next to him was a woman as round as she was tall – the school matron, Betsy Pollock. The old man turned pages and tutted and cursed before walking off, his cane tapping his way out of the dormitory, Betsy following in his wake. Bearded and walking with a stoop, Jacob had a strong feeling he recognised the man, and slipped out of bed to see what had annoyed him.

The book was open at a chapter entitled: *Desire*. Scattered on the floor were ten of Jacob's drawings – each depicting a girl with a striped parasol in a different pose, the girl from the National Gallery.

Jacob gathered up the drawings, shoved them back in the book and crept out of the dormitory with it under his arm. He caught up with the pair just before they turned a corner into the Corridor of Alumni. As Jacob turned the same corner the man was nowhere to be seen; Matron waddling away down the long straight corridor, alone. Jacob passed under the portraits of earls and generals, prime ministers and the aristocracy, pressing himself against the oak panelling for fear of being seen.

When he was directly under the portrait of Greenwold Hall's original owner, the illusive Frenchman who had betrayed King Charles, the panel gave way and Jacob fell into a cobwebbed stone stairway. The panel slammed shut behind him. Down in the distance he could make out a lantern flickering as it moved away. He quickened his pace. The stench of dank walls. Water dripping. Mice scurried, frightening him. Black fungi shapes reached out from the walls as if to grab him. He was becoming more anxious and about to turn back when the stairs opened into a labyrinth of cavernous tunnels bathed in flickering candle light, with shadows blacker than black cast in every alcove and up onto the high vaulted ceiling.

'Hello?' he called out, nervously. 'Is there anybody there?'

Jacob peered into the caverns, but could neither see nor hear a thing, until... Voices. Whispering. Echoing and laughing.

'Find the secret. I will, Papa. I promise. A tanner to smile. Imagine bottling that.'

Jacob squeezed his eyes closed, stood perfectly still. The voices faded away.

Then, breathing. Behind him. He turned. Startled. The old man's huge wrinkled nose an inch in front of his own.

Alchemy crashed onto the flagstone floor.

'I'm... I'm sorry, sir,' Jacob stammered, staggering backwards. 'I didn't...' He scrabbled on the floor, picking up his scattered drawings for a second time this evening, shoving them back in the book.

'What is it you're trying to bottle, young man?' the old man said.

'There's a secret, sir. I promised my father I would find the secret,' Jacob responded nervously. 'How the old masters found immortality.'

'And you believe there is such a secret?'

'My father was seldom wrong, sir. He said Newton was on to it.'

'Indeed he was. But Newton wouldn't listen, would he? Not to Da Vinci, nor anybody else,' the old man said, extending his bony hands to take the book from Jacob. He opened it on a low wall that resembled a sarcophagus.

'Newton *met* Da Vinci, sir?' Jacob questioned, but it wasn't answered. After turning a few pages the old man swung back round to Jacob.

'Well, come back next Thursday and we'll get started, shall we?' He touched his nose then ran his fingers through his ragged beard. 'Our little secret, mmm? Not a word to anybody, eh?'

Jacob picked up the book.

'The girl's a distraction. Come back without her.'

Jacob turned but the old man had gone. He called out, 'Hello?' Then louder, 'How should I address you, sir?'

Out of the shadows, '*Professor* would be appropriate. Same time next Thursday, Jacob?'

'Have we met before, sir? Are you the gentleman from the Institute?'

The sound of water dripping was the only response as the light from the professor's lantern faded in the distance.

In moonlight, as boys slept in a line of beds, Jacob crept in and fell onto his bed. It was after two in the morning.

Muxlow sat up and wiped his eyes. 'Heavens, Jake. Thought you'd bunked off back to London.'

'No. I'm starting to like it here,' Jacob said happily. He undressed, took off his leg braces and crawled into bed.

'This came for you,' Muxlow said, passing Jacob a letter.

'It's from my aunt,' Jacob said, opening it enthusiastically by the window. Tears welled in his eyes within an instant. Muxlow quietly waited until his friend composed himself. 'My mother passed,' Jacob finally whispered.

'I'm so sorry,' Muxlow said, placing a hand on his arm. 'You must take some time off. I'll let your tutors know in the morning.'

Mother's remains were collected from the prison by his aunt and Jacob had two days off school to travel, attend the funeral, and return. During the journey back to college, he contemplated the meaning of religion in his short life. The ill-attended church service that preceded the burial of his mother had affected him, so much so that he vowed to worship only one god in the future – science. Saying a last goodbye to his mother, he opened his loyal companion, *Alchemy*, and looked forward to his first lesson with the professor.

Arriving back at the college late that evening, Muxlow soon cheered him.

'Grabbed this at supper,' he said, unfolding a napkin filled with grub. 'My sisters arrive tomorrow, remember?' Muxlow reminded him.

Jacob nodded, stuffing his face with a contented grin.

Jacob was napping across a bale of straw in the stable yard when Muxlow shook him.

'Jake? Jake! Rebecca and Emily.'

Jacob regained his senses to find two beautiful creatures in their finery, the elder smiling and seeking attention. The younger hid shyly behind her sister. Rebecca Muxlow was eighteen and appeared to Jacob to be of such beauty and perfection he was convinced right then that she peed holy water. Giggling, Rebecca curtsied deep and low to ensure he saw her cleavage. Staring with his mouth open, Jacob jumped to his feet, bowed and kissed Rebecca's hand.

Utterly amused, Rebecca hauled her reluctant sister forward – a spitting image, just two years younger. They could have been twins. Equally beautiful yet immensely shy, Emily proffered her hand with her chin lowered.

Jacob bowed and kissed it, but clung on, and their eyes locked. Emily's face was so familiar – the subject of a thousand sketches. He knew no other nose or pair of eyes better. As the sun glinted on her golden hair, he said, 'My pleasure, Emily, but I feel I know you both.'

Rebecca put a finger to her chin, twirled, posed this way and that, and tried to catch Jacob's attention – or more precisely, draw him away from Emily. 'Tommy says you'll paint us given half the chance.'

But Jacob couldn't take his eyes off Emily. 'You had a blue-and-white-striped parasol, at the National Gallery. You bought my portrait.'

'The Mona Lisa? That was you?' Emily said, surprised. She looked down at his leg braces. 'My. You've changed so.'

Rebecca swooped between them. 'I'm studying the history of art in London.'

Jacob leaned around Rebecca, ignoring her and catching Emily's eye. 'I must paint you. You'll sit for me?'

Rebecca hopped in the way to block his view. 'Yes. Paint us. I'd love to see you working. I could learn a lot. You can do us both after Open Day, if you've time. But me first, I'm the eldest. We're staying with the Bedfords for the summer.'

'He'll make time, won't you Jake?' offered Muxlow.

'Do us half as good as my Mona Lisa and we'll love you, won't we Becca?'

Rebecca laughed and pressed against him, provocatively. 'Make us immortal.' She giggled. That was when Jacob's sharp artist's eye discovered Rebecca's imperfection – pox scars. Piled with powder, her attempts to completely conceal them had failed. Jacob would soon learn that these and other stains on Rebecca's character were quite sufficient to turn holy water to pee.

'The Bedfords expect us. Come on,' Tommy said, dragging Rebecca away. Looping both their arms he led his two sisters off across the yard.

Jacob fell back onto the bale of straw, elated, visions of Emily with her parasol floating through billowing cloud. How glad he was to be at Greenwold on this glorious day.

The blackboard was crowded with hieroglyphics. The professor called out ingredients as Jacob wrote them down.

'Ergot fungus; psilocybe semilanceata and peyote cacti. Now begone. It's well past midnight.'

Jacob sneaked back into the college corridor through the secret panel and turned to check the hall clock.

'What are you doing out of bed?' the elderly school secretary, Miss Dunne, barked.

Jacob promptly stared up at the portrait of the school benefactor, and mumbled to himself before answering. 'I'm just sketching Old Nick. Isn't he fascinating?'

'Be off with you, or it'll be six of the best.'

Miss Dunne found him in the same corridor on two more occasions, in the early hours. He pretended to be in deep discussion with the portrait, claiming he was helping him with his homework.

Miss Dunne was as good as her word.

A line of nervous boys waited outside Housemaster Williams' office the following morning.

Thwack! Thwack! Thwack!

They cringed, their eyes blinking with every stroke, praying it would stop. Jacob came out of the office, wincing, rubbing his backside, grateful it was now someone else's turn. He would watch out for Miss Dunne more carefully in future.

Back in the catacombs, the professor stood at a bench full of bubbling chemistry paraphernalia as Jacob placed a sprig of purple-leafed deadly nightshade on the bench.

'How did such a deadly poison get the name belladonna?'

'Beautiful woman?' said the professor, holding a piece up to a lamp. 'Well, isn't she? In fact, she's had many names over the centuries: devil's berries, naughty man's cherries, death cherries, beautiful death, devil's herb and deadly nightshade. Wash your hands. It's lethal.'

Jacob rinsed his hands in a rusty pale of water. The professor gripped the sprig with tweezers, sliced the roots with a scalpel and put them in a glass beaker over a flame. Then he passed the tools to Jacob. 'Only the roots.'

'What will it do?' asked Jacob, chopping fine pieces.

'Drops of this deadly herb were used by women to dilate the pupils, make them more appealing,' said the professor. 'Hence its nickname *belladonna.*'

'Like peacock feathers?'

'Precisely. And used by artists. Concentrated belladonna in a final coat of varnish will oxidise, vaporise for years, spreading its deadly wings. Applied over a portrait, only the top most coat mind, as people stood and stared, their eyes would dilate. This signalled to others observing them that they had found the painting desirable, *come and see.* And so a crowd gathered, admiration soon to follow. And so an undeserving reputation expanded, exponentially.'

'The old masters did that?'

'Anybody who could daub paint on canvas did it – if they knew of the trick,' the professor said, his fingers running through his beard. 'You surely don't think *I* discovered this, Master Jacob?'

Alcohol was added and the concoction stirred, poured into miniature glass vials and then corked. Jacob wrote a label and made an entry in their lab journal.

'Desire. Tincture of belladonna.'

'And a cure for the pox,' added the professor.

'Really?' said Jacob, incredulously.

'Assuredly. Freckles too.'

Jacob placed the small bottle in a line along with another dozen of their discoveries.

'And we've a whole lot more sorcery to cover yet, dear boy,' said the professor, closing their manual: *Alchemy.*

Everyone was asleep when Jacob hovered over Muxlow. He dripped one drop from a glass vial onto Muxlow's freckled cheek, giggled and climbed into bed.

The following morning Muxlow sat up in bed, scratching his face like mad as Jacob awoke, leaped over to him and pulled his hands away from his face. In the middle of a face full of freckles, a completely blank spot shone in the morning sun.

'*Freckilitis!* It works!' Jacob yelled. Other boys sat up, wondering what was going on. Excited, Jacob ran off through the dormitory with his clothes in his hand – then collapsed.

The whole dormitory laughed.

'Legs!' Muxlow called after him, sliding Jacob's leg braces across the floor to him.

The following night, Jacob applied more drops to his sleeping friend's face, crawled into bed, and giggled himself to sleep. Jacob awoke the next morning to find Muxlow clawing at his face again. He leapt out of bed and held Muxlow's face to the sunlight. A miracle. The freckles on that side of Muxlow's face completely gone; red-raw skin in their place.

'I've cured you,' laughed Jacob. 'You're normal, now.'

'Cured me? Are you the reason I'm scratching my face off?' yelled Muxlow, lashing out at Jacob.

'No. I'm the reason you'll be favoured by the fairest in the land,' said Jacob, leaping back onto his own bed. The whole dormitory burst into laughter as Muxlow chased Jacob around his bed, waving his fists.

Suddenly, Muxlow stopped and vomited. A dozen shoes flew at him as disgusted boys grimaced and heaved bed covers over their heads to avoid the stench.

'Should see Matron about that, Muxlow. Might be catching,' Jacob warned.

Banners and bunting; laughter and revelry on Open Day. Mother hens mollycoddled their boys. Pompous fathers boasted and bragged, sipped champagne and scoffed unashamedly from hampers fit for kings. A rugby ball bounced across the courtyard with rowdy boys in pursuit. It was kicked again, harder.

Alone on the edge of the quadrangle, Jacob watched as the ball soared high into the sky and then bounced in front of a coach-and-four – startling the horses. They reared and whinnied. A coachman grabbed the bridles of the leader pair, fought to calm them, the others becoming frantic. The carriage lurched, knocking the coachman aside. Then they bolted.

A group of women directly in their path chatted and laughed, oblivious. Rebecca looked up, terrified. The horses tore towards them. Rebecca screamed. Pushed Emily aside, grabbed her brother. Dived out of the way. The coach tore past, missed them by inches and, passing close to Jacob, headed directly to the largest group gathered – Bateman and his boys. Jacob, his leg irons clunking, strode into their path and leapt onto the leading horse's bridle. The boys scattered – but for the smallest boy, timid and terrified little Rachman, directly in line with the stampeding horses: frozen.

Jacob struggled with the leaders, but the wheelers, behind, were stronger, pushing harder. He hung on for his life, got a boot up onto the troika and pushed hard against it. He turned the frothing horses into a tight circle. Bateman was off to the side laughing his head off, ridiculing little Rachman peeing his pants, inches in front of the halted panting and sweating horses, their eyes vibrating in terror

The coach, its forward steering wheels hard over, angled over, the horses still rearing and lurching, sweat pouring off them. Jacob unfastened some straps and suddenly, the horses broke away, galloping off to adjacent fields.

The carriage teetered.

Observers stood aghast, pointing, fearing which way it might fall.

Rachman glared at it, screaming as it crashed down onto its side.

On the ground, a dress fluttered in the wind – Emily. Rebecca screamed. Ran to her. Jacob clanked over to her side, agony etched in his face.

'Emily!' he yelled, tapping her face. He turned to the staring Lord and Lady Bedford, his lordship still clinging onto a glass of champagne.

'Get a doctor!' Lord Bedford barked, sipping champagne as others did his bidding.

Little Rachman quietly approached Jacob, his face expressionless. Spots of blood appeared on Emily's dress.

'Blood,' Jacob screamed, scrabbling around trying to find Emily's injury. More blood dropped onto his hand. He looked up.

In Rachman's hands – the source of the dripping blood.

The Trial: Day 4

'Please state your name and occupation and address your answers to the jury,' Mr Ponsonby instructed the young man in the witness box. From where I sat in the gallery his head barely appeared above the parapet.

'Ralph Rachman. Estate manager, sir,' came the barely audible response.

'And just to make it clear you are the fifth son of Lord Rochford and the estate to which you refer is the Rochford Hundred Estate in Essex, is that correct?'

'Yes, sir,' came another quiet reply.

'I must ask you to speak up, young man, so we can all hear. Now,' Mr Ponsonby showed him a sketch, 'do you recognise this drawing?'

'Yes, sir.'

'Exhibit 6, m'lud.' Giving the jury only a brief glimpse, and we in the gallery no idea what was drawn, Mr Ponsonby turned back to the witness, 'Tell the court how you acquired it.'

The little man looked nervously at Jacob over in the dock. 'I... I took it, sir.'

'You took it. I see. From whom did you take it?'

'I watched *him*,' he pointed to my Jacob, 'Silver, draw it and give it to Muxlow. Then I took it.'

'When was this?'

'When we were all at Greenwold College, sir. After Muxlow was duffed up by Bully's boys.'

'Bully?' asked Mr Ponsonby.

'The boy in the drawing, sir. Bateman. Bully Bateman, sir.'

'Are you referring to the late Bradley Bateman the Earl of Burrington.'

'Yes. That's him, Bully,' Rachman chirped.

Mr Ponsonby passed the drawing to the jury. They gasped. After they had each examined it, the drawing was handed back to Mr Ponsonby. He held it up to the court and ensured we in the gallery saw it clearly. Those with a good view gasped. I examined it through my opera glasses. While we could not have known if the caricature bore any likeness to the late Earl, or not, it was the *finishing touch* which caused so much dismay – his head severed by a guillotine, watched by a host of bewigged and laughing young aristocracy – his peers no doubt. Terror was very apparent in the young earl's face.

'Were you a witness to the incident in the quadrangle at the college on Open Day that same year?'

'Yes, sir.'

'Describe what happened to the boy in this drawing.'

Rachman, frightened and stammering, described a runaway carriage overturning, and then added: 'His head– The coach– In front of me. He– He was– Decapitated.'

Oh dear. Gasps rose again from the gallery – recalling the decapitated head in the drawing, of course.

'And what happened to the head?'

Rachman cowered, glanced at Silver in the dock. 'I carried it over to Silver, sir.'

A buzz swept through the gallery; ladies either side of me crossed themselves repeatedly.

'You carried a severed head over to the accused?'

'Yes, sir. It was exactly like – Like the drawing. Like Silver predicted.' Rachman cowered at the back of the witness box, shielding his face.

I noticed he was afraid to look Jacob in the eye.

Mr Ponsonby left him to stew a moment.

'I still have nightmares, my lord,' the pipsqueak added, looking to the judge for sympathy.

'And what did the accused say when you offered him the earl's head?'

'He just said: "Bugger off, Rachman. It's dripping all over Emily."'

Groans circulated the courtroom.

'One moment, sir, one moment. Are you telling us that despite a noble earl of the land losing his head in a most gruesome accident, all the accused had to say was "Bugger off"?'

'Yes, sir.'

'After the incident, what were your sentiments towards the accused, Mr Silver?'

'We– It was like he– We were frightened, sir. Nobody messed with him anymore.' Turning to the judge, he added: 'We thought he was the devil, my lord.'

How absolutely absurd. Where's Mr Ecclestone? Mr Ponsonby

is staging more drama to have the jury harbour the worst thoughts towards my Jacob.

'My lord,' yelled Mr Ecclestone, defence counsel, jumping to his feet and proving, at last, he was awake today. 'This is absurd. An innocent sketch and the prosecution are demonising my client because of ridiculous superstition.'

Well done, Eustace, if I may be so familiar.

'I agree,' the judge said, turning to the jury. 'The jury will ignore the witness' sentiments.'

Well done, my lord.

Turning to Mr Ponsonby, the judge said, 'More facts, Mr Ponsonby, and less theatre, if you please. I hope it will not be necessary to warn you again.'

'Obliged, m'lud,' said Mr Ponsonby, popping up as Mr Ecclestone popped down.

But I was extremely annoyed. Just *how* a jury could forget that drawing and what Rachman had so vividly described, would not cause Mr Ponsonby the slightest concern. The image would remain in the jury's minds until the final day, the day of judgement, and he well knew that. Jacob was now a demon as far as the jury was concerned. Mr Ponsonby is a bounder. But more shocking, was what now followed. Mr Ponsonby had one further angle to exploit with this little upstart, obviously calculated to add further weight to the prosecutor's cause: that the accused was far more wicked than a mere five counts of murder suggested.

'Tell us about the boy Muxlow, Mr Rachman,' Mr Ponsonby asked.

'He was a mate – a friend of Silver's. I wanted to be his friend, too. But Bully wouldn't let me.'

'What happened to Muxlow, do you know?'

'He left college early, sir. After Silver got expelled.'

'Do you know *why* he left?'

'He was ill, sir.'

'Had the accused been treating him for some ailment?'

'I don't know, sir.'

'Come lad, everybody in the school knew. Removing his freckles? Remember that?'

Mr Ecclestone jumped up. 'M'lud! Perhaps you should ask my learned friend to take the witness's place in the witness box, as he much prefers the jury benefit from his own version of events.'

Well said, Mr Ecclestone. You are beginning to earn my respect, sir.

The judge held up his hand; defence counsel sat.

'Mr Ponsonby, you know better. The witness said he didn't know. Now, bearing that in mind, how do you wish to proceed with this line of questioning as I fail to see it has any relevance?'

And neither do I, my lord, I wanted to shout out.

'If it pleases, my lord,' Mr Ponsonby continued subserviently, confident that *removal of freckles* was stuck firmly in the jurors' minds from his last trick – along with Jacob supposedly *getting away with* Bateman's decapitation, 'Where is young Muxlow now, Mr Rachman?'

'Finchingfield, sir.'

'Finchingfield? Where in Finchingfield?'

'In the family tomb, sir.'

'He's dead?'

'Yes, sir.'

As if you didn't know, Percy Ponsonby, QC.

'What from?'

'Cancer, sir. It ate away his whole face,' Rachman said, turning to the judge again. 'It was horrible, my lord.'

'Your witness,' said Mr Ponsonby to the defence, sitting down with a smirk on his face.

Get in there, Mr Ecclestone. *Get in there, sir.*

Defence counsel leapt up. I was delighted to watch Mr Ponsonby squirm. 'Mr Rachman, do you have any knowledge of the accused,' pointing towards the dock, '*ever* having treated Master Muxlow?'

'No, sir.' Rachman said. Mr Ponsonby tutted and showed his disgust.

'And have you *ever* had a spell cast on you by the accused, Jacob Silver?'

Rachman cowered back in the witness box. Then, a whisper, 'N-no, sir.' Titters rose from the gallery.

'Quiet!' yelled the judge.

'Louder, please, Mr Rachman.'

'No, sir,' Rachman called out.

'You are sure of that?' He was. 'And can you name anybody, one pupil, master or member of staff, dog, cat or hamster for that matter, who was, or was rumoured to have been, put under any spell at Greenwold College by Jacob Silver?'

Rachman paused, looked over towards Mr Ponsonby and shrugged as if to apologise to the prosecutor. 'No, sir.'

'No more questions, m'lud.' Mr Ecclestone sat and glared at Mr Ponsonby.

Well done, Eustace. *Well done!*

'The witness is excused,' said the clerk.

Mr Ponsonby flicked through his notes and consulted with junior counsel behind him.

'Any more acts before lunch, Mr Ponsonby?' the judge asked.

I noticed Mr Ecclestone slamming his hand over his mouth, presumably to avoid laughing out loud.

'Acts? Er... Am I to take it your lordship is referring to witnesses?'

'If it pleases,' the judge added, a broad smirk on his face. Defence counsel grinned at the judge. Mr Ponsonby was not so amused. Before he could summon a rejoinder:

'Then we shall adjourn until two o'clock,' the judge said.

'All stand!' called out the usher.

Jacob's hateful chains clanked as he rose, and he glared piercingly into Rachman's eyes across the courtroom, the little man frightened he might turn into stone, perhaps. Rachman crossed himself repeatedly as he fled from the courtroom.

I saw him later, fleeing to the sanctity of an alehouse. I presumed he would seek to drown all thoughts of the devil in pursuit.

Bless him.

Chapter 3

Emily lay in a huge four-poster bed surrounded by collectibles. Lord Bedford had an eye for a bargain. Louis XIV cabinetry and chairs, drapes from Lady Hamilton's own boudoir, Emily was reminded almost daily, and pictures that had once adorned the walls of the most wealthy now suffering hard times, apparently.

Lady Bedford, sister of Emily's mother, never missed the opportunity to boast of an item's provenance. She led Jacob into Emily's opulence with his sketchbook.

'Someone to cheer you, Emily,' Lady Bedford announced. She then dragged a Louis XIV gilded chair about as far away from the bed as was possible and commanded, 'You will sit here, Master Jacob, while I'll go and fetch Rosemary to sit with you both.'

Emily smiled and struggled to sit up in bed, a large swelling on the back of her head, delighted to see Jacob. No sooner Lady Bedford had left them, Jacob went and sat on the bed.

'Everybody's talking about you. You're very brave,' Emily said, taking one of his hands.

'But Bateman—' Jacob began.

'Shh. Don't fret over that bully. He almost killed my brother, did you know?' Jacob nodded. 'God works in mysterious ways.' Emily took his other hand, Jacob fearful, initially, that milady would return and catch him, but relaxing once indulging in what lay before his sharp artist's eye.

'I never forgot you,' Jacob said shyly, producing sketches of Emily with her striped parasol from inside his sketchbook.

Emily giggled, as she looked at each in turn. 'These are wonderful. But she's far too beautiful to be me.'

'Never. And I'll finish a portrait in oils, next time,' Jacob said enthusiastically, 'show the world how beautiful you are.'

Although pale, Jacob thought Emily looked radiant and he was totally content to sit and do little else other than admire her beauty. For the first time he could see deep into Emily's eyes, the sparkle there; deep pools of brilliant green, chips of emerald melded with joy; and in them an excitement for living. Vibrant and brilliant, he had loved those eyes from the very moment he caught sight of her in the National Gallery. Now, an eternity later, and after a chance meeting he had never imagined possible, he was with her, beside her; touching, feeling, and caressing if he so dared. He spoke softly to her, about her brother, his kinship, life at the school, omitting the darker side of life there. He made her laugh – all the while studying her every move ready to encapsulate them in his sketch. As he looked deeper and her pupils expanded, he felt the warmth from within and, if his study of the biology behind those pupils was correct, he was elated to find she was as much pleasured by his presence as he was hers. For one so young, Emily struck him now as so advanced in years. Barely older than he, she was comforting him over the nightmare of Bateman, disregarding her own brush with death. What a fine woman this young girl will turn into, he decided.

But what Jacob did not see was the excruciating yet secret pain Emily concealed behind those glorious eyes. A pain so bad, so overpowering, however brave the girl was bearing it, she would need him and every ounce of his healing powers, and all those he could make available to him, to endure her condition much longer. The bump on her head was a godsend. It distracted her from her real ailment, the secret about which all in this household knew very little – except Lady Bedford. Rebecca, her own sister, knew of some ailment, but not what it was, and certainly not how serious it was. Deadly serious. The news of it had been held back, for fear of upsetting Rebecca unnecessarily, on her mother's order.

But Emily herself felt this youth, Jacob, this young dream of an admirer sitting with her now, deserved to know. She would tell him she was ailing, she determined. He deserved that. And he deserved better, a *whole* woman. And he must be free to develop a love such as theirs might have been, with another. Some very lucky, *other* young lady. While that very thought distressed her, at the same time it made her feel proud that, one day, if all she wished him came true, he might compare another's affections with what *they* shared now. That he would learn of her woes was inevitable. So it was better coming directly from her. She would tell him – as soon as the time was right.

What Emily could not have known then during these earlier private liaisons, was that the brilliant genius before her now would become so besotted and so obsessed that he, and he alone, had the means to save her, from this and any other ailment she might succumb to.

'At least I have you all to myself,' he said, edging himself away and retrieving sketching materials from his bag.

'My hero,' Emily said, not taking her eyes off him.

Hearing someone approaching outside the door, Jacob was forced to dash back to the Louis XIV chair as Lady Bedford entered.

'Now, Master Silver, I can't find Rosemary and Emily must rest. I can only allow a few minutes more.' Lady Bedford said, turning to leave again, her numerous silk skirts swishing behind her.

'I'm grateful, milady,' Jacob said, pretending to be engrossed in the chair's architecture.

'Yes, exquisite, isn't it? Napoleon Bonaparte thought so too, when he sat on that very chair,' she said, finally leaving but ensuring the door was left wide open, this time.

'And his seductress, Josephine, slept in this very bed, Jacob,' Emily added, laying back and stretching out her arms seductively. 'Isn't that interesting?'

'And who's Rosemary?' Jacob asked, amused.

'Our maid,' Emily said.

'Your brother lent me this jacket and tie. Is her ladyship still afraid that, as well-dressed as I am, I'll kidnap you?'

'Would you?' Emily joked. 'Go on, I dare you. Drag me off and...' she paused. 'Actually, I'm not sure what's supposed to happen then.'

'Oh, we'll think of something, I'm sure,' Jacob said. Emily giggled. 'Anyway, I've no need,' Jacob continued. 'When I've finished this I'll have a true likeness of you all to myself. Permanently. Take it wherever I fancy. And better, it won't disagree with anything I desire to do to it.' He laughed, continuing to sketch.

'But I thought the finished painting would be mine?' Emily complained, pouting her lips.

'I'm only teasing,' Jacob assured her. After a while he took two small vials from his satchel and smuggled them under the blankets by her hand. He whispered, 'Two drops, no more. Twice a day. You'll feel a lot better.'

'Just seeing you makes me feel better,' Emily said, reaching out for his sketch. 'And I doubt *I* would object to anything you cared to do with me,' pulling at his shirt so hard that he fell onto her. She grabbed the sketch.

Jacob snatched it back. 'When it's finished,' he teased. Though the door remained wide open, Jacob chanced leaning right over her, laid back in the bed. He looked deeply into her eyes, caressed her face, watched her pupils expand. He kissed her cheek softly, gently – a pillow of wholesome cream.

Emily pulled him to her, stared into his eyes and ran a finger softly over his lips.

'You really are the most beautiful man.'

And so, so gently their lips touched, her tongue teased his mouth – and Jacob was lost in the paradise of his first kiss.

Rosemary giggled from the landing and popped into an adjacent room.

Jacob shot off the bed and rapidly tidied his clothes as he bid the giggling Emily good day and rushed towards the stairs.

'Her pupils! I knew she liked me,' Jacob told the professor, as his tutor pounded a mortar and pestle angrily. He unrolled his sketch of Emily. 'Don't you think she's beautiful?'

'A distraction!' shouted the professor. 'We've work to do. Science. Discovery. Remember?'

Jacob rolled up the sketch. 'But I need *some* recreation, or life would be quite dull.'

'*Dull?*' the professor shouted, throwing down his tools. 'I can make your art revered the world over, make you immortal. And you find that *dull?*' Fuming now. 'Leave this place. Go play with your trollop!' He swept glassware crashing onto the flagstone floor.

Jacob turned to leave, got only a few paces, and then turned back. He slipped an apron over his head, knelt and began to clear up the broken glass.

Jacob was sure that the elderly professor taught the only way he knew how. When he spoke, the pupil was expected to listen. He never repeated himself. One was expected to find out what one had missed or misunderstood from the dozens of ancient volumes on chemistry and alchemy lying around the place. Jacob soon learned there was no room for distraction, in particular of the feminine kind, in the professor's classroom; or in one's life, if the tutor had his way.

Jacob wondered what kind of life the professor's was, burrowed deep down there in the catacombs. He lived like a white-haired mole, blind to all activity above ground. The man had not introduced him to a soul and Jacob had never seen him talking to other pupils or colleagues, above the ground or below it, apart from the matron on that first night. What had been made clear on many occasions was that Jacob's tuition, where he had a professor of science all to himself, was to be kept secret.

'Don't speak of your tuition here in this sanctuary to a living soul, you understand?' the professor warned him as he left one night, 'or else they'll all want the same.'

'There are two other brighter boys that could be as worthy as I of your personal tuition, Professor,' Jacob had suggested at one stage, aching for a companion with whom to share his discoveries.

'There's only room for one, Master Silver,' the Professor had replied sternly. 'Remember that. The moment your secret is disclosed will be the day you leave.'

Jacob never had reason to question the professor's outstanding mind. The old man never referred to notes and yet knew the answers to all things. On occasion, Jacob had thought to outwit him, asking impossible historical questions no one could possibly know all the answers to; questions relating to wars and plagues, revolution and scandal.

'I have to write at least a thousand words about the Krakatoa phenomenon,' Jacob enquired innocently during one session. The professor stopped the lesson on sulphuric acid and built a mound of ash over a Bunsen burner.

'Watch closely, but keep well back,' he said, as he ignited gas flowing through the ash. The pile of ash became molten in minutes, dripping off the bench before exploding into the air. 'That's Krakatoa. Just imagine it several billion times larger and below the surface, rising out of the ocean.' The professor gave him *five* thousand words, explaining in detail, with great drama and much gesticulation, what had occurred, precisely at what hour, who reported it, the effect on world climate and the drop in temperatures throughout the world.

'What do you know about the South Sea Bubble?' Jacob asked the following week, toying with his tutor again. Jacob was fully aware of the swindle from the last century, and what caused it, but the professor explained everything remotely connected to it and rattled off the names of twenty or so noblemen who had lost significant fortunes when the bubble burst. Once again, it was as though he had stood there and watched those events occur. On other occasions, Jacob raised questions on ancient concoctions he had found right at the back of *Alchemy*, sure the professor would have forgotten *something*. But whether the data was five hundred years old or five thousand, the professor *did* know everything about it.

'That was something its inventor, Karl Skillet, swore would remove bunions in one lunar month,' the professor explained about one such potion. 'He applied it to his assistant, Erica Banoile, at an exhibition in Paris in the month of May, 1386, at four o'clock in the afternoon. Remarkably, Miss Banoile was able to peel off her particularly enormous bunions after only eight days – and Skillet was paid a fortune for his invention. But it was a fraud. When he was sentenced to prison, his assistant admitted her bunions had been glued on. Now, does that answer your question, Master Silver, or are you simply hoping to waste more of my time?'

And so it was with anything Jacob found in *Alchemy*. The professor was infallible. He knew every potion, every charm, and every ingredient however anciently described and in whatever language – for there were many. He could quote instances of any potion's uses, whether it was a cure or prophylaxis, dates it was first concocted, whether and when it was improved or failed, the names of the alchemist and sometimes his assistant, and the reason for their exaltation or eventual downfall – most often their downfall. The professor was a living pharmacopeia and encyclopaedia combined, and no person alive had more respect for his knowledge than Master Jacob Silver.

And later, through lessons learned, no person alive would have more respect for Master Jacob Silver than the professor, for Jacob's superior mastery of *Alchemy*.

After building a repertoire of half a dozen concoctions that the lesser old masters might have cheated with to draw people into their art against their will, Jacob became aware that the professor had an ulterior motive for making his prize student continue to toil on the treasures described in *Alchemy*. It concerned an item comprised of five lines, labelled *essential ingredients ~ the catalyst*. The rest of that page was in Latin, but the questionable piece was not in any language or script that Jacob was aware of, it was a jumble of characters from many cultures. Jacob had asked himself: If these ingredients were *that* essential, then why hadn't the author written them in plain language? It would remain a mystery a lot longer.

However hard Jacob tried to race ahead, the professor would haul him back to *that* page and those five lines.

'Find a solution, boy! There is so little time,' the professor had shouted after Jacob's persistent refusal to attend to it. 'Think, boy! It's what you're here for! It's what we are *all* here for!'

Only then did it occur to Jacob that here was the first and only occurrence during their working together, that the professor was beaten. This puzzle, he hadn't solved. And had claimed he was running out of time.

'*He* couldn't solve it,' Jacob screamed to himself on the way back to his dormitory one night, 'so how the devil am I supposed to?'

As September arrived, Jacob became aware of additional pressure upon him from the irritable professor: apparently it was imperative that the five lines of essential ingredients were deciphered before the twenty-ninth of the month – Michaelmas Day. Short-tempered and more aggressive as the fateful day approached, the professor gave him a hard time at every opportunity, until, fearful of the repercussions, Jacob declared openly that he had no idea what the solution was. Cursing, the professor threw another tantrum, breaking whatever was within reach. A beaker of acid overturned and smashed on some stone steps – the pair having to flee out into the fresh night air for fear of choking to death.

Jacob was convinced that the five lines in question were not ingredients at all, but an absurd attempt at disguise; red herrings, detractors to the worthy student. And so he, Jacob, continued to ignore them. He determined that these five lines of gobbledegook made no difference whatsoever, not an inkling, to the subject matter before or after. They were a fool's errand. And he just wished the professor would forget them, as he told him often he should, and stop pestering him; let him move on to complete the book.

'What difference would it make whether we solved it Michaelmas Day or Christmas Day?' Jacob had asked the professor the day after Michaelmas Day. The old man had been in a black mood all day.

'Because it's another opportunity lost!' the professor had shouted and stormed off.

Jacob was none the wiser until he found an explanation – on the last page of *Alchemy*.

Do it, in each and every way. Do it all on Michaelmas Day.

He decided to make himself scarce for the best part of a week, claiming other tutors needed him to attend important examinations.

It was the middle of another night, soon after, when Jacob awoke, suddenly overcome with the realisation that the professor had known something quite profound all along which he had failed to share with him; the fact that Jacob's search for immortality through his art, as he promised his father, and what *Alchemy* explored, were two entirely different kinds of immortality. Yes, *Alchemy* did assist him in bringing to fruition his potion of *Desire* and their wider *mood collection*. Father's *tanner to smile* was now accompanied by twenty-five other potions all proven to assist with general wellbeing. Their concoctions had successfully removed freckles, courtesy of guinea-pig Muxlow, warts, verrucae, boils on schoolboy barons' bums, stubborn sties on young earls' eyes, and more stubborn faeces in constipated counts. A scullery maid at the school quietly lost her syphilis as did the fourteen pupils she'd infected and another certain young lady, closer than Jacob dared admit out loud, had lost her pox scars – but Jacob had not disclosed that particular case in their laboratory journal. Yet *Alchemy*, Jacob now knew, was not itself constituted for such mundane purposes. *Alchemy* explored and set out to answer man's wildest dream, the darkest of all shades of immortality – the elixir for eternal life. Living forever.

Quite absurd, Jacob thought.

After secretly unravelling and translating the last few chapters of the tome, Jacob harboured his first doubts about his mentor's mental condition. *How could such a wise man believe in such tripe?* For in those pages the very darkest of dark learning lay before him – resurrecting the dead. How could such a learned man accept there was such a thing within man's power? Jacob dreaded reaching those pages, knowing the easily-annoyed old man would not accept his refusal to continue. But he never let on to the professor about his discovery. Had he done so, and spoken out against the absurdity of everlasting life and resurrection, he feared their relationship would be severed at a stroke. That would not only end his glorious independence and freedom from regular classes with those snobs and bullies he hated so much, but also limit the number of opportunities for tender moments he could share with Emily during the day. Those days were precious to him. Essential.

The only time the professor allowed absence was when Jacob needed to attend compulsory studies in other subjects. Since he was not allowed to mix classes with his peers for fear of embarrassing them, all other studies took place when his tutors were otherwise free; evenings, weekends or holidays included, to their chagrin. But the professor didn't know that. And need not know, Jacob decided, swanning off, ostensibly to whatever class he lied about for an occasional clandestine rendezvous with Emily, or to somewhere quiet to complete her portrait.

The benefit of so much individual tuition from all his tutors, was exponential to Jacob's learning.

'The boy's a genius with an unquenchable thirst for knowledge,' his tutors agreed in the staff room during a heated discussion about the risks to their own skins.

'He's way ahead,' said one.

'Too far ahead,' said another, adding: 'We risk being embarrassed, or worse, bled dry of all we know.'

'Thinks he knows it all. Soon he'll be demanding that *he* teaches our subjects,' a grey-beard quipped, 'and demanding a salary, no doubt.'

'Find an excuse,' one declared. 'Find a reason to remove him altogether.'

And they would have all been most pleased to learn that, as Christmas approached, such a reason was beginning to take shape.

Tommy Muxlow sat on the bed next to tearful Emily.

'I care for him so. It's breaking my heart,' she said, busily twisting her golden hair into ringlets. 'I manage to sneak out twice a week but that only gives us an hour together. We get rather, well, rather passionate talking about what we'd like to do but what with the farmers and shepherds constantly tending their stock, what can one do in such a short time down by the river?'

'You'll be better soon and then you could meet more often, I'm sure,' her brother assured her, stroking her hand. 'His tutors drive him fiercely hard but I know he would rather be with you,'

After what seemed an eternity to Emily, Jacob did make an appearance. Emily sat alone in bed, the bump on her head now subsided, as Lady Bedford entered with her portrait.

'Your young beau dropped this off. It really is most extraordinary!' She placed the picture on the bedside table. 'I sent him away. He wore neither jacket nor necktie and there's no one to sit with you. I suggested he return after lunch on Saturday when your brother can sit with you in the orangery.'

Emily squealed, excited at seeing the painting. She ran to the window. Outside, Jacob walked away across the manicured lawns, past the fountain. Emily turned to admire her portrait, picked it up and danced in a circle holding it at arm's length. Lady Bedford laughed and left the room, confident the child was well and truly on the mend.

Emily closed the door quietly, grabbed the glass vials from under her pillow and bit off the corks. Drops exploded onto her tongue. Eyes closed tight, fists clenched, she stamped her feet. Opening her eyes again, she shuddered and ran to the open window, leaned out and put two fingers in her mouth.

In the garden below, Jacob whipped round, trying to locate the loud whistle. Up at the window, Emily, in only her nightgown, beckoned excitedly and pointed to ivy climbing up to her. Jacob laughed and clanked back towards the house.

Moments later, Emily giggled as she hauled Jacob in the window by his belt. They tumbled, his leg braces clunking on the floor. They laughed hilariously. Jacob caressed her face, stared into her eyes. Her pupils were about to burst. They kissed passionately. Again and again. Emily got up off the floor.

'The medicine?' Jacob enquired.

Emily nodded. 'What it's doing to me, I don't know. But I love it. *Love it!*' she squealed, straddling him, her thin nightgown billowing in the breeze from the window, her fair ringlets flowing in the wind. That image, her radiance, was indelibly etched into his mind and would remain with him for the rest of his life.

'An angel,' Jacob sighed.

Emily giggled and then slowly slid her shoulders out of her nightgown. The garment slid off, floated down onto his face. She laughed, infectiously. He laughed, as her foot teased his groin.

'Angel?' she questioned, menacingly.

Jacob peeped up through the nightdress at the wonder of her body. Emily threw her head back in raucous laughter – then plunged onto him.

The door burst open.

A scream – from Lady Bedford.

A squeal – from Jacob.

A yelp – from Emily as her ladyship yanked her off him by her hair.

'*Out!*' screamed Lady Bedford, lashing at Jacob with her boot.

Chapter 4

I fled from Emily's boudoir, leaving Lady Bedford yelling and screaming at her, and dashed down the hallway towards the main staircase and freedom – certain her ladyship's wrath would soon follow me. But Rebecca, no doubt curious about the commotion, came out of her room in her night attire and blocked my path. She dragged me into her boudoir, slamming the door quickly behind her, locking it and laughing before sliding the key down her heaving cleavage. She came straight to the point, pinning me against the door.

'My sister says you're doing things to her,' she said, and then smirked, raising her finger to her lips and whispering, 'Shhh.'

'I've not touched her!' I quietly protested and tried to push her away. She resisted. With Rebecca dressed only in a flimsy nightgown, and I being locked in a room with her, and a bedroom at that, I listened intently to the pursuit outside fearing discovery and a thrashing from Lady B. Fortunately, still yelling, milady rushed past Rebecca's door. In retrospect, I wish now I had suffered capture and torment from her ladyship rather than endure the next few hours locked in there with Rebecca.

'The potions?' Rebecca said, releasing her grip on my wrists and stepping back from me. 'They're making her so... so much more interesting.'

She had walked over to the windows and I'm sure was quite aware that the sunlight streaming through her nightgown put every inch of her on display. But I am only human and having just seen one sister stripped completely naked, cannot deny I was aroused by the other blatantly egging me on. Or was I imagining things?

'Jake, darling,' Rebecca began, sidling up close to me seductively. She entwined her fingers with mine. 'I need–'

'I don't think Lady Bedford would approve right now,' I blurted out. But she suddenly appeared embarrassed. Was that possible? Did such a condition actually exist in Rebecca's repertoire?

'Can you keep a secret?' she asked shyly. 'I have a problem.' She could tell I didn't understand. 'Down there,' she said, casting her eyes downwards as she pressed her breasts into me. I must have looked puzzled for she pulled my hand between her legs. 'There,' she said, cheekily.

She let go of me, turned and looked out of the windows towards the woods yonder. 'Fell for the gamekeeper's charms. Became his *poachee*,' she said, her back to me.

I couldn't say anything. I didn't know what in damnation she was talking about. After a few moments, she turned and faced me. My lack of understanding of her apparent plight angered her. She lifted her nightgown and unashamedly showed me she wore no drawers. Raising her voice, she said, 'A poach-*ee*, poach-*ed* by the poach-*er*.'

At last, I got it. Understood. The lady has the clap. Christ! And I'm locked in her bedroom with my hand on her privates. And if my ears didn't deceive me, Lady Bedford was below that window within shouting distance.

'Get the hounds!' I heard her ladyship call out. 'There's a scoundrel loose in the grounds!'

Rebecca pressed me up against the door again. 'I was wondering…' she continued bashfully, running her finger down my chin. 'D'you think–'

I opened my jacket. She saw the line of little pockets, a selection of glass vials all in a row. A cure was surely on its way, she must have thought, for she relaxed immediately. I picked one.

'Sit. Relax,' I ordered her, and was pleasantly surprised she obeyed, plopping onto the edge of the flouncy bed and frankly, looking a picture. 'Got just the thing. Naughty man's cherries.'

'Er – no! Had my fill of those,' Rebecca said, grimacing. 'The state of them when I refused to do what he asked. But he did persist so.'

I smiled and uncorked the vial. 'Now promise me, once you've taken this, you'll let me go.' She nodded. 'Head back. Open wide,' I barked. And she followed my instructions precisely.

Three drops of the nectar drizzled onto Rebecca's tongue and watching her reaction was sheer delight. Her mouth open wide, her salivating tongue waggled and she smiled, breaking into laughter.

'Quiet or you'll have Lady Bedford onto us,' I warned her, placing my hand gently over her mouth as she clutched onto me. Squeezed me. Gripped me between my legs and pulled me close to her. She writhed and twisted – but she wasn't in pain. She was in ecstasy. Small waves of flesh formed and rippled down her face, down her wonderful neck and, as she ripped off her nightgown, I watched as they passed down through her voluminous breasts to her stomach.

She winced, grabbed herself between her legs and threw her head back. Anticipating a yell I covered her mouth again and she bit my hand, dug her teeth into me, drawing blood. I fought to free it but she gnashed her teeth at my face – a tiger loose in her boudoir. I cannot deny, it was exciting. Wincing and whining, she hissed and spat at me, keeping me at bay until I smothered her head in her discarded nightgown to drown any noise about to break through.

After a few moments she was quiet. I removed the nightgown, aghast at what was happening to her face. Eruptions all over. The pox scars were popping open all over her face. Each rose like a dark volcano and then erupted – leaving raw new flesh as the evidence of change. One after the other they quietly exploded, alarming her. She was aware something extraordinary was going on with her face – but frightened she was losing her one vital asset, I don't doubt. I fought to keep her hands away, struggled to ensure she let the potion do its work. Eventually, the eruptions desisted. There were no more to erupt. Rebecca's face was completely new, the skin on her face like a baby's. She became silent but for harsh panting, like she'd run through a forest; sweating like she'd run through a waterfall. Her eyes closed.

I knew what would happen next; the scullery maid I'd treated with this same potion became uncontrollable, wanton. I had to get out of there, before she awoke. But this was Rebecca, sister of my beloved. Could I risk leaving her, with Emily so near? Would she blurt out our little secret? And Lady Bedford still hovered somewhere out there on the other side of the door. Exhausted from all the excitement, I decided to lie next to Rebecca and wait.

I awoke to find the tigress with the newborn face on top of me – riding me like a stallion, fumbling with my trouser buttons.

'Off!' she yelled. 'Get them off!'

'You promised you'd let me go!' I yelled back, fighting her off.

'But you *knew* this would happen, didn't you?' she yelled.

'That's why you must let me go, girl!'

She settled for a moment, panting. Still on top of me. And she did look a picture with her new pink face. As her breasts rose and fell to her deep panting, and so very close my face, I found I was getting aroused. Her reaction was immediate.

'Yes, yes, yes!' she whispered. 'Show me you want me.'

'No. No, it wouldn't be true. It's Emily I–'

'Are you a man or a mouse?' she snapped, still working on my trousers. 'Boys of thirteen could marry, just a few years ago.' She grasped my manhood. 'What d'you think it's for?' Her boudoir skills were certainly well polished. She raised herself and had my trousers off in seconds. I was tortured with embarrassment as my ugly leg braces were revealed – but she took not the slightest notice. Within moments she had lowered herself onto me.

'Oh thank you, Jacob!' she gushed, as she moved her bottom slowly and rhythmically. I suddenly forgot all about my dilemma and Lady Bedford. Every part of me was enjoying her. Her groaning became more rapid, the rhythm faster, until I feared reaching a point of no return.

'We'll have to–' I tried, half-heartedly. 'We must stop!' I gasped, hoping she never would. But thoughts of my sweetheart on the other side of the house were giving me second thoughts. 'Emily might–'

'Emily?' she replied, 'She won't mind a bit.' Her pelvis rose and fell faster than ever. She was gulping for breath now. 'You really are… the most beautiful man and…' her face screwed up as she gulped back an inward scream. 'She wants us… to share you. We share… everything. We want you to… love us both.' I felt myself explode inside her. And with that her whole body shuddered, my hand tight over her mouth lest the whole neighbourhood came running.

She rolled off, panting heavily beside me, before curling herself into a foetal position, her thumb in her mouth like a small child. I was satiated. Sore, but completely satiated. And Rebecca appeared content, at last. But I was confused. What had happened had been entirely against my will – to begin with – but I had developed feelings towards her. A lust for her which she rewarded so admirably. As I looked at her naked on the bed, I found myself growing hard again and was thrilled that my further enjoyment would have had Emily's blessing. I would have taken Rebecca again, under my own terms, had it not been for that knock at the door.

'Becca, the door's locked. Let me in.'

Emily.

I was half naked and, for a moment, had no idea where my trousers were. Finding them under the bed, I slipped them on hastily over my leg irons and headed out of the bay window. I prayed there would be ivy climbing to this window, too.

There wasn't.

Outside on the ledge I pressed my back to the wall, out of sight from those inside, but within sight of two gardeners busily tending to flowerbeds around the fountain below – fearful they should happen to look up.

The window wide open, I heard Rebecca's door unlock and Emily rush in, giggling and gushing with news.

'You'll never guess! Lady muck caught me earlier with– Oh! I see you've been... busy.'

I feared Emily had seen the untidy bed and I leaned forward to look. Trembling, I glimpsed Rebecca taking a seat at an array of mirrors on her dressing table in plain sight within the bay window, brushing her hair. She glared at me through the glass, a discreet nod of her head warning me to steer clear.

'What's this?' I heard Emily yell. I saw Rebecca duck as one of my glass vials shattered a mirror on the dressing table. 'He's been here? You've been canoodling with my beau?' Emily yelled, standing right behind Rebecca now, pulling her hair. So much for *we want you to love us both*, I thought. I screwed my eyes shut, and leaned back against the wall for fear of being discovered.

But I was too late.

One of the gardeners laughed, distracted by the girls shouting, he pointed me out to the other. They stood and stared, leaning on their garden forks, laughing.

'You don't own him, dear. I can't help it if he finds you so dull!' Rebecca's bitchiness was on top form. And I could do nothing about it. 'He's a bloody cripple. You can't be *seen* with him anywhere! Can't take him to any debutante's ball; so you might as well share him with me.'

Then the fighting began. I heard them screaming and hissing at one another, glass being broken and a final expletive I would not have expected from Emily, as a complete triple-mirror came thundering through the bay window and crashed into the fountain below.

My dilemma was heightened as one of the gardeners pointed at Lord Bedford's carriage approaching in the distance. I decided not to hang around and faced the dangers head-on, sidling across the bay window in front of the two girls fighting until reaching some ivy to climb down. Fortunately, they were too occupied with each other to notice me. The gardeners applauded my departure when I finally reached the ground and fled.

Hearing Rebecca's harsh words about my legs confirmed the girl was a vixen and as I applied some precautionary lotion to my genitals later that night, I vowed never to give her the time of day thereafter. But time is a great healer and no one would be more surprised than I how I would, once again, lust after her.

Chapter 5

'You took advantage of her, Silver,' Muxlow growled the Sunday after as they sat on the riverbank. 'Lady Bedford demands you don't go near the house. She could have you expelled.'

'I did no such thing. If anything...' Jacob began in protest.

'Let's leave it at that, shall we? I'd like us to remain friends. What you did to Emmy—'

Jacob grabbed Muxlow by the shoulders and spoke firmly.

'Friend, I did *nothing* to Emily. I promise you. Emily was happy, elated. She got carried away, that's all. But nothing happened. Her honour is preserved.'

They sat in silence, skimming stones, free from the pressures of the Bedfords and the school bullies. In fact, since Bateman's unfortunate accident, the others left them alone. Rumour had it that Jacob had more control over events that day than he would admit, and all were wary of him wreaking vengeance upon them. If he decided only to get even it would cause them much mischief.

'Do you really care for her?' Muxlow ventured, breaking the silence.

'More than I can describe. How I'll cope, not seeing...'

'She's missing you. Chronically. Cries all the time.' After a few moments Muxlow added, 'And if you're truly missing her... Well, I'll arrange something. As long as you promise...'

Jacob shook his hand like a gentleman. 'I promise. She's safe with me. I'll protect her.'

'She's not well, our Emmy.'

'I know that. I was there when it happened, remember. Concussion can—'

'Oh, *that*. No, it's a bit more than a bump on the head, old chap.'

'She's ill? Tell me. Tell me everything, Muxlow.'

'She's here for the fresh air. She can breathe properly here.'

'Asthma, is it?'

'Mama wouldn't say. Thought it best I didn't know, stop me

worrying, she said. Nor Rebecca. Emily has to wait and see what a year with the Bedfords will do for her.'

'Apart from drive her mad, you mean?' Jacob smiled.

'She's all right, the old lady. Worries for her little niece, that's all.' Jacob smiled again. 'Becca took a fancy to you, too. Did you know?' Muxlow quipped, catching a passing duck with a bouncer. The duck squawked repeatedly, paddling rapidly and scooting across the surface until it took flight, making them both laugh. 'That's the kind of noise Becca made, hearing you were banned from the house.'

'Really? Oh, dear. Going to have to disappoint your Becca, sorry. Emily wouldn't approve.'

It was half-past midnight, mid-January, when Jacob returned to the dormitory from his latest session with the professor, two nights later.

'Christ, Jake!' Muxlow whispered to him, dragging him out onto the landing. 'Emmy's here, catching her death waiting for you. Thinks you've got some other filly in tow.'

'Emmy? Where?' Jacob pressed, looking into the dormitory.

'Not there, stupid. I took her down to the boathouse. Nobody'll see you there.' Muxlow led him away.

Moonlight reflected off the flooding river as Muxlow, not finding Emily where he'd left her, led Jacob through a back door into the boathouse. They heard giggling.

'She's in here. You'll have an hour at least but don't press your luck, old chum. I'll be out here.'

'In case I go too far, is that it?'

'No, you idiot. In case anybody comes,' Muxlow said, clawing at his face.

'Mosquitoes?' Jacob asked him, pulling his hand from his face.

'Something bloody nasty. Eating me alive it is.'

'We'll see to it later. I promise. Least I can do.' With that, Jacob disappeared inside the boathouse.

Jacob called into the pitch dark, in a loud whisper, 'Emmy? Emmy? It's Jacob.'

A soft feminine hand grabbed his wrist and pulled him tumbling into a scull alongside the dock. Loud giggling from both of them followed before the rocking hull settled.

'Keep it down in there!' murmured Muxlow from outside the door. 'You'll wake up the whole bloody college!'

Their giggling controlled, Jacob held her face in his hands. 'I missed you, darling,' he breathed.

He held her face between his hands as her hands slid into his shirt, flicked open a couple of buttons and then tugged at it, signalling she wanted it off. Jacob obliged, caressing her; and the whole time her hands were kneading his firm body, handfuls of flesh squeezed with excitement. A cold, wet hand suddenly shot down into his trousers. He yelped. Fumbling with her bodice and petticoats, he did the same, dipping his hand first in the water and then on to her now naked breast. She giggled, a faint inward chuckle of delight, then urged him on top of her, unfastening his belt and yanking his trousers off his hips.

More water splashed onto his rump. Yet more smeared on to her heaving breast.

As she panted and urged him on, his hardness was unbearable. God, what promises had he made to Muxlow? How could he stop now? This girl needed him. Needed him inside her. He needed her. He had to have her. It was a duty. And what of honour? Loyal to friend outside, or lover here, inside? Beside him. Panting. Urging. How could he possibly–

'Hello?'

The voice: unmistakable. In the dark, up a mountain, in a forest, in hell or heaven – he knew that voice so well.

'Is anybody there?'

Emily.

'Jacob, darling?' Her voice nearer now.

Rebecca giggled loudly, grabbed his sagging manhood in two cold wet hands.

'Do it, for fuck's sake! Do it!'

The twenty-foot boat rocked. Someone had stepped on the far end.

'Becca? I know it's you.'

Muffled giggles rose from the girl next to Jacob in the boat.

'What in damnation are *you* doing here?' Emily shouted.

'I couldn't sleep,' Rebecca lied, peering into the blackness as she tried to unravel her drawers.

'*You bitch!*' Jacob breathed into her ear, struggling to stand up before leaping out of the boat onto the dock, his leg irons clunking.

The narrow boat rocked violently. Yells came from Emily's end, then two huge splashes. Gurgling. Choking. Floundering. Emily and Rebecca, arms flailing, tried desperately to stay afloat, creating a shocking din in the small boathouse.

A flood of moonlight lit up the spectacle as Muxlow threw open the door. Before it closed, he had dived into the water after his sisters. But he was too late.

Jacob had them – hooked with a boathook. He pulled all three Muxlows out of the water.

Coughing and spluttering out in the moonlight on the riverbank, Emily could not conceal her anger. Jacob feared who would feel the edge of her tongue the most and sat well away from both girls. But poor Emily, still struggling to catch her breath, was in no fit state to squabble, needing to recover from the pneumonia that was about to invade her lungs, before thrashing her sister.

Two weeks later, Emily was seriously ill. Messages, conveyed to Jacob by her maid, implied she was in fear for her life.

'I don't care for your rules, Lady Bedford. I am in love with your niece and I'm not prepared to sit and wait while you and those other quacks sit by and let her die,' Jacob said, bursting into Emily's boudoir.

Lady Bedford yelled, summoning the butler, the footman, and the maid, in that order, to rid her of this intruder. When, finally, Rosemary the maid answered her call, she found Jacob kneeling at the bedside of an unconscious and wheezing Emily, stroking her hand. Closing and locking the door to keep Lady Bedford and her smelling salts out, Rosemary pleaded with Jacob.

'She pines for you, Master Jacob. Every day, ten times a day she pines. Don't fret over milady. Just tell me what to say to Emily when she next wakes – so I can put her out of her misery.' Jacob looked at the maid, puzzled. 'She thinks you don't care, master. But I know that's not true. I've seen the way you look at–'

'Rosemary, open this door at once, I command you,' Lady Bedford cried out, kicking the door. 'I will not have this insolence in my own home, you hear, gel?'

'It'll be a thrashing for me, master. Make it worth my while. She's dying, sir. Leave something nice for our dear Emily to remember you by.'

And Jacob did. Taking two vials from a row sewn into the inside of his jacket, he passed them to the maid.

'Rosemary, not a word to her ladyship. I could go to prison, you understand?' She nodded. 'But I've trained in these things my whole life. See that Emily gets two drops from each vial, three times a day, in a glass of water, for seven days, understand? Don't mix them. Whatever you do, don't mix them. D'you understand?' The maid nodded again, smiling this time. 'Emily need not know we're treating her, in fact it's best if she doesn't. And her ladyship must never know. But I promise, with all my heart, we'll all find a great improvement in poor Emily.' He prepared to step out of the window. 'I'll leave this way. Can I count on you to do exactly as I ask, Rosemary?'

Rosemary bobbed a polite curtsey, holding up her pinafore, 'Swelp me God, you surely can, Master Jacob.'

'Only two drops from each vial, three times a day, in a glass of water, for seven days, understand?' Jacob reminded her.

Rosemary, her back raw from a beating with a broom handle, concealed the vials under the blankets in her room high in the attic. Once she was sure the household were all in bed, she made her way down to Emily's room. Emily was fast asleep, pale and still wheezing heavily. Taking out the vials, Rosemary removed the corks and counted the drops onto a spoon.

'Seven drops, three times a day for two days,' she murmured under her breath. 'Do I mix 'em or what?' she asked herself, hesitantly holding the second glass vial over the spoon. 'Why not?' she settled on, 'All goes down the same 'ole.'

Tilting Emily's head up from her pillow, Rosemary slipped the tip of the spoon between Emily's lips, which parted conveniently allowing fourteen drops – a mere ten drops too many, neat, without water – to percolate down the girl's throat.

By morning, twenty drops too many, undiluted and taken together against all instruction, had passed Emily's lips – and she was rampant. She climbed the walls, fought Rosemary to try and jump out of the window, swore at and cursed the maid, milady and all who came to listen, with words they thought only thieves and beggars used – or Rebecca occasionally.

Late the next night, after a priest called and blessed the child with holy water, he was about to begin performing an exorcism when Rosemary fell to his knees and gasped for forgiveness, confessing everything before sobbing her heart out.

Headmaster Fellows had Jacob by the ear and frogmarched him out through the large oak doors. 'After what you did to that poor girl, you're banished from these hallowed halls – *for ever!*'

'I didn't touch–' Jacob kicked out and tried to break free, but was thrown onto the front lawn; his worn satchel followed.

Begone with you, boy!'

The Trial: Day 3

My bully of an escort made a swathe through the usual hangers-on on the way upstairs to Court Number One. At the top I was confronted by a particularly scruffy urchin offering me a silk kerchief with a motif. Exquisite, it bore a family crest depicting two exotic birds supporting a shield bearing three purple fleur-de-lis orchids. The tanner it was offered at made it particularly good value for money. Nevertheless, I called my escort with his horsewhip to assist with negotiations.

'The boy is offering me this for sixpence,' I told the man who towered over the lad menacingly. 'Tell the boy,' I continued, glaring at the snotty lad, 'I'll pay him double if he can name the birds in the motif, and quadruple if he can name those items in the middle of the shield. If he fails, the scarf shall be mine.'

The boy tugged on my man's sleeve and whispered in his ear.

' 'E says: *what's a quad-duple*, ma'am?' asked my man.

'Quadruple. Four times. Two bob in your tongue,' I said directly to the boy.

'A deal then,' he began, pointing into the kerchief. 'Them's chickens and them's fevvers,' he blurted, grinning and holding out his grubby hand.

Withdrawing a silk handkerchief from my purse I pointed at the same motif. 'Them's peacocks and them's fleur-de-lis orchids,' I told him, snatching the kerchief from him, adding, 'you snivelling tyke. You stole this from me yesterday on my way up these very stairs.'

My man had the boy by the ear as he thrashed out. 'Take yer furkin flurtle leezes. I don' wan' 'em, yer ol' cow,' he yelled. After my man clumped him, he added through tears, 'Was after a crust is all.'

I left with the booty and heard the yells behind me when the boy's minders succeeded in freeing him. I decided that my man deserved the two bob, one for each shiner.

It would prove to be an interesting day.

Sergeant Beck was continuing with his evidence, Mr Ponsonby

posing questions. I found counsel styling his questions in such a way as to throw the worst possible light on poor Jacob's character. The jury could be forgiven for thinking this was a witch hunt rather than a murder trial.

'You asked Jacob Silver why he was expelled, sergeant?' Mr Ponsonby began.

'I did, sir. He replied: "They said I administered substances, maliciously. But what I had given the poor girl had been improving her for weeks. So who gives a tuppenny toss what it was?"'

'You have your notes taken at the time, sergeant. Please continue through the interview you conducted with the accused,' Mr Ponsonby said, turning to face the jury through the sergeant's evidence.

'I asked Silver: Did you mean Emily harm when you administered these *substances*? He replied: "Of course not. I cheered her. Every day she improved." I said: But you weren't there when the maid administered those last concoctions. He said: "Unless she was stupid, my instructions were quite clear. Two drops, three times a day. How could anybody get *that* wrong?" I said: But as far as you knew these medicines, these potions, were working, improving her condition? He replied: "It was the same medicine I had given her before. There was no reason to suppose she would respond differently, only positively."

'I asked Silver: Who else have you administered substances to? He laughed and replied: "To many. Where shall I start?"'

Murmurs rose in the courtroom and gallery above. I noticed jurors were looking at each other with some dismay.

'At the beginning, I told him. Let's have them all. You've told me about Muxlow, your friend. What about the others?'

Sergeant Beck read out a long list of ailments that Jacob had supposedly treated, unofficially, and the Latin names for what he had treated them with. Most of them were problems caused when disgusting little boys attending the college, mostly titled I might add, mixed with one particular scullery maid, who took a liking to all boys, titled or no. Others treated were boys of a shy nature whose ailments were mostly minor embarrassments, indigestion, or tummy upsets, or constipation and the like, for which those boys preferred not to consult the school's nurse, Miss Primm. This lady, no matter what end of their body the ailment, always insisted they drop their trousers for closer examination, Jacob had explained to the sergeant. The court found that element quite amusing.

One other patient's complaint was of a more serious nature – a certain young lady named Rebecca Muxlow. Since she later became one of the murder victims, Sergeant Beck was questioned for over an hour about Jacob's consultation with her – a consultation that had cost him dearly, losing something he could never possibly regain – his virginity.

The sergeant described, in Jacobs own words, how this hussy had forced herself upon him. I had no sympathy for the girl. He had openly offered to help her, without questioning the consequences – and she took advantage of him.

I was eager to learn how she met her demise, later.

My respect for Jacob was completely renewed when the officer next detailed the administration of substances to Emily. For that was the Jacob I knew so well, and loved. A saviour. He would do anything to help *anyone* in distress – even though it led to his expulsion from college.

'So, in the accused's eyes,' asked Mr Ponsonby, 'he had *saved* Emily, from certain death?'

'He was sure he had saved her life. Yes, sir.'

'And the family's only appreciation of his interference led to his expulsion?'

'That is correct, sir.'

'Sergeant, at the time of *this* interview, Jacob Silver had led you to believe that Emily Muxlow was back in normal health by the time he was expelled. Is that correct?'

'Yes, sir.'

Chapter 6

Ashamed and expelled, I arrived back home in mid-February, 1888. The Thames, visible from the front windows, was frozen over. Left empty, the house was extremely cold with ice on the inside of the windows. I broke up old furniture to make the first fire and slept in front of it on a mattress pulled down from upstairs. I used every blanket in the house just to keep warm. Numerous jars of vegetables, preserved by my mother, remained in the larder and I feared that once they had gone I would starve to death without an income.

After a couple of days, I went to visit my aunt and explained my shame at being expelled. I didn't tell her about my encounters with Emily or Rebecca, only mentioning the medicines I had offered to those I had considered in need. Aunt Alice didn't hesitate to provide me with a large box full of food and provisions but, herself being a widow surviving on a meagre military pension, insisted I seek work, of any kind, in order to be able to stand on my own two feet. She promised, in the meantime, she would call and ensure everything was in order and bring me five shillings a week to cover essentials.

My father's wholesaler remembered me well and gave me some casual work helping in his warehouse. I also drew caricatures of every one of his staff, selling them for a few coppers to bolster my meagre income. Customers were soon to catch on. I raised the price five-fold yet they continued to come eagerly for sketches of their family members. When one of the warehouse's employees decided to go and take his chances in America, I was offered his full-time position, working sixty hours at a starting wage of six shillings and nine-pence a week, measuring and packing orders for chemicals. My aunt said she would keep up the allowance for a month or two longer and I couldn't have been happier.

But on a chilly morning in early April that year, my life was turned upside down completely. I was setting off to work when a shy urchin, no more than eight and shivering in little more than a ragged shawl, begged I visited her ailing mother. When I apologised and explained that I was neither an apothecary nor a doctor she pulled at my jacket and pointed to the grimy sign still affixed above the boarded-up shop window: 'S. Silver & Sons ~ Apothecaries.'

I tried to explain but she either did not understand or simply refused to accept that I could not help her, pulling at my coat-tails until I went with her. I begged she wait until I packed my father's old Gladstone bag, and coming back to the front door, seeing she wore so little to combat the cold, I went back inside and fetched her a warm jacket of my mother's. Inside the hall she marvelled at seeing her full length reflection in the hall mirror, the jacket touching the floor, her arms somewhere up inside the long sleeves. Wrapping a woollen scarf tightly around her neck, I told her to lead the way.

Clasping my hand the whole way, she led me eastward towards the docks. The squalor that lay less than a mile from my front door was a different world, the noise and bustle always exciting.

We dodged past scavengers outside the fish market at Billingsgate as they fought over bloodied fish heads in the gutter and pressed on through a throng entertained by street peddlers and jugglers. Tents by the Tower offered private sessions with prostitutes. Tents alongside those were equally busy; quacks offering cures against ailments the prostitutes next door gave their clientele. A multitude of huge sailing ships were tied alongside the dock. On the dock itself, crews of all nationalities manned stalls that offered animals I'd not seen before; monkeys of every shape and size and caged birds, their feathers every colour imaginable. But the slight girl in front of me was not distracted, pulling me on with much determination.

We proceeded on to narrower, darker streets, into a more deprived area of the East End, where a cloak of misery appeared on almost every face we passed. A sign told me we were in Wapping. At a narrow alleyway, my young guide muttered, 'Here,' and standing on a wooden crate, reached into a letterbox and hauled out an iron key on a length of string. She unlocked the door and led me inside.

'Hello?' I called out in the pitch black inside, covering my nose from the stench. The girl led me upstairs and into a squalid bedroom where a woman lay quite still. Her face was covered in black pustules. I recognised them, and the fear of God ran through my bones. 'You go back downstairs,' I said to the girl, but she shook her head and remained at my side, clinging onto my coat.

Trembling, I touched the dead woman's brow, expecting it to be cold as stone. I was startled as her eyes opened.

'Save Nell,' she gasped. 'Too late for me.'

I grabbed the girl and rushed from that room.

'Nell? You must come with me. It's not safe here.' Reluctant to move, I tried to reassure her. 'I have to get some medicines for your mama. But you cannot stay. You–'

She pointed to an adjacent room, its door closed.

'It's not safe, Nell,' I said kneeling down beside her. 'Come with me, you can help me find the right medicines.'

She jabbed her finger at that other door again. I had no idea what to expect as I slowly turned the handle. How I would regret not sending the child away before opening that door.

The room was dark; thick sacking draped across the window. What little light there was came from the landing where I stood. On an iron bedstead I could make out a shape, the bedclothes pulled completely over it. I heard my leg braces vibrating as I trembled; not through cold but through abject fear of what lay under those covers. I went to the window, pulled down the sacks. The room was flooded with light streaming through the grimy glass, and at once, the buzz of flies filled the room. Thousands of flies.

'Nell?' I called out. I didn't want her near. I couldn't see her. Had she gone downstairs? I approached the bed, the stench overwhelming. I held a handkerchief tightly over my nose and took hold of the top corner of a grubby blanket, inhaled and quickly pulled the covers back.

My God!

A deafening, high-pitched scream shattered the silence. There was a tug at my leg as Nell slid to the floor behind me.

I grabbed her and rattled down the stairs on my leg irons as fast as I could, slamming the front door behind me. Nell was unconscious, and white as a sheet. My legs gave way and I slid down the door to the frozen step, clinging onto the child. I feared we had only a short time to live.

'Brought me a customer, Nellie?' The voice startled me as Nell shook me. I looked up to see a woman, nineteen or twenty, standing over me, her petticoats tickling my nose. 'Ain't had one in leg irons before,' she laughed. 'There's a novelty.' She reached over me and fished the key out of the letterbox, my head smothered in her undergarments. 'Lookin' an' smellin's free, chum,' she laughed, uncovering my red face. 'Gotcha pecker up, 'as it?' She shoved the key in the lock. 'Shift your arse, then.'

'You live here?' I asked, struggling to my feet. She nodded. 'Sorry, but you can't go back inside. It's not safe.'

She laughed in my face. 'Want one on the doorstep, ducky?' she giggled. 'Catch me deaf out 'ere, for sure.'

I drew her aside and checked we couldn't be overheard.

'In there, madam,' I said sternly, 'is certain death. Plague, madam. D'you hear me?' As the colour drained from her face, it was quite obvious she had heard.

She screamed inwardly, like a muffled bleating lamb.

I slammed my hand over her mouth, pulled her back into the doorway. 'Keep it between us. Until I've spoken to a constable. They'll need to isolate you all. Keep Nell safe. You have somewhere to go?'

'It's me 'ome, innit,' she replied. 'Ain't got nowhere else.'

'A friend, maybe?' She shook her head. 'Anyone?' I pleaded. She shook her head again.

Of course, I knew of one safe place, one uninfected and isolated and well away from there. 'Then you'd best come with me. We'll stop at a doctor's on the way.'

'No doctor's willing to come. Ma tried. For the lodger,' she said, rolling up the sleeves on Nell's new jacket. 'An apothecary at Blackfriars helped her out once, gave her credit. She never forgot him.'

'That would be my father,' I said. 'This lodger? Where had he come from?'

'Merchantman, landed a month ago. From India he said.'

'*He* was from India or his *ship* was from India?' I pressed.

'No, 'is ship. 'E's an Eastender. Brought up 'ere. Ma knew his ol' man. Why, what's 'appened to 'im?'

I spoke quietly. 'When was the last time you saw him?' She began to think. 'Saw him alive,' I pressed.

'Christ!' she blurted out. 'Oh, my fucking Christ, Nellie.' She broke down into tears and hugged Nell.

'He's been dead for at least two weeks,' I told her quietly.

'Ma said he wasn't to be disturbed. A shipmate of 'is paid 'is lodgings, all the time 'e's 'ere. Ev'ry Mond'y.'

'Follow me,' I instructed her, as Nell took my hand. 'With any luck it can be contained. But we'll not know who's infected, or otherwise, for a week or two. I'll send medicine for your mama. The council will have to pay. They won't want this spreading.'

Her name was Polly – and she was stunningly attractive; her hair black and long with ringlets. The woman she called her mother, *Ma* to be precise, had taken her in as a baby after finding her abandoned on the chapel steps near Billingsgate fish market.

'From that step to Wapping pier,' she explained to me, sitting near a blazing fire in my father's home. 'I ain't got far. Nothing so grand as this.'

'I've lit the fire under the copper in the scullery. I'll draw you a bath,' I offered, 'soon as the water is hot.'

'An 'ot barf? In the 'ouse?' she said, tugging at Nell's jacket. ''Ain't never seen that before, 'ave we Nell?'

'Then you can choose which bedrooms you'd like.'

'A bedroom to *meself?*' Polly exclaimed. 'Wait 'til I tell the gels. They'll all wanna come.' She giggled, and hugged Nell.

After their bath I found them night clothes from my mother's wardrobe and showed them their bedrooms. Nell, without the grime on her face, truly was an angel; a cherub if ever I saw one. She had light, blond hair, dimples to each cheek and large, round bright-blue eyes. While she sensed something untoward so far as her mother was concerned, she smiled almost constantly, and that always brought me good cheer. With her fair hair and pale skin she did so remind me of my lost love. But right then, I had the distraction of plague taking my mind off Emily.

Polly made a point of coming to thank me immediately she stepped out of her bath, completely naked as she spread the towels on a rack in front of the kitchen stove. Long wet black hair stretching halfway down her back, she was a picture of femininity, a nymph. But I would neither admit nor give in to the feelings she aroused, even after she curled up at my feet and asked me to comb her hair.

'I find you very attractive,' I said to her quietly and strode over to the sideboard. She appeared quite disappointed when I took a sketch pad and crayon from a drawer, drew the curtains and sat down in an armchair opposite. 'May I draw you?'

As I was finishing the outline there was a knock at the front door. I passed Polly a dressing gown and went to answer it.

It was a constable. He stood at a distance, back at the kerb. 'They identified the illness, sir,' he called out. 'Bubonic plague, like you suggested. Fleas, sir. Spread by fleas. You should be safe here. But we need you to remain isolated for a month or two at least. Just in case, like.' He came forward and reached out to me with a sheet of paper. 'Write down the names of all the occupants and their ages and pin it on the front door. I'll collect it later. Then I've got to seal the place up. Nobody goes in or out. Got that?'. I nodded.

The officer kindly agreed to the safe delivery of a note to my aunt, explaining my predicament and the need to be brought regular food supplies; and another to my employer apologising for my absence. I closed the door and returned to Polly. She slid the dressing gown off her shoulders so provocatively that I readily accepted the terrible situation in which I found myself.

'A month or two?' Polly giggled, throwing her arms around my neck, the dressing gown falling to the floor. 'What on earth shall we find to do, kind sir?'

Nell was fascinated by Papa's many books in the library. In particular she loved anything with animal pictures and Darwin's drawings in one precious volume occupied her for hours on end. I decided Polly and I should use the opportunity of our enforced imprisonment next to a library to teach Nell to read and write. It was quite a surprise to hear Polly's reaction.

'Well, I ain't no good wiv letters, meself,' she admitted, looking a little embarrassed. 'I fink the pair of us should knuckle under and take them lessons.'

And so it began. Day and night. By day, I taught Nell and Polly to read and write the alphabet and improve their diction. I also sketched both girls as they studied, and, in the attic room with the skylight, that my father had converted into a studio, made portraits from the sketches in oils. Fortunately, there was a good supply of pigments and ample linseed oil and turpentine. My aunt kindly supplied a roll of artist's canvas after I sent word to her. By night, after Nell was tucked in bed, Polly tried her hardest to return my teaching favours, offering to give me instruction of a more personal nature, in the bedroom.

'The bestest lessons money can buy,' she promised, adopting such provocative poses that I would often have to leave the room to hide the discomfort in my trousers. However, I fought against the temptation – although she never ceased to surprise me with her tales and descriptions of the imaginative games other folk were playing in this same city.

As difficult as it was, I resisted temptation and made no approaches towards Polly. One woman, Rebecca Muxlow, had already taken my virginity. And were it not for her badgering me with continual references to the age of consent being just thirteen only a few years earlier, I'm sure I would have struggled harder to hang onto it. I vowed from that day I would abstain and save myself for my one true love, Emily. Ever in the forefront of my mind, I knew that somehow, no matter what stood in my way, I would find Emily and bring her back into my life.

I soon had quite a collection of paintings, my favourite being one of Nell whom I'd dressed in a guardsman's bright-red jacket. It was a souvenir of my great-grandfather's, dating back to Waterloo. Having seen in the newspapers, before our incarceration, which art was currently fashionable, my portraits of Polly had her posing in various states of undress to compete with the high volume of similar, titillating works arriving from Paris. Once I gave Polly an idea of any pose I intended, she soon understood, and would sprawl out on the chaise longue in the most provocative manner. I knew then that all I had to do was capture that look, that temptation, and my work would easily sell.

It was four months before Nell demanded she see her mother, soon, having asked after her almost every day and been given vague reasons why it was not possible.

After a doctor attended us and the constable agreed our quarantine period was over, the three of us made our way to Wapping and to their home, or more precisely, the charred remains of what had been their home. The borough councillors had thought fit to control the outbreak of plague as best they knew how – they burned down the whole squalid terrace. Former neighbours confirmed to Polly that Ma and her lodger had been carted away and cremated. Nell was heartbroken, Polly uncertain of where their future lay.

'We can't impose on your kindness no longer, Jacob. Leave us 'ere – *here*,' she corrected herself. 'We'll find something, I'm sure.'

'No,' I insisted. 'Wouldn't dream of it. Come back with me. Nell and I both need looking after. I couldn't think of a nicer lady to do it.' I really didn't want to see her go.

'Jacob,' she said, taking both my hands. 'We's from a different class. It won't do. You'll never be proper comfortable pretendin' to live in our world. You– We don't live like a couple. Don't– Y'know? One day you'll find a nice young lady and then where will we be? On the street again, I 'spect. And it'll be much 'arder then, 'aving got used to a nice 'ouse and stuff.'

'Polly, please. Don't do this,' I pleaded earnestly. 'I'd never forgive myself if anything happened to either of you.'

'No. We've decided, Jacob,' she insisted. 'I'll ask around and find somewhere safe and come for our things in a coupla days.'

Nothing I said would dissuade Polly from leaving. When she returned at the weekend I gave her two large bags full of mother's best clothes and something I thought she could sell to help her on her way – the portrait of Nell in the red guardsman's jacket and one of herself. Polly explained that she had found a room for them to share with a friend in Whitechapel, just a mile or two from their former home.

It was mid-August, 1888, when they left; a very bleak day for me as I watched them drag their bags down onto the pavement out the front, a day I was sure to remember in view of what followed.

Aunt Alice said she would continue with my allowance for a little longer and I returned to the warehouse, although they could now only offer a couple of hours a day instead of ten, my position having been filled. Down in the dusty laboratory at home, I found significant quantities of ingredients which I intended selling back to the warehouse – but that was before Polly's acquaintances called. They claimed she had recommended me after saving her life. Every one of them suffered ailments associated with poor living conditions or malnutrition and most left my dispensary carrying as much food as medicine. I was willing to wager that the food was soon exchanged for gin or some form of alcohol before they arrived back in the East End. The small payments they were able to offer barely covered the cost of the food and soon ran out.

I knew then I had to offer my portraits for sale; sell them or starve. Selling what remained of my parent's clothes enabled me to purchase another roll of artist's canvas and some stretchers, for framing it.

Two weeks after Polly and Nell departed, on the last day of August, 1888, I ventured along the Embankment to the offices of the *Evening Standard* in order to invest in a small advertisement. A bustling crowd were clambering over each other for copies of that evening's edition. I become alarmed when I caught a glimpse of the headline: 'Brutal Murder in Whitechapel'.

I bought a copy and scanned the front page. My heart stopped upon reading that the victim, a Mary Ann Nicholls, was also known as Polly. I found myself in a blind panic.

I spent my last shilling taking a hackney to Whitechapel where I made enquiries as to the whereabouts of the murder. I had with me sketches of Polly and upon arrival in the repulsive neighbourhood of Buck's Row I entered an ale house.

'The murdered lady,' I asked the landlord, showing him a sketch of Polly, 'was this her?'

He laughed, grabbing the sketch. 'Lady? Polly Nichols ain't no lady. What, leave you with a dose, did she? Want your money back, that it?' His customers found that greatly amusing. The overweight landlord squinted his eyes as he held my sketch up to a lamp. 'Didn't know she'd scrub up that well, that's for sure. Difficult to say. But I guess–Yeah, could be 'er.'

'She would have shared a room, with Nell. Nell or Nellie she was sometimes called.'

'Nellie,' the landlord added. 'Yeah, Nellie Holland.'

I felt ill and sat down. My Polly. I'd sent her into the very depths of hell. I went outside and retched. My poor, poor dears. What a callous fool I'd been, sending them away – nothing could have been more cruel. And what of dear Nell?

I must have knocked on every door in Whitechapel before I finally returned home after midnight, grief-stricken over dear Polly and worried stiff about poor Nell. No one could help me with finding the sweet girl. I mourned the loss of my little family and the joy they'd brought into my life for those few short weeks.

After a miserable month, with little left in the larder, I headed towards the Savoy where I knew that, close by, *The Strand Gallery* exhibited some of the finest art I'd seen in London. I had with me a business card handwritten in my best copperplate script and two portraits, the oil barely dry. Both were of Polly. I couldn't bear to part with them, but it was that or starve.

I found the front of the gallery surrounded by a lively group of well-dressed folk bustling to get a glimpse of something in the window. Obviously, the proprietor had chosen wisely once again and was causing quite a stir outside. None had ventured inside and the fact I would not be causing too much of a disturbance improved my confidence as I opened the door and made my way in.

The proprietor was a flamboyant toff with shiny, flat hair and a waxed moustache, who might have thought he sounded French but his version grated on my ears, my fluency in that language being far superior to his.

'*Monsieur, bonjour*,' he greeted me with and then, continuing in French, told me his name was Jean-Louis and, twisting the ends of his moustache, asked how I was, how was the weather pleasing me and how could he, favoured expert in art in all London, help me invest in a work of art.

I answered in French only to find he didn't understand. When I offered to explain the purpose of my visit in English, he was visibly relieved and broke into perfect Cockney.

'Winder-dressin',' he replied, referring to his French, 'but I'll learn it one day. Them haristocrats adores it.'

I offered him my card. 'I hoped you could exhibit my work.'

'I doubt that,' he said dismissively, conjuring a huge purple handkerchief from his breast pocket and dabbing his nose. 'I'm known only for the best, you know.' He pointed to the small crowd outside peering in at an easel standing in the window. 'People buy from me because I can sniff out a good investment,' he dabbed his nose again, 'heirlooms, something they can 'ang on to or make a profit if they don't. Look at 'em stare. Guests from the Savoy, mostly. I tips the commissionaire. Jean-Louis, gets first butcher's. Them out there,' he said, pointing to the crowd through the window and tucking his handkerchief away, 'are making a note in their 'eads. *The* place to come for London's finest art.'

He strutted over to the back of the easel. 'Take this little gem,' he said, holding the legs of the easel. 'Brought in this morning for her ladyship. Sold within minutes. Could've sold a dozen if I 'ad 'em.' He turned the picture to face us. A card showed the price, one hundred guineas, with *Sold* written boldly across it. I did my best to conceal my surprise.

'Her ladyship?' I asked him.

'Sent her lady-in-waiting,' he whispered into my ear. 'And she could wait on me anytime she liked.'

'You could have sold more like this?' I asked him.

'By this artist, yes. But tell me, what kind of thing do you paint, young man?'

I pulled the two portraits of Polly from my bag and leaned them against the wall.

'How exquisite,' he said, picking up one of the paintings and taking it into the daylight in the front window. It featured Polly bent over backwards on the chaise. 'You knows the gel, then?'

'Gel?' I asked.

'There can't be *two* such beauties in all of London, surely? This is the lady-in-waiting I referred to,' he said, pointing at the other painting on the easel. 'She'll be calling soon for her ladyship's money.' He ran his hand over Polly's thrusting breast. 'My God, you've captured her well. I can sell these. Betya life.'

I felt elated. Polly *wasn't* the victim of the man the newspapers were now calling *Jack the Ripper*. She was alive and well. And that could only mean Nell was in safe hands, too. How delightful! And they had the means to make a good start in their new home. I laughed out loud, surprising Jean-Louis, and referred him back to my card and my signature on it. Then I held the card against the signature at the bottom of the portrait on the easel before us in the window; an angelic child, Nell, wearing a guardsman's crimson jacket.

His mouth gaped as I turned to leave.

'I'll bring more like her ladyship's paintings in a couple of weeks, Jean-Louis,' I said, leaving the two portraits of Polly behind, for him to sell. 'Please let her lady-in-waiting know when she comes for her money that Jacob Silver the artist called and would she leave her address that I might call on her and renew our acquaintance.'

'And maybe she could continue to *pose* for you, sir?' Jean-Louis said suggestively, running his fingers over Polly's breast again. 'Very marketable. Very marketable indeed.'

'Yes, indeed,' I smiled and opened the door. '*Bonjour, monsieur.*'

Once home, I raced up to my studio and pulled out sketches of Emily. I was determined my next paintings would be special and after the daylight faded and I could no longer work on the canvas I sought out formulae in the old tome: *Alchemy* that might make the finished work even more desirable than the pretentious Jean-Louis could ever imagine.

Two weeks later I returned to collect eighty pounds from the sale of the two portraits of Polly and took along my new offering. I watched proudly as an excited Jean-Louis examined what I felt was my best ever painting.

'Between Manet and Monet, I think,' he proposed, holding it up on the wall. He moved along further, 'After Rubens, before Turner, maybe?' He sashayed over to the window with it. 'No. It deserves a place of its own.' He pulled another painting off the easel in the window and put my *Emily* in its place.

Out through the window, people stopped in their tracks, cooed and pointed. A small crowd soon gathered. And they all had something remarkable in common. All their eyes stared – their pupils huge.

And I knew exactly the reason why.

'You must promise me exclusivity, Master Silver, I insist,' Jean-Louis said as he offered me two sovereigns. 'An advance. Bring me everything, you 'ear?'

By the time I left his gallery a crowd had gathered outside, clambering to get a glimpse of my very own Mona Lisa.

The following day a messenger called at my home and said he'd been instructed to await a reply.

'*Emily* sold,' the note read, 'When can you bring some more?' It was signed Jean-Louis St Clair. There was a sealed envelope inside.

'Tell him two weeks. I'll work day and night,' I told the messenger. After he left I opened the envelope; a bank cheque for an awful lot of money – one hundred and fifty pounds. My first cheque. And the first I'd ever seen. Papa had a bank account but I don't ever recall him writing or receiving cheques. People we traded with insisted on cash. 'Cash before you kill 'em,' the supplier's carrier would say on every delivery, before attempting to unload anything off his wagon. And Papa said the same terms applied to those we dispensed our medicines to. Cash before *we* killed them.

I opened my own bank account and now that I was in funds decided to invest in some fresh food to fill the larder, and just as importantly, someone to cook it.

I wrote out a cardboard sign but surprisingly, before I could hang it on the front door, there was a knock at the side door and a lady who looked rather familiar asked if the housekeeper vacancy was still available.

I nodded, and the rather large woman, as round as she was tall, barged her way past me and headed indoors.

'How did– Who sent you?' I said to her back.

'The Institute,' she replied, heading upstairs. 'Which room's mine?' she called out from the top landing.

'Turn right, box room at the–' I offered, but the box room door slammed shut before I finished.

From outside her door I could hear her unpacking and humming happily. 'You're Betsy Pollock, the Matron at Greenwold,' I called out. The humming stopped, but she didn't answer. 'We haven't discussed your duties. Your hours.' She still didn't answer. 'What am I to pay you?' The door opened and she stuck her large round and dimpled face out. 'We agreed two shillings and sixpence and all found. Thank you,' she said, closing the door sharply.

'*We* agreed?' I called back to her.

'The Institute,' she called out.

How the Institute would know of my needs or, for that matter, know anything at all about me I found bewildering, especially as I neither knew nothing of who or what it was, and why they should interfere in my business. While I could recall, vaguely, that they'd something to do with my receiving my treasured tome *Alchemy*, it would be sometime before I discovered that the Ancient Institute of Apothecaries and Alchemists was, in fact, a co-sponsor behind my scholarship to Greenwold College.

It was such a relief to find Betsy performed well in the kitchen. After finishing my first proper meal for months and then settling into a regime of long spells in my studio, painting variations of Emily, interspersed with regular meals, I found myself quite content with the decision to employ her.

But I had no idea she was conspiring against me.

Chapter 7

As time passed, and having informed the wholesalers I was no longer available for work, I hadn't so much as stepped out of the house. I realised I had no need of people to complicate or clutter my life. I would spend a little time each morning in the laboratory topping up the tincture that I had grown accustomed to taking – and that ensured I had all the company I needed, in the privacy of my locked studio. It was something from the mood collection that I had mastered with the professor back at the college and which, I discovered later, of all the potions listed in my wonderful book *Alchemy*, would have the most profound effect on me.

It was my little secret, something I made sure Betsy was not aware of. It was the same tincture I had used on Emily, back at Greenwold, and I could never forget what it did for her and how it cheered her so. Imbibing her remedy made me feel part of what she and I had together; part of *her*. And what harm was there in a wee drop every now and then – or two drops, occasionally more, depending on how my mood took me?

The lure from the bottle of pale green liquid standing on the windowsill, particularly when the sunlight streamed through it, throwing a perfect spectral array across the wall opposite, was quite irresistible. Consuming that nectar always brought her to me, but oh, how I missed touching that girl!

Whatever I created on canvas would sell. With Jean-Louis continually insisting *eroticism is the future*, and with Emily so eager to please, I did find my art leaning in that direction. While she would do anything I asked, I found she never ceased to surprise me with new, ever more provocative poses.

I could paint what I liked, as long as I wished, and someone else ensured that I ate properly; the house was cleaned and there was a clean shirt to put on if I needed one. How many others were as fortunate? I was emperor of my own domain. Everything was within my control. How could I not be content? What could possibly go wrong?

My artist's palette, prepared each morning, consisted of a healthy daub of burnt umber, one of chrome yellow, a French blue, another of crimson or vermilion as the fancy took me, purest white and blackest black; ample turpentine and linseed oil alongside, together with a small dish of the most important ingredient of all – *Desire* – my wonderful pale green tipple. I always began by dipping the brush in the delicious *Desire*. I liked to suck that dry, leaving the bristles damp, at the same time gaining my first pick-me-up of the day. Dipping again and mixing that with the paint, I was ready to paint anything my imagination could conjure up.

If the canvas was blank, from a fresh start, I knew it wouldn't be for long. No sooner the outline wet the canvas, Emily would arrive and whet my appetite to continue with gusto. Another quick dip or two and she would laugh; yet more, and her infectious giggle would fill the air and I would soon be sharing a private paradise with an angel.

There were times when I would look at that pale green liquid in the bottle and sense its comradeship – and how much I was in its debt.

I found I was only content painting Emily. Day after day, building her image in front of my eyes, I felt I was a part of her and she of me. She would respond; I learned what pleased and displeased her; and before long, I heard her respond – her sweet angelic voice.

'You got a woman in there, master?' Betsy called out from the landing one day.

I opened the door and assured her I was alone. To my surprise she passed me a full bottle of my favourite green tipple, adding, 'I made you this up. So's you can carry on working, like. And I think it's high time you opened the dispensary again. It'll provide an income until your paintings sell reg'lar.' And before I could comment, 'I'll go start tidying things up down there.'

'I only have one certificate. I need to study, sit more exams,' I called after her, hoping she would drop the idea.

'I have the certificates,' she insisted, 'You've no need to concern yourself about that.'

I wanted to ask to see them, but she walked away with such a stern face I decided to leave it until another opportunity arose. But I was so surprised she was aware of my secret tipple, as I had always kept it in a concealed compartment in the back of a cupboard in the studio.

Later, I was away from the house for three or four hours replenishing art materials. When I returned, Betsy was as good as her word, opening up the dispensary. She had ripped away the boarding from the old shop front and cleaned some eighty years of grime off the plate glass windows beneath. A man arrived and leaned a ladder against the outside and began scraping the paintwork.

Within a couple of days, *S. Silver & Sons ~ Apothecaries,* above the windows, shone brightly and it looked like we would soon be back in business.

'People are pestering for medicines and we don't have any stock,' I told Betsy early one morning, after a rude awakening from a hoard of people banging on the windows.

'All in hand, Master Jacob,' Betsy told me as she swept past me on her way from the laboratory, her arms full of merchandise. 'Credit,' she assured me. 'You pay the suppliers end of the week.'

I hoped she had remembered Papa's adage: *cash before you kill 'em,* in order to repay the supplier. Following her, eager to see for myself exactly what she had achieved in her new shop – bearing my name above the door – it was a pleasant surprise, not at all as I feared. What had become a disused, dusty and dilapidated storeroom full of old furniture and empty containers of every shape and size had been transformed into what must have been one of the trendiest pharmacies in all of London. Bright lights shone down on shelves loaded with coloured bottles and jars, medicines and cures, powders, dried leaves and plants. It was truly breath-taking – and I had contributed nothing. I felt ashamed. I realised Betsy had been with me just six months and was now virtually in control of my life. But I was quite content to float along with her.

'You get back to your art,' Betsy insisted, pushing me out of the door. 'Can manage here quite well on my own, thank you.'

Before I reached the top of the stairs I heard the shop bell ring and the first customer enter. I looked out of the window to see customers impressed by the window displays making their way inside. Betsy would do a roaring trade.

Returning to the sanctuary of my attic studio and locking the door, I consumed another tall glass of my green inspiration and eagerly awaited the wonders that would manifest themselves before my eyes. I was soon wrapped in the ecstasy of Emily engaging me with her imaginative sexual fantasies, finding it difficult to choose which pose should finally appear on the canvas.

I could never have known then that, three floors below me, Betsy was plotting murder.

The Trial: Day 4

A bottle of pale green liquid stood in a ray of sunlight on a table before Percy Ponsonby. I found myself almost mesmerised by a perfect spectrum cast through the bottle, the jurors' faces striped with the brilliant colours of the rainbow. Alongside the bottle, numbered jars contained different coloured powders.

The elderly witness stooped in the witness box and lowered his right hand, passing the Bible back to the clerk.

'Your name and profession, sir?' asked prosecuting counsel, Mr Ponsonby. 'Please address your comments to the jury.'

'Dr Horatio Pincher. Principal of Toxicology at the Royal London Hospital, sir.'

'Dr Pincher, were you given these items to examine by the police?' Mr Ponsonby pointed to the jars and bottle on the table.

'I was, sir.'

'Exhibits 16 to 22, m'lud,' Mr Ponsonby said to the judge. 'Tell the court what you discovered, doctor.'

'One jar contained a chemical compound: thujone; the other five, pulverised dried herbs and fungi. Ergot; psilocybe semilanceata; peyote cacti; belladonna, commonly known as deadly nightshade; and the last, thapsia villosa, commonly known as deadly carrot.'

'And, in simple terms, what do they have in common, doctor?'

'They are all hallucinogenic and deadly poisonous, taken sufficiently, sir.'

'Taken sufficiently?' asked Mr Ponsonby.

'A mere drop would cause hallucinations. A teaspoon or two of some of them would poison an individual. Half a cup would just about do all this lot in,' said the doctor, waving around the court with a wide grin on his face. Gasps came from the public gallery and some people crossed themselves. The judge sneered and pushed his glasses up his nose.

Mr Ponsonby held up a jacket and turned it inside out to reveal a line of corked glass vials supported by webbing, sewn into the lining. He passed it to Dr Pincher.

'You examined this selection of potions, doctor?'

'Yes. I identified all the ingredients of Exhibits 16 to 22,' the doctor said, pointing to the table, 'contained within these glass vials.'

'And this?' said Mr Ponsonby, taking back the jacket and passing the witness the bottle of pale green liquid.

Coloured light danced over the doctor's face as he waved it about. 'Closely resembles absinthe, sir. But in this case, seventy per cent proof. Considered to be an addictive psychoactive drug. The Green Fairy. But in this—'

Laughter erupted from the gallery as, up here, they imitated a toast, chinking imaginary glasses of the stuff.

'But in this particular sample, the chemical compound thujone, from the exhibited jar Number 16, normally present in absinthe in trace amounts is way, way above tolerable levels.'

'And what, in your expert opinion, doctor, would be the effect on anyone drinking this *adulterated* concoction?'

'Well, absinthe is the favoured tipple of many artists and bohemians, well known for its hallucinatory properties,' the doctor continued as he tapped the bottle. 'A mere few drops of *this* concoction would likely have a nun swinging naked from the chandeliers in Saint Paul's Cathedral during Sunday Mass.'

Raucous laughter rose from the gallery as vulgar men and women shouted and reached out for it.

'Make mine a double, guv'nor!' one toothless old lady called out.

'I'll 'ave a pint for the missus, mate!' a stout man shouted.

Even Mr Ponsonby found himself smiling as the room filled with laughter. The judge, not at all amused, hammered his gavel for a good few moments before order was restored.

'And suppose, doctor, one were to consume this concoction regularly,' Mr Ponsonby continued, staring at the accused, 'habitually?'

'It is my professional opinion that any person consuming such a mixture would find their mind distorted, and probably not be in any fit state to do anything about it. It would be akin to suffering an exaggerated bout of the DTs – delirium tremens; bottle-ache, barrel fever. Delirium from acute alcoholic poisoning.' He pointed up to the public gallery, 'I'm sure *they* can tell you what that's like,' and laughed. 'It would distort their vision and impair their judgement, perhaps beyond repair. Hallucinations might last months, possibly becoming permanent. Frankly, they would be considered quite mad.'

'And if this noxious substance were *withdrawn* suddenly, say? Like it might be if the person were incarcerated, for example?'

'Provided the brain wasn't already damaged permanently, that person would suffer severe withdrawal symptoms until hopefully returning to normal,' the doctor proposed, the bottle standing on the ledge in front of him, adding: 'Those withdrawal symptoms would be horrific, mind. He or she would have to be secured to keep them from harming themselves.'

'But they *could* return to… to normality?'

'Yes, sir. But there's an equal chance they wouldn't.'

Then Jacob had been tortured so – hung out to dry. This explained his terrible appearance, his sunken, black eye sockets and pale face, a profound change from when I had seen him last in my own home.

'Dr Pincher, did you find this same concoction, this same elixir shall we call it, present in any other samples given you?'

'It was present in each of the five jars – the liquid in which the five severed heads were suspended; in a glass in a bathroom cabinet next to a toothbrush; a cup in the kitchen, another in the laboratory; and traces were found in the accused's blood, from a sample taken.'

'Traces in his blood?'

'Sufficient to determine that the accused would have been a regular consumer of the elixir – and without doubt addicted.'

'As he admits, Dr Pincher. Could you draw any conclusions from it being the suspension liquid inside the five jars?'

'The accused admitted to tasting samples from Emily's jar. As her head decomposed, a stronger concoction would have resulted – and only *that* version would have appealed to him; or more simply explained, have given him the kick he desired. It is my opinion that, given the volume found in his blood, he likely drank from all the jars.'

'Can you be sure of that?'

'No, to be fair. No, I can't. But why not? His state of mind then, meant he was dependent on the stuff. And here it was in abundant supply. Cups and glasses everywhere proved he had imbibed regularly.'

'No more questions, m'lud,' Mr Ponsonby called out and promptly sat down.

The behaviour described was disgusting. I desperately needed fresh air. Jacob had admitted his addiction but the prosecution were making far more of it than was the case. Surely?

Chapter 8

Bloodshot eyes sunk deep into his skull, Jacob painted furiously. Another picture of Emily erotically posing on the chaise rapidly took shape on the canvas, her delicate arm draped over the back. His eyes flicked back and forth – from easel to chaise.

But the chaise was empty.

Emily's infectious giggle echoed through the air. Her voice in his head, teasing: *Angel?* Jacob was intoxicated with her. Then father's voice: *Find the secret…* The professor's: *I can make you immortal and you find that dull?* Everyone competed for his attention.

On the canvas, Emily laughed and giggled, teased and tantalised him, slid her blouse off her shoulder and fondled her breasts; pouted her lips.

Jacob drained the last of the green nectar into a bowl, sucked it dry. But it seemed like it was only a few minutes before he grimaced and shrieked as Emily faded – became transparent. In panic, his brushes flashed across the canvas, desperately trying to capture what they could until, finally, she disappeared altogether.

Housekeeper Betsy entered carrying the apothecary's bible: the pharmacopoeia. She flopped onto the chaise and took up Emily's exact pose in the portrait, an arm as thick as Emily's waist draped over the back – a beached whale imitating the angelic mermaid.

'Paint her enough, Master Jacob, and she'll surely stay,' Betsy breathed to herself. Tapping the book, she beckoned Jacob to come sit beside her.

'Got three with whooping cough, two mumps, a measles, and a chicken pox. Knock up something by teatime, there's a good boy.'

At dinner, after Betsy served Jacob a huge meal followed by his usual tall glass of pale green nectar, she plonked *Alchemy* next to him.

'Finish up your medication, won't you? There's a dear.' she said, pushing the glass close to his hand. 'And you won't forget your studies, Master Jacob, will you?' She opened the book at 'Immortality'. 'You promised your father,'

Jacob screwed up his face, puzzled. But Betsy left the room before he could ask how she knew about his promise to his father. After a few sips of his nightly nectar, the matter dropped out of his head completely, along with anything else of importance.

Later, in the laboratory, Betsy stood at his elbow egging him on, throwing in ingredients while Jacob stirred the pot. She offered a spoon of steaming brown sludge up to Jacob's mouth. After slurping the spoon dry, Jacob lost his balance, the room twisting and turning.

'Long as it don't kill you, we know it'll do,' said Betsy, giving a raucous laugh.

And so it was, day after day: customers' requirements demanding he spend hours in the laboratory between heavenly painting sessions up in the studio; Emily's giggles as much a necessity to his happiness as the green stuff until suddenly, something he never dared dream of occurred – his inspiration dried up. Emily no longer came to him. She refused to appear on the canvas, no matter how much nectar he poured down his throat, no matter how strong his demands. She wasn't coming out to play.

The shop, open nine months, was now making a little profit but he had become accustomed to living at a much higher standard compared to that of his parents. Wine accompanied every meal; as did a cigar afterwards and a glass of port or two, not forgetting the all-important potion that he had relied on for so long. And Betsy needed paying, of course. He was becoming a celebrity, he considered, and so had invested in new clothes for his gallery appearances, although of late, most often due to his addled and addicted state, he was able to attend on only very few occasions.

And as Jacob's inspiration dried up, Jean-Louis' demands increased for more works of Jacob's special erotica for his gallery. He was beginning to lose patience with the young artist and refused an advance, after Jacob had requested one.

'We need more port,' Jacob asked Betsy on her way out one December morning, 'there's none in the house. And sherry. It's Christmas. Get them to send a bottle or two, if you will.'

'I'm off to the wine merchant's now, Master Jacob, to pay off a little towards his account,' Betsy said in a huff as she scooped up what little change there was out of the till. 'He insists there's no more credit until the account is cleared. And the grocer took that side of bacon back, that you ordered, since I couldn't pay. We must cut back, Master Jacob, Christmas or no. Cut back or close down. *You* choose.'

Before Jacob could complain, an advertisement he spotted in *The Times* would prove to save his bacon. A symposium of science was to be held at the Crystal Palace in ten days' time on New Year's Day, 1890, and contributors were welcomed to submit applications. Noting numerous well-known quacks and clairvoyants had already been accepted, Jacob decided to make an application to contribute. He would speak about the history of modern medicine. His application was accepted.

After preparing meticulous notes, his lecture proved an enormous success. Wiser men than he stood to give him applause. Another contributor asked to speak with him after his presentation; he was a senior official from the Pasteur Institute in Paris, a foundation that had opened recently, in 1888. Jacob had heard of Louis Pasteur and his work on anthrax and rabies, *pasteurization* fast becoming a universal process it seemed. After cunningly avoiding questions about which college of medicine he had studied at, Jacob was surprised by his admirer's request to consider joining their institute as their London representative. They wished to study English strains of diseases they were attempting to eradicate – and Jacob was an apothecary who lived at the heart of the densest populated area in all England, harbouring every disease under the sun. What better? No sooner had they finished speaking when a very talkative Polish woman, in her twenties, joined them, a personal friend of Louis Pasteur she claimed – Marie Curie. She, too, complimented Jacob on his presentation and soon had Jacob engrossed in what she and her husband were studying, something they had decided to call: *radioactivity*. By the time Jacob left the Crystal Palace that day he had made the acquaintance of no less than four scientists from Europe, including the Pasteurs and the Curies, all agreeing to share experiences and experiments. Two had promised him a small income to assist with expenses. He had learned a profound lesson from all the important speakers that day: *not to let the imagination stifle progress – let it run wild – exciting discoveries did not lay in the mundane.*

After Crystal Palace, Jacob flung himself back into studying the sciences, down in his laboratory. And he did let his imagination run wild – imbibing prolifically in his favourite nectar. For a while, since she had refused to come at his beckoning, Emily was put aside.

By New Year's Eve, 1890, Jacob was selling patents of his own medicines. Working with a Dr Adolf Behring from Berlin, whom he met at the Crystal Palace Symposium, he had assisted in the discovery of an antitoxin for diphtheria, a disease labelled the scourge of the nation at the time. He left Dr Behring to work privately on his own, against a disease that had devastated many and in which he had a very personal interest – polio. Needing to *prove* his results to himself, alone in his laboratory while revellers celebrated in the street, he injected his own body as a human guinea-pig – a fact not divulged in his patent application, later. That night was one of extreme torment as his mutilated knee and shin bones started to grow again. It was more than he could endure – but morphine was close at hand. The final test, three agonising months later, attempting to walk without the leg braces that had supported him for almost five years, was as emotionally painful as the bone distortion itself. But it worked. He cried for hours with sheer joy, fearful of going to sleep and waking up to find it was all a dream; continually rubbing his new legs to satisfy himself the leg irons had really gone.

By March, 1891, the Pasteur Institute had agreed to assist with further testing and licensing of his discovery to enable marketing of the drug throughout Europe. It was by no means a cure for polio, it was more of a repairing agent for those it left crippled, and since scientists at Pasteur's saw no cure or vaccine on the horizon, they felt it worth the investment. By December that year, *Silvesteur*, the product of their joint venture, was on apothecaries' shelves to support its launch in all the medical journals. For the first time, Jacob felt assured about his future.

Visiting his attic studio for the first time in over a year, he stood at the easel staring at a half-completed portrait of Emily – dying to share with her his joy over his legs and his discovery. But Emily wouldn't materialise, however much he desired her to. He became distraught, fearing life without her, that he might never see her again. Despite the possibility of untold wealth, he considered life unbearable without his Emily. He turned to his faithful nectar again, but it failed him, no matter how much he drank or how haphazardly he topped up the ingredients, hoping to trigger her vision to appear. Finally, he came to the conclusion that the nectar itself was the cause of his lack of inspiration – his body having built an immunity to it.

'No more of this nectar,' Jacob instructed Betsy one night in early April, 1892, pushing the green glass away. 'I have no need of it. I must have Emily, the real Emily. I must find her – wherever she is.'

That night he wrote a letter to his old friend Muxlow at the college, apologising for not keeping in touch but begging him to pass his best wishes to Emily. He explained about his new legs and his successful branded medication and pleaded for an address where he might write to Emily, with a view to asking her to join him.

That same night, Betsy sat by the oil lamp in her room and penned a letter that would change both their lives forever:

I think the time is right for the mistress to join him.

On the fifteenth of April, 1892, late in the afternoon, Betsy Pollock served Jacob with a huge glass of a decidedly darker-green nectar.

'I thought we'd agreed I didn't care for this anymore,' Jacob complained.

'Try it,' Betsy said persuasively, 'I've used a different recipe. It'll calm you.' She passed him the glass. 'A very pretty young lady came into the shop today, asking after you,' Betsy said, urging him to finish the drink. 'I asked her to call back this evening, when you were free.'

'Pretty girl? Asking for me?' Jacob asked, his eyes glazing over, the nectar getting the better of him. 'Did she leave her name?'

'No, master. She didn't.' Betsy, content her master's curiosity was at its highest, waited a few minutes before placing a gramophone record on a turntable and wound the handle. An orchestra playing a spirited waltz soon filled the room.

'Master Jacob,' Betsy said, nervously wringing her hands together. 'A surprise for you.' She opened the drawing room door and brought in a visitor to join them.

Jacob, by now heavily intoxicated from the new beverage, screamed in terror, gripped his face in his hands and fell to his knees.

The Trial: Day 3

Mr Ponsonby continued questioning Sergeant Beck.

'Sergeant Beck, may we please now move on to what the accused said concerning the time when Emily Muxlow joined him in London. *When* did he say she had returned?'

'Silver was certain of the date, he didn't have to think about it. It was the fifteenth of April, 1892, he said.'

'Sergeant, let us be clear about the dates here. Emily had been ill, and apparently *close to death,* according to the accused, in February, 1888, having fallen into an icy river in Northamptonshire in the middle of a fierce winter, while recuperating from some other illness.'

'That is what Silver led me to believe, sir, yes.'

'Despite all these difficulties she had to overcome, she joined the accused, he told you, four years later, in London. Is that correct?'

'Yes, sir. At his apothecary's shop. He lived above, sir.'

'Did he say *why* she took so long, before joining him?'

'No, sir.'

'Did he say he had *invited* her?'

'He had written to the young lady's brother, but as yet, had no reply.'

'Did he *know* she was coming on that day?'

'No, sir. He made it clear it was a complete surprise.'

'Very well. Now, what was his reaction, when she, completely out of thin air, surprised him on his doorstep?'

'He said he screamed. Screamed out loud. The shock, you see.'

Chapter 9

The new concoction Betsy had prepared for me was far more powerful than anything I'd taken previously. It seemed to take control of me. My arms and legs felt quite numb. I told her I wanted no more, pushing her hands away, spilling some – but she kept insisting, topping up the glass until I had consumed what she considered a full measure. I felt powerless to stop her. And I was losing what little control I had left of my limbs. My head was in a spin, the room revolving about me.

After only a minute or two, the revolting taste and smell of the obnoxious nectar on my lips had me gagging and retching. I tried to stand up but my legs failed me, my whole body trembled.

What was happening to me?

Betsy herself was becoming more and more nervous before she said something about a young lady that had called into the shop and was asking after me. Then she announced:

'Master Jacob, a surprise for you!'

It was like a dream. A nightmare. She seemed to glide across the room to the door and open it – wheeling in a wicker bath chair. Betsy then dashed out of the door, slamming it closed behind her. No sooner had my eyes fallen upon the occupant of the wheelchair, my heart was in my mouth.

I screamed.

The room closed in about me; bile filled my mouth as the floor rose up and sucked me down into a disturbing, bottomless void.

Smelling salts, waved under my nose by Betsy, caused me to regain consciousness. I was still on the floor; with Betsy's aid, I sat up. Vaguely, I recalled what had happened. The bath chair. It was horrific. But I couldn't remember why. I became frightened again. Trembling, gibbering:

'Make it go away! Send it away!'

'It'll take a bit of getting used to, Master Jacob,' Betsy said softly. She handed me another glass of her distasteful nectar, refusing to move away until I drank it all. Again I waved it away but she insisted, forcing me to drink the vile potion. Finally, she took the empty glass from my hand.

'Shall we try again?' She reached behind me. I turned my head slightly and was startled upon noticing the wickerwork edge of that wretched bath chair again, so close to me. I crawled away to take refuge behind the sofa, my head throbbing from what appeared to be my own boiling blood pulsing through my brain. But then everything began to change – for the better. The ceiling gaslight transformed into a thousand twinkling stars; every corner of the room lit up with coloured light, pulsating, floating on a gentle breeze about the room. My head no longer throbbed and a glorious feeling of euphoria came over me. I was happy. I wanted to laugh. I *had* to laugh; share the happiness of my elation.

The sofa moved away and the wicker wheelchair gently rolled up to me. I kneeled to look inside again.

And there she was.

Emily.

And I laughed out loud, joyously. Emily looked radiant in a long evening gown, a glowing aura about her. Her eyes were not as bright as I once knew – but bright enough to bring me inward happiness again. Her hair was different, lighter and thinner; and her face... I noticed she had succumbed to the latest fashion of a tinted foundation. She had matured somewhat, but she was absolutely beautiful, as magnificent as when I'd last seen her.

There was music, a huge orchestra played a waltz – its elevating spirit matching my own. I cannot recall how Betsy had arranged everything – but it was a wonderful reception. Of a sudden, at least a hundred guests arrived, smiling, applauding and congratulating me. Half the aristocracy was there, thrilled by Emily's presence. And no sooner had we gone through to the ballroom there was Her Majesty, patting a seat for Emily to sit beside her. It was glorious. Emily was the centre of attraction – their new princess. Everybody rejoiced.

At breakfast the following morning, my recollection of the night before was far vaguer than I would have wished – but my throbbing head forbade me to dwell on it. Betsy served another glass of her mysterious and revolting nectar before attending to Emily. It lifted my spirits immediately – I felt I could float on air. She had persuaded me of the necessity to imbibe in the nectar frequently, to avoid dangerous ill-effects.

I recalled that Emily hadn't spoken that first evening; she was surely as shocked as I was, the sheer surprise of our meeting up like that. Betsy impressed upon me that Emily would need time to adjust; she was in a delicate state – hence the wheelchair.

'But cheer her enough,' Betsy said, 'and she'll be all you ever expected.'

At last, Betsy brought my love into the breakfast room – and my headache vanished. I felt complete again.

'My dear, it is so wonderful to see you again,' I told Emily, as I kissed her cheek.

Emily stared at me, not saying a word – but her look was all I needed. She needed time. She had to adjust. I pledged solemnly to myself that I would give her all the time she needed. Although I hadn't imagined it would be quite that long.

Day after day we sat together at every opportunity, until Betsy determined Emily was too tired and needed to rest. And still she was not back to her old self – the gaiety and spontaneous sense of fun that I had known in her, so distant. But I said nothing. I waited – waited until, finally, she came out of herself.

The sun was streaming through the windows one morning about a month later, after I had finished breakfast as well as my regular glass of nectar, and Betsy brought Emily down to join me.

'Good morning, Jacob,' Emily said calmly, the first words she had spoken to me since her arrival. I was elated. 'As it's such a beautiful day, I thought perhaps we could go sit in the garden?'

'Of course, my darling,' I said enthusiastically, 'of course. But why don't we stroll along the Embankment?'

'Good heavens, no, master,' Betsy interrupted. 'Madam's nowhere near well enough for that.'

'Very well,' I said, 'Then it's the garden. But will you not eat something first, Emily?'

'I've not the appetite to eat right now,' she said. 'Maybe later.'

It was a glorious May morning and I prepared to wheel her chair out into the garden when Betsy came fussing with an extra blanket. 'You must stay warm, madam,' Betsy said, tucking the blanket tightly around her and affixing a bonnet. 'Don't keep her out too long, master,' Betsy told me, opening the back door, and assisting me to lift the wheelchair down the two steps into the garden. 'I'll come and fetch you later.'

In the garden, spring was under full swing. A cherry tree was in blossom and other shrubs were beginning to bud. Birds of all description chirped in the warm sunshine. Although Emily didn't have much to say, she seemed content staring up at the odd cloud floating by.

'So, you got my message from your brother?' I asked Emily under the cherry blossom. She didn't answer. 'Tommy? How is he?'

I asked. Again, she said nothing and continued to stare skyward. 'Do you see him?' I pressed. 'I do miss old Muxlow. We were best friends.' After another long pause I asked, 'How are your family?'

Emily stared and said: 'We don't have much to do with one another any longer. Everybody has grown up, gone their separate ways.'

After a long silence, I felt I must ask: 'And Rebecca?'

'I want nothing more to do with her,' Emily said, after another long silence. 'She seemed to think *you* were *her* property,' she snarled.

'I thought it was a misunderstanding,' I tried, but Emily was furious.

'You would rather it was my sister sitting here, is that it?' she snapped, angrily, her eyes piercing through me like a knife to my heart.

I didn't answer. After what seemed far too long, I put my hand on her wheelchair and made my confession:

'You know, Emily, you are the only person in the world I care about. The only woman I have had affection for. I missed you terribly after leaving college. It broke my heart. And when you nearly died...' I couldn't speak for a few moments, but then ranted on: 'You do know it was *I* who saved you, do you?' She didn't answer. 'Nobody could love you as I do; I will do anything and everything to see you fully well again. You mean the world to me. You *are* my world. I've been so miserable without you. Please, please, trust me. Allow me to be as close to you as we once were. For without you I am nothing. Nothing. I would not wish to go back to that loneliness again, and—'

'I trust you,' she interrupted. 'But you have to accept I'm no longer the young girl you knew. I'm not well. I will need a lot of looking after.' She took a long deep breath and sighed. 'You must love me. Always love me. You must care for me and give me time.' She took another deep breath. 'I'll then be yours – completely. But hear this now, Jacob Silver – never neglect me, you hear? Never turn your back on me for another. Never fail to be there when I need you; come when I need you. It is important to me. It means everything to me.' And then she fell silent, a fan covering her face from the bright sun.

'I hear you, my darling,' I told her, solemnly, 'I hear you and will do what you ask and so much more.' Laying my hand on her blanket, I assured her: 'I will always love you.'

'I need you to come inside now,' Betsy called out as she ran down the garden and took control of Emily's chair. 'Emily you'll catch your death out here.' And as Betsy passed: 'Your medication is on the kitchen table, master,' she whispered to me, referring to the potent nectar she was so sure I needed.

I grew used to Emily's condition. Precisely *what* was ailing her, she would not say and forbade me to investigate. After reminding her of the cures I had discovered for others and the huge medical resources I had at my disposal, she still would not let me concern myself with what was troubling her. Others had prescribed what was good for her – she told me sternly – and I was not to interfere.

'Let me speak to those fools,' I told her, 'and I'll soon have you cured.'

'Make one move toward diagnosing my ailments, and I will leave you,' Emily warned me, 'in an instant.'

Frustrated that I could not intervene, no one was more surprised than I as to how willingly and lovingly Betsy took care of Emily and saw to all her needs. The one odd thing that I never got to the bottom of, was that whenever I suggested showing off Emily to the shop customers or taking her for a walk in her wheelchair, Betsy declined to let her go, for one reason or another.

Betsy also mixed Emily's various medications, my being banned from the laboratory when she did so. Together, we endeavoured to give Emily all the joy possible. I was delighted to find that after I introduced her to my father's library, she found much consolation in reading, and set out to read almost everything on the shelves. She digested literature like an industrial machine. Soon after I had left her with a fresh volume to read, Betsy would come and complain she had finished it and needed another. And she learned languages quicker than I ever thought possible. Soon, we were gabbling on in a multitude of languages exchanging views on the works of Anton Chekov, Pushkin, Fyodor Dostoyevsky, Leo Tolstoy, Emile Zola and Victor Hugo, among others. Emily could quote verbatim, eleven of Lord Byron's poems – as I could. Her favourite book was *War & Peace* by Leo Tolstoy and often, just before she went to sleep, she would read it to me, softly, her voice as hypnotic as a songbird's.

Although I had held back one portrait of Emily that I held dear, my *prized Emily*, I called it, completed from the sketches I had made of her at Lady Bedford's over four years earlier, it had been at least a year since I had taken any newly completed work to the gallery. Jean-Louis had become quite annoyed that I had *cut him off so*, he said. *Had I found another gallery?* I explained that my attention had been fully absorbed in science, and all the experimentation going on in the laboratory proved that. But Jean-Louis was sure that I had obtained a better price for my art, elsewhere. Eventually, I promised him I would work on some portraits, telling him Emily had come to stay.

Having Emily around me did give rise to a new passion to paint her and I was soon sketching her at every opportunity. She enjoyed the attention and would chat away about everything and anything, from the stench of the horse manure left in the street below her window to the sounds of the bargemen calling across the Thames, plying their trade. I found it exciting to be putting oil on canvas again, and what better subject than Emily herself.

'I just want to paint *you*,' I told her on one of her brighter days, 'so that all of London can enjoy your beauty and feel my appreciation for you.' But she declined to show much of her body, however much I urged, drawing the line at anything suggestive of eroticism.

She looked at me – puzzled. 'Let's hope all of London agrees with your perception of beauty,' Emily said, 'otherwise you could end up penniless.'

Each portrait took three weeks to complete, and I took them to the gallery no sooner they were finished. Jean-Louis seemed as enthusiastic as ever, initially, although this enthusiasm did wear thin when not a single one featured a naked breast. And none had sold.

'They're different, I give you that. But they're all of the same subject, Jacob, in the same boring pose,' Jean-Louis complained. 'You must have her do things with her body or find other women to pose – and more provocatively, I would suggest, if you have any hope of attracting regular buyers.' But I had no intention of insulting my dear Emily in such a way.

It was December before I took the eleventh portrait to the gallery – and still none of the others had sold. Embarrassed, I offered a proposal to Jean-Louis to help clear the lot.

'What if I bring in the most beautiful *Emily* of all – one that is certain to sell, and we display them all together at a reduced price?' I suggested, 'Like a series of Hogarth's lithographs. Everyone will want one, and they can help themselves.'

'Since they will be of the same subject, Jacob,' Jean-Louis considered, twiddling with the end of his waxed moustache, 'I suppose it could catch on.' After more thought he added, 'An edition limited to twelve, I could inform patrons accordingly. Yes, that could work. Bring it in.'

And so later that day, I delivered to the gallery my *prized Emily*. The only difference between all twelve was that the *prized* version had a topmost coat of varnish laced with my *Desire* potion.

After eight months of our being together, at Christmas, 1892, so contented and so in love, I felt it only proper that I put a serious question to Emily during the festivities.

'You've made me so content, my darling,' I told her Christmas evening in the drawing room, passing her a package of hand-made chocolate from her favourite chocolatier in Regent Street. I knelt beside her bath chair and held her face between my hands. 'I would be the happiest man in London if you would consent to marry me.' Inside the chocolate I had concealed a modest diamond engagement ring. But she did not get to open the chocolate.

She seemed surprised. Startled. She immediately called for Betsy, tears streaming down her face. I laughed, so sure she was overcome with joy. But I was mistaken.

It was an hour or so later, after being settled in her room, that Betsy returned to the drawing room, barely able to compose herself.

'She's not herself, master,' Betsy said, screwing a handkerchief in her hands. 'She loves you, I know she does. With all her heart. But marriage…' Betsy blew her nose. 'Marriage and all those people coming to the church, gawping… The last thing madam wants is to become a spectacle.'

As Betsy cried and left the room I was deeply saddened. Our love for each other was of the purest kind. Marriage was inevitable, I had imagined. Was Emily happy to continue as a *mistress*? Her possessiveness had me think otherwise. I was confused and took the chocolate with the ring away, locking them in my writing bureau. I was devastated as I turned the key in the lock. Heartbroken. Perhaps she needed more time? Time for us to *grow closer* – if that were possible. But how long? How long was I to wait to make our lives whole?

For fear of upsetting Emily again, I kept my distance – and she didn't complain. Jean-Louis, constantly pestered me from the gallery to sell the *prized Emily* – as nobody had any interest in the other eleven – and I vowed not to paint anything else until some of that collection were sold. I instructed the gallery not to sell the prize, my favourite work of art, at any price. With the success of *Desire* so well proven, I confess I was seriously considering slipping Emily similar potions, something that might change her mind. But I never had cause to. Two months had passed since my spurned proposal of marriage, when Emily made a proposal of her own:

'I see no reason why we cannot live together as man and wife,' she said calmly, not raising her eyes from the book she was reading. I was even more shocked when she added: 'The commoners do it all the time – without ceremony. So, why shouldn't we?'

I sat quite still for a few moments, with mixed feelings, for I had hitherto been the subject of rejection – rejected by a dear one living in the same house. For two months I had felt unloved. Unneeded. I had contemplated leaving; getting away from her, sure that that was what she required. And now, with this simple statement, Emily suddenly declaring that she fully accepted me, I realised I had been completely wrong. She *had* wanted me. She *did* love me. My heart thumped with excitement.

'Well?' she pressed.

'Er, yes. That… That would be wonderful,' I finally blurted out, grinning at her.

'Then I'll have Betsy re-arrange things,' she said matter-of-factly, like it meant less than changing the laundry. 'Have Betsy take me up now, will you,' she continued. 'I need to rest.'

After I was alone again, I felt cross. *When* would Betsy be asked to re-arrange things? I wondered if I had heard Emily correctly. Had she asked me – or more accurately: *told me* – to become her husband, or not? Was she expecting me to rush up there in hot pursuit, or wait until she was asleep? Her manner had me favouring the latter. Let her be asleep and only find I had not slept in her bed the next morning, when she awoke. Perhaps she might then appreciate me more, appreciate what being a *loving* wife entailed. The least I had expected was an invitation to jump over a broom with her. And jolly soon. I couldn't stop thinking how so much more joyous it would all have been, and emotionally comforting, if Emily had simply told me that she, too, was in love and wanted to marry me.

And to my immense surprise, that was what the note said, brought to me on a silver platter the following week, the twelfth of March, 1893:

I love you so much – let us privately
celebrate and become man and wife. Emily.

But before that happy occasion, a visitor arrived who would change everything – and kill my darling bride.

The Trial: Day 3

'So how did the accused describe Emily's condition, sergeant,' Mr Ponsonby asked Sergeant Beck.

' "I was in shock," he said, and apparently collapsed. He went on to tell me:

"When I finally regained consciousness and had my wits about me, Emily looked radiant in a long evening gown, a glowing aura about her. She had matured somewhat, but, to me, she was absolutely beautiful, as magnificent as when I'd last seen her.

"There was music, a huge orchestra. I don't recall how Betsy," his housekeeper, sir, "had arranged everything – but it was a wonderful reception. At least a hundred guests were there, smiling, applauding and congratulating me."

'For clarity, I asked him to repeat where, exactly, this reception was held. He replied:

"At the house, moments after she came through the door."

'*Your* house? I questioned. A hundred guests, you say? Anyone we know?' He replied:

"Half the aristocracy was there. And no sooner had we gone through to the ballroom there was Her Majesty, patting a seat for Emily to sit beside her." '

Coos and murmurs rose from the court. *Her Majesty was there?* I was amused at first, but this was the first occasion during the trial when I began to doubt Jacob's sanity.

'Sergeant, I must ask you: How did you feel after hearing this?' Mr Ponsonby asked.

'I asked him again: Did you say: *Ballroom?* And he looked at me strangely. I suspected he was playing with me; trying to impress me how so upper class he was, perhaps. After getting him to confirm things again, I wondered if he was intoxicated in any way, taking anything – anything that would make him speak of such nonsense.'

'Such nonsense?'

'It's a flat above a shop. I've been there. All right, it's a big flat, but there's no room for an orchestra, let alone a hundred guests. And as for Queen Victoria, in the ballroom? Huh! There was no sign of alcohol on his breath. I thought he was hallucinating or spinning a yarn, sir.'

'Up until then, how would you have described his mental state during the interview?'

'He was obviously an intelligent young man, well-spoken and lucid. He didn't slur his speech at all, or seem to suffer any symptoms of intoxication. He was alert, and answered all my questions promptly and politely.'

'What did he then go on to say about Emily's condition?'

'He said that she was unwell, not on her feet. She was in a bath chair, attended to day and night by the housekeeper. But he swore he would never let her out of his sight again.'

'Who brought up the question of marriage?' asked the prosecutor.

'According to the accused, he, Jacob Silver, asked Miss Emily first, on Christmas Day, 1892 to marry him. But apparently she wasn't ready for marriage. Later, he said that Emily sent him a note asking *him* to marry *her*. That would have been early March, 1893.'

'But they didn't marry, did they?'

'No. A visitor arrived soon after they agreed to marry. Silver's exact words were:

"A visitor arrived who would change everything – and kill my darling bride." '

And I was confident that, after we had heard more about this visitor, Jacob would be vindicated.

Chapter 10

15th March, 1893

An eerie mist swirled around dark, ominous shadows in the cobbled street as the afternoon sun struggled to break through dense fog. A carriage pulled up outside the closed shop as thick yellow smoke billowed up from basement windows.

Down in the basement laboratory, Jacob, almost twenty-three, coughed and spluttered in a thick yellow smog.

'Emmy! Gagging here! Ask Betsy to help me open some windows.'

'Too much sodium I fear, Master Silver.' The man's gravelly voice startled him. He peered into the fog. As it cleared. . .

'By heavens! I don't believe it! Emmy! Emmy! A visitor.' The two men greeted each other fondly. 'You haven't changed a bit,' Jacob enthused, standing back to admire his old mentor.

'But *you* have, Master Jacob. Most surely,' replied the professor, now having to look up at Jacob standing a foot taller than he. He gaped around the laboratory at all the equipment, stroking his scraggly white beard. 'And just look what we have here.'

Jacob led the professor to each bench on a conducted tour. 'Mould on saddles cured the horses' saddle sores. I've managed to grow it and bottle it. I'm preparing a thesis for the Pasteur Institute in Paris.' At another cluttered bench, 'Bits and pieces sent me for analysis. I'm working with scientists all over Europe.'

Jacob pulled down a brass lever attached to the wall. Loud clanking and hissing filled the room as the whole wall opposite slid back to reveal various experiments on benches.

'Works by compressed air. My father kept this room for dangerous experiments.' He pointed down some stone steps. 'The river's just down there, if I need to put out a fire.' Stepping inside the exposed anteroom, they walked over to a piece of rock in a glass case. 'Working with a young Polish lady living in Paris, Marie Curie. She calls it *radioactivity*. Determined young lady, pesters me the whole time. Never gives up.'

After Jacob closed the wall again, the professor found *Alchemy* lying on a bench and tapped the cover.

'And. . .?'

Jacob puffed out his chest. 'The theory put into practice, my dear professor! Come, my turn to enlighten you.'

From the street, Jacob called back inside the open shop door, 'Emmy, we have business at the gallery and shall return soon,' before closing the door behind them and hailing a hackney cab.

'Not to be. . . You're walking–'

'The old leg irons?' Jacob laughed, doing a little hop and a skip. 'Tonics I made. Re-grew the bones. And calcium carbonate. Ten spoonfuls a day. Farted like a pig. Betsy kept her distance. But not bad, eh? Sells like hot cakes.'

A hackney cab pulled up alongside them, the horse sweating. As they embarked, 'Savoy!' Jacob called to the cabbie.

The professor waved to Betsy, smiling at them through the shop window as they left.

*

When I entered the gallery that morning with the professor, Jean-Louis was greeting a distinguished couple.

'*Monsieur, madame. Quel plaisir de vous rencontrer à nouveau.*'

'One day, a real Frog will come in and castrate him,' I laughed, leading the professor through a selection of modern art. I hadn't noticed these particular offerings before, and feared that Jean-Louis' eye for quality was failing. Macabre horror paintings, scenes from the Ripper murders almost five years earlier, left nothing to the imagination. Blood and guts and yet more vivid, scarlet blood. A scrawled signature meant nothing to me.

'Why such talented artists feel the need to shock is beyond me. Jean-Louis will have his gallery wallowing in the gutter,' I told the professor.

I led him to a larger salon and my own special exhibition. I smiled when the professor stopped abruptly, stunned, his mouth wide open.

'Odd, I know. But it's an experiment,' I started to explain.

All in a line, two yards apart, twelve of my portraits, absolutely identical. And all of my favourite subject – Emily.

A crowd had gathered around the painting at the far end, but there was not the slightest interest in the first eleven – as was always the case whenever I visited. I led the professor towards the crowd at the far end.

As we walked past the first eleven portraits, 'All identical in the minutest detail. These first eleven are for sale. A hundred guineas – half the normal price,' I told my former mentor, before we mingled with the admirers of the twelfth painting.

'This one is *not* for sale. My *Prized Emily,* I call it. Watch this,' I said, catching Jean-Louis' attention. The gallery proprietor waded into the crowd.

'*Mesdames et messieurs, puis-je présenter l'artist.* Zhaycoooob Seelverrr.' Jean-Louis bowed in front of me.

The crowd became almost hysterical, clambering over each other to touch me. A refined woman fell to her knees, to my surprise, and pulled at my cloak.

'Sir, please, sir. Sell me this. . . this masterpiece, I beg you!' she pleaded, with tears in her eyes.

'For my dying mother, sir,' another lady called out, as she shoved the kneeling woman aside, her purse held high. 'I offer a thousand guineas, sir. I can leave a substantial deposit.'

I backed away as two gentlemen, one in a dog collar, made their demands.

'For the archbishop, sir. He must be given priority,' said the cleric.

Very upright and distinguished, the next gentleman wore a cravat bearing a coat of arms. 'I represent Juan-Carlos Fernando Frederik Geraldo Francisco Laurencio the Fifth, Count of Catalonia, squire, and I'm instructed to pay whatever price you demand.'

I broke free and led the professor to the street door. 'Potion One – *Desire. Quod erat demonstrandum,* Professor,' I told him.

Jean-Louis was grinning by the door, rubbing his hands together. I took him aside and quietly told him, 'Sell it. Highest bidder. It's time to move on.'

A few minutes later, the professor and I were enjoying tea and cucumber sandwiches in the orangery at the Savoy, overlooking the River Thames.

Something must have upset the professor, for he neither ate nor drank.

'A most frightening experience,' he exclaimed, as he dabbed sweat from his face.

'Frightening?' I asked, laughing.

'Those women. Throwing themselves at you. Gross and immoral.'

I laughed out loud, banged the table. Not for the first time, snooty diners around us turned up their noses. A very elderly woman close by, dripping in diamonds, eyed me through her monocle, scowling.

'The look on that old trout's face,' I said to the professor as I pulled out a sketchbook and some crayons. This was too good an opportunity to miss. My hand flashed across the page as the professor looked at his cucumber sandwiches and turned up his nose, pushing the plate aside.

As I was finishing the sketch, the professor looked startled when two women came up behind me, giggling as they peered at the sketch forming on the page.

I turned to see them point at the diamond-clad octogenarian opposite and walk away laughing.

A waiter approached me, whispered in my ear.

'A complaint, sir.'

'From whom, pray?' He indicated with a discreet nod. 'And who is the good lady?'

Once he gave me a name, I stood and bade the professor follow. 'Lady Jane of Sherston demands we be thrown into the street, Professor. Shall we?' I made my way to her table and dropped the finished caricature into her lap. A toff at her table took it, unfolded the silver sixpence I had enclosed in one corner, and read out loud:

'A tanner to smile, Lady Jane.'

What didn't help the old lady's embarrassment was his insistence in showing the drawing to all and sundry.

The whole place was in uproar before an attendant thrust my cloak into my hands and hurried us off the premises.

*

Soon after Jacob and the professor had left the gallery that afternoon, Jean-Louis sent the Count of Catalonia's agent to enquire as to what price he was willing to pay, and then placed the *prized Emily* on an easel in the window, writing a price ticket he was sure was unattainable – unless a blind man should take a fancy to it.

'Some fool may care enough for it,' Jean-Louis declared, as barely fifteen minutes later a liveried carriage pulled up abruptly in the Strand outside and an upper-class, genteel woman in her mid-twenties disembarked, rushed over to the window and stared inquisitively at the portrait.

With a snooty air of superiority she wafted into the gallery demanding attention. An assistant was soon put in his place and sent running for the proprietor.

Jean-Louis attended the lady and bowed as deeply as he felt she deserved. '*Madame, bonjour. A votre service,*' he said in his best French, offering a hand to lead her to a comfortable chair from which to peruse. His hand and chair refused, the lady produced her business card.

'I represent a collector,' she began, avoiding eye contact. 'In your window. Twenty thousand guineas. Yet the artist's unknown.'

'Unknown to madame, perhaps,' Jean-Louis quipped, having exhausted his continental vocabulary, 'but zis very day an agent for El Conde de Cataluña comes to buy it.'

'And you suppose I would fall for such a trick?'

At that very moment, the door opened and in walked the count's agent. 'If it is a trick, madame, then I am the one tricked. For here is the count's agent, now. Excuse me, one moment.'

But before Jean-Louis had completed his turnabout to go and greet the noble agent, 'Twenty thousand it is, then,' the young lady barked, pulling a cheque book from her handbag and hastily scribbling.

Jean-Louis, perplexed, hovered – but the bird in the hand was worth more than the count's in the bush. '*Un moment, s'il vous plaît, madame,*' Jean-Louis said as subserviently as he knew how, bowing again before he left her side to escort the count's agent deeper into the shop, out of harm's way.

Returning to the genteel lady, Jean-Louis swept her into his office and closed the door. The count's agent, suspecting skulduggery, crept back to the closed office door, pressing his ear against it.

He gasped.

His noble employer had been promised first refusal of that twelfth portrait in the long line of *Emily's*, the one now whispered about behind that office door, the first day it was displayed. The count had considered it a miracle, the portrait bearing a remarkable resemblance to his granddaughter, deceased only days before. Fuming, the trusted agent strode over to the easel in the window, whipped out a canvas bag bearing a coat of arms from inside his coat and quietly prised the portrait out of its frame, concealing it inside the bag.

Outside, the gentlewoman's carriage waited patiently at the kerb. A footman and coachman gossiped idly. But from the window of the carriage, a veiled, elderly lady observed the count's agent as he slyly wafted deeper into the gallery, selected a lesser *Emily* off the wall, prised that one from its frame, and brought it back to the easel, where he secured it in the empty frame there, replacing the priceless portrait with a mere imitation. Then, clutching his crested bag, he quietly sneaked out of the front door and closed it behind him, dissolving into the shadows of the Strand.

Turning towards the nearby Savoy Hotel, the agent frequently glanced furtively over his shoulder, the bag held tightly under his arm.

The footman leaping out in front of him quite startled him — the dagger suddenly pricking into his throat, more so. Terrified, he sought a means of escape. The coachman, who pressed up close behind him wielding a horsewhip, had him trembling, stuttering and shooting his arms into the air. The crested bag dropped on to the pavement. The dagger drawing a trickle of blood from his throat ensured little resistance.

'Our *Emily*, honourable sir,' the coachman urged from behind, 'and not a whisper, or the next breath will surely be your last.'

Back in the gallery, Jean-Louis, twenty thousand guineas happier, glided across the gallery floor waving and blowing on madame's freshly-inked cheque, two steps behind his lady client.

'I'm sure the portrait will give your client so much pleasure, madame,' he gushed, until he saw the enraged expression on madame's face.

She didn't say a word. She jabbed a finger at the portrait now resting on the easel, snatched the cheque from his fingers, turned and stormed to the door. Aghast and puzzled, Jean-Louis would never forget her icy stare before she stomped out of the gallery and slammed the door behind her. He watched open-mouthed through the window as a footman opened the carriage door and his lost client, together with twenty thousand guineas, climbed inside.

'The man is a bounder and a scoundrel!' the young lady said to the elderly veiled lady inside the carriage. Dressed all in black, the old lady clutched a canvas bag bearing a familiar coat of arms. Once her companion was seated comfortably beside her, she lifted out the extraordinary prized *Emily* portrait.

The young lady's eyes widened in shock, her jaw dropped open.

'Thank you so much, Rebecca dear,' old Mrs Muxlow said tenderly, 'I shall treasure it until my dying day.'

The carriage continued down the Strand.

Chapter 11

We returned to my laboratory in good spirits. I knew Emily would be concerned how much longer our uninvited guest would keep me from her. Since her proposal to me, she had become more possessive than ever and I needed good reason not to always be with her.

'Yes, my darling, I'm back,' I called up the stairs, 'I won't be long.' And when I finally closed the door, I explained to the professor, 'She doesn't like to be left alone, dear thing.'

The professor seemed to understand, but was pulling at his beard and I sensed he had something he needed to get of his chest. He opened our old scholarly book at the page headed 'Immortality'.

'This particular piece is the work of Paris's finest alchemist, Perenelle Flamel. Extraordinary woman. Rumoured to have made her husband, Nicolas, immortal.'

'Yes, I was aware. She died just under five hundred years ago, in 1397. But strange, is it not, that Nicolas, a popular scribe of his day, recorded not a word about immortality in any paper he wrote during his whole lifetime. I'd wager the tale is not true. Rumour and gossip, you ask me.'

'But perhaps that was the Flamels' intention,' the professor argued, searching inside his pocket and bringing out a fold of papers. 'Keeping it secret.'

'The discovery that has evaded all mankind – and a news scribe wants to keep it secret? Come, come. He would want to shout it from the rooftops. Look how many papers he would have sold. Malicious rumours. Mark my words.'

The professor unfolded a faded sepia facsimile of a manuscript and passed it to me.

'Couldn't agree with you more, Master Jacob, except. . .' he delighted in spreading out the document before me, 'this surfaced in the Vatican archives, two hundred years later.'

Written in Latin, some of the lettering was faded but the

message was quite clear. I held it up to the gaslight and read out loud:

'*I have no doubt that Alchemy was written by Nicolas Flamel – but the science is certainly not his. That belongs to Perenelle Flamel, close to death by the time it was completed. The science is dark – too dark for mere mortals. But alas, it works.*'

I burst out laughing. The professor's face turned decidedly sour. I recalled such rapid changes of mood in him, during my youth. But I stood my ground, flinging the document down.

'Ah. Right then. That proves it. And what bright arse wrote this? Some pimply-faced junior at the British Museum? Frankly, Professor, that means less to me than a fart in St. Paul's.'

The professor turned the document over to reveal a rhyme and a signature above it – a signature I recognised only too well.

'A pimply-faced junior by the name of Leonardo da Vinci, actually,' he said, stabbing the signature with a crooked finger.

Heavens.

I tried not to show my dismay. Leonardo, my lord and master? *He* had appraised *Alchemy* thus? I studied the signature; ran my fingers over it. They trembled. *Leonardo da Vinci, 1507.* I was quite sure it was indeed the old master's. I was lost for words. Had I been sitting on this divine master's approved work for years and not taken it seriously? But there was something I had to tell the professor, tell him before–

'You've learned to capture desire. Today's demonstration proves that without doubt. But of all people, you, Jacob Silver, are the only man I know alive today who could crack this, that one thing that has eluded man for–'

'But it doesn't work,' I blurted out. There. I'd told him. I held up a glass of golden liquid – the liquid that *was* the elixir the professor sought so badly, made exactly as prescribed in *Alchemy*. Every ingredient meticulously researched, over a hundred. This was his prize. And it didn't work. Gaslight shining through the glass caused a full array of coloured light to dance across the professor's face. He seemed taken aback; reduced to a pupil awaiting his master's lesson. *My* lesson.

'You– You've solved this one, too?' he asked incredulously.

'It took a while. A good deal of effort. But, yes. After deciphering one hundred and twenty-seven medieval ingredients, I had it. I've named it *Elixir 32* – my thirty-second attempt at getting it right – but it just doesn't work, Professor. To even think it would in the first place is complete and utter madness.'

Crash!

His cane smashed down on the bench. I was startled as he snarled into my face. I backed away.

'If I'm mad for believing immortality *is* possible, then let me be called mad – but only by any man that can prove it is *not*.'

'But– I tried everything. It didn't–'

He turned to a certain page and pointed to the five lines of gibberish that had evaded him back in my college days. 'You deciphered *these* ingredients? The catalyst?'

I looked closely at the text, an assortment of characters from a dozen or more languages and alphabets. 'Well, no. Not that. That's all gobbledegook. There's no such–'

Crash!

The cane again.

'Then you haven't cracked it, boy! Like the three hundred before you who didn't crack it, either!' His stare was intense. I feared he might turn the cane on me. But this was *my* house. *My* home. He had no right to be there, insulting me. I was not his enslaved pupil in the catacombs any longer.

'Er. . . It's late,' I said, although not as boldly as I had hoped. 'We're both tired. I dare say you have a long way to travel.' I opened the door and nervously ushered him out. His mood changed in an instant.

'No. I've nowhere more important to go. I'll stay as long as it takes. Till we solve this riddle. Prove the formula. Break this infernal code,' he said quite politely, as Betsy sprang from the hallway shadows, curtsied and offered him his cloak and hat.

'The master will put it to Emily, sir,' Betsy offered, without consulting me. 'Come back in the morning, can you?' And then the two of them headed to the front door.

Just get rid of him, I wanted to scream after them, still trembling from his outbursts. I heard them in the vestibule.

'And how is Emily?' the professor asked, as if he actually cared.

'Wonderful,' Betsy assured him. 'Never been better. They must be the happiest couple in all London.'

And we don't need you coming along, spoiling it, I wanted to shout up the stairs.

But the professor's response disarmed me. 'One seldom comes across such joy in these miserable times. Good night to you, madam.'

And then he was gone.

The faded manuscript copy was still on the bench and I decided to take it up to bed with me – amused by the rhyme above Leonardo's signature. Well, at least one person had cracked it – and claimed it works.

Betsy met me on the stairs. 'It's a wonderful opportunity, Master Jacob. You could make a name for yourself, solving this one.' Then she bade me goodnight.

Of course, I knew she was right. I would have an enviable reputation if I could equal Leonardo's findings and prove the formula worked, publishing the result to the world. But I somehow doubted the professor had any intention of popularising our discovery.

Emily had stayed awake to learn what had taken place. I sat on her bed and told her the full story.

'I know what you're thinking, Emmy. But I won't neglect you, I promise. I'll get rid of him as soon as I can. But he's right. We probably are the only two mad enough to try this. Even so, you mean the world to me. I'll find his wretched solution and then we'll be rid of him. Six months, that's it. I'll give him until Michaelmas Day. If the end's not in sight by then – I'll heave him onto the street.' I turned the manuscript over to read the rhyme. I hoped she would find it as amusing as I did. 'Listen to this. . .

Be warned thou prying eye,
These formulae thou dost espy.
Only those who dare ferment
Each and every experiment
Shall find the door and turn the key
To mankind's dream: Immortality.

'And signed by the man himself, my own master and father of all science: Leonardo da Vinci.'

I wasn't sure that Emily realised the significance of that endorsement, or understood that I now felt it essential to drop everything else and solve that one last riddle which I had so foolishly ignored. Leonardo had turned it into a more worthwhile quest, a challenge. I kissed my darling goodnight and switched out her light, my mind racing with endless possibilities for getting back to work.

'Stark raving mad, you ask me,' Emily called out as I went off to my own bedroom. 'Night-night.'

Chemistry paraphernalia bubbled when, dressed in my apron, I led the cloaked professor into the laboratory the next morning.

'And Emily approves?' the old scholar asked cautiously, slipping on an apron.

'Indeed. I think she's just as excited as I am. I rose early and dealt with the day's prescriptions. So, let's get started on this elusive riddle, shall we?'

Betsy Pollock waddled into the lab and took the professor's cloak and hat. She smiled at him in his apron and left.

I pored over the questionable text in *Alchemy*, puzzled. 'I bow to your superior knowledge and experience, Professor. Not gobbledegook – a code of some sort.'

'Precisely, Master Jacob. Apply your mind. Stretch the imagination. We don't have much time.'

'Much time?' I asked him.

'Michaelmas Day is not that far away,' he answered. It was as though he had been reading my mind. But then I recalled that Michaelmas Day was the date upon which *Alchemy* instructed that, once these illusive ingredients had been added, the concoction should be consumed.

I took some rice paper, placed it over the text. 'First, I'll trace it. Then, my father's library. Everything on medieval medicine. Look for similarities.'

The professor, Betsy and I filed into the laboratory with our arms piled high with ancient books. Betsy blew off the dust. The professor and I spread them over the benches, studying each and every one closely, comparing the text from *Alchemy*.

Later, by gaslight, we were exhausted, having examined hundreds of pages between us.

'Betsy's made the bed up for you in the spare room, Professor,' I told him, as he headed for bed with a candle. 'We should finish the rest of these books tomorrow. I hope that yields something.'

'And if it doesn't?' asked the professor, yawning as he shielded his candle from the draught.

'The Ancient Institute of Apothecaries and Alchemists,' I said, 'wherever they are.'

'Er, no, Master Jacob,' the professor said nervously, placing his hand on my arm. 'We shouldn't go disturbing them, not unless it's a last resort, you understand?'

I didn't understand, but thought that perhaps the professor had good reason. Was it that he did not want the institute to know he was close to perfecting the elixir? Had they forbidden him to work on it? I had no idea, but found the whole thing intriguing.

'Of course, we could try the Apothecaries Hall – I heard when I was taking my examination there that they boast of a huge medieval medical library,' I said.

'Er, no, no, no,' insisted the professor, becoming flustered. 'We don't want to disturb them. It might resurrect ill feeling over dealings I've had with them in the past.'

'Ill feeling?' I pressed.

'Not now,' he said, edging off towards his bedroom, 'but I will tell you one day.'

'The British Library, then,' I called up the stairs, sure that he would have to agree. 'Everything ever written on the subject,' I added, heading upstairs after him. 'I'll find it, never fear.'

But he had gone to bed.

The magnificent dome of the British Library Reading Room within the British Museum at Bloomsbury was believed to have covered more books than any other place in the world when Stanley Silver put his unborn son's name down for a pass upon its inaugural opening in May, 1857. The pass duly arrived on Jacob Silver's tenth birthday, twenty-three years later, and the library became the fountain from which young Jacob sated his thirst for knowledge when his father or teachers could not provide the answers he so eagerly sought.

As a child, Jacob knew every square inch of the huge spider's web-like floor arrangement, and the librarians, stymied by awkward requests from visitors, would often seek out Jacob to guide them to the correct shelf. In those days, if it were outside school hours, he was sure to be present.

Now he was calling daily to crack this code, it was the librarians' turn to assist Jacob. They introduced him not only to their more serious members in the reading room but to department heads in the British Museum itself. That handful of lines copied from *Alchemy* tied up acknowledged authorities on chemistry, physics, cryptology, Egyptology, calligraphy, ancient Greek, Aramaic, Chinese and Japanese texts, Sanskrit, numerology, and astrology, for weeks on end.

Convinced he was on to something revealing, one official took Jacob to the library of St Paul's Cathedral where, in the cool and eerie catacombs, they were given cotton gloves and access to illuminated volumes on witchcraft and curses over five hundred years old. Hundreds of hours of mind-numbing scrutiny resulted in Jacob learning exactly, and precisely, nothing to help him crack his code – but an awful lot he didn't know about witchcraft.

Enquiries went on for month after month. The first Michaelmas Day came, and although the professor was as irritable as sin, it passed without a murmur, due to their level of concentration. Jacob did detect a degree of frustration coming from the professor from that day forward.

Almost every expert Jacob consulted was adamant that such an array of symbols in his five-line riddle could *only* be a *code*, of some sort, and *not* any specific language.

The Riddle

He finally received a letter from the British Museum staff:

'You have letters from the ancient Greek Cyrillic alphabet, others from Arabic, Sanskrit, Chinese and Japanese, Latin and bits from before Christ. Some symbols are reversed; some are inverted; others are rotated. Someone is challenging you. Testing you. It is most certainly a *code*. And a number of us here are sure that the writer was concerned with religion,' wrote the Head of Languages. 'If and when you do solve it, we would be delighted to learn of the result. Good Luck!'

Jacob showed the letter to Emily that night, as proof that he was onto something – and assured her he would soon solve the mystery, emphasising how much he was missing their time together during the day.

'Then the sooner you crack it, Jacob, the better,' Emily urged, 'We can get back to life as normal once that wretched man has gone.' After he straightened her pillows and kissed her goodnight, she asked: 'What of the gallery and the paintings they have yet to sell?'

'No word yet. Jean-Louis has buyers for the prize painting but none have yet come forward for any of the others, people just stop and admire, he says, every day.'

'And may I remind you that you haven't painted a thing for over six months,' Emily said, tutting, as Jacob blew out her lamp. 'Next, we'll have the grocer knocking at the door yelling to be paid. Do some proper work and get rid of that damn man and his puzzle, or we could end up in Carey Street.'

While the professor frittered away valuable chemicals with innumerable failed experiments in the laboratory, other wild-goose chases led Jacob to Great Queen Street, near Covent Garden, and the archives of the Freemasons' Grand Masonic Lodge, and the ancient Order of the Knights of St John, at St John's Gate, Clerkenwell. Another three months were wasted. It was only then, at the point of exhaustion and walking home to Blackfriars, that Jacob found himself in Black Friars Lane, less than half a mile from his home, passing a grand building, with the grander title of The Worshipful Society of Apothecaries, the very place he had taken his first examination at his mother's insistence – Apothecaries Hall. It was now a whole year since he had begun work on solving this riddle. Was there no end to it? Reminding himself that this was the place the professor had insisted, twelve months before, that he should not approach, Jacob, so frustrated from his failures thus far, decided to ignore his over-sensitive mentor and take matters into his own hands. With any luck, he imagined, the professor would have forgotten all about it. Jacob clung to the high iron gates and made up his mind to return during office hours.

'Is that the Institute?' Jacob asked Betsy that evening after arriving home, aware she somehow had a connection. *Wasn't it the Institute that sent her for his housekeeping vacancy?* he recalled. He never did get to the bottom of that.

'You'll need to ask the professor,' she replied, making excuses to leave him and go to bed. 'But don't disturb him now; he went to bed early with a headache.'

Jacob was sure he heard them whispering down in the basement before retiring himself. He had heard the word *institute* quite clearly. As he climbed the stairs he could hear the professor shouting and hoped he would be in a better temper in the morning when Jacob told him that he was going into Apothecaries Hall – like it or not.

If, indeed, The Worshipful Whatnot *was* The Institute, from whence *Alchemy* came, Jacob was confident that he would find a solution there. He sensed he was close to solving the riddle. And, ever the optimist, that was what he told Emily as he kissed her goodnight and turned out her light – and had told her just as confidently almost every night for over three hundred nights.

If Emily was annoyed over the exorbitant amount of time Jacob was devoting to the professor, and *Alchemy*, rather than herself, despite the old man's agreed tenure having well expired, she did not choose to convey it, just then.

But she surely would, soon enough.

And what of her offer of marriage? Had he forgotten? Did he no longer care? She had proposed that they lived as husband and wife in common law – and he had accepted – over a year ago. But each time Jacob had attempted to fulfil their arrangement, and there had been many, and tried to persuade her to move from her room to his, Emily had complained.

'Not while *that man* remains in our house,' Emily had decreed, referring to the professor sleeping at the end of the corridor. 'I need privacy, absolute privacy.'

In an effort to appease her, after four months Jacob had removed the professor from upstairs and, after much explanation and apology, accommodated him in the anteroom, off the basement laboratory. On what was to be their first night together as *man and wife*, Emily had insisted on being wheeled straight back to her old room after being disturbed by a serenade of clanking and hissing coming from the basement – the pneumatic wall separating the professor's anteroom being opened, or closed.

'Is he shut in, or shut out?' Emily yelled, making her way out of Jacob's bed. 'This isn't good enough! I need to feel safe and secure in my own house. Get rid of that man!'

And no matter how hard he tried to share her bed over the ensuing months, Emily would not succumb, insisting that the professor had to go – or she would. In addition, Emily made it quite clear that whenever Jacob finished his duties, whatever they were, he was to call in on her, on his way to bed.

'I then have the added security of knowing you are close – to protect me,' she had informed him. 'The day I am neglected by any man,' she had stressed upon him many a time, 'is the day I leave.'

Dutifully, Jacob had done as requested and not missed a single night. He paid homage to his darling mistress, praying inwardly outside her closed door that, one night, she would invite him to come inside, close the door behind him and crawl into bed bedside her. And every night she denied him with a crushing excuse:

'A headache.' 'Too tired.' 'It's rather late,' or 'It's too early.' 'You're too excited,' or 'You're not excited enough.' 'I haven't brushed my hair,' or 'I've just brushed my hair; you'll mess it up,' or 'I need to be in the mood.' 'I've had a hard day,' or 'I'll need all my energy for tomorrow.' 'You smell of chemicals' – or 'old books'; 'London smog' or 'laboratory fog.' And so on...

Jacob wore the same brave face, whatever the excuse, every night, quietly kissing her goodnight, closing the door behind him and going off to his own, deserted, soulless room where, more often than not, he would lay for hours with tears in his eyes. She meant everything to him. She was the only reason he had for living. Every night, before drifting off to sleep, he vowed to try harder to be a better person and fulfil Emily's every wish, bring her comfort, bring her security, and earn her respect – because he loved her so.

The following morning the professor declined to confirm whether or not *The Institute* and *The Worshipful Society* were one and the same. He had thrown a tantrum and forbade Jacob to make enquiries there – against all reason, in Jacob's view.

Having run out of other options, Jacob chose to ignore him and ventured into the grand entrance of The Worshipful Society of Apothecaries at Apothecaries Hall, with the baffling riddle written on a sheet of paper. Jacob lied to a clerk, explaining that he had a dilemma with a test question from a university syllabus on historic medicine that he was studying, and wondered if somebody there could assist him. He gave his name and sat on a hard bench in a marble reception hall that resembled a mausoleum.

'Jacob Silver. Jacob Silver,' a very tall and painfully thin official was repeating, as he followed the clerk out to meet Jacob. He held a finger to his high forehead and asked, 'Jacob Silver? Jacob Silver, son of Stanley and Ethel Silver, Victoria Embankment, Blackfriars?'

Jacob was startled that they knew his name. The Institute's director, Dr Joseph Jensen, shook hands vigorously and introduced himself. He towered over Jacob, constantly pushing half-moon spectacles back up his nose. 'Winner of our 1886 Scholarship. Of course I would remember you. Yours was the highest score ever achieved in the first examination. But you didn't return? Didn't take up your dear father's profession?'

'I. . . Well, I found another calling, sir, but–'

'Ah, yes! The artist. I clear forgot. *We* lost a great student. The *world* gained a great artist. My congratulations.' He bade Jacob follow him deep into the bowels of that place, down stone steps which led into cavernous cellars, leading the way with a lantern. 'I notice a Miss Pollock is licensed for your father's old business, now,' the doctor said. Jacob nodded.

'You said I won a scholarship, sir?' Jacob asked as they proceeded below ground.

'Of course. To Greenwold College. Were you not aware?'

'Ah, of course. I didn't recall it was Apothecaries Hall, that's all. I thought it was from the Institute.'

Dr Jensen stopped dead. 'The Institute!' he said, alarmed. 'What do you know of this Institute?'

'I wondered if the two organisations were connected, sir. Apothecaries Hall and the Institute.'

'No. Definitely not. The Ancient Institute of Apothecaries and Alchemists were a scandalous and anonymous bunch who brought our trade into disrepute. Be proud, young man, that no such institute sent you to Greenwold. That was *our* honour, young sir. I assure you. Although, I must confess, the Institute did make a small contribution towards your expenditure, clothing and such. But that was all. A tiny contribution when compared to the total sum involved.'

'Well, I've not completely given up on medicine, sir. I'm studying ancient remedies, since it was my first love.'

'Ah, yes. A problem with a formula of some kind?' he asked, putting out his hand. Jacob passed him the note, the five lines from *Alchemy*. The director held up his arms and led Jacob into dark dungeons within the cellars. 'The answer, if there is one, is likely to be in here.'

Jacob stared with incredulity at dusty, cobwebbed shelves lining every nook and cranny, piled high with ancient tomes. Here were thousands of books like *Alchemy*, arranged into subject then date order. Dr Jensen lit a second lantern for Jacob.

'Do you have any idea when this might have been written?' Dr Jensen asked. 'Within a century or two?'

'1350 to say, 1400, I would imagine.'

'And in what context?' asked the director.

'Medical. . .' Jacob hesitated, 'concoction or potion.'

'Cure or curse?'

Jacob laughed. 'There were such things?'

'My boy, the medical world survived on such things. Quacks and charlatans benefitting from the patients' own healing powers made a good living during those times of plague and pestilence.'

'Mind over matter,' Jacob offered.

'Exactly. And many a sugar pill is still being palmed off, as we speak,' he kept walking, 'I'm sure with the best of intentions, by educated physicians with many letters after their names.'

The director stopped at a gap in the shelves. A whole line of books were missing; a note sat on the shelf, which the director unfolded and read.

'1350 to 1400 you say?'

Jacob agreed.

'Odd. Very odd. What, pray, is the work you are studying?' he asked, placing the note back on the empty shelf.

Jacob became nervous, felt cold sweat on his neck. 'It's a compendium of formulae, Latin, Turkish and Greek,' he lied, fearing any clue as to the subject matter could give rise to a thousand questions.

The director gave Jacob a piercing look. 'Latin, Turkish and Greek. I see. The volumes that once occupied this particular shelf were on French and Italian alchemy – for the same period. Coincidence, mmm?'

'What happened to them?'

'Stolen. One after the other.' The director walked on into another section where a heavy antique table stood in the middle of the room. In its centre was a fixed wooden surround with a hinged glass top. But the case itself was empty.

'You lose many books, sir?' asked Jacob.

'Not for hundreds of years. Then those on that shelf, and. . .' tapping on the glass of the empty case, 'the one that was locked inside this, disappeared without trace.'

'Oh,' Jacob said, curiously. 'Was it valuable?'

'Priceless, in the right hands. Some of the world's greatest scholars have claimed it held life's most profound secrets, Mr Silver.'

Jacob calculated immediately that *Alchemy*, opened, would fit snugly inside that case. He feared his next words could have him dashing out through the front door with the Worshipful Society's staff snapping at his heels. He changed the subject.

'So, where else might we look, Dr Jensen?'

'Was the answer in there, I wonder?' Dr Jensen asked, pointedly, his eyes rapidly moving back and forth between Jacob and the vacant case.

'I wonder,' added Jacob, looking for a distraction and stepping into a Greek section in the next bay. 'But perhaps among these?' he asked, taking down a crumbling book.

'No.' The director took the book, placed it back on the shelf and led Jacob deeper into the cellars. 'I think you need to study the earliest works on Hindu-Arabic numerals – mathematicians of the twelfth century. Get back to the source and build from there. All kinds of cryptology derived from those patterns. And another thing you need to ask yourself is: *Why?* What was the point of a code? Why was it so necessary? Who cared? Who would benefit if it were unravelled?'

'I'm thinking that it might have been secret ingredients, so that competitors couldn't imitate the potion, even if they found the recipe,' Jacob offered.

'Like this American and his *little liver pills?*'

'Samuel Carter? Yes, that's what I had in mind,' Jacob said, knowing he could not drop the smallest of clues as to what his riddle really protected. 'Any apothecary could sell the same formula profitably for a penny, but folk'd rather pay a tanner for Carter's because his had a *secret* ingredient. That's it, precisely.'

Dr Jensen laid Jacob's note on the table.

'The power of advertising. God help us if any more businessmen learn how to promote their wares as forcefully.' The director pulled out a gold pocket watch from his waistcoat pocket and snapped open the lid. 'I have to attend to other matters, but you're welcome to stay as long as you wish. Call again, if it helps.' He turned to leave. 'If all else fails, jump into the next section. Fibonacci. Extraordinary character and a great code maker. Ignore Da Vinci, and Nostradamus, both cryptologists, but they came after – although both often referred to Fibonacci as a guiding light for four centuries or so.' And as the director disappeared into the shadows, 'Huh! Plenty there to keep you busy, young man.'

'Where exactly did our manual on alchemy come from, Professor?' Jacob asked innocently over dinner that night.

'Been in my family for centuries, Master Jacob,' the old man replied, after regaining his composure from having choked on a mouthful of pea soup.

'But I thought it was *The Institute* that sent it for my fifteenth birthday?'

The professor put down his soup spoon. The conversation appeared to have affected his appetite.

'They did. My family loaned it to them.'

'Bequeathed it, you mean? Gifted it?' Jacob offered.

'Not exactly. The story my grandfather told me, and his grandfather told him, was that The Ancient Institute of Alchemists was awarded the work for a period of one hundred years, *or*, until it solved this same puzzle with which we are currently struggling – whichever should come first – after which the Institute would have to return it.'

'When were they loaned *Alchemy*?' Jacob asked, hoping this run around the mulberry bush might end before daybreak and the professor would simply admit that he had stolen it.

'1522.'

'*That* long ago?' Jacob exclaimed, genuinely surprised. 'So what happened?'

'The Institute was considered a secret society. Its members met in the great cloister of a former Dominican friars' monastery, close to here.'

'Blackfriars Monastery, a victim of Henry VIII's Dissolution, in 1538,' Jacob threw in. 'My school was built on the same site, hundreds of years later, of course.'

'Interesting. The Grand Master of the Ancient Institute, rumoured to have been the fugitive abbot, was finally doomed after being recognised by Catherine Parr, later to become Henry VIII's sixth wife. She was born and raised close to the monastery. The king wanted the abbot's head but he fled to France – apparently taking the book with him.'

'Back to its birthplace. So, it was lost to your family?'

'After dear Henry persecuted and murdered most of the remaining members, survivors joined The Worshipful Society of Apothecaries who miraculously had enough funding to acquire premises on the very same site.'

'Without paying a brass farthing, one surmises. So what looked like a merger of interests was in fact a change of name, perhaps? Monks disguised as alchemists and magicians, no doubt. Could cure or curse anyone they chose. I learned that from the archives under St Paul's Cathedral,' Jacob said, but the professor didn't answer. 'But how did *they*, the new society, acquire the book – if it was in France?'

'You don't know that they did.'

Jacob thought quickly, remembering the specific instructions not to go near Apothecaries Hall. 'I extrapolated that this was to where this was all leading.'

'Extrapolated correctly, Master Jacob,' the professor said, a glint of suspicion in his eye. 'My family, I'm told, satisfied they would never see the book again, forgot about it. Until,' the professor leapt up, 'following a little fire that burned down the whole of London—'

'The Great Fire? 1666?' Jacob interrupted.

'Indeed. The leather-bound book was raked from the ashes, entirely intact.'

'So it didn't go back to France? They lied?'

'Yes. And yes again, Master Jacob. I had searched for the book, and my forefathers had, too, to no avail. Until a fellow alchemist invited me to join the new Institute, recently.'

'*New* Institute. Another secret society?'

'More secret than even the last.'

'A secret, secret society. And who are the members?'

'Nobody knows. Or it wouldn't be a secret, would it?'

Jacob laughed. 'That's absurd, Professor. You had to know who you were dealing with.'

'Not at all. Why was it necessary to know *who* had found the cure for the Black Death? It was a cure.'

'Black Death? You said you joined *recently*,' Jacob asked.

'That was just an example.'

'Give me another?'

'Turned silver to gold.'

'Impossible,' Jacob snapped.

'Oh, yes? I'll show you one day, I promise.'

'Anyway, back to *Alchemy*, sitting in the Worshipful Whatnot under lock and key,' Jacob urged.

'You *know* that?' the professor enquired, leaning into Jacob's face.

'I guessed. It was considered a valuable book, after all.'

'Then I stole it.'

'What?'

'Can you *blame* me? It was my property.'

'Did they prosecute you?'

'No.'

'Did they know it was you who took it?'

'Probably.'

'You mean they didn't know?'

'They noticed it gone along with my absence; so must have deduced something of the kind.'

'And the full shelf of other books along with it?'

'What?'

'Simple enough. Did you or did you not take all the similarly dated books on alchemy along with it?'

'I. . . I did not.'

'You don't seem so sure.'

'I'm not a liar.'

'A thief but not a liar. Such high morals have you.'

'*I* did not take them, Jacob,' he said, hand on heart. Then, 'I only took what was rightfully mine. But I know who did.'

'Really?'

'Students of mine.'

'You would need to explain that.'

'Students set exactly the same task as yourself. Searching for that key to mankind's dream. The elusive formula.'

Jacob placed the slip of paper on which the puzzle was written in the middle of the table. 'For immortality?'

'Yes. What else is there? Nothing has eluded man as much.'

'And so, the answer wasn't there.'

'Obviously.'

'So, no point in tracking down the missing volumes?'

'Unless. . .' the professor hesitated. 'They might be grateful to get them back and reward the finder with further access to their archives.'

'You have the stolen books?' Jacob asked.

'I was. . . looking after them.'

'Where are they?'

'Greenwold.'

'I'll mention it to the director, tomorrow.'

'You can't go there. They'll throw you in prison.'

'Throw *you* in prison, Professor. *I* haven't put a foot wrong.'

'You wouldn't. . .'

Jacob stood, threw down his napkin and turned to the door. 'I wonder what they would offer for the return of *Alchemy*, together with the current abode of the man who stole it?'

Banging his fists on the table, the professor shouted as he watched Jacob leave, '*I did not steal it!*'

Installing himself early the next morning in the archives at Apothecaries Hall, Jacob decided to take the director's advice and closely examine the revered work of mathematician, Fibonacci. The works astounded Jacob, considering they were recorded before the mid-thirteenth century, but applying anything he read to his unsolved five lines of gobbledygook brought nothing new. Until. . .

Late-afternoon, a clerk delivered Jacob a glass of lemonade, standing the glass by his scribbled extract from *Alchemy*. He warned Jacob that the hall would close shortly.

Starting afresh, Jacob numbered every character. Then, playing with prime number sequences, for which Fibonacci was most noted, he selected letters or symbols from the coded message, according to prime numbers: the first, second, third, fifth, seventh and so on, writing the result, a line of thirty-three characters on a fresh sheet of paper. But these results, although looking almost like words, made no sense in any language he knew, and according to his research, in any language the Flamels knew. Or so he thought.

Reaching for the lemonade he saw something odd. Something astounding. He moved his scribbled extract in closer to the front of the glass.

This wasn't just anything; it was revelatory.

'Eureka!' he yelled, leaping up and running through the cavernous cellars, up the stone steps and barging through the door into the marble reception hall. 'Eureka!' he yelled at the startled clerk who had delivered the lemonade. 'I could kiss you!'

The clerk scrambled to his feet and raised his chair between himself and his attacker – ready to fend off any amorous approach. A kiss would not be appropriate. His embarrassment was spared by the appearance of the lofty Dr Jensen.

'I have it!' yelled Jacob. 'Thanks to your man here.'

'Fothergill?' the director looked puzzled.

'Thank you, thank you, thank you!' Jacob yelled as he ran out of the front doors.

'Well, Fothergill, it seems you have helped solve the mystery of more than just a liver pill, I trust. Well done.'

Fothergill, looking perplexed, sat back down at his desk and loosened his collar, before picking up the empty lemonade glass and scrutinising every inch, inside and out, searching for the wondrous solution it held.

Back in the laboratory, the professor was tutting over a pan of smoking ingredients as it shot up in flames, singeing his eyebrows for the third time that day. It was getting dark outside.

Jacob screaming 'Eureka!' as he rushed down the stairs towards the laboratory, sounded promising. Perhaps the boy had something. At last.

'Eurekaaaa!' Jacob burst into the smoky laboratory, grinning. 'We have it, Professor! We have it!' and was promptly overcome by the smoke, coughing violently.

'I'll open some windows,' said the professor, flustered and hoping he hadn't killed his student before he revealed a five-hundred-year-old secret.

Forcing Jacob to sit down, he brought him a beaker of water and patted him on the back. After a couple of sips from the beaker, Jacob placed it on the bench and placed a lantern nearby, moving it from side to side until he was content it was precisely where it needed to be. Then he unfolded his copy of the riddle taken from *Alchemy* and placed it in front of the beaker, before picking up a pen and fresh sheet of paper.

'Madame Flamel was obviously an admirer of Fibonacci,' Jacob began. Pointing at the beaker, 'In there,' he said proudly, 'is what everyone's been searching for, for over five hundred sodding years.'

The professor leaned towards the beaker, shook his head. 'I. . . I don't see it. . . Sorry.'

'Reflected. Inverted. That's why it meant nothing. She made it nigh on impossible to solve. Three-quarters of it is mumbo-jumbo, the other quarter mostly mucked about – reversed or inverted. She hoped nobody would solve it; didn't *want* her recipe used again. First, I wrote down the code – numbering every character. One hundred and thirty-one in all.' He showed him that version. 'Now, take out all those characters that are *not* prime numbers. What do we have left?' Jacob showed the page of his workings. 'Still looks like rubbish.'

He pushed the glass above the remaining single line of text. 'Now look in the glass at the first characters – inverted: *V anima!*'

'*V anima!*' the professor yelled, seizing the text.

'Now I was onto her! I soon figured out the rest. Latin, most of it rotated, or inverted, or reversed; but it's all here. *V anima. Puella, vidua, saga – uxor & canicula.*'

'V, the Roman five. Anima. The soul. Five last breaths, I'll wager,' the professor rejoiced. 'The soul was believed to leave the body with the last breath.'

'And she's named them all for us,' Jacob said, 'Precisely whose souls they should be.'

'*My God!*' the professor yelled, '*You have it! You damn well have it!*' He grabbed Jacob's shoulders, kissed him on both cheeks then danced around the lab with him. '*V anima, V anima, V anima!*' he sang out loud.

Betsy Pollock stood in the doorway aghast, before breaking into laughter. The professor grabbed Betsy as they passed and led them all into a jolly dance until, exhausted, Betsy fell onto a chair.

'Enough, gentlemen, please,' the very much overweight Betsy

pleaded, struggling to get her breath as sweat poured off her. 'I'll go and prepare dinner.'

Stopping only a few minutes to eat, the two alchemists bade Betsy goodnight and talked on through the night. At last, they had a solution. A year's work – although precisely how they would use it was not clear.

At least to Jacob, the way forward was not clear.

The Trial: Day 5

'. . .and swear to tell the truth and nothing but the truth.'

'Please state your full name and profession, sir, and address your answers to the jury,' Percy Ponsonby began.

'Dr Joseph Jensen, Director of The Worshipful Society of Apothecaries, sir.'

'And where is the society's central office, Dr Jensen?'

'Apothecaries Hall, in Black Friars Lane, in the city, sir.'

'Close to S Silver and Sons, Apothecaries on the Victoria Embankment?'

'Very. About half a mile.'

'Could you describe, briefly please, the society's role?'

'The society was granted a Royal Charter in 1617 by James I and recognised as a City of London livery company after apothecaries broke away from the Grocers' Company. Its first notable role was to challenge the College of Physicians' monopoly over practising medicine. In 1815 the society was granted the power to license physicians and pharmacists alike, with apprenticeships and hospital internships becoming compulsory.'

'And I understand you boast of an historical library?'

'The society has a vast archive of medical publications dating back centuries, second only to the British Museum.'

'Do you know the accused: Jacob Silver?'

'Yes. My first introduction in person was about a year ago when he came to me with a riddle to solve. Before that, I was the person responsible for his father's licensing and inspections, and marked Jacob Silver's first society examination myself, sir, in December 1885.'

'How did he score in his apothecary examination?'

'One hundred per cent; the first ever to achieve this.'

'He was clever, then?'

'Obviously, sir.'

'Had you met him *before* that examination?'

'Yes. Although I wasn't introduced. He called once a week to study in preparation for the examination. '

'For how many weeks?'

'The syllabus is twenty-two weeks.'

'When he approached you more recently with a *riddle*, you say, were you able to find the solution?'

'It concerned ancient medicine. I took him down into our archives.'

'And yours was the most comprehensive archive for all medical precedents, was it not?'

'It was – until particular volumes were stolen.'

'Particular volumes?'

'Those relating to the very period that Mr Silver was investigating.'

'How many books were stolen?'

'Twenty-two lesser volumes, all from the same shelf, and one particular treasure – kept separately in a locked case.'

'Over what period did these volumes disappear, doctor?'

'Over a period of five or six months between June and December, 1885.'

'Twenty-two to twenty-six weeks of the precise period during which Jacob Silver was on the premises studying for his examination?'

'Yes, sir.'

'Never to be seen again?'

'Well, the missing twenty-two turned up recently, surprisingly. A carter brought them.'

'When did they turn up?'

'About a month after Mr Silver last visited us.'

'Delivered from where?'

'A label said Greenwold College, in Northamptonshire.'

'Well *there's* a coincidence.' Ponsonby exclaimed, looking directly at Jacob. 'Was Mr Silver made aware the books had been stolen?'

'Yes, sir.'

'What were the subjects covered by the twenty-two books?'

'They mostly contained historical pharmacopeia, remedies for ailments together with their recipes, from the fifteenth century with modern translations added, identifying the ingredients. Others covered mostly alchemy, some experimental chemistry, human anatomy, biology and pathology.'

'Pathology?'

'Dissections of bodies, that kind of thing.'

'Decapitation?'

'Yes. For the purpose of analytics.'

Gasps from the public gallery. Jurors looked at one another in dismay.

'Was the subject of the human soul mentioned in any of these books?'

'Indeed it was. The soul was thought to remain in the body until exhaled in the very last breath, in those days.'

'Those days?'

'The fourteenth and fifteenth centuries.'

'Was a method described of how to capture said soul?'

'Numerous methods. But the favoured one involved what became known as *purging and splurging*. *Purge,* or force the soul out with a particularly rancid concoction into a balloon of sorts; then let the soul loose in the same, but boiling concoction, in a sealed vessel; until the soul became acclimatised. All gibberish, of course. There is no such thing as a soul, is there?' Groans rose all about me. Dr Jensen looked about the court, becoming more nervous as none of those souls present volunteered any sign of agreement. 'In a tangible sense, that is. It's spiritual, of course.' Smiles of acknowledgement renewed the witness's confidence.

Mr Ponsonby picked up the old book, bound in flaking leather: *Alchemy*. 'Do you recognise *this?*' he said, passing it to Dr Jensen.

'Oh yes. That's *Alchemy,* the treasured item I spoke of, stolen from the glass case, sir.'

'On what date did it disappear?'

'I reported it to the police on the seventeenth of June, 1885.'

'You have with you Mr Silver's examination application?'

'I do, sir,' said the doctor, unfolding it.

'What does he show as his date of birth?'

'The seventeenth of June, 1870'

'So, coincidentally, it would have been his fifteenth birthday, the day this treasured book was stolen?' Percy Ponsonby asked.

'Yes, sir, indeed it would,' replied Dr Jensen.

Mr Ponsonby chose that moment to pause, for calculated effect, I guessed, feigning the need for a sip of water. So, now he had painted Jacob as a thief.

'How sure are you that this is the same book?'

'There's only one of its kind in the world. Here. . .' he opened the book and turned to a page. 'This is the code Mr Silver was trying to solve. He wasn't the first. Students had been trying to unravel it for five hundred years. Many famous former members of the society had been recorded borrowing the book to do just that. But none succeeded.'

'What is the code for? What would it enable, if *unravelled,* as you say?'

'The legend is that whosoever unravels this code will have the key to. . .' Dr Jensen looked around the court, 'it's only a legend, you understand. . .'

'Key to. . .?' Mr Ponsonby urged.

'Immortality, and. . .' he hesitated, 'the ability to raise the dead. It lists the last ingredients required in a potion, the catalysts.'

The silence was palpable, broken by murmuring from the public gallery; people praying and crossing themselves.

The judge looked over his spectacles at the witness, sniffed crudely and spat into a handkerchief before he returned to making notes.

'And did the accused crack the code?'

'I can't be precise. . . But he implied that he had, yes. He was. . . how should I say? Ecstatic. Hysterical. Wanted to kiss everybody. So, yes. I feel sure he had cracked it. Or thought he had, anyway.'

'No more questions, m'lud,' said Mr Ponsonby, sitting down sharply.

'Your witness,' the judge nudged Eustace Ecclestone after a long pause, the defence lawyer slowly rising to his feet while still scribbling notes.

'Dr Jensen. Apart from the examination you spoke of, was this most recent meeting your first with Jacob Silver?'

'Yes, sir.'

'Do you have any reason to suspect that Jacob Silver stole anything from your secure library?'

Dr Jensen hesitated. 'I suppose not.'

'Yes or no, Dr Jensen? If there was suspicion tell us why?' A pause. 'There was no suspicion, then?'

'No. Not really.'

'Not really. However, it is more likely, is it not, that following your pointing out to Jacob Silver the loss of these volumes, he was responsible, directly or indirectly, for their safe return?'

'I suspected that.'

'That he was a good person?'

'Yes, sir.'

'Indebted – doing a good deed in return?'

'Yes, sir.'

'Dr Jensen, did you, or any of your staff, ever report at any time during Jacob Silver's frequent visits to Apothecaries Hall before he took his examinations, seeing him in the cellars, prior to your escorting him down there, more recently?'

'No, sir.'

'You are a learned man, Dr Jensen?'

Dr Jensen looked surprised. 'I have had an education, yes.'

'Would you describe your education and experience to the court, please.'

'University, post graduate doctorate in medical studies and pharmacology, seven years in practice as a physician, twenty-two as a pharmacologist.'

'And did your studies include Latin?'

'Yes, sir.'

'Dr Jensen, would you mind stepping down and translating something for us?' turning to the judge, 'With your permission, my lord?'

His lordship turned to Mr Ponsonby. 'Unless you have an objection to Dr Jensen being an acceptable expert, Mr Ponsonby?'

'No objection, m'lud,' Mr Ponsonby said, bobbing an inch off his rear. The judge acquiesced, waving his hand.

Mr Eustace Ecclestone whipped a white sheet off the foul exhibits in jars on the table in front of the jury and led the now very nervous Dr Jensen along the line of severed heads.

'On the front of each jar, doctor, is a word written in Latin, I believe?'

'Yes,' the doctor said, raising some spectacles to his nose and peering closely at the first, 'that's Latin, yes.'

'Would you be so kind as to read out a translation of the Latin after I read out that victim's name?' Defence counsel proceeded to read the name off the first jar: 'Polly.'

'A wench.'

'There is no doubt, Polly was a wench. She was a *woman of the night*. The next, Letty.'

'A widow.'

'Indeed, Letty was widowed. The next, Nora.'

'It says: A witch.'

'Nora was a fortuneteller, she read tea leaves for an ha'penny.'

Whisperings in the gallery became louder as Mr Ecclestone avoided the next jar and pointed to the maggot-ridden skull. 'Emily.'

'A wife.'

'Emily and the accused were betrothed, she was to become his common-law wife. And finally,' Ecclestone returned to the jar he missed, 'Rebecca.'

Dr Jensen smiled a half-smile. 'A bitch.'

'Thank you, doctor. If you wouldn't mind returning to the witness stand.' Mr Ecclestone turned to the jury, tapping along the line of heads in the jars.

'A wench, a widow and a witch; a wife and a bitch.' He turned again to Dr Jensen in the witness stand. 'Would you just confirm for us, doctor,' he began, placing his hand on *Alchemy*, 'that there are those you consider more educated than yourself who have made it known that they believe what is contained within the pages of this book, to quote them: *is possible, is true, is profound,* and, according to a certain scientist, Leonardo da Vinci: *too dark for mere mortals.*'

'I. . . Well. . .' His eyes searched the court, before he quietly replied, 'Yes.'

Uproar in the court had reporters dashing from the public gallery. A cleric alongside me in the gallery pulled out a large cross and shouted down to those below, 'God protect us from this evil. Repent I say. Repent all ye!' before being clouted about the head and dragged away by ushers.

The judge pounded his gavel. 'Another outburst like that and I'll close the gallery! You hear me, up there?' After they quietened, he turned to defence counsel. 'Continue, Mr Ecclestone.'

'Finally, Dr Jensen, you are still under oath and I want you to be candid with me. Do you, Dr Jensen, a scholar in medical science and anatomy, believe the formulae contained in this tome to be viable?'

The good doctor paused, a little too long for Mr Ponsonby it seems, as he attempted a rescue, jumping to his feet. 'My lord! Dr Jensen's own beliefs are not on trial here.'

The judge sniffed, became a little flustered, then, 'I think I'll allow it. Dr Jensen, try to be as candid as you can. Be assured this court has no axe to grind, and,' grinning, while pointing up to the gallery, 'I don't think you need fear being struck by lightning.'

But I was sure that the silence in the hushed court had many there believing and fearing that lightning could indeed be preparing to strike.

Mr Ecclestone reminded everyone of the question, 'Do you believe the formulae viable, doctor?'

The doctor's lips moved, but nothing came out.

'Again, please, doctor,' Mr Ecclestone urged, cupping his ear.

'Y-y-y-yes.'

'No more questions, my lord,' defence counsel said, as a crash boomed across the court; not a thunderbolt but Dr Jensen's head hitting the side of the witness box hard. The poor man had fainted.

I watched, bemused, as forty pairs of arms covered heads below, including the judge's, as a hundred pairs of boots thundered on the public gallery floor above them, amid howls from those trampled underfoot.

Chapter 12

'A wench, a widow and a witch; a wife and a bitch. So, five souls. But, how do we catch one, and what do we do with them, Professor?' Jacob pressed him after calming down from their celebrations. 'And how will we know if we've got one?'

'I've no doubt we'll recognise one, Master Jacob. Once they appear.' The professor tugged at his beard, considered before continuing, then, 'Capture, then infuse them into the elixir.' He went over to the urn of *Elixir 32* that Jacob had claimed did not work, poured a full wine glass and held it up to the light. Once again, an aura of coloured light danced across his face, sparkling in his eyes, making him look quite grotesque. 'It was in one of the Italian volumes at Greenwold, if I recall correctly. *Purge & Splurge.* The resultant fluid to be administered to the subject – providing eternal life, something like that,' he quoted, unable to contain his excitement. He held his hands up in praise – to some god or another. 'We have it! My word, we have it! After five hundred years!'

'Woah, now!' Jacob cried, trying to calm the professor down. 'Deciphering all those ingredients, fair enough. What was it. . . a hundred and twenty-seven to be precise. But capturing souls? Just how dark is this going to get? And whose poor souls do we capture?'

The professor appeared unaffected, patted the book. 'This will guide us. And I don't give a gnats knees *whose* souls. We're on the verge of man's greatest discovery. Bringing a five-hundred-year-old recipe back to life.'

'And highly probable it never worked. Ask yourself: how many wrinkly five-hundred-year-olds d'you see walking around?'

'I'm sure they're lurking somewhere, Master Jacob. It'll work, trust me.'

'With so little evidence, Professor, I wish I had your confidence.'

'Just need to find a wench, a widow, and a witch; a wife and a bitch. How hard can it be?' the old man suggested. Jacob laughed uneasily. The professor slapped him on the back. 'Have faith, young man. It'll work, I assure you.'

'Da Vinci said Perenelle was dying. I'm thinking *hers* was the *wife's* soul she refers to. Would make sense if she was making her husband immortal. A means of her joining him in a way, spiritually, on his journey.'

'How romantic,' the professor added, solemnly, 'sacrificing herself for him like that.'

For the first time, Jacob sensed maybe there was a mite of compassion in the man. But he also found himself wondering about his own *wife* – his bride-to-be upstairs.

A cock crowing jarred Jacob to his senses. He pointed up at daylight breaking through the basement skylight. 'Heavens! I'm off to bed before Emily discovers my neglect,' he said, rushing to the door and pelting up the stairs.

'And neglect her you surely did, Master Jacob,' the professor mumbled to himself. 'God bless her soul.' And with that, the professor ticked off from his list of five – *a wife*.

Upstairs, Jacob rushed into Emily's bedroom. He yelped, rammed his hand into his mouth. The bed had not been slept in.

'Emily!' he breathed, tearing into the bathroom. Nothing. Perhaps she had taken refuge in his bed, he thought proudly. But that dream soon disappeared; she was not there either.

Where is she?

He winced as he piled down the stairs into the drawing room, concerned more than ever now. No sign of her there, either. Echoing inside his head, his broken promises:

You mean the world to me. I won't neglect you. I promise.

The dining room – empty. The kitchen and finally out in the garden.

'Emily!' he moaned, collapsing onto this knees. Tears streaked his face as sobs racked his body.

Give it six months. . . Then he goes. . . I promise. . . I promise. . .

The professor had *Alchemy* open on the bench when Jacob entered.

'What to do with the souls. It's all here, Master Jacob.'

'Emily's gone! You'll have to leave!' Jacob shrieked.

'Leave?' The professor looked flabbergasted.

'Yes! *Leave now! Emily has gone!'* Jacob shouted, pointing to the door.

The professor stuttered, stabbed the book with his finger. 'Look!

Capturing souls. It's all here. We can do this.'

'Don't you understand? *YOU MUST LEAVE!*' Jacob screamed, clenching his fists.

'But we're on the verge–'

'I CAN'T GO ON WITHOUT MY EMILY!' Jacob screamed, grabbing him by the throat. He released him only after he began to choke and splutter into his face.

'Master Jacob, she was a mere. . . a mere mortal. Crack this and you'll be a *god. Inspiration* for mankind–'

'She was *my* inspiration! I can't go on without her! I'm dead without her. *GO NOW! LEAVE THIS PLACE!*'

That was when Betsy entered the laboratory, her round physique blocking the whole door frame. Distraught, she wiped her eyes with her pinafore.

'Mast– Master Jacob!' she pleaded, sobbing. 'I found– It's– It's–' Betsy pointed upstairs.

The darkness up in the apothecary's shop was broken by the light from Betsy's lantern as she led them both in.

Jacob, shaking, face awash with tears, feared the worst. Betsy pointed to a nightgown protruding from behind the shop counter, on the floor.

Horrified, Jacob fell to his knees.

On the floor, surrounded by broken glass, her lips black, her purple tongue out, her hair floating in purple liquid – Emily.

Agonised.

Dead.

Jacob would never forgive himself.

The Trial: Day 3

'And he described this visitor, the professor?' Mr Ponsonby continued questioning Sergeant Beck.

'He said the same man taught him science at college.'

'Did the accused tell you *why* the professor returned?'

'He wanted Silver to finish working on a formula, in their book: *Alchemy*,' the sergeant said, pointing down to the old book lying on the table in front of the prosecutor.

'*Their* book, you say?' asked Mr Ponsonby, slapping his hand on top of the book.

'Well, Silver said it was the professor who presented it to him on his fifteenth birthday, in June, 1885. '

'But it wasn't *theirs*, was it, sergeant?'

'So our enquiries ascertained, no sir.'

'So what were they working on, did he say?'

'Immortality, sir. And raising the dead. They had a formula for an elixir of some kind.'

Oh dear! I wondered if I should listen to much more. Jacob was surely not capable of such sorcery. How much darker was this wicked trial going to get?

'Immortality. An elixir. Raising the dead. That's quite profound,' Mr Ponsonby said, looking up to the gallery, seeking support, no doubt. 'Did you have to *persuade* him to yield this information? *Force it* from him?'

'No, sir. He gave it quite freely. He seemed quite proud of what he was setting out to achieve. Like it was quite a normal thing for a man of science to be doing, raising the dead and all.'

More gasps rose all around the courtroom. I was quite shocked as to what my beloved had been up to. Raising the dead? My goodness, what had I missed in my assessment of Jacob?

'The accused described this professor well, did he?' Mr Ponsonby asked.

'He did, sir.'

'Did it sound like an accurate description, like a *real* person?'

'Very real, sir. He even provided a sketch of the gentleman, to help us find him.'

'And did you, or any other officers that you know of, speak to this professor?'

'No, sir. We didn't.'

'Did you make enquiries as to his whereabouts?'

'According to Silver he shared the same premises at the time, above the apothecary's shop. And he apparently had a corner in the laboratory. But we found no trace of the man.'

'No trace. But you looked everywhere?'

'Yes, sir. We couldn't prove he existed.'

'*Of course, he existed, you fool!*' Jacob screamed from the dock. '*I'd known him nine years! He killed my girls!*'

'*Silence!*' the judge called out, jabbing a finger in Jacob's direction. 'You'll have your turn later. Continue, sergeant.'

'We looked everywhere, sir. And someone went back to his old college to seek him out there.'

'Did Silver speak of anyone else that would prove the professor's existence?'

'His housekeeper. Oh, and the college, Greenwold college.'

'And what did the housekeeper say?'

'We didn't find, and have still not found, any housekeeper, sir.'

'Mrs Pollock, sergeant? You haven't found her?'

'Extensive enquiries have been made and no trace of the woman found, sir.'

'But the accused described her well, did he not? *As round as she was tall?*'

'He did, sir.'

'And you believed him, believed she did exist?'

'I did, sir.'

'*You idiots!*' Jacob yelled. '*She had the box room! The customers all knew her!*'

The judge hammered his gavel as a jailer put his hand over Jacob's mouth. 'Another peep out of you and I'll have you gagged? You understand?' Jacob did not respond. 'You understand?' the judge yelled. After a pause, Jacob nodded.

'All these characters, sergeant, and none to be found?' Mr Ponsonby continued.

'No, sir. Not one.'

'You asked shop customers?'

'Well, the shop was closed up after Silver's arrest, sir. It was difficult to find any customers. Those we did find found it all too distressing to discuss what went on there.'

'Shocking state of affairs – nothing to support his story.'

'Now, now, Mr Ponsonby,' the judge intervened.

I should think so! It was obvious to me the police had not looked hard enough for these two characters. Of course they existed.

Mr Ponsonby smiled at the judge. 'And, according to the accused, Emily suddenly died, sergeant?' he went on.

'Yes, sir. She committed suicide, the professor told him. But Silver was suspicious. Didn't believe him.'

'So, *who* was chosen to become their first subject to *raise from the dead*, I wonder?'

'Emily died, and he was devastated, he said. They knew how to make the elixir work, so Silver said it was only natural to complete a batch and use it on Emily. Revive her. Bring her back from the dead.'

There were groans from all about me. Poor Jacob must have been out of his mind with grief, thinking in such a way.

'So Emily's death was kind of convenient? It provided an instant guinea-pig for their first practical experiment?'

'Yes, it did. That is why Silver said he had a suspicion the professor had killed her. For her soul. For the formula.'

'Emily's soul was needed for their potion, but Emily needed to die before they could resurrect her. Is that it?'

'That's the strength of it, yes, sir,' the sergeant agreed.

A flurry of reporters dashed from their seats and disorder broke out. The judge was forced to hammer his gavel a number of times but it was a good while before anybody took any notice.

Chapter 13

'I'll need these ordered from the wholesalers for early delivery,' the professor told Betsy, passing her a long list of ingredients.

'I shall have to check with the master.'

'The master will approve, rest assured.'

'But there must be a hundred items here, and why d'you need so much?' Betsy asked.

'Science, my dear. Science. Work the master and I are perfecting.'

'Well, approval must come from his nibs, and I can't see him doing that when we've no money. His credit won't stretch to it.'

'No money?' cried the professor. 'But surely the shop has been open and taking money all this time, hasn't it?'

'It's a fledgling business. Delicate. I don't always get me sums right. We're not making much, and besides, without the master's paintings to subsidise it. . . We're broke. No two ways about it.'

'But he sells his paintings for hundreds of pounds, madam,'

'When he's painted something to sell, yes. But it's been over eighteen months now since he took anything new to the gallery. He's given up painting the mistress or anybody else, it seems.'

'And what about his invention – *Silvesteur*? Where's all the income from that?'

'That'll take years to filter through. All the research and testing costs have to be paid back to them Pasteur people, first. Don't count on it. You won't be seeing anything from that for a year or two.'

'Then I'll ask him myself.'

'Master's not to be disturbed. Still grieving,' Betsy said, rolling up her sleeves and ready to fight her corner.

'Grieving? How long will he need? We're on the verge of a major discovery.'

'He's just lost his wife!' she shouted. 'These things take time. Very sensitive, the master. Took it bad, he did.' She raised a clenched fist in front of his wrinkled nose. 'I forbid you to disturb him.'

But the professor wouldn't wait. He had the problem of a disposal of a body on his hands and leaving it to rot any longer was not something he cared to dwell on. No sooner had Betsy left, he made his way up the back stairs into Jacob's bedroom.

Jacob's appearance shook him. Gaunt, unwashed and unshaven, he hardly recognised the bright young man he knew so well.

'I'm sorry to–'

'*Go away!*' Jacob yelled, without looking at him.

'We have to–'

'How many times have I told you?' glaring at him this time. '*Leave this place!*'

'But we have a problem, Master Jacob, a serious one.'

Jacob ignored him, pulling the bed covers over his head.

'A body. And not the first one the police have found here, is it? We have to deal with it. Don't want to see anybody going to prison, do we?' After no answer, '*I* have to deal with it. I just thought you ought to know, that's all.' The professor left.

Down in the laboratory he pulled an old galvanised iron bath out from the back and poured in various liquids from large glass carboys.

Later, upstairs, morose and suicidal, Jacob reluctantly awoke from a drug-induced sleep, the same black shadow still hovering over him: how he could possibly survive without his dear Emily. He got out of bed and slipped into his dressing gown and wandered downstairs.

In the laboratory he saw the professor asleep, sitting at the bench with his head laid on his forearms, snoring quietly. In the back he found the bath tub covered with a canvas sheet, so reminiscent of his father's demise. He felt nervous. Losing her was bad enough, but what if she were discovered? Would he die in prison, like his mother?

He lifted the corner of the sheet gently.

'Don't touch that!' the professor called out, striding towards him. 'It needs another few hours.'

Startled, Jacob dropped the corner of the sheet. But they both watched in horror, cowering back against the wall, as the sheet lifted itself high above the bath tub. They slid down the wall onto their backsides, gripping each other's hands in mortal fear, as the sheet dropped and the smooth, wet, nymph-like Emily stepped gracefully out of the tub.

'I'm so hungry,' she said calmly. 'Did I miss breakfast?'

Terrified, Jacob yelled out loud – waking himself from his dream, his nightgown soaked through. Grabbing a dressing gown he flew downstairs into the laboratory.

There, at the bench, the professor snored, his head in his arms, just like in his dream. Jacob crept towards the tin bath at the back of the laboratory, a canvas sheet stretched over it. Nervously, expecting the worst, he gently lifted a corner of the sheet – and yelped like a wounded dog!

'Don't touch that!' the professor called out, 'It needs another few hours.'

But Jacob *had* touched it. And seen far too much. Something so horrible it brought bile right up into his mouth. He turned and grabbed the professor by the throat, spitting venom.

'What have you done with my Emily?'

The professor beat him off. 'I think more to the point, Master Jacob, is what have *you* done with your Emily?' The professor pulled the sheet off the bath. 'Acid. She'll be all but gone in a couple of hours. No trace. No evidence she was ever here.'

Jacob flew at him again. 'She was alive! You murdered her!'

'Alive?' the professor chuckled. 'You saw her. Nothing was ever more dead. Poisoned herself because of your neglect.'

Jacob reached for a fishnet on a pole and scooped what was left out of the tin bath – Emily's head, half of it eaten away to the skull, the other half still almost normal.

'SAVE HER! YOU HEAR ME? SAVE HER!' Jacob screamed, startling the professor.

'Save what?' the professor shouted back. 'There's barely anything left of the gel.'

Jacob took hold of the skull and held it close to his face, staring incredulously at all that was left of his dearest love. 'We must save her, Professor. She's all I have. We, of all people, have the means. We must do it! Save her.'

'Put her down,' the professor pleaded, taking the skull in his own crooked hands. 'I'll deal with her, save what I can. You'd better go and paint something. We need money to buy chemicals.'

Jacob snapped out of his morbidity, aware he now had an important part to play. He uncovered the urn of his Elixir 32. 'If Leonardo was right, then we must use it to revive Emily.'

'With only her skull?' the professor questioned.

'Whatever morsel is left of her – I want her back. You hear me?' Jacob insisted. When the professor didn't respond, *'You hear me, Professor?'*

'We'll have to make a full batch. Find the souls we need.'

'I'll get the money, one way or another,' Jacob promised.

'Paint something to sell. Take in other models. It's as simple as that!' the professor offered.

'*Never!*' Jacob yelled back. 'Emily would never forgive my painting other women.'

'Emily doesn't really have much say in the matter, does she?' the professor offered.

'She meant the world to me. And she *will* return. We will bring her back. I'm not about to desecrate her memory by painting other women,' Jacob remonstrated, storming out of the door. 'You have the formula now, the whole formula. I'll raise the money for the ingredients.'

At the gallery, Jean-Louis was wary and apologetic. 'Monsieur, eez no possible. Times is very 'ard, monsieur.'

'Jean-Louis, it's only an advance. Till I finish a masterpiece. A new girl, positively *beautiful*.' Jacob pleaded.

'Eez no possible, monsieur.'

'Cut the accent, you bloody fraud. You've made thousands from me. Just a few hundred pounds will do.'

Jean-Louis responded in perfect cockney, 'You haven't painted anything saleable for over a year. It's all a gamble for me. I can do you a ton. An 'undred. Take it or leave it.'

'You still have my prized *Emily*, worth thousands. Christ, people were begging for it and you can't even sell that.'

'There's not a lot of people with the means—'

'Should I take it elsewhere, perhaps?'

'Two hundred then. But no more of your *Emily*'s, you understand? There's demand for horror, masochism, sadism or Satanism, you understand? It'll sell like hot cakes.'

'Never!'

Jacob stormed towards the door where a bunch of people were crowded around a painting. He pushed through them to look for himself. A horror painting – a woman tied and blindfolded, cuts over her body. The label read: *Salute to de Sade*. The price tag: *300 Guineas*. And scribbled across it: *Sold*.

He approached Jean-Louis again and quietly growled at him, '*Damn you, man!* All right! I'll take it.'

As he handed over the two hundred pounds, Jean-Louis gave a further warning, 'No more of your ladies-in-waiting, d'you understand?'

'Ladies-in-waiting?'

'They sit, they wait. Wallflowers on these priceless walls. Get with the fashion, young Jacob, or you'll be left behind, I tell you.'

After he arrived back at his apothecary's shop on the Embankment, Betsy greeted him with a big smile, took his hat and cloak and bade him go straight down to the laboratory where the professor had a *nice surprise* for him.

'Well, I've a surprise for *him*, Betsy,' Jacob said. 'A wagon should call by later with my latest purchase.' He passed her a parcel, 'Take these up to the studio, will you? Paints and linseed. I shall need to start painting again before we starve to death.'

The professor had just covered a large pot with a cloth as Jacob entered. 'Master Jacob, I beg you stand still and observe,' he said as first he lit a candle, and then went round closing all the curtains to the windows bringing the place almost into darkness. '*Voilà!*' he announced as he whipped the cover off a large glass urn.

Startled, Jacob cringed, his back to the wall. Inside the urn, her hair floating like kelp on a tide of his golden elixir – Emily's mutilated head.

Half, to Jacob's eyes, was near perfect, his wonderful Emily. His inspiration. The skin was blackened – but that didn't matter to him. The flesh of the other half was eaten away to the bone – inspiration for many a nightmare. He stepped forward and pressed his nose against the glass.

'Can we do it?' Jacob, breathed, running his finger down the urn. 'Can we bring her back to life?'

'Alas, Master Jacob, this is all I could save.' The professor placed the candle on the bench and placed over it a metal frame supporting a glass plate, resting horizontally above the flame. From a tap at the bottom of the urn, he dripped just a few drops of the golden fluid onto a spoon then dripped these onto the glass plate over the candle.

As it warmed and swirled, a moving, vibrating, full-colour spectrum shone brightly as it danced about the ceiling – their private aurora borealis.

'With the souls added, I'm confident we'll bring all of her back,' the professor said.

Jacob was mesmerised. He knelt before the urn. Kissed the glass. He touched the tap; a drop wet his finger. He held it to his lips, sucked it dry.

'It's good!' he exclaimed. 'Not good, it's incredible! Invigorating! Enlivening!' He poured himself a small glass and gulped it down. 'Essence of Emily,' Jacob breathed, tears welling in his eyes. He placed his head by the candle and plate glass – the aurora swirling on his face, reflecting in his demented eyes, making him look stark raving mad. 'You've brought her spirit back, Professor,' Jacob breathed passionately, shaking his hand enthusiastically. 'Preserved her in my otherwise miserable life.'

Over dinner that evening, Jacob explained about the advance of two hundred pounds and that he had already spent it all.

'The box that arrived this afternoon is for your experiments, Professor. A large copper kettle in which to boil and ferment large quantities of our new elixir.'

'And the chemicals with which to fill it, master?'

'Nothing left, sorry. Spent the rest on paints and oils. But now my inspiration has returned, thanks to you, I'll get painting again. We'll soon be in funds. You can have everything Betsy makes from the shop, meanwhile. Until you've accumulated enough chemicals, I suggest get investigating those souls we need, and more importantly, what we need to do with them.'

'But I must have chemicals. Large quantities. How can we—'

'After I sell something. First, I'll pay back the advance and then we'll begin in earnest.' Jacob picked up an empty wine glass. 'Something to drink, Betsy?'

'I'm sorry, master,' Betsy cast her eyes down, 'there's nothing left.'

The professor came to his rescue. 'The elixir, Master Jacob. There was a little left over,' he said, pouring a small glass of the golden liquid and handing the glass to Jacob.

Jacob was already becoming touchy and irritable, Betsy having been unable to offer his usual medication for some nights now. He sipped the new offering and smacked his lips. 'Thoroughly recommend it,' he said, swallowing the rest in a moment.

Both Betsy and the professor cringed.

'Jean-Louis insists you paint horror, I understand,' said the professor, winding his beard around his bony fingers.

'And what does *he* know about art?' Jacob snapped.

'He knows what sells and we do need the—' the professor tried.

'I don't give a damn!' Jacob interrupted, slamming his knife and fork down so hard on the table that everything bounced. 'I paint portraits of quality and if he won't sell them, I'll find another gallery that will.'

'But while dear Emily is er... resting, master,' Betsy began, hoping not to irritate him further, 'might it not be a good idea to try another model just to—'

'*Enough!*' Jacob yelled, pushing his plate away and jumping up from the table. Standing over them, he thumped his fists down hard on the table, startling them both. '*No other women!*'

Jacob retired to his studio after ordering Betsy to take Emily there and sit her urn on the chaise, his preferred pose. He locked himself in with Emily's remains, and made it clear he did not want to be disturbed, assuring them that when he next came out of that room at the top of the house he would prove how successful he would remain, without the need of any woman other than his dear Emily.

Locked in the studio, determined to conjure up another masterpiece on the otherwise blank canvas, Jacob mixed a palette as he always did, except for that one sorely missed ingredient – his pale green tipple.

Emily sat patiently on the chaise, in her jar; Jacob's eyes rapidly switching back and forth between her and the canvas.

He wrestled with the blank canvas; yelled at it; commanded it to obey; willed something, *anything* to appear. But after a long and dreadful night fighting his demons until daybreak, appear it would not. And worse, Emily spoke not a word to him. Her presence gave him little inspiration; without a sign or word of support or encouragement, his depression worsened.

And so it went on. Day in and day out. Night in, night out. Jacob leaving his studio, exhausted, with nothing to show for it. Not a line, a dot or a jot, or the smallest dab of paint. Nothing. Emily had left him. His inspiration had left him. He feared, forever.

A depressed professor sat twiddling his thumbs in the laboratory, confident he was sitting on the solution to mankind's greatest discovery, but unable to buy the chemicals he needed to top up the pot – for the sake of a few pounds. And then he thought of something. Emily herself could provide the solution.

Over dinner that evening, the professor waited until a suet-pudding desert had been served, and Jacob appeared content.

'I believe I have a solution,' the professor offered.

'Solution?'

'Something to enable you to paint more.'

'As long as it doesn't involve other women, then go ahead,' Jacob said, causing a long silence.

'I think we should consult a medium.'

'A trickster you mean? A charlatan?'

'They're not all charlatans, Jacob. The same as not all doctors are quacks. Listen to what I have to say.'

Jacob sat back, swallowing the last of his desert, and taking up a small glass of elixir.

'Let's find a medium, a true spiritualist, and ask them to be in touch with Emily – on the other side.'

Jacob leaned forward, intrigued. 'And...?'

'You can then ask Emily to return to you, become your inspiration again.'

Jacob appeared surprised. 'Very interesting idea. She'll learn how much I need her. To be my muse. We loved each other so dearly, she's bound to want to help. What d'you think, Betsy?'

Betsy looked at the professor before answering. 'Well, at least you would know how Emily is getting along, master.'

And so a séance was arranged.

It wasn't long before Marianne Meridrew, *recommended medium to the discerning*, had them all holding hands around a table and conjured up taps on the table accompanied by billowing curtains in the flickering gaslight. All present were content that Emily was in their midst.

'Ask her how she is,' Jacob asked, holding the medium's hand on one side and Betsy's on the other.

'She's safe now. Out of pain, she says,' Marianne said in a ghostly voice. 'She misses you terribly.'

'Why did she take her own life?' Jacob asked, tears welling in his eyes.

'The loneliness, she says. It was all too much.' Dead on cue, the medium suddenly switched to a higher-pitched, younger voice, something akin to Emily's. 'Always waiting, not knowing if you would come.'

Jacob burst into tears.

The professor jumped to his aid. 'Ask her how the master might gain the strength to paint again?'

The medium obliged. 'Paint, Jacob, darling. Paint for all you are worth.'

'Paint what?' the professor pressed, tightly squeezing the hand of the medium.

'Will you come to me, my darling?' Jacob asked through his tears. 'Be my inspiration again?'

'I am weary of inspiration, and not as beautiful now as you deserve,' the voice told him.

'So?' the professor interjected. 'So what shall he do?'

'Remember I am with you in spirit, Jacob, and paint the fairest you can find, my darling, the fairest you can find.' That was when the medium fainted, her head crashing onto the table.

The séance was over and after a stunned Jacob had left them, the professor paid the medium the agreed fee – double her usual because of Emily's admirable spiritual cooperation.

The following morning, Jacob was back with Jean-Louis at the gallery after receiving a note by messenger. Jean-Louis produced a business card.

'Gentleman asked me to recommend a portrait painter – *the old-fashioned kind*, he said.' He passed Jacob the card. 'Your chance to repay the advance, quick as you like.'

Jacob read out loud from the card. '*Sir Robert Weston. Psychologist to the Queen.* Dare say he can afford the best portrait painter in London.' But Jacob had another portrait in mind – the fairest he could find. 'The girl, Polly, remember her? Brought you my child in the red tunic, from her ladyship, Summer of '88?'

'The lady-in-waiting? Yes, I remember.'

'Can you get a message to her? I'd like to paint her again. It'll be well paid.'

'Now that un brings back memories. Get *her* in a nice erotic pose, with some blood and guts; can make a deal of money out of 'er, ol' son. Been four years or more since I sees 'er. Now, where was it?' He scratched his chin. With some toff, doin' a bit o' hescorting they tells me. Working the Drury Lane crowd.'

'Theatregoers you mean?'

'Not 'er. Theatre owners, more like. Owners, playwrights, managers. Bit o' class, that un.'

'Drury Lane, you say?'

'Try the Old Mo, know it?'

'Of course,' Jacob replied, without having the slightest idea who or what Old Mo was, but it was enough to go on.

'Some foreign geezer made a packet in the city and lost it at backgammon, the story goes. Runs a line of our finest gels now for the hoity-toity. He won't take kindly to your interfering, mind. Tell yer that for nought.'

'The Old Mo?' Jacob asked the ticket tout outside the Theatre Royal in Drury Lane. Rain was lashing down. The tout had hoped for a punter, at least.

'T'other end of the lane, mate. Corner a Parker Street. Sign says

Middlesex Music Hall.'

'Looking for my sister,' Jacob said, showing him a caricature from his time with Polly. 'Know her at all?'

'Geddout! *Your sister?* Our Poll?'

Smelling a tip in the offing, the tout became very helpful. 'Be easier to make a date with Nell Gwynn than 'er, mate,' he said, stepping into the middle of the road and pointing up Drury Lane. 'Side door, sticking out up there. If it's our Poll use after, she'll be wiv 'is lordship 'aving dinner after the show. An' 'e won't wanna see 'er messing with no riff-raff.'

'She'll mess with me. I'm family.' Jacob scribbled on the back of the caricature a short message, passed it to him with a half-crown. 'Make sure she gets this, will you. I'll come back at midnight and give you another.'

At the stroke of midnight, Jacob peered out from the doorway of a store at Number 173, Drury Lane; *J Sainsbury ~ Grocer,* the sign said above the door. A shiny, liveried carriage pulled up near the stage door to the music hall. A footman helped down a wheezing, fat, elderly gentleman onto the pavement and closed the carriage door. Polly stuck her head out of the window and blew the old man a kiss through deliciously puckered lips. Just as the carriage was about to pull away, the tout Jacob had seen earlier rushed up to her, waving Jacob's message and caricature. He watched as her gloved hand took the message.

The carriage moved on, away from Jacob. A cloak of misery covered his face as Jacob paid the tout the other half-crown and watched Polly's carriage proceed further down the lane in the rain – and then stop abruptly. Polly looked out of the window and waved frantically back to him.

Jacob ran down the middle of the road in the pouring rain, hat in hand, the two of them squealing with laughter as she opened the door and he climbed in.

The professor mounted the newly delivered, five-feet high copper kettle in the corner of the anteroom next to the steps down to the Thames, and looked inside through the glazed porthole in the top. Satisfied it was entirely suitable for their needs, he pulled down the brass lever on the wall. Loud hissing and clunking accompanied the closing wall, protecting their latest adventure from prying eyes, as he attended a glass beaker bubbling in the main laboratory.

Betsy entered with some packages.

'From the wholesalers. Another four ingredients. Will there be many more?'

'Only another hundred and twenty or so,' the professor said, passing her a long list. 'I'll need these tomorrow. For a small sample batch.'

'You ought to catch a glimpse of that new gel, Polly, he's got up there. Good job the mistress ain't on her feet.' She giggled. 'Seeing as how quick she threw her clothes off for him, Emily would've scratched her eyes out.'

'But he has Emily's blessing, don't forget,' the professor laughed, touching his nose. 'I'll pop up and see how they're getting on later.'

'I should, if I was you. From what I see of her tits 'n' arse hanging out, it don't look much like no horror painting to me.'

Upstairs, Jacob worked rapidly behind the easel, his hand racing across the canvas. On the chaise, the delightful naked body he knew so well from her earlier stay, his very own *lady of the night* – Polly. Jean-Louis had agreed with him that she was *the fairest*, probably in all of London, if one ignored her jet black hair.

Displaying the body of a Greek goddess, she had her glorious flouncy pink, polka dot dress draped over her lap while she sucked noisily on a peach.

'Gonna put me name on it, ducky?' Polly said, twirling a ringlet of her waist-length hair around her fingers.

Jacob threw his brush down. 'I said: *Don't move!* And close your legs, Polly. It's not *that* kind of painting.' But Jacob was in good humour, his inspiration had returned, with no small thanks to the constantly full glass of elixir by his side. 'Anyway, who'd be attracted by *Polly?* And from what you've been telling me, girl, half the potential buyers already know you – too well, I fear.'

Polly giggled. 'Just business, innit.' Then, extremely well pronounced: 'Isn't it, squire. Like what you taught me.' She giggled.

Jacob laughed while he pondered, his hand flying across the canvas stroking on her beauty. 'I'll call you *Penelope.*'

Polly giggled again, spat the peach stone into the fireplace like any bricklayer would. 'Penelope. I fink. . . *think,* sorry, that's what Ma wanted me called but apparently she couldn't spell it at the reg'stry office. Nice, though. Pernel-O-Peee,' she mouthed, opening her legs again. 'Price of a shag'll 'ave to go up, name like that.' She giggled infectiously and Jacob joined her.

'D'you have to do it?'

She looked at him, puzzled.

'Sell yourself. I thought you might've got yourself away from that way of life, selling the paintings.'

'I tried, Jake. But, onnis truth, I found settling with any geezer a bit much. My way, I gets enough money for a good time wiv the gels, whenever I needs a break. Don't 'ave to be there at anyone's beck and call. An' I ain't met a geezer yet who didn't have no weird demands or who didn't feel he had every right to knock us about. Know what I mean?'

'Charming.'

' 'Ceptin' yourself, *mon-sure.*'

Jacob laughed. 'I'm nearly done. But tell me, what of dear Nell?'

'Wiv the gallery money I put her into a boarding school, paid a coupla years and I've been sendin' 'em money to keep her goin' ever since. 'Igh days 'n' 'olidays, me and the gels get a charabanc down to Brighton and give her a right ol' time.'

Jacob finally dipped his brush into a jar of turpentine. 'Belladonna! It's done.'

She ran to him behind the easel – and gasped. She started to cry. 'You . . . You made me so boootiful. Made me immortal, you 'as.'

'Well, I'm hoping that painting a beauty such as you, Polly,' Jacob said, placing a wrap around her naked shoulders, 'will one day make us both immortal.'

Polly slid back into her clothes, the finest silk underwear and the beautiful polka dot dress, fit for a day at the races.

'How d'you feel about more sessions over the next week or two?'

'Can't meself, duck. Got er. . . a client to service. Reg'lar. Can't let him down. Got some friends, though. They could do with a bob or two. The ones I go to Brighton wiv. Letty an' Nora. Both pretty, too. Makes me look like a drowned cat, our Letty.'

'Impossible,' Jacob laughed. 'But send them along. I need to make three portraits for a small exhibition.'

Letty's face did indeed paint a pretty picture, well before Jacob captured it on canvas. High, pronounced cheekbones set off her nose with its tiny upturned end. Her eyes, the colour of steel, pierced anyone so bold as to look into them, causing many a confession from those about to plunder her body, no doubt. Straight, long auburn hair broke at her shoulders.

Letty, surprisingly nervous after she took off her clothes in front of this, her first disinterested man, felt forced to wave at Jacob to remind him she was there, posing.

'Just getting some background in, my dear,' Jacob offered, his hand flashing across the page. He pointed to a painting leaning against the studio wall, her friend, Polly. 'D'you think you can take up that pose, for me?'

Letty did as requested, cottoned on instantly; she leaned back in the chaise, one arm draped over the back, her dress draped across her lap. 'Ain't never done nuffink like this, mister.' After Jacob didn't answer, 'Most men I know wanna get it over and done wiv, soon as yer like. Y'know what I mean, sir?'

'Call me Jacob, please,' then, after lifting his brush to arm's length and peering past it at her, 'So you're Letty. Magnificent.' He turned the brush horizontally, then vertically, then horizontally again. 'So that you don't get bored, why not tell me about yourself? I'd be interested to hear.'

'I's a widder,' she began, as Jacob daubed paint on the canvas.

'A widow? Oh, I *am* sorry,' Jacob said with genuine dismay.

'Accident, in the docks. They gave us five shillin's, me and the kids. Compensation they says. Five bloody bob, Gawd luv us.'

'My sympathies, my dear. Er, how do you feel about Leticia?'

'Leticia?'

'The name we'll put on your painting. For one so beautiful I want your portrait to have an extraordinary name.'

'Not back luck, is it? Changin' a name? Didn't I hear it said...'

'Ships, Letty; bad luck for ships, apparently. But for a beautiful woman? I see no harm.'

'I dunno, I...'

'Women are changing their names every day, aren't they? When they marry? Or when they elope with the gardener and stay at a shady hotel, perhaps. Lady Belcher of Belchington suddenly becomes Mrs Smith of Rotten Row when Mr Smith picks up the bill.' Jacob laughed. 'Trust me, there's no harm in it. And if *Leticia* becomes famous, I will see to it that you and your family share in the profits. How's that?'

Letty's eyes welled. She dabbed them dry on the cotton dress draped across her lap. 'You's a kind one, for sure, sir.' She tutted. 'Jacob.'

Letty could not have known then, just how famous her portrait would become – as an exhibit in her murder trial.

After another four sittings, making Letty five shillings better off, Jacob declared her portrait was finished.

'You've paid me same what I got for the ol' man,' Letty announced sadly, pocketing the day's payment. She stood clutching her dress to her bosom and, stepping towards the easel, asked, 'Can

I see it? That be all right?'

'Of course,' Jacob waved her towards him behind the easel. 'I hope it's to your liking.' He introduced them formally, bowing deeply to the portrait like she was royalty. 'Lady Leticia of Lexington meet milady Letty, my new acquaintance.'

Letty giggled, curtsied and looked up at the portrait – then burst into tears. She threw her arms around Jacob's neck, dropping the dress and blubbering. 'So… So bleedin' gorgeous. That really me?'

Jacob comforted her for a few moments, patting her naked back gently, and then finding his hands smoothing the cheeks of her bottom. Snapping out of it, he held her at arm's length, snot running from her nose as she wailed some more. Jacob pulled out a handkerchief. 'Wipe your nose, dear. Can't have you leaving here looking like that.' He laughed. 'They'll think I've been beating you.'

Letty laughed with him and blew her nose, handing the handkerchief back to him. Jacob folded it gently, popped it back into his pocket. 'I shall treasure it.'

Letty smiled, kissed his cheek. 'Thank you, sir, for making me…'

'Jacob touched her lips gently, with his finger. 'Shhh. I didn't do anything.' Gesturing to the painting, '*That* is what you are to me. I can never thank you enough. We shall offer it for sale – but only to someone who deserves it.'

Jacob could not, at that precise moment, have known where Emily was in the house – Betsy, or he, choosing to move her from time to time to give her a better view, or a warm by the fire. While Betsy and the professor were both certain Emily was a preserved piece of animal matter in a jar, Jacob had insisted they treat her as one of the family – as he fully intended she would become after their concoction for immortality had been mastered and he had resurrected her. And regardless of her being inanimate, to Jacob, Emily was as good as alive and well, due to his continued consumption of the elixir he and she shared. And *she* was very much back in control. Had he known she was within earshot, he would not have given the delectable Letty so much attention, nor stroked her curvaceous rump. In *this* house, Emily's house, there were rules – rules that had to be obeyed. Jacob had never contemplated disobedience; hell had no fury anything like this *reborn* woman now ruling his life – be she in a jar, or no.

But within earshot, she was. And those fingers caressing the girl's bottom would not go unnoticed.

When the professor and Betsy sat down at the dinner table that night and Betsy began to serve, Jacob startled them with his shouts and screams, upstairs.

'In the doghouse again?' the professor smirked, well aware that Emily was getting far more attention than she deserved.

' 'E's been confessing, I 'spect. Can't keep anythin' quiet, that one,' Betsy replied, spooning cabbage onto the professor's plate. 'Probably had his hands on the stock.'

'The stock?' the professor questioned. Then, chuckling into his beard: 'Ah. The fair stock.' Impatient to start his meal, the professor added: 'Was a widow, that one.' A thump and the sound of breaking glass caused them both to stare at each other.

'Think he'll be all right? All that medication…'

'It's never done anybody any permanent harm,' the professor assured Betsy. 'Anyway, we're nearly there. Just a couple more steps.'

When Nora threw her clothes off, Jacob was entranced.

'Extraordinary, your freckles,' he remarked, running his finger down her back, tracing the freckles to yet another delightful rear. 'You're completely covered.'

'My lucky charm, me mum says,' Nora giggled. 'She'd read 'em, like they was tea leaves.'

'Fascinating,' Jacob said, holding up Letty's portrait. 'D'you think you can take up this pose?' She nodded, sat down on the chaise and prepared.

With a more rounded face and fuller figure than slender Letty, Nora was still an extremely pretty lady. Her dark brown eyes sparkled in her freckled face which gave her a child-like, impish look. Shapely cupid's bow lips enclosed teeth that were as straight as a die.

Betsy knocked and entered carrying a silver tray. 'Tea, sir,' she said, 'There's milk, cream or lemon, whatever madam prefers.' She tapped a small bottle and smiled. 'And don't forget your medicine, master.' Betsy averted her eyes for fear of causing either herself or the naked girl embarrassment.

'Thank you, Betsy,' Jacob said from behind the easel.

'If you're havin' a cup, duck,' Nora said to Betsy, 'I'll do your fortune, if you like.'

'I'll be taking mine downstairs,' Betsy said, smiling. 'But if the master doesn't mind, the opportunity to have one's fortune told is too good to lose. I'll see you in the parlour, shall I, miss?'

'Nora, duck,' she said, smiling at Betsy. 'Just leave the dregs in the bottom of your cup and I'll take it from there.'

At the end of Nora's first sitting, Jacob cleaned his brushes in turpentine.

'Gonna 'ave a very long life, Jacob,' Nora said, reading his tea leaves after he obeyed the instruction to swirl the dregs in his cup three times clockwise, then three anticlockwise, and upturn the cup into the saucer. She then took hold of his hand and studied his palm. 'Straight as a rod, that lifeline. 'Ere,' she said. 'Never seen such a long 'un, I really ain't.'

'And does it tell you anything else?' Jacob sat on the chaise, his hand in hers. 'Will I have children?'

Nora dropped his hand suddenly, fluttering her eyelids, like she had something in her eye. She reached out for her bag. 'Summink in me eye,' she complained, and suddenly stood up. 'Gotta go now. I'll be late.'

'So, *will* I, Nora? Will I have children?' Jacob called after her as she flew out of the door.

'Maybe next time,' Nora said, hurrying to the stairs.

Nora was halfway down when Jacob leaned over the landing banister. 'Is something wrong, Nora? Something I said?'

She stopped on the stair, looked up.

'Just me. Ain' feeling no good. Bedder get meself 'ome.'

Jacob studied his palm, sure that Nora had seen something there – something sufficiently bad to frighten her away. He returned to the studio and closed the door, searching his palm again for evidence.

Soon after, Betsy knocked and entered. 'She was going to tell my fortune,' she said, a little dismayed. 'I was all prepared. Did you have cross words?'

Jacob shrugged. 'She just ran off. Perhaps she can do it at her next sitting, in a few days.'

Nora duly returned but there was something different about her demeanour. A little nervous, she stripped and sat on the chaise and continually touched a silver crucifix hanging from her neck on a thin chain, moving her lips as if muttering a prayer.

Jacob was quick to notice – he was a portrait painter after all – and silver objects reflecting light do get noticed next to pretty breasts.

'The necklace?' he asked. 'Something new?'

'I… I'd like to keep it on if I may, sir?'

'Of course, Nora. That won't be a problem. I'll ignore it.'

After that sitting Nora called on Betsy on her way out and did tell her fortune.

'There's two men in your life, Betsy, and one what's up to

mischief,' she said, pulling a solemn face, looking from all angles inside the cup at the scattered tea leaves. 'You've just gotta work out which one it is, duck.'

Serving more tea in the parlour, Betsy quietly began to pry. 'And er… his nibs,' she raised her eyebrows, signifying *him upstairs.* 'Anything fascinating, dare I ask?'

Unconsciously, Nora gripped the crucifix on her necklace.

'Promise you won't tell?' Nora asked, awaiting Betsy's solemn nod. 'His lifeline's longer than Soufend Pier. Goes on forever,' she said, checking over her shoulder lest they be overheard. Nora leaned in close to Betsy's ear. ' But 'e's gonna have a lot of tragedy in his life. Gonna bury everyone he ever loved.'

Betsy gasped. 'I must warn him before–'

Nora grabbed her arm. 'You can't. Breached his confidence ain' I. Besides, things get worse, you interfere. Mark me words, stay well out o' it.'

The line of three beautiful portraits of Polly, Letty and Nora, leant against the studio wall. Each showed a startlingly attractive girl, seductively laid back on the chaise, naked, with her dress draped over her lap, an arm over the back of the chaise. Each pair of attractive eyes showed the minutest detail and followed any observer from whatever angle, luring, beckoning – *come sample my wares.*

Jacob angrily swigged back the last of a large glass of port, standing *Penelope* on his easel. The professor sat on the chaise, sipping his.

'My best yet and he refused them all. The man has no taste! Damn him!'

'But we haven't the money to pay these girls. And the whole purpose of painting again was to enable us to buy chemicals, Master Jacob, was it not?'

'Of course it damn well was,' Jacob shouted disrespectfully. 'He gave me another hundred, for three lesser *Emily's* he just sold. You'll have to make do.' Jacob threw his glass, smashing it in the fireplace.

'Just a hundred for three masterpieces?' the professor asked meekly. 'I thought they were selling for thousands.'

'Only the one. Some collector wants to buy all the others. A job lot.'

'From your experiment?' the old man asked. Jacob didn't answer. 'And what of the *prized Emily?* Why hasn't that been sold? People were fighting over it.'

'He couldn't even show it to me. Said it was away being

appraised. Soon as he gets it back I'll take it somewhere else. He doesn't deserve it. He just wants blood and guts plastering his walls. Torture and pain seem to be the current fashion. Pleasure is very much out of vogue, according to Jean-Louis.'

'Thanks to Monsieur De Sade, no doubt,' the professor added. 'So what is it exactly that disturbs you about painting horror, Master Jacob, like he suggests? It's not as though we don't need the money.'

'Does one have to *shock* to survive? Paint like a sheep after the herds of perverts copying these… these sadists and masochists?'

The professor stood and approached the portrait on the easel, stroking *Penelope's* face with the knuckle of his bony forefinger. 'Here you've captured beauty and emotion, a dazzling smile, a twinkle in her eye, desire and passion. In life, she's offered a shilling for the pleasure of a few moments. A pleasure that, in private, takes a lonely man's breath away.

'*You* on the other hand, a master craftsman, you are denied even that shilling, offered not a penny for a masterpiece that'll bring pleasure and public applause, not just for moments, but for a thousand years – and take *everybody's* breath away.'

The professor went to the studio window and pointed down into the street. 'And what is the difference, pray, between the pleasure she brings down there in the street, and the fear, dread, terror and horror that the gallery clientele demands? Purely shapes on a face, is it not?' Jacob did not answer. 'How many guineas, I wonder,' the professor continued, picking up and dashing a huge butcher's knife across *Penelope's* throat, 'to *frighten* her a little?'

Fumbling in his pocket, Jacob came across the business card Jean-Louis had given him – the gentleman wishing to commission him to paint a portrait of his daughter. Using the card just like the professor had used the butcher's knife, Jacob ran it across *Penelope's* throat in the portrait.

'Jean-Louis would love me to paint her head on a plate, ready for lunch. I wonder if Sir Robert would agree to his daughter being portrayed like that?' He laughed sarcastically. 'I'll make arrangements to see the old boy before we all starve to death.'

Chapter 14

At the gallery, a dignified and upright gentleman introduced himself to me as Sir Robert Weston. I recalled his profession: By Royal Appointment, Psychologist to Her Majesty Queen Victoria; but with his weather-beaten face, wide handle-bar moustache and a neatly trimmed, grey goatee beard, one could easily mistake him for an explorer or adventurist. He was well over sixty but there was still a sparkle of youth in his eyes.

'I need an artist, young sir, and you come highly recommended,' he said. 'I was here some months ago and Monsieur St Clair showed me your exquisite painting: *Emily*. I was hoping you would agree to paint my daughter?'

'I would be honoured, Sir Robert,' I told him, producing my three latest and rejected works: portraits of Polly, Letty and Nora.

'My goodness, they are wonderful,' Sir Robert exclaimed, 'I can see why the gallery are so proud to represent you as an artist.'

Jean-Louis, who, from a distance, had watched their proceedings thus far, suddenly concealed himself behind a curtain.

'Yes, Monsieur St Clair truly does appreciate my work,' Jacob said loudly, to ensure the scoundrel had heard.

'Congratulations. You have the kind of talent I seek. But some decorum would be necessary, sir. Clothes would be essential.'

'My apologies, sir. I meant no impertinence. I show them purely to give you the confidence I am able enough for the task.'

'My daughter is very special to me. I want you to capture her. . . before. . .' he was suddenly overtaken with grief and obviously in great distress. Tears rolled down his face into his whiskers. He regained his composure and blurted out:

'She's dying, Mr Silver.'

Chapter 15

I knew it would cause me much discomfort but I hoped I could manage to sit the hours required without spoiling the occasion, as it did mean so much to dear Papa. The last thing I wanted was to have to sit as rigid as a post, smile and make small talk with some crotchety old gentleman smelling of linseed and turpentine.

And then a carriage arrived, bringing Jacob Silver.

Well, as he took my hand and looked into my eyes I became overwhelmed by his innocent beauty. I was quivering, stuttering and stammering like I could never recall. His eyes, the colour of steel; hair, jet-black and swept back; angled features as perfect as I have ever witnessed. And then he smiled. I felt alive once more, shaken from the slumber I had been driven into by remedies for this wretched disease.

'Millie,' Papa called to my maid, pulling my hand from the young visitor's. Millie appeared and curtsied to our guest. 'Show Mr Silver upstairs. Jacob, I'll leave you with Lizzie just a few moments to introduce yourselves.' Papa whispered something to Millie – probably a command not to leave me alone with our delightful visitor. I wasn't sure whether that was to stop him devouring me, or vice versa. 'And then perhaps we can all agree on how you would best like to proceed.'

I knew exactly how *I* wanted Jacob to proceed – but Papa would surely not approve. I watched the artist's every move as he unpacked his tools in the upstairs drawing room, a sketchbook and a few crayons, and then he erected an easel before facing me on the chaise.

'May I ask how old you are?' I asked him. My chaperone, Millie, giggled. 'My father spoke of your success but I was expecting someone. . .'

'Someone older? A wrinkly old sage, perhaps? Taking snuff and sneezing all over you?' he laughed. 'I'm twenty-four, Miss Weston. And you?'

Being so carefree, he was obviously unaware of the poor

manners in asking any lady her age. Was he showing off his modernism or just being impertinent, I wondered?

'How old do I look, Mr Silver?' Millie was quite shocked.

'I would guess way younger than I. Eighteen perhaps?'

Shrewd. Exactly right. How many other eighteen-year-olds had he painted to compare me to, I imagined? And how many had thrown their naked bodies at his feet and demand he capture their innermost secrets for the world to ogle at? The very thought brought a flush to my cheeks. And couldn't he see from the tremulous condition in which he had put me, unable to conceal my heaving bosom, that I was quite old enough.

'It'll be wonderful to paint you. But if I disappoint, you will let me know, won't you? I won't leave until I've completely satisfied you.'

This was beginning to sound very interesting.

*

Meeting Lizzie Weston was so much a pleasure. The girl, although pale, was positively beautiful. And everything about her was refined to perfection. Underneath the brightest blue eyes I could ever remember seeing, she had fine high cheekbones, providing the opportunity to add depth to what was already a beautiful face, playing with light and shadow. Swathes of finely brushed golden hair, secured at the back with a jewelled comb, hung to her waist. And despite her ailment, she was very amusing.

After I had prepared my tools of trade, Lizzie and her father gave me their views on how best to capture her. Lizzie wanted to wear her mother's favourite, a glorious white gown. It was a wise choice, complementing her fair hair and complexion. Sir Robert was particularly interested in capturing some of the landscape viewed from their drawing room window – something I had perfected with the prized *Emily* – a feature I had borrowed from the *Mona Lisa*. From this opulent room, furnished with the finest Chippendale cabinetry, that view was enchanting; most of London stood below them. After one or two suggestions from me, purely to make the sitting more memorable and interesting, I stepped outside on to the landing with Sir Robert and pulled the door to. I felt I had to ask a burning question.

'What, pray, ails the child?'

Sir Robert spoke sadly. 'Consumption. Been to every specialist in London. There's nothing else–'

I took his arm. 'My sincere condolences, sir. I can sense the immense love between you. I'll get started.'

'And I'll see you at lunch, Mr Silver. Join me in the conservatory.'

Sir Robert returned downstairs and as I entered the drawing room again I witnessed for the first time how ill his daughter was. Lizzie was coughing her heart up. Her little plump maid, Millie, became quite concerned.

But between her bouts of coughing Lizzie was the perfect artist's model. I soon had an outline and spent a good deal of time on her magnificent sparkling eyes, bringing them to life. A vivid blue, there appeared to be a touch of oriental in the way they pointed upwards and outwards; they were her main striking feature although everything was perfectly formed over a fine bone structure. A great sadness came over me as I tried to come to terms with the fact that this young beauty before me would never experience love, happiness or romance and all the good things life had to offer, and would likely be snatched away from her dear father before the paint was properly dry. I fought hard to prevent her from sensing my sadness, but somehow, when she spoke, always softly and eloquently, I suspected she was aware of my sorrowful thoughts and was trying to put me at ease.

'I've experienced wonderful things,' she told me, 'seen my father at his happiest; and his saddest, after poor Mama. We've travelled much of the world together, all the parts Papa thought it worth my seeing. I've danced with most of the kings and princes of Europe and enjoyed, or suffered, most of their hangers-on. It's been a wonderful life. I can't complain. And now I've met you.' She giggled while elegantly cooling herself with a fan.

Then she began coughing again, a deep retching cough that racked her whole body however much she tried to conceal it. She signalled to Millie to go fetch something. For a while I felt helpless and knew I should do something to ease her pain. Finally, after the coughing caused her so much distress, I made the decision.

A jug of water and a glass stood on a sideboard, close to my easel. Pretending to seek better light I moved my easel nearer the jug, blocking Lizzie's view of it. Once there, I ensured I was concealed behind the easel and selected a glass vial from the line of medicines secreted inside my jacket. While Lizzie was completely distracted, bent over double with coughing, I dripped two drops of the chosen medication into a glass of water. As Lizzie sat up straight and wiped her mouth I squatted beside her and offered her the glass.

'Sip this, it'll help,' I told her. She smiled down at me with a very brave but exhausted smile. I prayed my efforts would give her some relief. And then Millie returned with her usual medication – a strong painkiller. So had her doctors given up treating the disease itself?

I continued sketching and ensured she finished my potion. Almost instantly she was calmer, coughing less. She smiled more often and I managed to complete an outline without further interruption; the portrait would build from that, nicely.

'Forgive me if this is upsetting but may I ask Miss Weston's prognosis, Sir Robert?' I asked him in the conservatory over lunch. Lizzie had asked for her lunch to be served in her room.

'Six months ago they hoped for a year or so, God willing. But she deteriorated in a way I didn't think possible. I've been watching my darling die...' Sir Robert struggled to continue, 'I fear we have only a month or two. She's in so much pain between the opiates.'

Opiates – painkillers. I had heard nothing positive about the treatment she could have been receiving and so desperately needed.

'This is so sad, sir. She has immense love for you.' He remained still, staring into nowhere, and I broke the silence, 'Does Lizzie–'

'Know?' he interrupted, 'No, no. I thought it best she didn't. One wonders what lengths one would go to in order to save a dearly loved one such pain. I have surprised myself, Mr Silver. I must have visited every quack, faith and psychic healer within a hundred miles. And with my credentials you would have thought I'd have known better. Right now, I would willingly trade my soul with the devil, were a cure possible. Meanwhile, I hope my denying her the knowledge of precisely what ails her, spares her some of the pain.' He sipped some wine and looked at an empty chair at the other end of the table. 'Her mother passed just three years since. We both miss her so dearly.' He paused, a tear made its way down his cheek. 'I'm not sure how I will...' he tried, dabbing his wet cheek dry.

Millie, the young maid, interrupted and whispered into Sir Robert's ear, giggling. Sir Robert cheered and stood up, throwing down his napkin.

'Apparently, there's something we must observe upstairs, Mr Silver,' he said, standing and beckoning for me to follow him.

At the top of the grand staircase I could hear singing, a delightful voice. As we approached, I realised it was coming from Lizzie in the drawing room. Sir Robert and I looked at each other, smiling. He eased the door open an inch or two to glimpse inside and then bade me look, too. Lizzie, oblivious to everything about her, had the sketched outline in her hands and danced joyfully around the room holding it out at arm's length, singing at the top of her voice. Sir Robert pushed the door wide open and we both stood there, gaping and bemused. We stepped inside and Sir Robert clapped to her rhythm, as she sang and danced.

'Papa! Papa, isn't it wonderful? Mr Silver, you've made me soooo happy.' She put the sketch back on the easel and dragged Sir Robert into dancing with her. Soon the pair pranced round the room like it were a debutante's ball. Sir Robert stopped in front of me, introduced us formally, and I bowed deeply, taking Lizzie's hand before she pulled me into a lively polka. Lizzie provided the music, vocally, but I was as sure as she that there was a full orchestra present for such a glorious occasion.

After two more sittings to complete the under-painting, each as enjoyable as the first but not quite so energetic, I took Lizzie's portrait away to finish it in my studio. I had continued to ply Lizzie with my most special tonic surreptitiously, fearing I would never be comfortable explaining my unprofessional behaviour to her father regardless of how much relief it brought Lizzie.

When I arrived in Hampstead to deliver the completed portrait the butler took my cape and top hat and I was shown into a huge library downstairs. Lizzie, more effervescent than I had ever seen her, ran to me and kissed me on both cheeks. I was rather taken aback, and then her father joined us. I placed a large bag with the portrait inside on a chair and prepared to remove the cover.

'Shall I?' They both nodded enthusiastically. I whipped off the bag and stood back.

Both pairs of eyes widened. They were silent, but I noticed their pupils dilating. Then Lizzie squealed with delight, thrusting her hands to her mouth. She ran to the portrait and knelt in front of it, gushing with admiration. I could see that Sir Robert was in tears and saved him any embarrassment by keeping my eyes upon Lizzie. She kept squealing. The little plump maid, Millie, whom Lizzie appeared to treat like a sister, curtsied and gave Sir Robert a look of: *may I?*

Lizzie jumped up off the floor and grabbed the maid by the shoulders, pushing her in front of the portrait. The maid's face was a pleasure to watch, and she happily joined Lizzie dancing and prancing around the room.

'Extraordinary! Most extraordinary!' Sir Robert said as he shook my hand robustly. 'The Dalmatian at her feet is exactly like her Spot. She loved him so dearly. It'll bring her many joyous memories.' He finally let go of my hand and took something from his wallet. 'The happiness you've brought my daughter will surely stay with me for the rest of my life. I doubt I could ever reward you enough, my boy.' He passed me his folded cheque, quietly. 'If ever anything troubles you and you feel you need a friend to confide in, do please consider me that friend. I would deem it an honour, sir.'

I felt quite humble. A knight of the realm, an advisor to Her Majesty, had called me *sir*.

By now, Lizzie had grabbed the butler and stood *him* in front of her portrait; the elderly gentleman stood dabbing his face with a handkerchief as tears rolled down his cheeks. Then the maid appeared with Cook, still in her pinafore and flour in her hair, and ran out again. A moment later, a coachman and gardener were shown in to join the celebration and Sir Robert poured them all a glass of sherry as they stood admiring firstly, the portrait, but more importantly, Lizzie's joyous antics and newfound zest for life. To witness such affection from household staff towards the master and his family was a joy indeed. Their house brimmed with love. And to think I had something to do with the happiness they exuded that night made me extremely proud. At the same time, I felt immensely sad. How would this loving household deal with the loss of the master's daughter, when the time came? The very thought cast a dark shadow over me.

As Sir Robert chatted with them all, I felt it an opportune moment to leave, and quietly collected my cape and hat from the lobby, leaving by the front door and closing it quietly behind me.

Before I reached my carriage, the black thoughts of a change of fortune about to befall this house still very much on my mind, I heard the door open and turned to see possibly the most heart-wrenching sight I had witnessed since the loss of my Emily – Lizzie running after me in her mother's billowing white gown.

She jumped in front of me, her delightful bosom heaving.

'When will I see you again?' Perplexed, she screwed both her hands tightly.

'My work here is done, Lizzie. I hope it meets your satisfa–'

She lurched forward and kissed me, hard on the mouth, wrapping her arms around my neck. I was startled and strained to keep an eye on the front door for fear of being discovered. How would I explain? She kissed me again and again, all over my face. I managed to hold her off.

'You can't go. I won't let you. I'll die without you.' She lurched forward again. 'I'll kill myself!' In tears now, she began pounding on my chest.

'Tonight. I'll kill myself, tonight, if you leave me.'

I struggled to hold her still, and thankfully, she calmed a little. I caught a tear on her cheek with my finger and felt honoured that such a beautiful creature should have such feelings for me, her portrait painter. But I needed to tell her why I couldn't respond in the way she so desperately desired.

'Lizzie. Lizzie, my dear, sweet thing. These past weeks working on your portrait so endeared me to you, too.' I passed her a handkerchief. 'I've helped repair your broken wing and now you're a bird ready to soar once again into the skies.' I took a deep breath; I had to tell her. She had to know that it was not that I wasn't attracted to her – that would have been completely untrue. 'But another has my heart, Lizzie.'

She stood back abruptly. 'How will I survive without you?' she said, wiping her tears. 'And without your tonics?'

'I don't–'

'Father would not be best pleased if I–'

'I did it for you,' I sighed, squeezing her hands gently.

'Are they legal? These potions that make me feel this way?' I couldn't answer that. 'I'm sure not. It's prison or me. You must choose, Jacob Silver.' She turned but didn't let go of my hand. Turning back, she pressed her face right into mine. 'You have a day to think about it. Then I'll tell my–'

The front door opened. My heart sank.

As she stepped towards the house, I blurted out: 'I choose you! I will come. I promise. If you'll wait a while. Until I–'

Lizzie squealed. Threw her arms around my neck then reached inside my jacket, fumbled and located the glass vials there. She took two and clutched them close to her breast. I was startled. Until then I had had no idea she was aware I was administering potions to her.

'I'll wait, then. You promise you'll come back for me?'

I nodded.

'Lizzie, you'll catch your death,' Sir Robert called out from the door. 'This is most unsatis–'

'Coming, Papa,' she called out to him. She turned, smiled, and mouthed me a kiss.

'Three drops. Twice a day. And each week, reduce them by one drop a day. No more, Lizzie,' I whispered. 'Understand? No more.'

She ran back towards the house. I climbed aboard the carriage Sir Robert had kindly put at my disposal and, as it pulled away, watched her white gown flowing in the wind behind her like the wings of an angel.

I would never forget that image of Lizzie. I felt so sad that I would never see her again.

The Trial: Day 3

Sergeant Beck was finishing his evidence.

'So the accused admitted to you that having found Emily dead, they didn't go to the authorities to report it.'

'Correct, sir. Silver feared that since his father had been found dead there, unnecessary suspicion would fall upon them – *him* – with a second body.'

'So they sought to *revive* her, instead?'

'Yes, sir, with this *Elixir 32* that Silver had perfected.'

'But it needed *other* ingredients, is that right? To work properly, they said.'

'I wrote it down,' the sergeant said, reading from his notes. 'Essential ingredients. A catalyst, he said. Souls. They hadn't got any souls yet. He left that side of things to this professor.'

'And on the twenty-eighth of September, Silver miraculously, without any prior knowledge, found the souls had not only been acquired but had been administered. Is that right?'

'Yes, sir.'

'Did the accused say he had *tested* the elixir – Elixir 32 that is – on some other body? Brought it back to life?'

'Not a body, sir, no. He used it on someone living, sir. Slipped it into her drink, surreptitiously, he told me.'

'And who *was* this, did he say?'

'Yes, sir.'

'M'lud!' Mr Ecclestone called out, getting up on his feet. 'The prosecution and the defence agree that it is not necessary for the person's name to be announced in open court.' He passed a note to the judge, who passed it back to Mr Ponsonby, who, in turn, passed it to the sergeant in the witness box.

'Sergeant, is this the name of the person the accused plied with *Elixir 32*, against their will?'

The sergeant looked down at the note and nodded. 'Yes, sir.'

Mr Ponsonby passed the note to the jury. 'May I enquire how he came to *slip it into her drink?*'

'Her father had commissioned a portrait of her. She posed at her home in West Hampstead.'

My goodness! I looked about me for support. They are referring to me. It can only be me. My God! *That* is what it was! I drank his wretched potion? I clutched my chest, feeling quite ill.

'And what was her reaction to this potion?'

'The accused said it relieved her symptoms; brought her a new zest for life. He actually admitted he became quite fond of the lady,' the sergeant continued, blinking rapidly from what looked like a tear in his eye as he added: 'But she was dying, sir. He only wanted her last days to pass without pain.'

'Did the accused see her after her portrait was complete?'

'I asked him if he had, sir. He replied: "I'm ashamed to say, I did not. She would have passed soon after, I fear, as I heard nothing more. I just hoped that I made her last days easier." '

My heart was pounding; my temperature rising. The courtroom below turned to a blur. But echoing in my head were those last words. Passed? Jacob thinks I'm dead? Gone from him? Was that why I never heard from him? I felt a little better and strained to hear every word.

'I asked him: Are we going to find this is another girl you've killed with your concoctions?' Sergeant Beck said. 'He replied:

"Get it into your bony head, sergeant, I haven't killed any of my girls. No man alive could have prevented the consumption from killing her at that advanced stage. And as for the others, I cared for them all. I had no control over what the professor did with them.'

'We shall see, sir, I said to the accused. He replied:

"Yes! You will see. See that you've made a terrible mistake. D'you think I go around killing people for the fun of it, is that it? I am a healer, sir. From four generations of healers, you hear? I did not kill those girls! Go order your Bobbies to Blackfriars and arrest this demon, this professor.'

My darling, darling Jacob! How I remember so well those glorious days, sitting so close to you. And how sadly now, I recall our parting. Dutifully, you returned to your ailing loved one – and I so understand that now. But I'm not dead, my darling. On the contrary, I live only for you. If only you would look up and see me, see how I care and how willing I am to help you in your hour of need.

But he didn't look up. He continued to cower in the dock, a vacant look on his face.

Chapter 16

Soon after the funds received from Sir Robert ran out, and egged on by an empty larder and belts that could not be further tightened, Jacob mellowed towards producing works of horror. A child dying in the neighbourhood after Betsy was unable to supply a simple remedy due to lack of stock, was almost the last straw. This added further pressure on him to earn money by whatever means, or risk losing the business that had been in his family for generations. Finally, having increased his daily intake of *Essence of Emily*, his worst fears, his ultimate nightmare, occurred: her urn was about to run dry. And what was left of her head began to rot. As he watched gangrenous blotches erupting all over what was left of her face he knew he *had to* preserve her – at whatever cost. Without her, he saw his life crumbling before him. There was only one solution: paint horror and earn some money to buy chemicals, and save Emily.

'Damn him! I'll do it,' Jacob finally succumbed, summoning his girls to report for duty. Polly was the first to return.

'The usual, is it? Clobber off and plant me fanny on the couch?' she asked, her clothes falling to the ground at her feet.

Jacob, pounding away with a mortar and pestle behind his easel, was quite taken aback. 'So quick, Polly. In a hurry?'

'Sorry, habit. Never 'ang around getting' me togs off. Sooner they get it over wiv the better I like it.' She turned to him, thrusting out her bosom, teasing, pouting her lips. 'How would you like me, kind sir?' Polly turned around, her back to him. She bent double and touched her toes, giggling, then poked her face through her legs. 'This way?' she cackled, then stood up straight and turned back to face him again, arms and legs stretched apart, 'or this way?'

Jacob laughed, holding up the club-shaped stone pestle. 'Gosh, you take my breath away,' he admitted, the tightness in his trousers causing him to turn about. 'But I want to try something different. An experiment.'

'Not wiv that you ain't, mister,' Polly cried out, grabbing her clothes off the floor and beginning to step into them. 'Fort you was a quiet one. This wha' you 'ad in mind all along?'

Jacob laughed out loud, throwing down the tool. 'Relax! It's for the paint, that's all.' He went over and coaxed her to sit on the edge of the chaise, carrying a bowl of hair accessories. 'I want you to fix your hair, Polly. Try and get it to look like this.' He showed her a *Harper's Bazaar* clipping of a high coiffure exposing the neck, then passed her the bowl of beads and hair clips.

'Blimey. Done up like a dog's dinner,' Polly said, after she had fixed her hair using the huge mirror that hung behind the chaise.

'Like royalty,' Jacob countered, going to her. 'Superb. I just want to…' He threaded some pink beads into her hair. 'Now, if you'll just sit upright on the edge of the chaise with this hand-mirror. Hold it like this. Imagine you're dressing up, for the ball.' He went back behind the easel. 'I need you to shift your bottom about an inch that way,' he pointed towards the door. 'Now, your head. Turn it just a little more towards the window, and… Fine. Superb.' From his point of view, behind the easel, it was perfect, the mirror behind Polly reflecting all of her back and head, and the hand mirror just visible.

Polly giggled infectiously as Jacob mixed his pallet and added the all-important *Essence of Emily*. He then began work on the outline; sweeping strokes, lightning fast. A dip of burnt umber, a dab of precious essence – a sip from the very last glass.

'Will I be able to see it, as it goes, this time? Steal yer secrets?' Polly laughed.

'No, sorry. But I'll show you when it's done.'

The next day, Polly returned and this time was asked to hold a plain, white-porcelain masquerade mask on a stick, instead of the hand mirror. During the third sitting, Jacob made a more unusual demand. After relishing a long slug of essence, he asked Polly, 'I want you to pretend you're frightened. Scared out of your wits. D'you think you can do that?' She looked puzzled. 'I'll demonstrate.' Jacob threw faces of terror and torture – succeeding in only making Polly laugh. 'You can do that?'

Polly attempted to impersonate Jacob – and burst out laughing. 'S'no use, Jake. I ain't no actress.'

Jacob demonstrated again how she should show fear and dread; how to grimace and scream – all to no avail. He knocked back the rest of the essence in anger. Finally, he ran downstairs into the kitchen, returning with a tool that was expected to help. Surprising Polly, he jumped behind her wielding a huge butcher's knife.

'Scream, damn you!' he yelled, thrusting the knife towards her naked neck.

Polly's face twisted into horror; her eyes frenzied, mouth widened, and she yelled the place down, shoving her arms up into his face to protect herself.

'*That's it!*' Jacob laughed. 'Exactly it! Keep it like that, will you?' He held up the knife again – she yelled again. Rushing back to his canvas, Jacob finally captured the moment.

But Polly witnessed that it was *his* eyes, *his* face that now took on the mask of horror. She became fearful as his frenzied eyes vibrated in his skull, his mouth spitting and hissing as he tore at the canvas with wide sweeps of his brush, wielding it like that butcher's knife. Crimson splashed everywhere; on the portrait's neck, the dress, in the hair; and on *his* clothes, on *his* hands, in *his* hair.

Polly jumped up, fearful of where this was all leading. 'Gorra go now,' she squeaked timidly, easing herself into her clothes, her eye constantly on the madman at the easel.

And then the spell broke. As quickly as it began. Jacob was his old self again, calm and collected like always; but exhausted by this nerve-racking sitting. He stood back from the easel and admired his work, his shirt soaked from sweat. He was confident the fake Frenchman would snap up this new offering – from his darker side.

After Polly pocketed the extra shilling Jacob awarded her, she quickly dressed. He opened the door to the studio. 'I'll show you out, Polly. And thanks again for being such a great actress. Exciting things going on here. Send Letty next, would you? And you might prepare her for what's to come. Don't want to intimidate the poor girl.'

'S'okay, I'll see meself out, no trouble,' Polly said. 'You get back and finish me paintin'. Can't wait to see it finished,' she said edging out of the door, not caring whether she saw the finished painting or not. She just wanted to be out of there. Away from him.

At the bottom of the stairs Polly was met by the professor. He spoke quietly, 'Master Jacob wanted me to show you his new beauty treatment. It's down here,' he said, indicating the stairs down to the laboratory.

The professor led Polly through into the anteroom where a pot of light-brown cream sat on the bench. 'He's working on a new perfumed balm for making women's skin younger. Here,' he held out her arm and dabbed a knob of what looked like butter into her palm. 'Best applied just under your nose. Takes years off,' the professor said, stepping back three paces and taking out his handkerchief.

Polly caught a whiff of the foul butter. 'Jesus bloody Christ. Like fuckin' pig's sh–' Her eyes rolled. The professor stuffed the handkerchief over his nose. Polly trembled, stammered, 'W-w-what have you–'

Polly shook and wobbled; her eyes rolled up into her skull. She reached out, grabbed onto the five-feet-high copper kettle, and then collapsed, her head bouncing off its glass porthole.

Her face flat on the ground, the last thing Polly saw and heard was the hissing and clanking of the whole wall closing beside her face – before she passed out.

Nora duly arrived to pose for her horror painting. Jacob found she was a better actress than Polly and didn't need much frightening at all. He found it fun working with her.'

'You saw Polly, Nora? She told you what I'm after?'

'Ain't seen 'ide nor 'air of 'er. You said you might have some extra work. Thought I'd pop by.'

After he'd finished explaining the pose, the hairdo, the hand mirror, and the porcelain mask, Jacob began painting in the background on the canvas as Nora prepared. 'So where is Polly?' he asked. 'She wanted to see her portrait.'

'Got that rich geezer in tow, ain't she just. Spect he's makin' demands,' Nora told him.

'I told her, I don't know why she does it,' Jacob said, concentrating on the canvas.

'She needn't. There's another sly ol' bugger got a place in Brighton. Says he'll set her up good and proper. Live like a queen he tells her. We all said we'd go down and take a butcher's one of these days.'

'A butcher? Why would she need a butcher?'

Nora laughed out loud. 'Butcher's hook, *look*. Take a look. Geddit?'

Jacob nodded and smiled. 'Be great for her to live near Nell's boarding school.'

'Boarding school? That what she calls it now?'

'Well, isn't it?'

'That's a posh way 'o puttin' it, I 'spose. Was called *reform school* when I last saw the sign outside. Girl's clepto. Nicks anything that glitters. Beatin' her ten times a day ain't knockin' it out of 'er either, they tells Polly.'

Jacob sat, astounded. He needed a while to compose himself. 'The poor darling. She truly was an angel when I last saw her. What could have gone wrong? What got into her?'

'Ask me, it's the life our Poll leads. Left the kid with any bugger who'd take 'er, to foller 'er trade. And this is what it's led to.'

Jacob pressed a few more pearls into Nora's high hairdo and demonstrated how she should hold the hand mirror. 'I would like to call the painting *Isadora*, if you have no objection, Nora.'

'Call it wha' yer like, guv'nor long as I get me dosh.'

It would be another two sittings before Jacob broached the horror element of Nora's portrait.

'Just pretend you're scared. Scared out of your wits,' he told Nora.

Her first attempt was nothing more than a mild grimace. 'I ain't no drama queen, sorry,' Nora apologised. When the carving knife came out she improved tremendously, like her life depended on it.

'*Murder, murder!*' she yelled out, her face terrified.

'*Hold that!*' yelled Jacob. 'Perfect,' he said, splashing on the crimson.

A few moments later, Betsy burst into the studio closely followed by a uniformed policeman, Constable Owen Williams, thundering up the stairs, his truncheon drawn. He forced Jacob up against the wall, the truncheon across his neck.

'Now then, what's your game, mister?' the constable demanded, turning to Nora. 'Y'alright, miss?'

Jacob fought for his breath.

Nora, stark naked, raced over from the chaise and burst out laughing. After tugging at the truncheon to prevent Jacob choking, she explained, 'Only muckin' about, constable. No harm done, look.' Her breasts almost touched his nose.

Embarrassed, Constable Williams hurried back down the stairs where Betsy let him out.

Nora approached the easel. 'Dying to see it,' she said.

'Nearly done, dear. Nearly done,' Jacob said.

Back on the street, Constable Williams met another patrolling constable and shared the tale of the actress and the painter. The two roared with laughter right outside the shop. Behind them, at street level, the basement laboratory windows splattered with blood, striped this way then that.

Nora's screams were met with a 'Now then, what's your game, mister?' followed by hoots of laughter, from the two policemen.

Dying to see it, Nora had earned her five bob well.

An overfed fishwife arrived outside the closed apothecary's shop early one evening. Dressed in a disgusting bloodied apron, wielding a scaly mallet in one hand and a scrawny five-year-old girl in the other, she asked the girl, 'This the gaff?' The girl nodded. The woman rapped hard on the shop door with her mallet until Betsy opened it.

'Me gel, she 'ere?' the fishwife bellowed.

'Girl, madam? What girl pray?' asked Betsy.

'The painter. He's 'ere?'

'He's indisposed at the moment. Can I help?'

'What's he done wiv our Nora? Came to 'ave 'er pitcher done. Ain't bin 'ome since.'

'Well, I assure you she's not here. She had five shillings to spend and spoke of going to Brighton. I suggest you go and look there, madam,' Betsy said firmly, shutting the door in her face.

Jacob had a bounce in his stride as he unloaded the three horror paintings from his carriage and took them inside the art gallery.

'Bonjour, bonjour,' Jean-Louis gushed, putting the paintings to one side for a moment, facing them to the wall. 'Monsieur Zhaycoob, this is a coincidence indeed, there's a dealer here buying some of your lesser *Emily's*. I'll introduce you,' he offered, gesturing for Jacob to join him in the smaller salon at the rear of the gallery.

Jacob noticed an attendant lifting the last of three *Emily's* down off the wall as a youngish and well-dressed, well-to-do lady stood by, her back to him.

'Who is she? What's her name?'

Jean-Louis pulled out a business card. 'Muxlow. Rebecca Muxlow.'

'Good heavens,' Jacob gasped, Rebecca turning around to greet him. 'An old friend, Jean-Louis. This calls for a celebration.'

'Jacob darling, how nice to see you after all these years,' Rebecca said, greeting him with open arms and offering him her hand to kiss. She looked him up and down. The absence of his iron legs must have pleased her. She smiled broadly. 'My, how you've grown so.'

'And you have matured into a fine lady, Rebecca, I must say,' Jacob said, taking her hand and kissing it. 'My goodness, such beauty.' He gave her a twirl. She laughed. 'Say you'll pose for me, please. I can't wait to capture your very essence.'

Rebecca giggled. 'Did he tell you? I've bought every one of your *Emily's*. For... for a client. She had to have them all.'

Jean-Louis, eager to see the new works Jacob brought in, made an excuse and left them to catch up.

Seeing Rebecca after all these years almost overwhelmed me. With her now looking so much more like Emily, the memories came flooding back. I wanted to touch her, hold her close, to bathe in sweet memories – of her sister. And what of Emily's demise? Rebecca, of course, could not have known. While Emily and I were together, Rebecca had never called. Emily insisted she didn't want anything to do with her, and never mentioned her. And I knew better than to mention her name myself. I had always presumed her animosity towards her sister was because of the incident in the boathouse, which Emily never once referred to in our time together.

Having to tell Rebecca that her dear sister was dead, filled me with dread. How could I? How would I explain what we did with her? That she is unblessed, cold in a jar. Preserved, so that I might study her for eternity, drink her essence to keep my sanity; use her golden light to keep my miserable flame burning. How could I subject Emily's dear sister to such pain? I chose to remain silent on the matter. If Emily's name should arise I would deny having seen her since college, spare Rebecca the anguish. It was as simple as that.

What I couldn't deny was that there, in front of me, was a replica of Emily. A new-born Emily. In the flesh. Perfect and provocative. A living, breathing, sensuous Emily. Alive! I almost felt ashamed, but I wanted her, wanted to touch her, caress her, envelope myself with her bosom, run my fingers and tongue over every inch of her. I almost felt I could have taken her right there in the middle of the floor, in a public window. I didn't care. The blood rose in me. I could feel the flush...

'Yes. I would like that,' Rebecca said, interrupting my thoughts.

I was puzzled. She would? On the floor? Now? 'Sorry?' I said.

She looked at me, a little confused herself. 'I'd be honoured to be painted by you, Jacob.' She smiled uneasily.

I needed to concentrate, take my eyes off her cleavage and stop these yearnings. 'You were so alike,' I told her, looking deep into her eyes for a signal; surrender; acquiescence.

Rebecca tenderly touched my hand. I gripped hers; more to feel her flesh than for support. Her long fingers, just like Emily's, entwined with mine. For a few moments it was divine. It was like Emily had returned yet again – as I knew she would, as she must, for me to survive.

'You still miss her, don't you?' Rebecca asked, a deep sadness in her face.

Rebecca *knows?* She *knows* Emily has gone? How could that be? We dared not tell. It was the most secret of all secrets. After dear Papa, another loved-one's body found in my house, I could not risk telling a soul.

'She had a secret, Jacob. It's my duty to tell you.'

I looked down at Rebecca's fingers stroking my hand, sensing more pain was on its way. She approached Jean-Louis and pointed to his office. We were both then guided towards it where Jean-Louis left us and closed the door. My heart was thumping. I dreaded what Rebecca was about to say.

'Those medications you gave her made her the happiest I'd ever known – after she got over Rosemary's overdose, of course. She would never stop telling me how much you meant to her. I was quite jealous. My little sister had the most beautiful man all to herself.' Rebecca lifted our joined hands and kissed the back of mine. 'But the light-hearted jolliness Emily always portrayed was an act, Jacob. She had consumption. She was dying. Jolly on the outside, dying from the inside. She couldn't bear the thought of deteriorating in front of you – you watching her die, mourning her. She came to me, asked for the means. I...' tears welled in Rebecca's eyes and then she burst out with: 'I supplied it. She took rat poison. Ended it all.' Tears ran down Rebecca's face.

I needed to sit down. So, they *had* seen each other, and Emily had not breathed a word. Had she feared Rebecca would have taken me from her? And then I remembered who I was to Rebecca: *the crippled boy she couldn't take anywhere.*

'I'm so sorry,' she finally breathed.

After composing myself in Jean-Louis' office, I scowled at Rebecca. I could easily have throttled her. 'You helped Emily take her own life?' Rebecca stepped away, held her hands up to ward me off. 'You killed her as sure as stabbing her in the heart!' I yelled.

'No, no. She was in pain and–'

'You killed your own flesh and blood. You bitch! If I had known what her ailment was, I could have cured her. Why wouldn't she tell me? Why didn't *you* tell me?' I went to strike her across the face but held back my hand, inches from her cheek.

'Jacob!' she yelled. 'I was trying to save her pain...' Rebecca dropped to her knees in front of me, gripping my hands, pleading. 'If you had seen her begging me to do it, making me swear I would not tell you. You, her darling dear boy, would have done the same. A wounded animal, put out of its misery.' She began to sob, her whole body convulsing. After regaining a little composure, through her tears she added, 'I loved her. Truly, I loved her, Jacob. I could not let her suffer any longer. I begged someone tell me what was best. Mama just wanted her preserved, through whatever pain the poor girl had to endure. I thought of you. And what you would do. But neither Mama nor Emily would permit me to tell you of her deterioration.'

I sat in silence with Rebecca still at my feet. I must have then asked about the colour of the poison.

'Purple. It was vivid purple,' she said.

Purple. How could I ever forget? The purple puddle around Emily, her helpless body behind my shop counter. It was true. She had as good as murdered Emily.

'You should have told me! Someone should have told me!' I said, somewhat harshly, forgetting she was equally as bereaved as I. 'I would have found a cure.'

'There was no cure, Jacob. Only tonics to ease the pain, and you gave her ample of those. And you yourself were one such tonic,' Rebecca said, remaining calm.

'I would have created a cure, I tell you. I would have made it my life's work to save her,' I snapped, thumping on the desk.

Jean-Louis tapped lightly on the door before stepping inside his own office, clearing his throat quietly, then, 'Forgive the interruption, a footman is here, asking for madam's parcels. He's anxious that the lady outside is growing impatient.'

'My mother,' Rebecca explained. And then to Jean-Louis, 'Give him the paintings while I finish with Mr Silver, if you please. Do you have brandy? I think he needs it.'

Jean-Louis obliged, extracting a decanter from the sideboard and providing just one balloon glass.

'Jacob, sit quietly. Sip the brandy. I shall be back in a moment or two. Then we'll make plans for my portrait,' Rebecca said, patting my head before leaving the office.

*

'Show me those paintings he just brought in, Monsieur St Clair. I want to see what he's up to nowadays,' Rebecca asked Jean-Louis quietly.

Jean-Louis took her to the back of the salon where Jacob's new offerings leaned facing the wall. On the reverse of each canvas, painted in burnt umber, the portrait's title: *Masquerade* ~ followed by each girl's name: *Penelope*, *Leticia* and *Isadora*. Jean-Louis turned all three of the paintings around to face her.

Rebecca sucked in her breath. 'Oh my God!'

'The artist's first in a new line of horror paintings, madam. Highly fashionable.'

'My God! I hope he won't paint me like *this!*' she gasped, picking one up and holding it at arm's length.

'Very much in demand, right now, madam. I'll have no trouble selling these.'

Each girl, naked, sat on a chaise with her back to a large mirror. The hair, full of beads and pearls, was stacked high on her head. Dressing-up for the Masquerade Ball. Each face was identical – a plain white porcelain mask. Blood dripped from under the mask. The eyes in the mask were missing; one saw right through the empty eye sockets into the mirror behind.

In their hand, each girl held an ornate stick with an oval frame at its end – where one would normally find the masquerade mask. But in Jacob's version the girl's *real* face was portrayed – horribly distorted and screaming in terror.

Reflected in the mirror behind, one could see the headless torso behind the porcelain mask, the beaded hair floating above in mid-air. The reflection showed the back of the severed head, dripping with blood, attached to the stick held in the hand.

Rebecca winced as she ran her fingers over the horrified face. 'You can sense the terror. So incredibly unique. I can sell these. I'll take this one on approval, if I may?' Rebecca said, selecting *Penelope*. 'I have just the client, a perverted letch in Putney. With any luck this'll frighten him to death,' she laughed. 'As long as it's after I get paid.'

Jean-Louis smiled and bowed, took the work of art and placed it into a canvas bag, taking it to the door to give to the footman from Rebecca's carriage. Rebecca then returned to the gallery office where she made an appointment with Jacob to call at his studio and sit for her portrait.

'Above the apothecary's shop,' Jacob told Rebecca, handing her his business card. 'I've a large studio.'

She would call on the last Friday of the month, the twenty-eighth of September, she explained, when her mother had no need of her services for the whole weekend.

'I daresay we'll find something to do with ourselves over a whole weekend. What fun!' she exclaimed as she left, the assisted murder of her sister Emily quite forgiven and forgotten.

What fun indeed.

In Berkeley Square, Rebecca arrived home having put her mother on a train to Finchingfield. It was late evening and she took *Masquerade ~ Penelope* upstairs, placing it in her bedroom on the chest of drawers at the foot of the bed. A little later, she climbed into bed and sat mesmerised by the painting for a few minutes. Every detail had been exquisitely executed, she mused. There was no doubt in Rebecca's mind that underneath that veil of terror, a beautiful woman posed. In her hair, pink pearls reflected the pink polka dots of her dress, draped across her lap. She thought about Jacob and how the crippled moth had developed into an elegant butterfly.

Rebecca finally turned out the gaslight and pulled the covers over herself. After tossing and turning for a while, unable to sleep, she jumped out of bed and turned *Penelope* to face the wall. Only then was she able to drift off and dream of what she might do to Jacob, once she had him all to herself.

On the River Thames, between Blackfriars and the Tower Bridges, a uniformed police constable leaned out of a rowboat as two boatmen pulled on the oars. Swinging a hurricane lamp, he was searching the river. The constable called out and pointed off the bow.

A boathook snagged some floating cloth. They eased alongside and while one of the oarsmen made excuses and retched over the side, the other assisted the constable to lift the object into the boat – a female body. She wore a pink polka dot dress.

Her head was missing.

Further down the river, Big Ben struck midnight.

At precisely that same moment, in Berkeley Square, horrific screams awakened Rebecca, terrifying her. She jumped out of bed, raced over to the portrait and turned it around.

The last thing Rebecca would remember before collapsing on the bedroom floor were the screams coming from *Penelope's* gaping mouth.

Chapter 17

At Stepney police station in East London, five days after the discovery of the unidentified woman's headless body in the Thames, middle-aged and poorly-shod, Gertrude Cummings, dragged in her four mischievous boys, aged between six and sixteen, to report to the duty officer at the front desk.

'It's me gel,' she began. 'Letty. Got me worried,' Gertrude announced.

Constable Higgins put down the worn copy of the *London Illustrated News* and tutted. 'If everybody worried about their kids came in here we'd have people lined up to Buckingham Palace, madam. Spent the night out, did she?'

'That dress in the paper. The spotted one what the gel with no head was wearing,' Gertrude continued, the constable now listening more closely.

'Your girl, she's got a dress like that?' the constable asked, picking up a report sheet and pencil.

'No,' said Gertrude. The officer threw down the pencil and sighed. 'She did have,' Gertrude continued, 'but she swapped it wiv a friend of 'ers, Polly.'

'And where will we find this Polly?'

'Dunno. That's why I come 'ere,' Gertrude said, as she commanded her youngest boy to come and have the snot wiped from his face. 'See, my Letty's missin' and she's often at Polly's. But I couldn't find Polly neither, see. She ain' 'ome, that's for sure. Then I see the pitcher in the paper.'

The two eldest boys began squabbling. The constable warned Mrs Cummings that their language would frighten a police horse and demanded she shut them up before the superintendent appeared. Gertrude went over and clumped them both about the ears. 'Be'ave!' she yelled.

'What makes you think it's the same dress, may I ask?' the constable pressed, sure this was a non-runner and eager to get back to his magazine.

'Cos one of the dots is missing; near the arse – same as Letty's. I mended it wiv a piece I cut from a sheet.'

The constable pricked up his ears, and said, 'Keep your kids under control a few moments, I'll get someone who can help.'

The constable returned with a detective in plain clothes, Sergeant Thorpe. Lifting the counter flap, Sergeant Thorpe invited Mrs Cummings to follow him to his office. The constable smartly banged the flap down to ensure her rowdy flock didn't follow.

'Wai' 'ere, you lot!' Gertrude yelled at her kids, 'and bleedin' be'ave or you'll get the back o' my 'and! You 'ear?'

'I think they heard, madam,' the constable said, grinning at the kids. The youngest poked his tongue out, and as soon as a door closed behind his mother, blew a loud raspberry at the constable.

After a poor connection and having to ask for the Scotland Yard number three times, Sergeant Thorpe replaced the telephone receiver on its pedestal and turned back to Gertrude Cummings, a solemn look on his face.

'It does look like this could be your daughter's dress, Mrs Cummings,' he said. Gertrude chewed on her fingers nervously. 'But let's not jump to any conclusions, shall we? When did you last see your daughter?'

'She said some well-to-do geezer was paying to paint her pitcher. She came 'ome wiv some flowers and left her little un wiv us to go sit for 'im again.'

'She say where the gentleman lived?' Sergeant Thorpe asked.

'The city, she said.'

'Where in the city, did she say?'

Gertrude shook her head and started trembling. 'Anyfink 'appens to her I'll kill the bastard meself, I'll tell yer that for nothin',' she said, fidgeting and twisting a dirty handkerchief into knots. Tears welled in her eyes.

'You watch, you'll get home and she'll have a nice cup o' tea waiting for you, eh?' Thorpe said, trying to settle her. But Gertrude was not consoled.

Just then, the sound of a howling youth broke through into the sergeant's office. The constable from the front desk knocked and entered. 'Scuse me, Mrs Cummings. But I felt obliged to clip your eldest's ear.'

'What's he done now?' she asked.

'Peed in the gutter out the front. So I clipped him and showed him the lav.'

'Bloody good job. Clip 'em all, willya?' Gertrude said, adding, 'No man about the 'ouse, that's my bleedin' problem.'

'Be much longer, sarge? Dunno if the super can take too much of these little blighters,' the constable asked Sergeant Thorpe, 'No offence, ma'am.'

'Shoulda drowned 'em at birth,' Gertrude quipped, ' 'ad a much quieter life.'

'Few more minutes,' Sergeant Thorpe replied, adding, 'Close the door behind you, constable.' After the door was closed, 'How well do you know Polly?'

Gertrude was leaving with her kids when she passed by the noticeboard in the lobby. 'That's our Nora. She missing, too?' she called out to the sergeant, looking perplexed and stabbing her finger on a faded photograph pinned to the board. It was pinned among a half-dozen others with a label above them: *Missing*.

'Her mother reported her missing a couple of nights back. Why, you know her, too?' Detective Thorpe asked.

Detective Inspector George Neville, by the rule of numbers, was the Metropolitan Police's finest detective. He had always been outshone by an inspector with a better record of detection – but Jack the Ripper helped him out, bringing Neville to the top of the pile sooner than expected. The Whitechapel murderer's rampage in 1888 left seven murders on Inspector Frederick George Abberline's sheet *unsolved* – destroying his detection rate. Abberline, bitter as he became further overshadowed by Neville's continued success, accused Neville of cherry-picking, only accepting the easier, solvable cases – as if Neville had a choice. The fact was that Neville was thorough to a point of obsession. He would not advance a case until he had sound reasoning to back up his deductions. 'Hunches are for amateurs,' Neville told his junior officers. 'Sound and logical evidence is what convicts. It's there somewhere. If necessary, go back and find it. Dig it out of people, dig it up from wherever it is, from whatever it's buried under, but woe betide you if you *make it up*.'

Stood in his Scotland Yard office looking out onto the River Thames – the murky waters of which had delivered up two female headless bodies in as many weeks – Neville had feared this case could ruin his record. Unidentified bodies were the hardest cases to solve. And worse, Abberline would be laughing at him or claiming he could have solved it, within days, no doubt. But then came along Mrs Cummings looking for her Letty, and the unsolvable seemed, at first glance, to have turned into another cherry for picking. Thank God.

The second body found had been identified – Letty Norton, née Cummings. Her mother, Gertrude, had identified her by an appendix scar and a birth mark, a brown mole on her forearm in the shape of an old boot. Having her picture painted by someone in the city, the mother had told them. That was all they had. Suspecting the body in the faulty polka dot dress was Letty's friend, Polly, Neville had only one means of identification open to him – the only known living relative, her adopted much younger sister, Nell, according to Mrs Cummings. The child was easy to track down. But quite how she could make a meaningful identification, without a head, was of grave concern. But murder is murder, and without certain identification of the victim the investigation was held back. Neville had no better choice open to him. Nell *had* to be brought to London – and suffer the consequences.

Nell was escorted by a lady from the reform school in Brighton. To make things easier on the child it was decided not to tell her about the missing head. The pathologist's assistant used an inflated balloon in a wig to replace the missing part of Polly's anatomy. This was then covered with a separate sheet down to the shoulders. Under no circumstances was the fake head to be revealed, warned the inspector, we don't have to frighten the kid to death.

Detective Inspector Neville led Nell into the mortuary anteroom where the victim's body was completely covered with a sheet. The reform school officer stood by, to help soften the blow.

'Nell, dear, we are truly sorry that you have to do this,' the lady officer began, 'but if this is Polly we do need to know. She would surely want you to help us catch whoever did this to her, wouldn't she?'

'Can I see her face?' Nell asked, innocently.

'Best you don't look dear. Bit upsetting,' the officer explained.

'What did they do to her?' Nell asked shakily.

'She was left to drown in the river, my dear.' Then, before removing the sheet that covered only the top half of the body, 'May I show you her, now?' Nell nodded. The top sheet was drawn down as far as the victim's waist, the head remaining covered.

Nell immediately shook her head. Then in a quiet whisper, 'Can't tell. I hope it's not her.' She then went to the foot of the trolley on which the victim lay and lifted the sheet. She caught her breath, pulled an agonised face and screamed.

After quietening Nell down, Neville heard the child say: 'It *is* Polly. It's her toes. I can tell from her toes. She had funny toes.'

Nell was led out after confirming she was beyond doubt that it *was* her sister's body. Inspector Neville had evidence better than blood grouping – of no use with stepsisters, of course – because of Polly's deformed inner toes on both feet. Each was joined to the next, up to the first joint; Polly had slightly webbed-feet.

Once Polly was identified, Neville was confident, thanks to Gertrude Cummings, they had a link between all three missing girls and a painter – the prime suspect paying a shilling a day to his victims. Neville hoped that, provided his searches were thorough enough, he could still find Nora, alive and well – before she turned up in the river like the others.

Neville had invited an old friend from the Marine Police at Wapping to talk the case through, Inspector Charlie Morgan. The biggest question was: *where* did each body get thrown into the river. On his desk, a chart of the River Thames bore crosses where each body was recovered.

Next to the chart was the pathologist's estimate of how long each body had been in the river, together with printed *Tide Tables* for the River Thames.

'If the killer got rid of the bodies immediately he took their heads, time and place of death would be around the same place as they were chucked into the river,' offered Charlie Morgan, experienced in dragging bodies and every other kind of detritus from the river. 'But if he kept the bodies and travelled to the river later, we've got a much harder job on our hands. Could have killed them anywhere. But transporting a headless corpse across London unseen, would be difficult.'

'I agree. Let's first speculate they were killed near the river, Charlie,' said Neville. 'Apply some science to the investigation. How far would that first body have travelled in the tides?'

'Discovered at midnight. Pathologist estimates six hours in the water.' Morgan referred to the tables by the chart. 'The tide was three hours after high water. So...' he ran his finger from a cross between Blackfriars and Tower Bridge. 'She would have drifted downstream for three hours or so, and upstream for three hours, all the way back to where she was dropped in. So not far from where she was found, is my guess. Someone hoping she'd end up miles away under Southend pier wouldn't have known the tides. My guess is she was put in the water around...' Morgan placed his finger on Blackfriars Bridge, 'here.'

'Now the other one. Only four hours in the water, a week later,' said Neville.

Morgan used a pair of callipers to step off tidal streams. 'Found at Chiswick. Working backwards, according to the tides, downstream from Chiswick, to Wapping, then upstream to...' the finger on Blackfriars Bridge again. 'Blimey,' Charlie Morgan remarked. 'Right on the button. Might be something to go on, George.'

'I need to be certain. Could you confirm all this with live demonstrations, Charlie?'

'What, throw something in about the same weight, and see where it arrives?' Neville nodded. 'We'd have to wait over three weeks, for the same state of the tide. Lunar cycles, you see?'

'But I can't wait for the bloody moon.' Neville looked out of the window again. 'Odds are, you're not far out, since we have two bodies pointing in the same direction. And the prime suspect is apparently an artist in the city. Blackfriars, may be near enough.' He turned back to the river chart. 'Our killer wouldn't risk being discovered. By all accounts it was broad daylight when they were shoved in the water. He wouldn't have risked doing that in the open. He had to be secreted somewhere away from prying eyes.'

'I'm guessing it won't be someone working on the river. They would know the tides only too well and wouldn't want a body snagged on their own anchor chain the next day,' Morgan offered.

'Charlie, get your river patrols to mark every property on this chart, say a mile either side of Blackfriars Bridge, that has direct access to the river. We'll then go house-to-house based on what you report.'

'Looking for...?'

'Artists first. Artists or sculptors, those kind of people. But doctors, butchers, mortuary attendants, and anatomy students, should all be included. Pathologist said both heads were severed professionally, not just hacked off. It's as though they needed to preserve them for some purpose. So anyone who uses a sharp knife for their work with a knowledge of anatomy or muscle structure.'

'Taxidermist?'

'There's a thing. Well done. Charlie. We'll add those to the list. Wouldn't come across many of them on a day's march, eh?' He tapped on Blackfriars Bridge on the chart again. 'But I feel we're getting somewhere.'

Inspector Morgan left Neville pondering over the photographs of the two headless bodies. He pulled a bell pull and an assistant arrived to take notes. Neville ordered one hundred copies of the unsold daily papers, since they were free, containing the circulated photographs of the three missing girls, Polly, Letty and Nora. Neville had been reprimanded by his superintendent for circulating missing girls so soon after their disappearance, asking for the public's assistance, claiming it was irresponsible as the public would now expect this in every case and they would be inundated. Inspector Neville argued that at least two of these three were *dead missing girls* and that was an exception. And he desperately needed to find the third girl before she too, ended up in the river without her head. The superintendent was not satisfied, and would not be unless a murderer was soon apprehended, he told Neville. Neville took it all in his stride, ignoring the superintendent. He then dictated a report for the duty sergeant, instructions to all divisions each side of the river to provide every uniformed officer with a copy of the photographs and begin asking all their contacts, shop and innkeepers, brothel madams and ticket touts if they knew of the girls, their contacts, and in particular, of course, of an artist painting their portraits. Another order informed detectives to begin seeking out art galleries in all of central London and asking if they had seen portraits of any of the girls. It was a long shot, so soon after their murder. But Neville survived on long shots. Until his river patrols reported back to him, in a day or two, he decided he wouldn't start house-to-house – for fear of warning the perpetrator before he had enough evidence.

At 10.15am the following morning, on the twenty-eighth of September, 1894, Constable Basil Bennett left the Savoy kitchens where he had dropped in for his usual cup of char and hot garibaldi biscuits straight from the oven, compliments of the head chef, strolled up Savoy Street and turned into the Strand. A small group of people blocked the pavement outside an art gallery, voicing their disgust at some of the art on show in the window. One woman turned and vomited into the gutter, apologising to the officer and demanding he arrest the gallery owner instantly for indecency and disturbing the peace.

'The gels with the masks,' Constable Bennett asked Jean-Louis inside the gallery.

'Masquerade, Leticia and Isadora, constable. They appeal?' Jean-Louis asked.

Bennett laughed. 'Take somethink like that home and my misus'd thrash me with the yard broom, that's for certain. No thanks. It's the freckled gel, caught my attention. What's the gel's name, d'you know?'

'Isadora. Why d'you ask? Know the girl perhaps?'

'Who is she, where's she from?'

'You'd have to ask the artist that, my friend. Here, I'll give you his card,' Jean-Louis said, taking a business card from inside a folder.

'Jacob Silver,' the constable read out loud. 'Victoria Embankment, Blackfriars? That where I'll find him?'

'Yes, he has a studio there, above the apothecary's.'

'And the other gel, she 'ave a name?'

'Leticia. Beautiful isn't she? How much would you pay to wake up against that body every morning, constable?'

'I'd pay a bit more if they had their 'eads,' Bennett said, but he wasn't laughing.

'Fashionable horror, constable. It's the *in thing*. Tell all your friends, won't you? These won't hang around for long. They'll have to be quick about it. Tell them that, will you?'

'Rest assured, I shall, Mr St Clair. Be very sure of that. I've a feeling they'll be finding these gels quite an attraction, right away.'

'One has freckles and the other's name is Leticia. A third one's named Penelope but I didn't see her picture, he's sold it. Bet your life that's them, guv,' Constable Bennett said to Detective Inspector Neville, pointing at the three missing girls' pictures cut from the daily papers.

'Jacob Silver, Portrait Artist, 72 Victoria Embankment,' Inspector Neville read off the business card. 'Well done Bennett. I'll see you get a mention.' He patted Bennett on the back, 'Good work. Who's the duty sergeant?'

'That'll be Sergeant Beck, sir. Frank Beck.'

'Ask him to join us would you?'

Uniformed Sergeant Beck was as excited as Constable Bennett when he joined Scotland Yard's finest detectives in the parade room at Charing Cross police station in Agar Street, less than a half mile from the Savoy. Within minutes of Constable Bennett's report from the gallery, Inspector Neville had ordered his strongest team to Charing Cross. They would set up shop and run the murder enquiry from there – away from his nagging superintendent. Seldom excited, Neville found the blood rising in his veins at the thought of closing in on this one – an early arrest was imminent, he was sure.

'Message from the River Police, sir, Inspector Morgan.' Sergeant Beck said after entering and saluting his senior officer, passing Inspector Neville a folded note.

'Thank you, sergeant,' Neville said reading the note and putting it in his pocket. 'Got him!' Curiosity covered the faces looking at him. 'Number 72 Victoria Embankment has access to the water,' Neville called out. He signalled his officers to sit while he sat on the edge of the table to address them. 'With any luck he'll not be on City's patch. If he is just over the line, we'll go in anyway and serve him up on a plate to those taller chaps in their big hats – after I get a confession.'

Everybody laughed.

'If it's the house I think it is, inspector, I've been there before,' Sergeant Beck said. 'An apothecary named Silver was preserved in a bathtub after he kicked the bucket. His old woman got life for carrying on the business. Killed a few patients, she did. Place lies about twenty yards on our side of the boundary.'

'Great news, Frank. Thank you. The more I hear of our painter friend, the more I fancy him for the rope.'

Frank Beck thrust out his chest, proud to be of assistance in the case and on first name terms with the notorious inspector.

And in case Inspector Neville was in any doubt, Constable Owen Williams, of *What's your game, mister?* fame, called in to describe what he had seen above the apothecary's shop: the actress and the painter.

'I've just come back off leave,' PC Williams said, 'saw all the commotion. But they said they was playing, when I caught them at it.'

Now fully aware the prime suspect was based on their patch, Neville turned to address his team.

'This is how we'll handle it, gentlemen.'

The Trial: Day 5

'...And nothing but the truth. Detective Inspector George Neville, Metropolitan Police, Scotland Yard, sir.'

'Inspector Neville, please would you describe to the court the events leading to Jacob Silver being detained,' Mr Ponsonby began.

Inspector Neville was extremely handsome and dressed as a true gentleman, not at all as I would have expected. His high starched collar and silk tie tucked into a waistcoat in his pinstriped suit – he might have been a model for Saville Row or *Harpers and Queen*. Clean shaven, his hair oiled and flat, I noticed more than one fan flutter at nineteen to the dozen amongst the women in the gallery, along with my own. He pulled a notebook from his inside pocket – but *his* appeared bound in red leather as against the poorer sergeant's in grey cardboard.

'Acting on information received,' he began.

'My lord, I must object!' Mr Ecclestone shouted, jumping to his feet.

'Now what?' said Mr Ponsonby, sitting.

'Yes, now what, Mr Ecclestone? The witness hasn't got to any point yet, has he?' his lordship enquired. 'Or did I miss something?'

Mr Ponsonby smirked, I noticed.

After requesting the court be cleared and both the jury and accused were removed, Mr Ecclestone proceeded. 'My lord, *acting on information received*. He implies someone called and said: There's a murderer at number 72, go and get him. Had he had such information? No. Does the jury think he had such information? Maybe. I therefore ask that the officer rephrase his opening remarks and choose something less inflammatory.' Having said his bit, Mr Ecclestone stood waiting for a response, but the judge had another approach and began questioning the inspector himself.

'Inspector... Neville,' the judge said, referring to his notes. 'You acted on information and went to visit the accused, is that correct?'

'Yes, my lord,' answered Inspector Neville.

'The information didn't say *go there*, did it?' The inspector agreed, it did not. 'What was the nature of that information?' the judge continued.

Messrs Ecclestone and Ponsonby raised eyebrows to each other, appearing to presume neither counsel was required in the case any longer. To the amusement of their junior counsel, they both sat with their backs to the judge and let him get on with it.

'Investigations revealed that the accused had painted three headless women – and two of those women were found headless in the river, my lord.' Succinct. To the point. Damning enough for Jacob, I was sure.

'Mr Ecclestone, do you have any questions before I declare my findings and call back the jury?' the judge asked the defender.

'M'lud, I submit that the inspector's opening remarks are inflammatory and mislead the jury. It rings of tip-off. The jury will assume the police knew he did it, never mind what he says etcetera, etcetera. I would prefer he simply said he called on the accused during the course of his investigation. That is all I ask, m'lud.'

'Not too much to ask, Mr Ponsonby?' the judge said, raising his spectacles and addressing the still-seated prosecutor.

Mr Ponsonby rose only halfway to his feet. 'Anything for a quiet life, m'lud' he said, sarcastically, flopping back down again.

'Now, now, Mr Ponsonby. Anything for a fair trial, I think you mean?'

'As it pleases, m'lud.' Mr Ponsonby was obviously finding the whole thing tedious.

'It pleases, indeed, gentlemen,' the judge remarked before leaning over to the clerk and ordering the jury return and the accused be brought up. A full half hour wasted, the inspector began again.

'As a result of enquiries I called at the accused's home and place of business, Number 72, Victoria Embankment, in Blackfriars on Friday, the twenty-eighth of September, this year, 1894. Outside I met a Miss Rebecca Muxlow trying to obtain entry to those premises. She was carrying a portrait. I asked to see the portrait and now produce it to the court,' the inspector said, looking up at Mr Ponsonby for direction.

Mr Ponsonby leaned back to junior counsel and a portrait was produced. An usher placed it on an easel at an angle so that the jury and most of us in the gallery could see it. Next to it were two other vacant easels. 'Exhibit 14, my lord,' Mr Ponsonby announced and continued directing the inspector. 'Did you recognise the lady in the portrait, inspector?'

'The pink polka dot dress on her lap appeared familiar, and after careful consideration, although her face is depicted in an horrific manner, I thought the girl closely resembled a Miss Polly Daniels, a missing girl who had such a dress. On the back of the painting,' Mr Ponsonby obliged, turning the portrait around for all to see, 'I noticed the title of the work: *Masquerade ~ Penelope*, sir.'

'Was the painting signed by the artist?'

'Yes. *Jacob Silver*, sir.'

'And why did this painting interest you, inspector?'

'The painting was one of a set of three, I learned, taken into The Strand Gallery by Jacob Silver, featuring headless women. And headless women were being found floating in the River Thames. I produce the other two paintings: *Masquerade Leticia* and *Isadora*, sir.'

Mr Ponsonby guided two ushers to raise the two paintings onto the vacant easels alongside *Penelope*, in full view of the jury, and entered them into evidence. 'Exhibits 15 and 16, m'lud.' Turning to the inspector again, Mr Ponsonby said, 'Penelope, Leticia and Isadora. All of interest, inspector?'

'The three missing girls, Polly, Letty and Nora, were all known to one another and all had posed for a *city gent*, sir. Two of the girls' bodies, Polly's and Letty's, turned up headless in the River Thames, like their portraits. Both had been identified.'

'And the third body, inspector?'

'Whilst outside the closed apothecaries shop on Victoria Embankment, shortly after Miss Muxlow gave us her painting to help with investigations, a constable arrived from the River Police and I learned a third woman's body had been found in the river – without a head. It was later identified as the third missing girl, Nora.

'The accused arrived at the apothecary's in a carriage, a few moments later. Myself and five other officers were present. He was in a frantic condition, demanding to speak to Miss Muxlow. I heard him say to her: "Thank God you are safe." '

'Safe from what, inspector? Did you hear?' Mr Ponsonby asked.

'No, not then, but the accused would soon explain. But before he could, there were further developments outside his house. A group of women came seeking vengeance and the accused asked to be taken into protective custody without further ado.'

Chapter 18

I returned home in high spirits after leaving Rebecca at the gallery.

'One hundred guineas,' I announced to the professor and Betsy at the dinner table. 'For the last three *Emily's.*'

'One hundred guineas for *three*, master?' Betsy said, aghast. 'They giving them away now?' she asked as she served a mutton stew.

'And you'll never guess who from,' I said.

'Someone who recognised your talent, Master Jacob?' the professor asked, slurping the broth noisily.

'Three guesses,' I joked.

'The Queen?' the professor offered, with a mouthful of food.

'No. But it might have been,' I teased.

'Not the Prince of Wales, master? Surely not?' Betsy said.

I laughed. 'Give in?' I said to their questioning faces. They nodded.

'Rebecca Muxlow!' I blurted out and the professor nearly choked to death.

'Emily's sister?' Betsy asked, patting the professor hard on his back.

'Emily's dear sister!' I rejoiced. 'Can you believe how happy I was to see her?'

Betsy and the professor stared at one another dumbfounded.

'What does that bit–' the professor began, heatedly.

'Come to see how her old love is getting along, I spect,' Betsy interrupted, restraining the professor by gripping his arm.

'She wants me to paint her. And nothing will give me more pleasure.'

'You…' the professor hesitated, 'You spoke of Emily?'

'Indeed we did. A very sad moment, I assure you.' I took a few moments to console myself, deciding I should not mention the assisted suicide. 'But, sadness aside, I was relieved to learn that Rebecca knew I'd lost Emily. Knew already. Can you believe that?'

They could not.

'But how, master?' Betsy asked.

'Because Emily told her. Told of being in such dreadful pain from her illness. My poor angel kept it from me, to spare me the agony.' I could see that the professor and Betsy found the whole thing as incredulous as I did. 'Don't you see?' I continued, 'Emily and Rebecca had been in touch with one another the whole time. Emily didn't depart this world because of my neglect. She succumbed to the pain. Something I was completely unaware of.'

'It *wasn't* the poison she gulped down?' the professor said, incredulously.

'My brave angel took it to spare me from watching her die.'

'The poor darling,' Betsy murmured, catching a tear with a corner of her pinafore.

I almost broke into tears. Betsy consoled me. 'Having been diagnosed incurable the poor darling didn't dare ask me to search for a cure for fear of causing me discomfort. She couldn't bear me discovering that I, too, was unable to help her.'

'Thoughtful to the very end,' Betsy said, tears rolling down her cheeks.

The professor's choking spate had made him morose. We three sat for a good while in silence before I announced, 'After dinner, Professor, we'll go to the laboratory and you can show me what you've been up to. We'll calculate what is needed to complete your experiments; get them all out of the way before Rebecca arrives at the end of the month.'

'She's coming *here?*' the professor said, startled.

'For me to do her portrait. Won't that be grand? Of course, we must ensure Emily is well out of the way. Rebecca wouldn't understand.'

'No, that she wouldn't, master,' Betsy said, catching the professor with the corner of her eye.

'End of the month, you say? You have a day?' the professor asked.

'The twenty-eighth, Professor. The day before Michaelmas Day.'

'If you can now afford the final batch of chemicals, Master Jacob, I'll have all I need,' the professor said, suddenly far more enthusiastic. 'The final result should be accomplished in good time to coincide with your dear guest's arrival.'

'It'll be a special day, Betsy, let's make it a big surprise for Rebecca,' I said.

'Oh, we'll see she gets her surprise, Master Jacob,' the professor said, chinking glasses with Betsy. 'We surely will.'

The days flew by. Early on the twenty-eighth of September I went to make a final inspection of the professor's experiments in the laboratory. It had been quite some time since I had spent any real time with him. I was confronted by a pungent and musty smell on the way into the laboratory. The benches, walls and wooden floors had obviously just been scrubbed – but that hadn't removed the objectionable smell.

'What is that dreadful smell, Professor?'

'All in good time, Master Jacob. All in good time,' he repeated as he pulled down on the lever to open up the wall to the anteroom.

As it slid back, the smell became overpowering and I noticed Emily's glass urn on the bench, facing the wall. But there was a marked difference – her urn was full again, the vivid luminescent essence topped right up to the lid. And it was bubbling.

I approached it.

'Not yet, master. Let me explain the process,' the professor insisted, pointing to the porthole in the top of our recently acquired copper distiller. 'Pray, see for yourself.'

Down inside the cauldron the bubbling golden fluid gave off vapours, condensing on the glass porthole.

A screeching, black, knotted, thread-like object crashed against the glass, startling me.

'Gracious!' I yelled, staggering backwards.

The professor laughed in my face. 'Spirits, Master Jacob. Spirits of the dead.' He bade I looked again as he pointed to three such *creatures*, angrily darting about in the mixture.

'Spirits? You mean...' I looked at the reflection dancing on his face. He looked quite mad.

'Souls, master. Beautiful, living, thriving captured souls.' His eyes were frenzied yet joyful as he admired those horrible *things* screeching and flitting through the slime like agitated pond life.

Bending down over a canvas-covered tin bath, he yanked off the blood-stained cover. I dreaded what was in there – dreaded what explanation I was going to hear next. Over-powering vapours floated up from the steaming tin bath. That pungent smell again, took my breath away. I held my nose.

'Closer,' he demanded, 'look through the steam.'

The professor pulled up his sleeve and delved into the steaming, bloodied mess. And there it was, in front of my face. As the stinking and bloodied water ran off it, I soon recognised her. Her jet-black hair knotted in his fingers as he shook her severed head in front of me.

Polly.

I turned, staggered backwards and retched. My mouth opened wide but whether any noise came out or not, I cannot recall. The whole thing played like the most horrible nightmare.

With Polly's head dangling from one hand, the professor scrabbled around and produced another handful of hair and then another – hoisting out two more heads. Nora and Letty. He was drooling, wallowing in the filth.

My lovely, lovely girls. He had murdered them all. I was close to collapsing.

'You found it, Master Jacob. The apprentice has turned master.' He dropped the heads back into the mire and went back over to the tall copper kettle. Vapour condensing off its Turk's head dome drizzled down a long glass tube to the bench and dripped through a hole in the top of Emily's glass urn. 'The souls of your wench, widow and witch. So powerful,' he turned Emily around, 'they resurrected the dead.'

He turned the urn. Emily's head faced me.

Her maggot-ridden eyes opened.

Bubbles rose from her mouth as she smiled.

'So now we have the wife,' the professor announced, pointing at Emily. 'Only one more ingredient is required, and the bitch Rebecca's coming today, you say?'

That was when my legs gave way and I passed out. I awoke sometime later, stretched out on the couch upstairs. I panicked, becoming more and more distressed as what I had seen turned out *not* to have been a nightmare. If only I could turn back the clock, make it go away. I grabbed a cloak and rushed out into the street, immediately taking a carriage to the gallery. I needed Rebecca's address. I had to find her; warn her. Her life was in danger.

This monster was killing everybody I loved.

I burst into the gallery. Jean-Louis said Rebecca had just left there, she was on her way to my house, to return the *Masquerade* painting.

I raced home again only to find police officers everywhere, surrounding Rebecca. At least she was safe.

No sooner had an inspector introduced himself, an angry mob of women carrying knives and mallets descended upon us. They claimed I'd had their girls. Hissing and spitting as they called me horrid names, one lunged at me with a bloodied spike. I feared for my life.

Inspector Neville's men fended them off. I was forced to ask him to take me into protective custody.

The Trial: Day 5

Mr Ponsonby continued questioning Detective Inspector Neville.

'So, in the police station the accused admitted that, in his house, from whence you came, were no less than four heads – severed from their bodies – together with the paraphernalia to raise the dead. Is that correct?'

'That is correct, sir, yes. He said this professor had just shown them to him that morning,' said the inspector, 'and that they had been alive.'

'At the police station, did you believe him, that severing these heads was the professor's work?'

'Everything was explained in the greatest detail, sir. Yes. Yes I did believe that something awful had been going on there – and we did have the headless bodies from the river. But, unfortunately, when we went back to search the house, on that first visit I found nothing suspicious.'

'Describe what you did find, inspector.'

'Six hours after taking him into protective custody, together with Sergeant Beck and a team of detectives, I returned to Number 72, Victoria Embankment, and went inside, using the accused's key. We made a thorough search of the premises but found nothing directly incriminating.'

'You found none of these heads the accused had described as being there?'

'No, sir. And no sign of any mischief, I might add.'

'But you found portraits of three of the missing girls?' Mr Ponsonby said, indicating to ushers to bring in the three more attractive portraits of the dead girls, that we had seen during the commencement of the trial.

'Yes, sir. That proved to us those women had been there.'

'And you did bring away some... shall we say... noxious substances?'

'Yes, sir, which I passed to Dr Pincher for analysis.'

'You found nothing directly incriminating, you say?'

'No, sir. No heads in jars. No bodies. No blood. No professor and no laboratory journals of any kind. The laboratory was neat and tidy, freshly scrubbed I might add. There was a strong smell of some medical concoction or another. I don't know what. We went on to search the whole house and were satisfied only one person lived there – the accused. There was one toothbrush, four bedrooms with four beds but only one with a mattress and any clothes in the wardrobe. Every other bedroom wardrobe was empty. And there was just one plate, and one knife and fork in the kitchen sink.'

'No sign of another living soul?'

'None whatsoever, sir.'

'You questioned the accused for a further five hours, I understand?'

'That is correct, sir.'

'And he stuck to his story?'

'He did, sir.'

'So, without evidence…?'

'Frankly, after we didn't find a thing that he had described, I thought he was either spinning a yarn, sir, trying to get some attention, or, he knew where the women's heads were, and wasn't telling us. And, of course, I considered he could have been hallucinating; dreamt the whole lot up. Lacking any evidence to charge him, the accused was allowed home whilst we made further enquiries. We put a guard outside his home – Constable Albert Everett.

'Miss Muxlow, Rebecca Muxlow that is, said she was certain of Silver's innocence and went to meet him the next day. A friend of Silver's, a psychologist, persuaded me of his innocence, as he, too, knew the accused well. He said he would assist us and go to Greenwold College and investigate the professor there – to prove Silver's innocence.'

Chapter 19

Although it was a strange request, Sir Robert Weston did not hesitate to go to Charing Cross police station where his artist friend, Jacob Silver, had asked for his urgent assistance.

Jacob explained everything to Sir Robert and that he was suspected of murder. After speaking with Inspector Neville, Sir Robert returned to Jacob in an interview room.

'I'm concerned for you, Jacob,' Sir Robert said, passing him a handkerchief to wipe the blood from his nose. He had been beaten; the whole of his face was bruised. 'Three women fished out of the river. Their mothers said they sat for you and didn't come home. And you've made portraits of all three without their heads.'

'Don't you see what he's done? He's made it look like I did it. I only painted them.' Jacob became distraught.

'This professor? When did you first see him?' After Jacob didn't answer, 'Soon after your father died?' Jacob nodded. 'Kind, was he? Took you under his wing, did he? Look like dad, did he? Helping you find immortality, was that it? Like dad said?'

Jacob blubbered through tears. 'He brought me books with potions. We captured moods. It worked. Then we worked on immortality.' He banged on the table. 'They were my friends. He killed them. He showed me their heads – still alive.'

'You live alone, don't you?'

'No, of course not. Four of us lived together. The professor and my housekeeper, Betsy, Emily and I. They were both there when the professor came to join us. But Emily– She–'

'She another body they're going to find?'

'She… She died. She committed suicide. Her sister, Rebecca, will tell you. She knows all about it. Ask her. Can't you see what he's done? He's made it look like I killed them. Can't they see that?'

'Immortality? Capturing souls? Come on, man! It's all in your head. Jacob, this professor doesn't exist.'

Jacob clawed at his head. 'Of course he bloody exists! I've

known him since I was fifteen! We wanted... I needed to bring Emily back, raise her from the dead. Don't you see?' Grabbing Sir Robert's lapels, Jacob screamed into his face. 'You said you'd help me! I could swing for this! I did not kill my girls! I loved them; loved them all. Find this bloody madman!'

The door barged open to Detective Inspector Neville's office and Sir Robert strode in. Neville and Sergeant Beck looked up in surprise.

'You knocked the shit out of him!' Sir Robert shouted, 'Would've admitted anything. I know the boy. He's telling the truth. He painted them. He admits that. They're missing. It's this professor doing the killing. You have to find *him*! There's no way this lad's your killer. No bodies, no blood, nothing at all at the house. You've nothing on him. Find the professor; he's your man. Silver's terrified of him.'

Sir Robert produced a caricature of the professor. That got their attention. 'He drew this. Tutor at his old college. We must find him. There's another possible witness. Jacob Silver and your chief suspect were thrown out after insulting Lady Jane of Sherston at the Savoy. Someone would've seen them together. And this housekeeper. She worked in the shop. Customers must have seen her. Get onto it. You'll need to build a case against them. I'm sure the housekeeper was in on it. Not much could have gone on there without her knowing about it.'

'Send someone to the Savoy, quickly,' Neville instructed Sergeant Beck.

'And Sergeant,' Sir Robert said to Beck as he was leaving, 'speak to this art gallery owner, a Monsieur St Clair. Someone went with Silver to the gallery. What can he tell us? And these Ripper paintings, ask him how he got those, will you?'

'You think there's a connection?' Neville asked.

'Something pretty evil changed the gentle artist I knew from painting beauty to... Doesn't bear thinking about.' Sir Robert then referred to the glass vials on Neville's desk. 'These vials you brought back? Silver rattled off the recipes like he was baking a cake. Deadly plants and fungi. He was addicted to them. Helped him get over losing his mistress, I suspect. He was manipulated like a puppet to acquire women for this monster. This stuff about immortality is all balderdash! Who ever heard of such a thing. And yet my friend in there was hoodwinked into thinking he was raising his mistress from the dead.'

'We must track this professor down before he kills again,' Neville said.

'I suspect he'll return to the laboratory,' Sir Robert said. 'They were in the final phase of his experiments apparently. The professor needs whatever's in there and tomorrow is a special day, apparently, Michaelmas Day. Bail Silver, let him go home but keep someone posted outside – concealed. I've a feeling the professor will show up. Meanwhile, I'll go to Greenwold College. See what they have on him.'

The duty sergeant put his head into the room. 'A Miss Rebecca Muxlow is asking if we need her any more, inspector.'

'I'd like a word with her, inspector,' Sir Robert said.

'Her life is in danger if this professor does exist, Sir Robert,' Neville warned him. 'This professor told Silver she had an important role to play. She's the next ingredient.'

Sir Robert sat opposite a shaken Rebecca in the police station foyer. 'He painted my daughter. She was dying. He gave her a new zest for life. She developed quite an affection for him. He's a healer, not a killer – a good man. I'd stake my reputation on it.'

'My sister loved him dearly. So gentle. He wouldn't harm a fly. He told me he was a broken man when she died,' Rebecca told him, patting her tears dry. 'How he has got involved in this–'

'Don't upset yourself, my dear. I think losing Emily resulted in his taking . . . taking things to keep his mind off her. But he did tell me he finds great comfort in you.'

This cheered Rebecca. She stood. 'I must go to him. He needs me.'

'Not here, I suggest. They're taking him home. Meet him there tomorrow, but please, do be careful. And tell me, Miss Muxlow,' Sir Robert added as he stood to leave, 'did Jacob ever give you anything to take? His potions?'

Rebecca avoided his eyes, walking with him to the front door, catching her reflection in a mirror there. 'Only for minor ailments.'

'And did they work?'

Staring into the mirror, Rebecca touched the pure porcelain skin on her face. 'Yes. Perfectly. He certainly had a flare for medicine.'

Sir Robert opened the door for her.

'Sir Robert, forgive me, but when did your daughter pass?'

'Pass? Oh, no. Miraculously, she survived, you see. She lives life to the full now. All thanks to Jacob, I'm sure.'

Chapter 20

On Michaelmas Day, Rebecca stepped from a carriage outside Jacob's business. She looked up at the accommodation above and shuddered as she approached the front door where a uniformed policeman leapt out from the bushes, surprising her.

'I didn't see you,' the startled Rebecca said.

'That's the general idea, miss,' Constable Everett replied.

'Mr Silver is expecting me,' she said, knocking on the door.

The constable saluted and apologised for scaring her.

Jacob opened the door and waved her inside. She winced at his beaten face.

In the sitting room upstairs, Rebecca hugged him and kissed his cheek. 'I was so concerned for you,' she assured him, stroking his bruised face.

'He's murdered my girls. All three! I thought they were going to charge *me*. Thank God for Sir Robert,' he said, going into the kitchen. 'I'll make us some tea.'

He poured sugar into a bowl. From a pot marked *salt* he added a large pinch to the bowl of sugar. Licking his fingers, he squeezed his eyes tight and relished the sensation, shaking his head repeatedly.

Jacob looked down into the street below at the policeman on guard, concealed in the shrubs. He smiled. He served the tea on a silver tray in the sitting room, setting it down on a low table in front of Rebecca. 'This will cheer you,' he said, sitting opposite.

As Rebecca spooned sugar into her cup, he said: 'Drink up then we can go up to the studio, if you feel up to it. Painting you will take my mind off things.'

'I so missed you all these years, Jacob,' Rebecca said, reaching out for his hand. She squeezed his fingers. 'Emily always knew that I loved you, too. You the artist. Me the art dealer. I feel we've so much in common.'

Jacob felt uncomfortable and gently pried his fingers loose. He stared into his cup at the luminous green swirling there. 'I would wait for Emily to wake. The sun that rose within her eyes would penetrate every bone in my body. I felt everything she felt. Was touched when she was touched, hurt when she hurt. I was Emily. She, me. But she's gone, that light has gone. There's still a huge lump here in my heart that is—'

'Aren't we going upstairs?' Rebecca asked, unable to conceal her annoyance. She stood up abruptly and Jacob led her upstairs towards his studio. On the landing, Rebecca turned and took Jacob's hand, pressing it to her breast. 'Jacob, there *is* life after Emily!'

Jacob looked down at what she was doing with his hand – and then pulled it away, walking into the studio. The chaise was exactly as he left it and Rebecca sat on its edge, her eyes fixed on Jacob standing at his easel. Before being asked, she slid her clothes to the floor and leaned back provocatively on the chaise, sliding her fingers between her legs to tempt him away from the canvas. Her eyelids became heavy.

Jacob picked up her dress off the floor and placed it across her lap. Then he took one hand from between her legs, kissed her finger tips tenderly and positioned it on the back of the chaise, the other to her breast. Returning to his easel, he poured a rich luminous fluid into a dish.

Rebecca's eyes were now extremely heavy; a drowsiness overcame her as she watched his brush dip into the bowl then touch his lips. The room began to distort and spin. She held onto the back of the chaise with both hands as Jacob's voice drifted over her – unable to decipher the words.

He came closer to her, put his face in front of hers. 'I want you in my horror collection. To preserve your essence into eternity.' He pulled a long butcher's knife from a closet behind her. 'I want you to act frightened. That's the whole point, you see?'

Rebecca was disturbed by his more aggressive tone. She shivered and felt like she was falling, falling off the chaise into a dark hole.

'More! Like you're really scared!' Jacob yelled, raising the knife above his head; his eyes wild; tormented.

As his face became enraged, Rebecca realised for the first time that this was not the tender Jacob she thought she knew, the cripple she had seduced so easily.

This one appeared intent on killing her.

Chapter 21

At Greenwold College, Sir Robert Weston sat listening to elderly school secretary, Miss Delores Dunne, as she recalled Jacob Silver.

'The crippled boy? Expelled after administering potions and molesting a young girl. He was lucky he wasn't arrested for murder.'

'Come, come. I know the boy. You have no reason to level such accusations,' Sir Robert said sternly, pulling at one end of his handlebar moustache.

'Thomas Muxlow died of cancer of the face not long after Silver gave him something for his freckles. Proving it was Silver was difficult. The police didn't pursue it. And in any case he had been expelled. He gave Thomas's sister, Emily, things, too – to seduce her,' Delores added with a sharp tongue as she poured tea.

'But *he* says *she* seduced him.'

'That's highly unlikely, Sir Robert. She was an angel. The sweetest thing. The last you would think of taking their own life.'

'You heard about that?'

'It was the talk of the school. Our reputation was at stake. Rat poison they said. She died instantly. But I would wager Silver had something to do with it.'

'Silver had nothing to do with it, I assure you. He loved her dearly. She took her own life and her loss broke his heart. How on earth could her death, years after he left, affect your reputation?'

After Miss Dunne explained, Sir Robert was astounded. Fumbling in his briefcase, he produced the likeness of the professor which Jacob had drawn for him. 'This professor. Taught him science. What can you tell me about him?'

Miss Dunne studied the drawing, turning it this way and that. 'I think you had better come with me,' she said, leading Sir Robert into the Corridor of Alumni and through to the catacombs.

Sir Robert rushed back from the catacombs into the office, snatching the telephone receiver off its pedestal.

'Get me Scotland Yard! Urgently, madam!'

Chapter 22

Jacob swiped the blade of the knife in front of Rebecca's face. His eyes bulging, mouth drooling, he leapt behind her and drew the knife across her throat, without touching the skin.

'More, woman! It's your . . . last . . . bloody . . . breath!' he screamed.

Rebecca, trembling, turned her head to steal a glance at his face. With terror in her eyes, she clutched her dress, pushed the blade away, gashing the palm of her left hand. She squealed and leapt off the couch.

'Jacob! Stop!' she screamed, her clenched fist spurting with blood.

Behind him, the closet door swung open revealing an open panel inside at the back.

Staring at Rebecca, her maggot-ridden head in a glass urn, a young lady she thought she recognised.

'Your sister!' Jacob yelled. 'I'm given her new life!'

Emily's one good eye flicked open and she smiled. Bubbles rose from her mouth as she yelled a muffled, piercing, *'Bitch!'*

Rebecca, naked, shaken and trembling, yelped and flew downstairs. Jacob chased after her, the knife still in his hand. Screaming and yelling, she tried the front door. It was locked. She lifted the letterbox and yelled out into the street.

Laying on the step outside, she saw a pair of black boots smothered in blood, the legs attached extending into the shrubs.

With Jacob in close pursuit, Rebecca fled down more stairs into the laboratory, slamming the door behind her. Terrified and exhausted, she wedged it with a chair and slipped back into her dress, blood still dripping from her hand. Using her drawers as a bandage, she searched the room for something with which to defend herself.

Jacob pounded on the door. 'Trust me, it's only for the portrait,' he pleaded. 'I want to capture you at your most vulnerable, that's all.'

Under the skylight windows, Rebecca pulled up a chair and climbed up onto the bench. She could just reach the window latch.

'We must finish what we started, my darling,' Jacob cried out tearfully. 'Make us both immortal.' Rebecca became more nervous than ever when he added, 'You'll join us. Emmy and me.'

A brass lever attached to the wall caught Rebecca's attention. She pulled it down to use for a step up into the street above. But it gave way under her weight. She stumbled back onto the bench as a loud whirring, hissing and clanking noise filled the laboratory.

'*No! Not in there, Emmy!*' Jacob shouted.

Behind Rebecca the dividing wall to the anteroom opened up, revealing a dark cavern inside. She could hear water lapping, and climbed down off the bench, praying for a way out.

Jacob seemed more determined than ever, thundering on the door which began to ease open. His fingers wrapped around the door's edge as Rebecca nervously stole past him into the anteroom.

Once inside, she found a similar brass lever and yanked on it. The hissing and whirring started again as the wall closed and for a few moments, provided she held the lever firmly down, she felt safe. Rippling light from the grille out onto the river filled the anteroom. On a side bench she found a chisel and, as Jacob yelled on the other side of the wall, she wedged it into the lever's mechanism. She had escaped. Relief ran through her body. Scum marks on the steps leading down to the river showed it was almost high tide. At low tide, she would simply walk out – walk away from this horrid place and the beastly Jacob Silver, she thought. And he can hang for killing those girls.

'You won't like it in there, Emily,' Jacob pleaded outside, pounding on the wall. '*Please,* come out and let's finish what we began.'

Rebecca, incensed he had mistaken her for her sister, explored her surroundings. The bench had various paraphernalia covered with a canvas sheet and in the corner, a luminous golden light shone from the porthole on top of a large copper kettle. She glanced inside.

Phantom, knotted string-like demons darted towards her face, scaring her. The longer she stared the more agitated they became.

My God! What has he been doing in here?

Rebecca then turned to the bench and the canvas sheet. She lifted a corner. Startled, her face in terror, she pulled the cover off. Three glass jars sat there – their contents staring at her.

The heads of Polly, Letty and Nora.

She felt her knees give way and as she fell backwards onto the flagstone floor the last thing she saw and heard etched deeply into her brain – the three girls laughing at her.

The Trial: Day 5

'Inspector Neville, after hours of interrogation from both you and Sergeant Beck do you regret releasing the accused to return home?' the prosecutor continued.

'Obviously. In hindsight.'

'You were *persuaded* he was innocent?'

'Against my better judgement, yes.'

From what I had heard, thus far, he *was* and *remains* innocent. They should have been searching for this mad professor.

'Tell the court what happened the day after Silver was released.'

'After receiving information from the accused's old college I returned with other officers to the apothecary's on the Victoria Embankment. We forced entry and quickly searched the premises. We found the accused upon entering the laboratory. But things were different. The whole room was different.'

'Different? In what way?' Mr Ponsonby enquired.

'A wall which had previously been there when we searched the place the day before, was no longer there. We discovered it was mechanically controlled and concealed an anteroom with access to the river. Unfortunately, we had completely missed it before.'

Murmurs circulated the court as reporters lurched forward and began scribbling rapidly on their notepads.

'And what did you find in this *anteroom*, inspector?'

'It was a chamber of horrors, sir. I'd not seen anything like it in all my years in the service,' Inspector Neville said, raising his notebook and then reading on. 'The walls and ceiling were smothered in fresh blood. The accused was covered in mud and soaking wet. He was standing over a copper distillery device, in the corner, peering down inside through an open porthole.'

'And what did you find inside this distillery, inspector?'

'It was empty, sir – drained dry by a tube at the bottom.'

'And what did the accused say?'

'He said we were too late. "He's taken them." '

'*He?*'

'He was referring to this professor.'

'The mysterious professor that he told you earlier had conducted experiments there?'

'Yes, sir.'

'Was there any trace of this professor?'

'No trace whatsoever, sir.'

'Have you or your officers *ever* found any trace of this mysterious professor?'

'None, sir.'

'And what else did you find in that anteroom, inspector?'

'In front of a bench sprawled across the stone floor was a woman's body in a pool of blood.' Neville paused, whether for effect or to gather courage, I could not say. 'Her head had been removed. The left palm had been slashed – a defensive type of wound. On a bench we found four severed heads in jars.'

My goodness! What had the mad professor done now?

The gallery broke into loud chatter and the judge hammered his gavel repeatedly until restoring order. He then nodded to the inspector to continue.

'A large butcher's knife lay beside the woman's body on the floor together with a rubber tube attached to a balloon of sorts.'

Mr Ponsonby held up a butcher's knife and other items as he asked, 'Are these the said knife and apparatus?' Inspector Neville confirmed they were. 'Exhibits 17,18,19, my lord. Were you able to deduce the purpose of these items?'

'Later, yes. A medieval Italian book, laying on the bench, described the process. The victim's throat was cut and the tube fed deep down the throat.' Folk were swooning and passing out all around me as the inspector continued. Ushers dragged numerous spectators out. 'As the body bled out, at the last breath, elixir was poured down the tube to *purge* what remained there – drive it out. The balloon was fastened to the end of the tube and captured what was emitted.'

'And precisely *what* was emitted?'

'According to the medieval manual – *the soul*.' Sharp intakes of breath rose from the gallery. 'The balloon was then emptied into the large, copper condensing boiler – the still in the corner,' the inspector continued. 'The mixture was brought to the boil and vapour driven off, condensed into containers.'

Five ushers then carried into the courtroom what looked like covered vessels, placing them on the bench in a line in front of the prosecutor.

'And did you find any of the finished product?' Mr Ponsonby asked, whipping off four of the covers to reveal four of the glass jars we had seen at the commencement of the trial – each containing a severed woman's head. A fifth jar remained covered.

'Yes, sir. Inside those four jars with the heads of the three missing models: Polly Daniels, Letty Norton and Nora Perkins. The fourth was identified by her mother as belonging to Rebecca Muxlow.'

At that, a veritable stampede of reporters headed from the court, the judge's attempts to prevent them falling on deaf ears. Perplexed ushers were barged aside as the mob burst out through the courtroom doors to spread the word. The judge, furiously pounding his gavel, had a real job on his hands before order was properly restored and Mr Ponsonby was asked to continue. The four jars were formally entered into evidence.

'Was this the same Rebecca Muxlow whom you met the day before, inspector?' Mr Ponsonby continued.

'Yes, when she returned a portrait painted by the accused.'

'What was wrong with this painting? Why was she returning it?'

'It frightened her. She claimed it screamed, sir.'

Here upstairs, the gallery was alive with gasps and whispers. Two elderly ladies must have decided it was all too much and vacated their seats. I was of a mind to leave, myself.

'Did you find anything else of significance in the house that had not been noticed during your earlier search of the premises?' asked Mr Ponsonby.

'Yes. In the back of a cupboard in the studio, inside a secret compartment we found a decayed head in a jar. The accused was asked about it and said it was all that remained of Emily Muxlow, who had died on the premises.'

'Is this the jar, inspector?' Mr Ponsonby asked, unveiling the hideous jar containing Emily's rotting head.

'Yes, sir.'

'Exhibit 24, m'lud. Did you find anything else in the studio?'

'Yes. Blood. Identified as being in the same group as Rebecca Muxlow's, it dripped from the chaise longue all the way to the basement laboratory. This probably came from Miss Muxlow's hand wound and confirms she was first attacked in the studio, then fled to the basement. It matched blood we found on the knife.'

'And the accused admitted to being alone with her in the studio, brandishing a knife?'

'Yes, sir.'

'Scaring the living daylights out of her.'

'It would seem so. Yes, sir.'

'And now can you describe what you found *outside* the house, inspector.'

'Upon our arrival, lying across the front door we found the body of Police Constable Albert Everett – his throat had been cut.' More gasps from the gallery.

'And the murder weapon?'

'The pathologist found identical blood grouping to Constable Everett's, on the blade of the knife, Exhibit 17, found next to Rebecca Muxlow's body – along with *her* blood.'

'Meaning the same knife was used to kill both, and probably by the same person?'

'Probably, sir.'

'Did the accused say anything about the policeman's body outside his front door?'

'He said he found it there when he ran from the house to go across the road to the river, where there was another entrance to the basement. He said he could see the officer was dead, and feared for Rebecca's safety.'

'You arrested Jacob Silver and took him to Charing Cross police station. Did you record the accused's version of events?'

'He had nothing to hide, he said, and gave a full account. I wrote everything down.' Inspector Neville held up his notebook.

Now at last, my darling would prove his innocence.

'Read from your notes, inspector, if you will.'

'After I asked Silver what had happened since he left the police station the day before, he said: "Rebecca came to have her portrait painted the next day. We went up to my studio but she became frightened."'

'I asked him to explain. He replied:

"I wanted to add her portrait to my horror collection. There was a knife. It was just meant to frighten her. But she ran off. She locked herself in the anteroom in the laboratory – the room where the professor worked. I feared for her safety – he had already killed my other models – but you hadn't believed me earlier. That anteroom has access to the river. After she wouldn't let me in, I made my way to the river entrance. That was when I opened the front door and found the policeman with his throat cut. There was nothing I could do for the poor chap. But I feared for Rebecca's safety. I had to wait until low tide and by the time I got to her it was too late. She was already dead – her soul taken."

'Her soul? I questioned. He replied:

"The professor only needed hers – then his work was complete.

197

Don't you see? It's Michaelmas Day and he has taken all their souls – made himself immortal!" '

'Of what significance was Michaelmas Day, inspector?' Mr Ponsonby asked.

'According to their book *Alchemy*, sir, this was the date on which their concoction for immortality should be administered.'

'Administered to whom, inspector?'

'We never found out, sir.'

'And then what happened?'

'Then he broke down. After composing himself, he said:

"He's made it look like I killed them. But he killed them all. There's a journal. It's all in there. You must find that journal. Or he'll do it again."

'He then added: "He revived Emily. Then took *her* soul." '

The gallery was in uproar and the four remaining reporters down in the courtroom made to leave. I so wanted to believe Jacob, but each witness' testimony was making it more and more difficult.

'Remain seated!' the judge ordered. 'I will not have any further interruptions, d'you understand?' They returned to their seats, shamefully. 'Continue, Mr Ponsonby.'

'Inspector, did you find this journal he spoke of?'

'No, sir, only the old book: *Alchemy*.'

'What else did the accused have to say about the dead body and these women's heads found in his home?'

'After telling me that the professor had shown him the severed heads *alive* the day before, and complaining the police did nothing about it, he ceased cooperating and asked to see his friend, a psychologist. We were then advised that nothing more would be said on the matter. But he did agree to a psychiatrist interview, to prove he was sane, he said.'

'And after the psychiatrist's meeting?'

'I then made the decision to charge the accused with murder.'

'Thank you, inspector. I have no further questions of this witness, m'lud.'

Mr Ecclestone stood to begin his cross-examination. 'Inspector, you were in charge of this investigation, yes?'

'That is correct.'

'Somewhat incompetent, not finding this room of horrors the first time, wasn't it?'

'I wouldn't say that, sir. It was well concealed.'

'What steps did you take to find this missing professor?'

'After hearing from the college and the accused becoming irrational–'

'Irrational?'

'Speaking of immortality, talking heads and the like; I was convinced this professor never existed. This was corroborated by our earlier searches of the murder scene – that Silver lived and worked alone – and from other evidence.'

'So you made no effort to find the professor – whom the accused blamed for the murders?'

'Not really, sir.'

'Not really. You mean you made no effort.' Before the inspector could answer, 'What efforts did you take to find Betsy Pollock, the housekeeper?'

'We made a thorough search but could find nothing to suggest she ever lived there.'

'And after referring to a police psychiatrist, decided she did not exist either?'

'That's about the strength of it, yes, sir.'

'And what difference would it have made to your case if either or both of these missing persons *did* exist?'

'A great deal. We would obviously have needed to interview them, rule them out.'

'Or rule them *in*, inspector?'

Neville did not answer.

'Did you find any of Constable Everett's blood on the accused?'

'No, sir.'

'Is it likely that someone slashing a man's throat would remain free of blood splatter?'

'We believe the throat was cut from behind, sir. In which case blood would not necessarily be found on the killer.'

'Surely anybody could have killed Constable Everett? Anybody passing.'

'True, sir. But would they end up with the knife next to them, when they were discovered?'

'No more questions, m'lud,' said Mr Ecclestone.

'You may step down, inspector,' said the judge.

It had been another long and horrific day and, thankfully, the judge asked that the jury be given some respite to come to terms with the evidence they had heard, adjourning proceedings until the morning.

I prayed that Mr Ecclestone would have greater success in proving the professor and Miss Pollock existed – for Jacob's sake.

The Trial: Day 6

'Mildred Agatha Muxlow, Muxlow Hall, Finchingfield,' the elderly veiled lady said, after handing the Bible back to the usher.

This poor woman had lost two daughters and her son and my heart went out to her. Dressed all in black and wearing a veil, she looked so frail, but refused to sit while giving her evidence, scowling at poor Jacob throughout the whole proceedings.

'You are the mother of Thomas, Emily and Rebecca Muxlow, now deceased?' Mr Ponsonby began, solemnly.

'Murdered by *him!* Yes,' the old lady replied, pointing directly at Jacob.

'Mrs Muxlow,' the judge interrupted, 'you have our deepest condolences for your loss but I must instruct you to keep your opinions as to the guilt or otherwise of the accused, to yourself, madam.' The old lady remained silent. 'Is that understood?' the judge pressed. Mrs Muxlow begrudgingly acknowledged that it was.

'Can you confirm, Mrs Muxlow, that Thomas, Rebecca and Emily, spent their holidays between 1886 and 1888 at Lord and Lady Bedford's estate near Greenwold College?'

'Yes. 1888 was their last spring together.'

'Our deepest sympathies, madam, but can you explain to the court how Thomas Muxlow died?'

Mrs Muxlow dabbed back a tear under her veil before answering. 'He died of cancer. Of the face. After being treated by *him*,' she pointed again at Jacob in the dock, 'for removing freckles.'

'You were directly aware he was being treated by Jacob Silver?'

'He wrote and told me so – in agony, I might add.'

'Do you still have that letter?'

'No, the police took it. And now they've lost it.'

'What was Emily's condition, during early 1888?'

'She was fragile, often breathless. She had consumption.'

'For which she took medication?'

'The best we could find. But my sister, Lady Bedford,

discovered she had been administered other concoctions. *His* potions. Before he seduced her.'

That set tongues wagging around me. I wondered if Jacob had been *a naughty boy*, or whether the old lady was just bitter after *he* had cured her daughter and not the doctors she had employed.

'You know this for a fact?'

'The gel admitted it, before… before…' She did not need to finish.

'Forgive me, madam, but I must ask you to confirm; eventually, Emily took her own life?'

'Yes.'

'Do you know how she–'

'Rat poison. She was still holding the glass.'

In the dock, I noticed Jacob sobbing into his sleeve. He must have loved her so.

Mr Ponsonby gave Mrs Muxlow a moment to compose herself before asking, 'Was anyone else in the household aware she took her own life?'

'She told her sister she would,' and after blotting another tear, 'The pain, you see? She couldn't bear it any longer.'

'And precisely *when* did Emily die?'

'A month after Thomas. June the third, 1888.'

I caught my breath.

'1888?' a gentleman to my right quietly asked me.

That couldn't be right. I was as puzzled as he was, but nevertheless put a finger to my lips, suggesting he listen intently – expecting a correction. From the groaning around us, I guessed we were not the only people confused. If Emily died in 1888 who on earth had lived with Jacob till 1894? To whom had he proposed marriage?

'I want to confirm that we heard you correctly, Mrs Muxlow. Emily died in June, 1888? Over six years ago?'

'Yes, a month after her brother. They rest side by side in the family tomb.'

'So she could not possibly have run off to London to live with the accused?'

'Of course not. And I would never have allowed that, not for an instant.'

'If anyone said they had lived with your daughter, Emily, between April, 1892 and earlier this year, a period of over two years, what would you say to that?'

'They are lying. Or insane. She died and was placed in the family crypt, in 1888.' She produced three sheets of paper. 'Here are all my children's death certificates.'

Whispering circulated the gallery as puzzled looks on faces appeared everywhere.

'I believe there is something else you wish to tell the court?' Mr Ponsonby said.

Mrs Muxlow stared straight at Jacob and appeared quite overcome. She struggled to speak before finally announcing: 'Her tomb was desecrated a month after she was interred. Her head was removed.'

What?

I was startled. Everyone about me was as confused as I was. Had Jacob taken his lover's head? How awful! But that could only mean… Had he been living with just Emily's head?

God! Jacob, how could you?

Horrified, and unable to stomach any more such evidence, I stood and pushed my way towards the stairs and the street. But sitting at the end of the bench, next to the doors, was someone I least expected to see – Papa – and there was no mistaking the look of surprise on his face when he caught sight of me, snivelling into my handkerchief.

Papa stood, abruptly, and took me on his arm away from that place, the public gallery now in uproar. The judge was still pounding his gavel as we left, attempting to regain control.

In a street café, just around the corner from the court, my father quietly chastised me for disobeying his strict instructions: *not* to attend this trial.

'I know the outcome,' he assured me. 'He is mad, do you hear me? Completely mad!'

I sat and continued crying as people I recognised from the public gallery came into the café. The judge must have allowed a recess.

'I knew you had feelings for the boy – which is why I specifically informed you *not* to attend his trial,' Papa said sternly, stirring his tea. 'He cannot win, Lizzie. He will hang. And you will have to get used to that idea. I'm sorry. But that is how it is. Forget him. Forget everything. The boy is due for a very sad end. You will only upset yourself.'

'But if he *is* mad, then surely he should plead so. They don't hang the insane. He would be saved,' I tried.

'Guilty by reason of insanity? That was already thrown out – on day one. There is a rule, the M'Naughten Rule, which decides these things.'

'But why was it thrown out? They surely cannot doubt he is

completely mad? Taking her *head*, for goodness sake!'

'It's… It's complicated. You see, whilst he might have been stark raving mad when he lived with the poor girl's head, he later claims he went to *save* Rebecca – save her from certain death. *That* proved that he knew it was wrong; knew what he was doing was wrong. That is the basis upon which a man is considered fit or unfit to plead – whether he knew the difference between right and wrong. And Jacob knew.'

'Jacob knew it was wrong for *the professor* to kill Rebecca, not *him!*' I remonstrated.

'Well, you'll find that isn't so. They'll prove it was Jacob doing the killing.'

'So, these… these lawyers, have decided between them he is fit to stand trial? To hang, is that it?' I pressed.

'Acting on the advice of psychiatrists from both sides – yes, that is what they decided. It is the law of the land, Lizzie. As long as he gets a fair trial–'

'Fair trial? I haven't seen a shred of evidence that he killed those four girls. What makes you so sure he will be found guilty? They have nothing. Nothing at all.' Papa looked at me in silence – was that because he, too, had not seen any evidence? I continued to rant. 'Granted, living with just a woman's head… But I can't talk about that. It disgusts me. There were others in that house. Miss Pollock delivered the girl to him. What has *she* got to say about her part in all this?' Papa stood and took my arm. But I had not finished. 'How could she stand idly by while Jacob was proposing to a dead girl? And this professor. Where is he? He's the murderer. Isn't it obvious?'

'My dear, I see no other solution,' Papa insisted, looping his arm through mine and leading me out into the street. 'I think you had best hear the evidence for yourself.'

After offering a small bribe, Papa was able to take a place by my side at the front of the public gallery, when the court reconvened. The judge took his place on the bench and after everybody was seated he looked up to the gallery with a solemn look on his face.

'Another outburst like that and I will have the gallery cleared for the duration of this trial. D'you hear me up there?' He then turned to Mrs Muxlow who had resumed her place in the witness box, sobbing quietly to herself. 'Mrs Muxlow, are you well enough to continue?' She nodded that she was and the judge nodded to the prosecutor to carry on.

Mr Ponsonby soon got back into his flow. 'Mrs Muxlow, I understand you collected art?'

'Only as an amateur. My daughter Rebecca would recommend works.'

'And did your daughter, Rebecca, *recommend* you acquire a particularly good painting of your other daughter, Emily?'

'Well, yes. But I needed no persuading. We saw it hanging in the gallery in the Strand. It was such a good likeness that I felt I must have it.'

Mr Ponsonby ushered in two attendants, one carrying a framed portrait, the other an easel. The glorious painting was set up to face the jury and gallery. 'And is *this* the first painting you so acquired?'

The old lady acknowledged that it was and Mr Ponsonby entered it into evidence. 'Exhibit 1, m'lud.' It was the wonderful portrait of Emily we had seen at the opening of the trial.

'May I ask the price of this masterpiece, Mrs Muxlow?'

'What's the price got to do with it?' Mrs Muxlow said angrily. She couldn't look Mr Ponsonby in the eye and turned to the judge for support. The judge held up his palms and shrugged, suggesting she answer.

'I am simply trying to draw comparisons – between this and other *Emily's* you later acquired, madam,' Mr Ponsonby added.

'The price ticket said twenty thousand pounds. Or guineas. I can't remember.'

'Twenty thousand pounds then, or thereabouts. I see. Did you continue to acquire other portraits of Emily?'

'I acquired eleven in all, from a series of twelve, the gallery advised.'

Ever the showman, Mr Ponsonby begged his lordship's permission and an entourage of attendants brought in the remaining ten paintings, standing them on easels alongside the first.

I gasped. The whole public gallery was buzzing with gossip.

Turning to Mrs Muxlow again, Mr Ponsonby asked: 'And are these those ten other paintings?' Mrs Muxlow agreed they were. 'Exhibits 25 to 34, m'lud,' Mr Ponsonby announced.

I was shocked and looked at Papa in dismay. The line of paintings was nothing like what I expected, or what anybody else expected in that courtroom, for that matter, judging by the sharp intakes of breath.

'And the twelfth portrait, Mrs Muxlow? To complete the set?' Mr Ponsonby asked.

'I sent Rebecca to acquire it but it had apparently been sold.'

'And what price, madam,' Mr Ponsonby asked as he walked to

the portrait furthest from us, 'did you pay for *this* portrait?'

'The last one? They couldn't give it away. It was fifteen pounds,' Mrs Muxlow answered.

'I suspect that was to cover the cost of the frame,' Mr Ponsonby said, running his hand round the gilt frame. 'So, just to clarify, Mrs Muxlow: you paid twenty thousand pounds or thereabouts for the first one, and only fifteen pounds for the last. Both portraits by the same artist, Jacob Silver?'

'That's right.'

'Why were you so intent on buying the whole series when you clearly had such negative feelings over these later versions.'

' 'Cause I couldn't bear anyone else seeing my dear daughter like that. And I knew he murdered my son and daughter, that's why.'

Mr Ecclestone bolted to his feet – but the judge waved him to sit back down.

'The jury will ignore that remark,' the judge said, looking directly at the jury. He then turned to Mrs Muxlow. 'I am sure, being an intelligent woman, you were aware that kind of remark is not allowed here. This is the second time I have had to address this issue, Mrs Muxlow. If it happens again, I will hold you in contempt of court.' She stared at the floor. 'Is that clear, madam?' he said in a raised voice.

'Yes, my lord,' the old lady muttered humbly, still staring down at her feet.

'Do you have any idea, Mrs Muxlow, what happened to the last in the series, the twelfth Emily?' Mr Ponsonby continued.

'My daughter was informed by the gallery that it had been sold.'

'And did you learn how much it was sold for?'

'Twenty thousand pounds. Or guineas. Daylight robbery, you ask me.'

'And had you ever *seen* that twelfth portrait, the last of the series?'

'Yes. It was not too dissimilar to the one I bought, number eleven.' She pointed: 'That last one, there.'

'Not too dissimilar and yet you only paid fifteen pounds for yours. And do you know to whom it was sold?'

'To a Spanish nobleman, apparently.'

Chapter 23

Although Rebecca returned to the art gallery with the *Masquerade –
Penelope* horror portrait, on the twenty-eighth of September, intent
on telling the gallery owner what he could do with it, Jean-Louis put
a proposal to her.

'I was under the impression, madame,' he began, 'you were
hoping this might frighten some old letch to death?'

'And your point is, Monsieur St Clair?'

'Well, if the gent was taken by *Penelope*, I wouldn't be opposed to
a little incentive, if you get my drift, for you to flog him the full set.'
He pointed at the matching portraits of *Leticia* and *Isadora* hanging in
the window, a ticket for three hundred guineas swinging from each.
'Shall we say fifteen per cent?'

'Twenty,' Rebecca said, thrusting out her hand. 'I'll bring the
gentleman next week,' she told Jean-Louis as he shook her hand to
seal the deal. She then headed towards Jacob's home, with the
Penelope portrait.

It was to become a very prosperous day for Jean-Louis St Clair
and Jacob Silver. Their pockets would soon be lined with gold as an
unexpected course of events unfolded at the gallery. Unfortunately,
Jacob would never have the opportunity to enjoy his fortune.

Adjacent to Jacob's *Masquerades* of Letty and Nora, a *lesser Emily*
remained on the easel in the window, exactly where the Count of
Catalonia's agent had left it, albeit pushed to the side to give way for
more fashionable blood and lust. The price tag of twenty thousand
guineas from the *prized Emily*, remained attached to it. Jean-Louis
had yet to *catch* any unsuspecting buyer calling in from the Savoy, or
passing blind man.

Dusting a *Monet* hanging on the back wall, Jean-Louis was not
pleasantly surprised when an entourage of six scarlet-and-yellow-
uniformed guardsmen in big feathered hats entered his emporium,
clearing the way for their leader, the most colourful of all.

'Juan-Carlos Fernando Frederik Geraldo Francisco Laurencio

heir to Juan-Carlos Fernando Frederik Geraldo Francisco Laurencio the Fifth, esteemed and noble Count of Catalonia,' an equerry announced as the similarly-clad heir breezed in through their midst.

Trembling, Jean-Louis bowed low, staring at the floor, hoping the gentleman's Toledo-steel sword hanging from his belt might await his execution until he summoned an excuse to explain the missing *prized Emily*. But the god's, from Spain and elsewhere, appeared to align in his favour, as he kissed the nobleman's hand.

'In your window, squire, the *Emily* my noble father so dearly needs,' the heir began, Jean-Louis standing and brightening considerably. The nobleman approached the painting. '*This* is the one my father chose?' he asked disapprovingly.

'I believe he marked it with some secret code,' Jean-Louis replied.

The young heir eyed the frame closely and finally nodded his approval. An attendant approached the nobleman with an embroidered leather bag bearing the same crest as that emblazoned on all their backs. Its draw-strung mouth was yanked open. 'I will pay in gold, if that is acceptable?' the nobleman announced.

Four other attendants knelt down before him on all fours; a fifth, set a small crested table top upon their backs, upon which the sixth poured the glittering contents of the leather bag – Spanish gold coins.

'Fernando VI doubloons,' the count's heir explained, 'been in my family a hundred and fifty years.'

'I'm sure that will be satisfactory, my lord,' Jean-Louis gushed and assisted the attendants to bag the portrait off the easel. Jean-Louis felt he must ask, 'El Cont de Catalonia's agent, noble lord, you know of his whereabouts? I needed to ask him about a certain missing painting.'

'The scoundrel disappeared with my father's twenty thousand guineas. If you should lay eyes on him again, do let us know. There will be a handsome reward,' the young heir declared.

'Well, my lord, you should know that he stole a work of art from this emporium of extraordinary value – making off with it into the night.'

Stepping back, the nobleman swiped his sword from its scabbard, startling Jean-Louis, who fell to his knees, pleading for mercy. The six attendants fell to one knee, removing their tri-cornered feathered hats.

'I beg you noble lord, not my head. I knew it was–'

'Jean-Louis St Clair, I, Juan-Carlos Fernando Frederik Geraldo Francisco Laurencio, heir apparent to Juan-Carlos Fernando

Frederik Geraldo Francisco Laurencio the Fifth, esteemed and noble Count of Catalonia,' the nobleman announced, tapping both Jean-Louis' shoulders, 'anoint you with the Order de Santa Maria de Montesa y San Jorge de Alfama for your chivalry and services to Juan-Carlos Fernando Frederik Geraldo Francisco Laurencio the Fifth, esteemed and noble Count of Catalonia.'

Jean-Louis wept in appreciation of keeping his head.

'Arise noble knight,' the young count decreed, hanging a huge gong over Jean-Louis' neck and kissing both his cheeks.

The cockney Frenchman felt a sudden urge to use the lavatory.

The son of the fifth count of Catalonia, and his entourage, duly arrived in Barcelona where the ailing count was ready to receive them, eager to set eyes upon the prize.

The painting was selected by the count when visiting Queen Victoria. His carriage had passed the gallery in the Strand and he caught his first glimpse of the masterpiece – a portrait of his beloved granddaughter, Isabella Maria Katrina Madalena Anna Christiana of Catalonia – hanging in the window. His granddaughter, with whom he sang and danced every day, had sadly died from diphtheria just days before, at the tender age of fifteen. The count was heartbroken and bitterly regretted not having commissioned any portraits of her. Discovering this remarkable likeness, in a foreign land just days after her demise, moved him beyond measure and he immediately set in motion steps to make it his own.

Finding the work was part of an exhibition, a series of twelve paintings by a relatively unknown artist, the count had agreed to wait until the exhibition was over before taking delivery, appointing an equerry to look after the matter in his absence.

To avoid any doubt, the count marked the label on the frame of the precious painting with a red dot, above the letter *i* in *Emily*. Of the twelve portraits, only that one, which hung at the end of the line, interested him, but he gave no explanation as to why the others did not.

Unfortunately for the count, but fortunately for the gallery owner, the label on the frame that his son had just purchased, still bore the little red dot.

Proudly, the count's son led his entourage into his father's bedchamber. Both father and son were reduced to tears as the portrait, covered with the scarlet-and-yellow-striped flag of Catalonia, was mounted at the foot of the bed. Mopping his tears, the son blew his nose sufficiently hard and loud to cause the pigeons to fly from the roof, servants would tell the press later.

Attendants hauled the count up upon five silk pillows that he might enjoy a better view, and firstly, inspect his little red dot, above the *i*. And there it was – the genuine article. He waved his hand for his son to proceed, and smiled for the first time in months.

The portrait was dramatically unveiled to a herald of trumpets.

All eyes were upon the count – to witness his pleasure, a pleasure he had told them that would make his life worth living again.

But it was not to be.

What they actually witnessed was a look of horror on his face as he threw his head back violently against the wooden bedhead, his fists clenched, bony knuckles as white as marble.

A finale of gurgling and spluttering confirmed their worst fears – and the count was pronounced dead.

The Trial: Day 6

As poor Mrs Muxlow stood in the witness box in tears staring at the *prized Emily* painting, I was astonished by the row of other portraits alongside it. The first, and only the first, was a splendid portrait indeed, full of beauty and character and love, a portrait any person would be proud to own. It *was* a masterpiece. But as the eye travelled along the row of accompanying portraits, a noticeable deterioration was apparent in what they portrayed. Yes, it was the same girl. Yes, it was the same setting; the same room; the same chaise longue and even the same open window with the curtain billowing in the wind.

But the subject's face, her skin and eyes in particular, dramatically changed with each subsequent portrait. The first, the *prized Emily* was magnificent. The second showed a girl suffering, in pain. The third, deformities that made her appear quite ugly.

By the eleventh painting, Emily's face was no longer recognisable, eaten by gangrene and raw sores, dripping with puss. What the Spanish nobleman would have seen in the twelfth painting left me shuddering in my seat.

Emily was dying and decomposing, before our eyes.

I squeezed Papas hand. I owed him an apology, for there was far more to Jacob's madness than I had ever imagined.

As Mrs Muxlow left the witness stand, she went up to the prized *Emily* and reached up, touching Emily's face, tears streaming down her face. An usher looked up to the judge, wondering what to do about this woman holding up proceedings. The judge shook his head – to leave her a few moments – after which many handkerchiefs touched many a tear-filled eye in the public gallery. Finally, the old lady turned to the judge and bowed respectfully, a hint of contentment on her face as she took a seat at the back of the court along with other witnesses.

Ushers cleared all the paintings on display and Mr Ponsonby called his next witness.

'Delores Dunne, college secretary, Greenwold College,' the elderly lady announced quietly as she accepted the judge's offer to sit while she gave evidence. Dressed in shades of grey, she wore a thin veil beneath a neat, rounded felt hat.

'Miss Dunne,' Mr Ponsonby began, 'were you the college secretary at the time Jacob Silver was admitted to Greenwold?'

'Yes. I've been there thirty-two years,' she said proudly.

'So not much would go on without your knowing about it,' Mr Ponsonby continued, rhetorically. 'Would you please describe briefly Jacob Silver's progress at the college.'

'He was a genius, according to all those that tutored him. But because of his... his background, he was treated abysmally by the other pupils.'

'By *background*, you mean because he was poor?'

'Poor, a cripple, mother in prison, and Jewish – none of which suited the elitist bigots that thought they ran the college – and the country, for that matter. Barely a day passed when we didn't learn Silver, and any that dared to befriend him, had received a beating of one kind or another.'

'And so I gather *special steps* were taken to ensure his safety?'

'To ensure he didn't outshine any of them, more like. Their parents had threatened to withdraw their children since they regarded Silver as unhealthy competition. And so the headmaster made arrangements for Silver to be tutored alone.'

'And out of harm's way?'

'Yes. That gave him some respite. The bullying almost stopped then – and stopped altogether after the unfortunate death of one particular bully.'

'A certain gentleman by the name of Bradley Bateman, the Earl of Burrington?'

'Yes.'

'The science professor who taught Silver, do you–'

'We don't teach science. And never have, to my knowledge.'

'*He taught me for two years! In the catacombs!*' Jacob yelled from the dock.

I was stunned. Of course they taught science.

'*Silence!*' the judge ordered, frowning over the top of his glasses. 'Continue Mr Ponsonby.'

'Is it possible, madam, that Silver could have been receiving personal tuition in science without your knowledge?'

'I don't see how. Tutors needed to be paid. And none claimed expenses for teaching Silver science.'

'Is there a classroom in the catacombs? A science laboratory perhaps?'

'I hadn't been down there for years. It's a storeroom of sorts. After Sir Robert Weston visited the school recently I went there with him. It was full of old furniture we no longer had use for, and such. And rats and spiders.'

I looked at Papa in astonishment. I had no idea he was so involved. Was this why he was so certain Jacob was guilty?

There were a thousand experiments going on there, you fool!' Jacob yelled again, attempting to get to his feet before being slapped down by his jailer.

'Any more and I'll have you removed!' the judge shouted at the accused. 'D'you understand?' Jacob glared back at the judge, then nodded.

'You saw no evidence of experiments being carried out there?'

'None,' said Miss Dunne.

Why would they not believe Jacob? He learned so much from the professor.

Mr Ponsonby passed the old lady a drawing. 'Exhibit 35, m'lud. Do you recognise this caricature, Miss Dunne?'

'Yes.'

'Where have you seen it before?'

'It was shown me by Sir Robert Weston during his visit.'

'And the subject of the sketch? Do you recognise him?'

'Yes.'

Passing the sketch to the jury, Mr Ponsonby continued, 'This sketch was drawn by the accused whilst he was in custody and was offered to the police to help trace the professor. It is apparently a good likeness of the gentleman, whom, he claims, taught him science at your college.'

Miss Dunne tutted. 'Firstly, I have to say it is a good likeness but not of any person that taught science at this college or any other. He was a Frenchman and benefactor of the Greenwold Estate.'

'Benefactor? And when did you last meet him?'

'I've never met him. He disappeared in 1679 and has not been seen since.'

I looked at Papa with incredulity. He looked back at me through an embarrassed smile. Gasps rose from those around me and Mr Ponsonby had to wait to be heard.

'Since 1679? Over two hundred years! You are sure?'

'It is a matter of public record. After he disappeared, the estate was gifted to the state. Thereafter, to us.'

'So how would Jacob Silver ever have known what he looked like – in order to make such a *good likeness*, as you confirm?'

'His portrait hangs in the Corridor of Alumni, sir. Jacob Silver spent many an hour observing it – talking to it. I saw him myself, quite often, in the middle of the night.'

'So who *did* teach Jacob Silver science at Greenwold College?'

'As I said, we don't teach science. And never have. There are no facilities.'

Oh dear, Jacob. It does seem your imagination had run wild.

If the professor did not exist then this could only mean my poor Jacob had lied, or imagined him. Whichever it was, my passion for his innocence was waning. We returned to the courtroom in the afternoon, and I particularly hoped to hear anything that would support his story – that the professor existed. The appearance of the next witness did give me a little hope.

'Helen Carol Bates, waitress at the Savoy Hotel,' the young lady said firmly.

'Miss Bates, were you on duty in the orangery on the day of a certain incident concerning Lady Jayne of Sherston?' Mr Ponsonby began.

'Yes. I remember it well. That young man,' she said, pointing to Jacob in the dock, 'insulted Lady Jayne good and proper.'

'Describe for us, if you will, the events leading up to the alleged *insult.*'

'That young man came in…'

'You are referring to the accused, Jacob Silver?'

'Yes. I didn't know his name, but he was a reg'lar. Always left a good tip.' A titter rose in the gallery. 'I showed him to a table and he ordered tea and cucumber sandwiches for himself and his friend, the professor, he called him.'

At last. Proof that the professor exists.

'So, you saw this professor?'

'Well, actually I don't recall seeing any other gentleman. I assumed he was joining him later.'

Oh dear. Maybe she saw him later?

'And then something happened concerning Lady Jayne?'

'The young man, Mr Silver that is, was sketching and chatting the whole time and Lady Jayne objected. The Head Waiter went and asked him to leave. As he left he presented Lady Jayne with a caricature. It was very good. Funny, you know. Dripping in diamonds she was. But it upset her.'

'And what else do you remember?'

'After the commotion, when I went to clear the table, only one cup had been used. The other was still full. And the cucumber sandwich was left on the plate.'

'You're quite sure?'

'Oh yes. I shared it with my friend, Mavis.' The court laughed as she added: 'It's not stealing or nuffink. We're allowed.'

'And you cannot describe the mysterious guest who neither ate nor drank?'

'No, sorry. There was such a commotion by the time he left, I didn't even notice whether his friend had turned up or not.'

'No further questions, m'lud.'

The waitress was allowed to leave and I was still concerned that the professor had yet to be seen by other witnesses, when the prosecution called their next witness.

'Herbert Charles Wheeler, Director of Calligraphy, Victoria and Albert Museum,' said the bald-headed gentleman, clutching a pair of half-moon spectacles.

'Mr Wheeler, would you please explain the area of your expertise to the court,' began Mr Ponsonby.

'My life's work has been the study of handwriting and signatures for comparative and authentication purposes.'

'And how long have you been involved with such work?'

'Thirty-five years. I was with both Sotheby's and Christie's documents and art departments for a total of twenty-three years and spent the last twelve years at the Victoria & Albert Museum.'

Mr Ponsonby passed the witness a piece of paper on which there was a handwritten note.

'Mr Wheeler, would you please read this note out to the court.'

Mr Wheeler slid his spectacles onto his nose before quoting:

' "*I love you so much – let us privately celebrate and become man and wife. Emily.*" '

'Exhibit 36, m'lud.' Mr Ponsonby turned to the jury. 'The note the accused alleges was written by Emily Muxlow, and addressed to him, on the twelfth of March, 1893 – four years after the alleged writer had died.' Turning to the witness, Mr Ponsonby continued, 'Mr Wheeler can you confirm this is an original piece?'

'Yes.'

'Did you compare it with *this* document,' said Mr Ponsonby, passing another document to the witness. 'Exhibit 37, m'lud. The accused's examination paper for his apothecary's certificate.'

'I did.'

'And you being an expert in handwriting, what did you find

upon comparing the two?'

'I found thirty-seven points of similarity in the two specimens.'

'To which your conclusion is…?'

'In my professional opinion, both were written with the same hand.'

'You are saying, in so many words, Jacob Silver had proposed to himself?'

The gallery burst into laughter. But as I looked over at Jacob, I could see that he was extremely embarrassed by this declaration, attempting to hide his face in his hands.

Retrieving the two handwriting samples, Mr Ponsonby then took a small oil painting off the bench and handed it to the witness. 'Were you given this painting to examine by Scotland Yard?'

'Yes, by Detective Inspector Neville. He asked me to compare the work with another and comment on the signature.'

'Exhibit 38, m'lud, a macabre Ripper-scene painting acquired from The Strand Gallery. Mr Wheeler, did you compare the signature on this painting with that on *this* work, exhibit Number 1?' Mr Ponsonby asked, pointing to the *prized Emily* on its easel.

Surely the prosecution were not suggesting Jacob painted such horror? He had described to Sergeant Beck how he abhorred the work.

'Yes. I found sixteen points of similarity between the two signatures and it is my professional opinion that they were painted by the same person.'

Groans rose from the gallery around me. This was indeed bad news for Jacob. He had always denied painting such macabre works – and earlier, I had felt sure he was incapable of portraying such horror. So, had he painted them?

'I have no further questions, m'lud.'

Mr Ecclestone quickly rose to his feet.

'Mr Wheeler, you found thirty-seven points of similarity in the handwriting samples and were professionally satisfied they were by the same hand.' Taking up the Ripper-scene painting and pointing to the signature, he asked: 'So, how can you be satisfied with only sixteen points of similarity with this signature?'

'Simply because it is a smaller sample. The more words, the more similarities.'

'If I were an artist with years of experience and had a similar brush to that which was used and the same colour paint, is it possible I could copy Jacob Silver's signature well enough to obtain sixteen points of similarity?'

'Well, I suppose–'

'Yes or no, please, Mr Wheeler.'

'Well, if you–'

'Just yes or no, will do, Mr Wheeler.'

'Yes, I suppose–'

'Yes! That's the word I'm looking for. Thank you. No further questions, m'lud.'

So maybe Jacob didn't paint them. The gallery owner's evidence will prove that, beyond all doubt.

The prosecution then called their final witness, and it was not the art gallery owner. I looked forward to him being called by the defence.

'Lionel Hastings, KCB,' the witness announced as he lowered his hand and passed back the Bible.

'Sir Lionel, would you please tell the court about your professional credentials,' Mr Ponsonby began.

'I am a psychiatrist and head of psychopathology at the London Hospital and…'

Defence Counsel bobbed up from his bench. 'The defence accepts Sir Lionel as being an *expert* witness in mental health, m'lud,' and sat again.

Mr Ponsonby pressed on. 'You were present during various interviews along with Sergeant Beck, Inspector Neville and the accused, is that correct?'

'Yes, sir, I was. And I interviewed the accused with Dr Sigmund Freud, visiting from Vienna, acknowledged expert in the field he calls *psychoanalysis*.'

'Please tell the court of your findings.'

'We identified Silver's ailment as multiple personality disorder. He spoke freely about his life and the events leading up to his arrest. Silver described how, at an early age, he had become accustomed to people dying about him, due to his father's practice as an apothecary.'

'Did that give rise to any conclusions on your part?'

'His mother's method of dealing with father's demise was described by him rather more freely and openly than I would have expected. He admitted responsibility for some of the deaths his poor prescriptions had caused but had no shame or remorse. Having made a promise to his dying father to strive for *immortality*, and then losing him, the closest human being in his life, his father's subsequent preservation undoubtedly had a profound effect on him. He admitted that he would have liked to have preserved his father forever. With what we know now, I would submit that these events were the *seed*, resulting in the first shoots of his mental instability.

'Effectively orphaned and crippled by polio, he is then outcast at his college. Lonely, bullied and homesick, this extremely intelligent boy would naturally seek allies, and a replacement father-figure, and I believe this is what drove him to befriend a fellow outcast, the benefactor of the school – adopting him as his *professor of science.*'

'When you say: *adopted him*, can you expand on that for us, please?'

'Having engaged in conversations with the imaginary professor, or the artist's impression of him if you prefer, the professor crossed over from being imaginary, in Mr Silver's subconscious, to becoming a *real* person; another persona, co-existing in his own mind. So far as Mr Silver was concerned, from that moment on, the professor was real enough to touch, smell, talk to and argue with – just as the accused described to those interviewing him.'

'*He was real, you idiot! You're all idiots!*' Jacob screamed from the dock, amid many a sharp intake of breath from the gallery.

'*Quiet!*' the judge yelled back at him. 'It's your turn later!'

'Left much to his own devices, the boy's mind had him believe he was a master in all things; grandiose schemes that led to him, *apparently*, developing potions and concoctions that he believed could cure anything – even the incurable. Sadly, this was delusion and led to the eventual death of his best friend, Muxlow, and very nearly killed his sweetheart, Muxlow's sister – Emily.'

'So there was no malicious intent when he administered these concoctions?'

'Not at all. Mr Silver believed, above all else, in his own skills. He wanted rid of Muxlow's freckles – the professor, his other persona, informed him belladonna would achieve that. Mr Silver had no knowledge, in truth, whether that particular potion would work or not; his imaginary professor had *invented* the process. And it killed the boy. Likewise, Mr Silver imagined he was *curing* Emily – in fact, from what we can ascertain, what he gave her nigh on killed her. But against all the odds, for she was in a weak state from consumption, she survived. The other medications she was taking at the time probably limited the damage Mr Silver's harmful medications could inflict.

'Banished from the college, the boy's mind would have been in turmoil. He had lost the only two people who meant anything to him – including the one person he dearly loved – Emily.'

'He continued painting Emily from memory?' said Mr Ponsonby, standing at the side of the line of eleven portraits of Emily which had been brought back into court, and pointing to the *prized Emily.*

'Yes. A brilliant artist with a brilliant memory to match, he recalled her so well. Just look at the beauty in that first portrait. Her own mother vouches for its accurate portrayal of her daughter. Recalling her with such clarity, such detail, this reveals an utter infatuation with the girl, there is no doubt about it. He kept Emily alive in his imagination by continually painting her. But memories of her eventually faded away, probably due to the addled state of his brain, after becoming addicted. She would no longer materialise no matter what concoctions he swallowed.'

'Perhaps now you could explain why he went for her head and the meaning behind these paintings, Sir Lionel,' said Mr Ponsonby, indicating the line of eleven easels.

'His first rendition, his *prized Emily* he called it, would have been the most beautiful, because she was still fresh in his mind. But when his memory of her faded, it was akin to losing an arm or a leg. So he went off to bring her back.

'He denied that, at every opportunity, but he *had* to go and get her – to fulfil his need for her in his life again. To survive. There is no doubt that he had an enormous passion for the girl – a desperate need.'

'But Emily had died, years earlier.'

'He couldn't have been aware of that until his arrival back at Greenwold. There is no doubt that learning of her death would have devastated his mind. Pushed him over the edge. He lost all reason. Someone must have explained she was interred in the family tomb at Finchingfield – an unguarded place where he could go and help himself.'

'And so he desecrated the family crypt and took her head?'

'That is my professional opinion, yes. He took her head and preserved it, in formaldehyde – just like he did with his father. To him it was the natural thing to do.'

In the dock, Jacob was sobbing, covering his face with his arms.

'During his interviews, he spoke of Emily arriving out of the blue, four years after he'd last seen her,' Mr Ponsonby said.

'That would have been *after* her head was removed from the formaldehyde and embalmed. He had dressed her to pose as his mistress – in the bath chair. His inspiration returned, immediately. And so he was joyful, able to paint her again, his mind blocking out, completely forgetting, the morbidity of how she came to be there.

'He painted eleven portraits over the next nine months or so. In *his* eyes, it was the *same* Emily on the canvas. His *beautiful* Emily.' Sir Lionel looked over towards Jacob in the dock. 'When he described that line of paintings to us during his interview, he was adamant they were all identical. To *him*, they were, in every way – beautiful and identical. But his artist's eye, recording like a camera, tells *us* that this was not so. *We* see Emily as she actually was, picture by picture – horrifically decomposing before us.'

'How was it possible that Silver thought Emily was alive again?'

'Oh, to him, she *was* alive the whole time. And very much so. She became another persona in his imagination, just another of the *strangers* that we know of, taking up residence there. She would do anything his subconscious demanded. He spoke six languages – *she* spoke six languages. His favourite book was War & Peace – *her* favourite book was the same. He could recite eleven of Lord Byron's poems from memory – she could do the same. It was no coincidence – *he* had given birth to her, after all. Everything she did or said came from him; from his script; from his knowledge; from his desires. He proposed to her and she to him. But we can prove from the handwriting of the betrothal *she* apparently made, that it was *he*, in fact, who did all the proposing.'

Goodness, Jacob! You were so terribly ill.

I could not take my eyes off Jacob cowering silently in the dock. Murmurs rose throughout the courtroom. My heart went out to him. I felt he needed me now, more than ever. But where was Betsy Pollock while all this was going on? Why had she done nothing to stop it?

'Sir Lionel, the accused had the police believe he and Emily had intended to live together as man and wife, quite normally. Can you explain how such monstrous behaviour might have been considered *normal* by the accused?' asked Mr Ponsonby.

'So far as Jacob Silver was concerned, Emily was alive and well. We have his own confession about his extraordinary drug intake. This, added to a genius's wild imagination, and I am in no doubt that, as distasteful as this may seem, he lived, conferred, and would have slept with Emily, like any other couple, if they had married. Remember, what *he* saw was only what he *wanted* to see – a beautiful, desirable, and *whole* Emily. Had they married, she would have become the *perfect* wife he desired her to be – in every way. And he truly believed his art was making her, and him, immortal. His own Mona Lisa.'

I was beginning to feel unwell from the already sickening evidence and was quite unprepared for the next line of questioning.

'And what of his drinking the elixir in which her severed head floated?'

'The toxicologist has confirmed that the elixir in which Emily's head floated – Elixir 32, Mr Silver had called it, until it became his *Essence of Emily* – was indeed a derivative of the nectar to which he had become addicted. Whether medically, biologically, chemically or psychologically, I cannot be certain, but her decomposing head added to what the elixir meant to him. By drinking it, he shared her means of surviving so that he became part of her – *she* became part of him. And he needed to maintain that euphoria every day, by *topping-up* every single day.'

A juror vomited. Groans and grimaces rose from the public gallery. Mr Ponsonby paused while the juror composed himself.

'You're suggesting he drank this obnoxious substance to survive?'

'He couldn't do without it. Addicted beyond belief, it made him feel a part of his... his victims.'

'And when the *Essence of Emily* dried up?' he continued.

'Catastrophe! He was rapidly losing her to decay. But he was sure he had a way to save her – bring her back to life. Now, his resistance to taking innocent lives was thrown to the wind. He knew it was wrong. Wrong to kill. But his need for these five souls was a greater need. Their souls would resurrect and rejuvenate his Emily. He *had* to have them murdered, to survive himself, and commanded his evil professor to take their lives, steal their souls. By the time the last girl's soul was added – he was convinced he could raise Emily from the dead. Adding Emily's soul would mean *she* became immortal. And he, consuming the same elixir, would become invincible.'

All around me, a wave of nausea ran through those present, as a cleric retched into his handkerchief. Others fought to get out into the fresh air. A fat woman fainted, blocking the aisle. Folk piled over the top of her or vaulted over the benches to freedom. I felt so relieved when the judge was forced to order a short recess.

Papa was right. I had needed to hear this myself, for I would never have believed him, had he told me himself. Jacob was far more mad than I ever dared believe. The vision I had, once so glorious, was all but destroyed.

When we reconvened, Mr Ponsonby continued questioning the psychologist.

'And what of the *mysterious* professor and immortality?'

'As I have said, the professor was another invention of his mind and became part of him – an extension of himself. The professor loved alchemy – because Jacob Silver loved alchemy. The professor sought the elixir of life, immortality – as Jacob Silver had promised he would seek immortality, to his father. During our interviews, Mr Silver often remarked about the professor seemingly reading his mind. Of course he could, he was one and the same mind. As one of his *multiple personalities*, the professor was just as real a person to Mr Silver as any man in the street.'

'*He was real, you fool! I knew him nine bloody years!*' Jacob cried from the dock, as a guard slapped him down.

'*Silence, or I will have you gagged!*' the judge yelled back, pounding his gavel. The gallery became a cauldron of murmurs and groans before settling again.

'And what of the housekeeper, Betsy Pollock?'

At last, finally we may find out the truth. Why had she ignored what was going on?

And then, the final blow…

'Betsy Pollock, too, was just another persona. A figment of his imagination, a character performing in his play. A play to achieve his dream – Emily in his life, forever – both of them immortal.'

'*They were real, you idiot!*' Jacob yelled from the dock again, rattling his chains. As the jailer attempted to gag him, '*I knew them both from Greenwold!*'

Mr Ecclestone jumped to his feet and went over to the side of the dock, jabbing a finger in Jacob's face while admonishing him.

I felt devastated. The last inkling of *some* normality in his life – gone. I considered leaving to spare myself the cruel truth. But another part of me was urging me to stay – to have faith. Believe in this mad man. But how could I?

The judge was furious. 'Just once more, d'you hear me? Just once more and I'll have you gagged or withdrawn. You will have your turn. Wait until then!' he scathed. 'Continue, Mr Ponsonby.'

'Mr Silver told the police that he wanted to show Emily off to the world. Take her for walks, go to meet customers in their shop, but Miss Pollock forbade that, for one reason or another. He said she not only existed but took control of Emily. How would you explain that, sir?' asked the prosecutor.

'This is typical behaviour for one with multiple personality disorder,' Sir Lionel said directly to the jury, 'one personality working against another. Let me explain using an analogy. Imagine Mr Silver's mind, if you would, as a stage, putting on a performance. There is a cast of four: Mr Silver himself, Emily, the professor and Betsy Pollock. The audience is the big wide world but only one of the cast is *actually* real, and the only one able to step out from backstage and converse with the audience – Jacob Silver. The curtain rises. The play begins. Enter Jacob Silver, the only person on stage. And he tells us he dotes on Emily and wants her onstage – to *show her to the audience*, the big wide world. The others say, and that includes Emily: It's too cold, or she doesn't want to, or she has a headache, or whatever, and remain backstage, preventing him from showing the real world their best kept secret – that none of *them* are real.' Sir Lionel looked at the jurors in turn, quizzically. 'You might ask: But how do they come to do this? Well, simply ask yourself this: *Who* wrote the script?' He paused, a finger raised in the air, then pointed it towards a smiling juror. 'Exactly! Mr Silver! Mr Silver's subconscious *knows* Emily cannot be seen in public. And so cast members, for whom he wrote the script and directed everything onstage, *conspired* to prevent that from happening.' He turned back to Mr Ponsonby. 'I think that is the best way I can explain it.'

'Does this explain why the police could find no trace of either the professor or the housekeeper?'

'Absolutely. They don't exist. To Mr Silver, they were as real as you and I. But Mr Silver himself could not tell us what they wore, what time they went to bed, what colour were their nightgowns, what they ate, why they never ventured outdoors, nothing of that nature – and yet he claimed he lived with them. I attended the house to completely satisfy myself, and could find no trace of either, or any sign that they, or any other person, had lived there with him since his parents left. He was completely alone. Sadly, so sensitive and vulnerable, we know now that he should never have been left alone.'

'Accept for Emily's head, of course. Can you explain a little about his believing he had concocted a potion he named *Desire*, and why he thought immortality was achievable?' asked Mr Ponsonby.

'In his experiment at the art gallery, Mr Silver thought all his twelve portraits were identical – but for one which had a coating of his miraculous potion: *Desire*. All delusional. People didn't flock to that one painting because they were chemically induced. It was the *only* painting of the bunch that was any good! Look at them.' He pointed to the line of portraits. 'See for yourself. The first was, *is*, a masterpiece. But he believed it was only desirable because of this ridiculous potion – taken from his book: *Alchemy*. Add to this the fact that he then learnt that his lord and master: Leonardo da Vinci, endorsed the book, and he was certain, *absolutely* convinced without a shadow of doubt, that anything in *Alchemy* would perform exactly as described.

'Then Emily goes and dies – in his shop. My explanation for that is that one of his *characters* had had enough of her decomposing in front of them and dropped her head in a jar of rat poison, before smashing it on the shop floor. It is no coincidence they chose the very poison she had used when she took her life all those years before. Mr Silver was mortified. Could not survive without her.

'But he was aware, at that moment, that he had deciphered the code for immortality from his faithful *manual of murder*. He passionately believed he had the means of bringing Emily back to life at his disposal – he just needed those souls to complete the elixir. And so a plan was hatched. His *evil* personality, the professor, painted the Ripper paintings to persuade his *kindly* self that horror was a good thing. Their popularity, had him develop a taste for blood. And he developed quite an appetite for it – as his *Masquerade* portraits of headless models show. His *evil* side finally convinced his *kindly* side that after just a few distasteful acts, simply practising what the macabre paintings preached, and he could raise Emily from the dead. All he had to do was *use the knife* to free their souls – and not just frighten them with it.

'Taking the lives of those poor women for such special ingredients was merely incidental – a means to an end. That they were his friends or loved ones, did not enter into it, was of no concern. They were gifting their souls for a higher purpose – the greater good.'

'And what of poor Constable Everett, Sir Lionel?'

'Sadly, he just got in the way. Mr Silver, or his *evil* professor, either one, had to dispose of him.'

'And is it possible his *other* self, his *kindly side,* as you put it, would be completely unaware of this?'

'Absolutely. *Kindly* Mr Silver was none the wiser – and probably can only recall innocently stepping over the body.'

Mr Ponsonby turned to the judge. 'I have no further questions of this witness, m'lud,' and sat down.

'Mr Ecclestone?' the judge asked, after defence counsel had not risen.

'Yes, m'lud,' was the response as the defence barrister rose to his feet and took some time to flick through extensive notes.

The judge was becoming impatient. 'When you're ready, Mr Ecclestone.'

Finally, 'Sir Lionel,' the cross-examination began, 'you accept the accused's story that he lived *almost* as man and wife with just the head of his former lover, Emily Muxlow?'

'Yes, I do,' replied Sir Lionel.

'You accept that he loved her dearly, would you agree?'

'Yes. He was morbidly infatuated with her.'

'From your intensive questioning and his own admissions, he

told you the truth that he was an addict, yes?'

'Yes, he admitted he was addicted to mind-altering substances.'

'He told the truth about co-habiting with what we know now to be a dead person; that he intended marriage to her?'

'Yes.'

'Then why do you not believe him when he denies severing Emily Muxlow's head, six years ago?'

'He denies it because this dark event was blocked from his mind. *Kindly* Mr Silver was completely unaware of what the *evil characters* in his mind were doing.'

'Would you agree with me that if a third party had severed Miss Muxlow's head and delivered it to him, in his addicted state of mind, the strange and macabre behaviour he describes, could have been much the same?'

'Yes. But who else could have, or would have, done that?'

'So, your professional conclusion is that because the police can't find anybody else guilty of grave-robbing, the accused should take the blame?'

'Well, not quite…'

'Not quite? But what evidence have you, or the eminent Doctor Freud, after numerous conversations with the accused, that he travelled to Miss Muxlow's tomb and returned with her head?'

'Er… Well, I… Er…'

'I believe the word you are looking for is: *none?*'

'He could not recall *how* the head reached him, and–'

'And neither can you prove *how* the head reached him, is that not so?'

'Yes. But it is more likely his evil persona did not disclose the fact to his kindly persona.'

'You have no idea *how* that head reached him except this extraordinary hypothesis that he went and collected it?'

'I believe that is what happened.'

'There you go again! You *believe!* But there is no proof, no physical evidence, per se, that that *is* what happened. Is there?'

'No. There is no physical proof.'

'And if Mr Silver can *prove* he did *not* take Emily's head, beyond all reasonable doubt, would you agree that your whole hypothesis about all these imaginary characters in his head, falls apart?'

'Well, no. I would not. I mean, have you considered that perhaps he had someone go and obtain her head for him?'

Mr Ecclestone took a sip of water and studied his notes before asking the witness, 'Proposing marriage to a severed head. Is it your professional opinion then, that this man must be insane?'

'In that regard, yes.'

'And yet this *insane* man is here on trial?'

Mr Ponsonby jumped to his feet. 'M'lud–'

'Precisely, Mr Ponsonby,' the judge said, waving him to sit back down. 'I will stop this line of questioning right there, Mr Ecclestone. And for the jury's benefit I will say this: Direction was given before the beginning of this trial that the accused *was* mentally fit to stand trial. The reasons *why* are not open for discussion by you the jury. There is a precedent from 1843, that the defence has had to accept, which dictated the way we should proceed. You will be put in the picture before going off to decide the case.' To Mr Ecclestone he said, 'Please continue in a different direction, Mr Ecclestone.'

'Sir Lionel, my understanding of cases concerning multiple personality disorder is that all the characters are reachable by their analyst. Did you at any time have a conversation with the illusive professor?'

'No, sir. He would not manifest himself, however hard I tried.'

'Betsy Pollock?'

'No.'

'Dead Emily?'

'No, sir. No other characters manifested themselves.'

'So how can you be so sure they don't exist?'

'But they *do* exist – in Mr Silver's mind. Just not in the real world.'

'You say you went back to his house and found no trace of this professor?' continued the defence lawyer.

'That is so.'

'Did you search every cupboard and storeroom?'

'I think so.'

'There was one secret anteroom the police missed the first time, did you look for others?'

'Yes, and found none; apart from the compartment in the studio cupboard where Emily's head was found in a jar.'

'And the housekeeper, Betsy Pollock. Where did you look for her?'

'All over the house. There was no sign she ever lived there. Especially in the box room, which was empty.'

'Did you speak to any customers of the apothecary's shop?'

'No. The shop was closed down as a result of the morbid discoveries there.'

'So, you did not speak to a single customer of that thriving business to ask about the very stout, and very un-missable, Miss Betsy Pollock, who served everybody from behind the counter?'

'No.'

'I put it to you, sir, that if we can prove beyond all reasonable doubt that Miss Pollock existed, *that* would throw your whole hypothesis out of the window. Turn it to dust.'

'Her role was not so vital in all this. Unless she could prove the professor existed, it would not change my mind about the professor being a figment of the accused's imagination.'

'I put it to you, Sir Lionel, that the professor's accomplice, Miss Pollock, had done a very good job of clearing up nicely after her and the professor's swift departure following these murders and because you were so convinced of your own *theories* as to what happened in that dreadful place, you, and the whole of the Metropolitan police force, did nothing more than take a cursory look around – already satisfied as to their non-existence.'

'Had Mrs Pollock lived there I am sure there would have been more signs, more evidence. However, I still maintain the woman is a figment of Mr Silver's imagination.'

'And so you didn't try hard to find her, did you?' The witness did not think that question justified an answer. 'No more questions, m'lud,' Mr Ecclestone announced, sitting down sharply.

Mr Ponsonby bobbed to his feet, 'That concludes the case for the prosecution, m'lud,' and promptly sat down again.

'I think this is a good place to adjourn. We will assemble tomorrow morning at ten to begin hearing the case for the defence,' the judge announced and stood up.

Papa and I agreed that the last witness had not been as effective as the prosecutor had wished. The prosecution's case relied on so much *theory*. Since neither the police nor the psychiatrist had done much to trace Betsy Pollock, I was confident that, although Jacob's mind was obviously disturbed, he had been telling the truth. The butcher, the baker, the candlestick maker, the college, Apothecaries Hall issuing her certificate to practice, and shop customers – all knew Betsy Pollock existed. Papa agreed that finding these other witnesses and *proving* she did – would carve a large hole in the psychiatrist's theories and the prosecution's case could falter. My one remaining hope was that the defence could find the lady herself. And she would surely lead police to the murderer responsible for these morbid crimes – the professor.

If neither the professor nor Miss Pollock were traced, I had little doubt that Jacob would be found guilty – as Papa had expected when he first saw the evidence against Jacob, he told me. With

Papa's blessing, I made up my mind to seek out Jacob's lawyers and find out what progress they had made with tracing the pair, or at least, proving they existed and had fled.

Papa and I managed to catch Mr Ecclestone in a corridor, just as he left the courtroom. I was still wearing a cloak and bonnet. Taking him to one side, my father introduced himself and told him who I was.

'Ah, the lady in the note,' he said, shaking hands. 'I do hope we dealt with your involvement in sufficiently confidential manner?'

'Yes, of course,' I told him. 'I'm truly concerned for Jacob's position. It would seem that without the professor and Miss Pollock being traced, he will be found guilty.'

'Exactly, Miss Weston,' Mr Ecclestone agreed, 'but we do have three witnesses possibly four, shop customers, who can vouch for Betsy Pollock's existence.'

'That's good. But is it not obvious to these psychiatrists that she and this professor have committed these crimes and Mr Silver will end up being blamed?'

'Nothing so plain is obvious to the prosecution, Miss Weston. They are convinced of Mr Silver's guilt – and the fact that this illusive professor and Betsy Pollock have not been traced suits their case enormously.'

'Do you have any other witness that has actually *seen* the professor with Mr Silver?' I pressed. 'What about the gallery owner? Jacob took him there.'

'The gallery owner is my last witness, although I have not been able to reach him these last few days.'

'It's imperative he gives his testimony,' Papa added.

'Yes, proof that the professor exists would be *most inconvenient* for the prosecution, and would dismantle their whole case. It would mean freeing Mr Silver. They would have to start their investigation all over again. They certainly won't like that.'

'From what these customers at the apothecary's have told you, have you been able to trace Miss Pollock?' Papa asked Mr Ecclestone.

'No. They can prove Miss Pollock exists but nobody seems to know where she went. Disappeared into thin air, it seems.'

'Well maybe I can help in that regard,' I offered, 'make some investigations of my own. But before I do, I must ask you, and you do not have to answer if that would be inappropriate, but now Mr Silver is sober, out of reach of his potions and drugs, how are his feelings towards his past behaviour – knowing he was living with just his mistress' head?'

My question surprised Papa.

'He suffered a great deal before every last trace of those obnoxious substances were removed from his body,' Mr Ecclestone began. 'He was in custody, and there are no easy solutions there. No facilities. We must consider it fortunate that his detoxification did not cost him his mind – as it does with many. No longer addicted, he finds it incredulous that he could not have known Emily was dead. He is horrified that he spent time with her in that condition. And more horrified that anyone suggest he went and stole her head in the first place. He is a healer and artist, he says, both skills familiar with the human body and its condition. Yes, he knew Emily was ill, Miss Pollock was for ever making excuses for her, he said. But *dead*? The woman he cared for and spoke with, and proposed to marry, was *dead*? He suffered a complete nervous breakdown in custody. After I read the psychiatrists' reports and with the professor and Miss Pollock untraceable, I pressed Mr Silver to plead insanity – although we know now the prosecution would not have accepted that plea. They want him to hang. But Mr Silver would not go along with it, anyway. Whilst he admits his former addiction, he says he's quite sane. Somehow, he thinks the jury will accept his side of things – that the professor and Betsy Pollock schemed and connived to make him responsible.'

'And *why* does he think they did that? What had they hoped to gain?' Papa asked, so sure the pair only existed in Jacob's head.

'Mr Silver is convinced the professor needed the completed elixir for immortality for a *certain purpose*. To use it to raise a certain person, perhaps, *someone special* to the professor. The old man was always going on about a time limit – it had to be done by such-and-such a date. It was imperative, apparently.'

'Michaelmas Day, the twenty-ninth of September,' Papa added.

'And the day of Jacob's arrest,' I said.

'Yes, coincidentally, it was,' Mr Ecclestone agreed. 'With the police no longer looking for them, Mr Silver believes that, if the elixir failed for any reason, the pair would go on to repeat the whole process – kill more women for their souls. Mr Silver said the professor spoke of many other students before him – all working on immortality – and failing. We've tried to trace them, but no luck yet. Greenwold college protect their own, it seems. Won't allow us anywhere near former students, children of the aristocracy.'

'Michaelmas Day was the day the potion *was* completed; the last ingredient added. Rebecca's soul. According to legend, for the first time in five hundred years it was viable. Perhaps it has already been consumed.' I said.

'Unfortunately, we have been unable to *prove* anything concerning the professor, or what was intended with the now-missing elixir,' the lawyer said.

I asked Mr Ecclestone: 'How is Mr Silver taking all these terrible things being said about him?'

A steel door slammed noisily behind us.

'See for yourself, Miss Weston,' Mr Ecclestone told me, turning me about to look into Jacob's face. 'They're bringing him for an interview with me, before we commence with the defence. Would you care to join us?'

His head lowered, shackled between two jailers, Jacob looked beaten, avoiding eye contact with any passer-by. He did not see me as Papa and I followed the group to a dingy interview room. Jacob was sat down hard at a small table in the centre of the room, a chair either side. After telling the jailers that we were part of the defence team, Mr Ecclestone spoke softly to Jacob.

'Mr Silver, Miss Weston will join us today,' he said, placing his hand on Jacob's manacled wrist. Jacob raised his unshaven face revealing bloodshot eyes buried deep in black sockets, under a mop of dishevelled hair. He appeared very frightened. 'Are you happy for her to stay?'

Jacob said nothing and just stared in front of him.

'Bring another chair, can you?' Mr Ecclestone asked a guard. From the back of the room the guard placed another chair opposite Jacob. I took off my bonnet, sat and reached forward, placing my hand on Jacob's clenched hands. He stared into my eyes and it was some moments before I detected a flicker of emotion upon his face. And then he smiled; a short, embarrassed smile. He had recognised me. We sat silently for a few moments, both my hands now held in his, until:

'Lizzie?' he whispered.

I nodded enthusiastically, gripping his hands tightly. 'Jacob, I'm here to help. Help find the other people involved.'

He sat stiffly while his eyes welled and then tears trickled freely down his face.

'They're saying... They're saying I killed my girls,' Jacob said softly, squeezing my hands. He broke into sobs that racked his body, placing his head down on my hands.

'I'm here,' I breathed, 'here, my love. I'll help you.'

Jacob suddenly sat up straight, thrust my hands away and yelled at Mr Ecclestone.

'She's dead, isn't she?' referring to me. 'This is a trick, isn't it? Lizzie's dead! You want to prove I'm mad!' He stared into my eyes.

'*GET HER OUT OF HERE!*'

'Well, I *do* believe him. And I'm not content to sit idly by while Mr Silver is measured for the rope, for something he so obviously did not do,' I later told Mr Ecclestone in the corridor, dabbing my eyes. 'The madness and addiction that had him accepting Emily as being alive, has left him. He's obviously ashamed and embarrassed. But that's all in the past. He's cured. Is that right, Papa?'

Papa nodded. 'He does appear to have his wits about him, now.'

'Obviously, my presence upsets him at the moment,' I said. 'I was dying when we last met. He knew that.'

'Ah, I see. That explains his outburst,' said Mr Ecclestone.

'I must break it to him gently. I'll write to him. Explain everything. He'll become used to the idea. I'll do anything to help.'

'But we have so little time. The defence case opens tomorrow. If you are so adamant that those two characters exist, the best way forward is to prove it. And that they set out to cause Mr Silver harm. Either one of them could do it – prove that the prosecution have got it wrong. I will need whichever one you find to be brought here – if we are to save him.'

'How long can you delay things,' I pressed.

'I can stretch it out to four days – at the most. I'm sorry. That's all we have. Find them – or he'll hang.'

Chapter 24

I had attended Jacob's trial against my father's specific instructions not to do so. But I had not known of his close involvement. He was only trying to protect me, he had said before the trial began, since he was aware of my impression that the *extremely mad* Jacob Silver was completely innocent. Papa's mind appeared a little more open now. On the way home from the trial, having learned Betsy was a real person, thanks to Mr Ecclestone finding shop customers who knew her, I had Papa's blessing to help Jacob all I could. I had my footman acquire a train ticket to Northampton to journey the next day. I was sure that Greenwold College would reveal more about the illusive professor and Jacob's housekeeper, than anywhere else.

'There's a possibility they've now lost an important defence witness – the gallery owner,' I said to Papa on the way home.

'My darling, I sympathise. But I can see no other outcome, whatever the gallery owner had to add. At best, he might have confirmed the Ripper paintings were not painted by Jacob. But what difference will that make? Jacob needs someone to find the professor. That is all.'

'The gallery owner met the professor. He can confirm, like Betsy, that the professor *does* exist! Don't you see, this professor committed perfect murder? Poor Jacob took the blame for everything. They drugged him into oblivion and brought Emily back into his life. They made him their perfect scapegoat; their perfect madman. All they had to do was disappear and Jacob would be left as the only person under suspicion. It was perfect. And from the evidence piled up against Jacob, they'll likely get away with it.'

'I had no idea you were covering the trial so closely.'

'I couldn't just watch that beautiful man suffer. Someone had to believe him, Papa.' And then I confessed. 'I attended every day of his trial.' Papa looked stunned. 'But I can't describe how badly I felt today, believing in his innocence when the evidence against him became so overwhelming.' Then I broke down.

'I was unaware you had such feelings for the man, my dear,' Papa said, as I sobbed my heart out. He leaned over me and spoke solemnly. 'And if all goes badly, my darling, you should consider this episode in your life over. It's probably too late now for you to change anything. The defence will submit what they have and if…' He let out a long sigh. 'My advice is that you must forget Jacob and move forward, enjoy your life and your new-found health to the full. Promise me, that is what you'll do.'

I promised – just to placate him. But if things went badly for Jacob, this was one promise I knew I would be unable to keep.

First, I had to prove the existence of the illusive professor. Under the pretext of considering a donation, I had telephoned the college and made an appointment to visit Miss Dunne, the secretary who had just given evidence.

'The college boasts a sparkling alumni over its two centuries,' boasted Miss Dunne as she led me past the historic portraits of noblemen, statesmen and military leaders hanging in the panelled Corridor of Alumni.

I felt I should call out *'and Jacob Silver, of course'* but that might have warned her as to my real purpose for being there.

'Our benefactor,' she said, stopping at the portrait of a distinguished-looking gentleman, a brass plate underneath declaring his name. The name meant nothing to me – at that moment. His white hair and beard covered a skeletal face that carried an oddly-wrinkled nose. His eyes were dark and piercingly sharp, following one when moving past. The caricature Jacob had drawn, produced at the trial, and later reproduced in newspapers nationwide, bore a remarkable likeness and looking up at the old *professor* now was like greeting an old acquaintance. His was the face of someone interesting, someone one would like to meet, engage in conversation perhaps. 'Born in Paris,' Miss Dunne said as she moved towards her office. 'Early seventeenth century, it is believed.'

'Has any record of his life survived?' I asked nonchalantly.

'We have a *Thank You* note signed by Oliver Cromwell himself, in appreciation of him handing over Charles I, who had taken refuge here. And a document from 1679, recording his last wishes upon his demise, that the splendid house and grounds be donated to the government of the day for, I quote: *providing amenities that would promote youth education.'*

Once we were seated comfortably in her office, Miss Dunne confided in me that former students had referred to their benefactor as *Old Nick,* and it was rumoured that his ghost toured the dormitories after lights out to *frighten the life out of anyone found awake.*

'And was anyone so frightened?' I asked.

She shook her head. 'It did ensure quiet after lights out although *Old Nick* did get blamed for anything and everything that went wrong; every lost or stolen possession and any bruised or broken limbs, from bullying and the like.'

'And no one ever met his… ghost?'

She tittered. 'Well, maybe.' I spilt my tea. 'On All Hallows Eve the older boys would terrorise the youngest. Sheets over heads and wicked laughs echoed from every nook and cranny in the old place. It was the only day of the year when the *lights out* rule of silence was not observed.'

'You speak as though this no longer occurs today?'

'No,' she replied, suddenly becoming more serious, distracting herself with a ledger. 'Er, you came to discuss a donation?'

But she had been about to tell me someone met the ghost. I was determined to find out more. 'Did something happen?' She acted as though she hadn't heard. 'Was someone hurt?'

She pushed the ledger aside and removed her glasses. Staring out of the window, she said, solemnly, 'They never got to the bottom of it. Of the various students admitting they played ghosts that night, none confessed to being in the same place as the… the incident.' A tear welled in her eye.

'Something serious?'

'Someone died,' she said softly, catching the tear with her knuckle. 'Heart attack they said.'

'But young men don't die of heart attacks,' I suggested.

'Oh, no. This wasn't a student. This was a master.'

'And had he suffered a heart condition?' I pressed.

'That's just it. As well as teaching French, he taught games and physical education. Of all the masters, Mr Beauchamp was probably the strongest and most fit.'

'Beauchamp? That's French isn't it?' She nodded, tearfully. 'When was this?' I asked. Miss Dunne was obviously distressed and I knew she would soon cease to continue, finding it all too much. I was convinced this master had not died of a heart attack, and something far more sinister was involved.

Finally, 'Fifteen years ago or more,' she whispered.

'And where, precisely?' After she didn't answer, 'Where in the college, Miss Dunne?'

A carriage clock on the mantelpiece chimed midday, loudly, the interruption giving Miss Dunne the opportunity to change the subject. Pulling the ledger towards herself again and appearing to snap out of her misery, 'Now, about your donation?' she asked.

We then attended to business and it was only after she wrote down my name that Miss Dunne connected me with my father.

'Sir Robert came regarding that dreadful Silver matter, you may have read about it in the papers? I've just got back from testifying.'

I pretended to have no knowledge and spent another hour discussing the college prospectus and how I was so sure that it was ideal for my imaginary cousin to attend after his sixteenth birthday, all the while hoping Miss Dunne would drop her guard and tell me more of the incident with Mr Beauchamp. I promised I would recommend the donation to my father. And if the day's events were sufficiently fruitful, I was determined the college would get it.

'My own interest is in the architecture of this magnificent estate,' I lied, standing and indicating our discussion in that office should come to an end. 'My father mentioned that you took him down into the catacombs. Is it possible I could have a quick look around? There was evidence down there, he told me, that the hall dates back far earlier than the façade would have one believe.'

'Yes. A gentleman from a new organisation interested in preserving Britain's heritage was interested to make a donation to help us maintain the roof. It's falling into disrepair. After looking in the cellars, he sent a couple of specialists in historic buildings recently and they were quite intrigued with some of the history. They thought they could dig up some more information from old government papers on Greenwold.' She stood and went to the window. 'It's very dirty down there. Are you sure you want to see it? So much mess.' I assured her it was of great interest to me. 'All right, then,' Miss Dunne replied, 'I'll get a lantern and we can go there directly. I'll find you something to cover your bonnet. And you're not afraid of spiders, I hope?'

Spiders were by no means my pet subject. I was afraid to ask *How big?* The answer might have frightened me off.

She took me outside to an ancient flight of stone steps at the rear of the hall which led down to double, heavy oak doors with huge locks. Adjacent was a well maintained playing field with rugby posts erected and I could not help but notice a huge puddle, some twenty yards in diameter, centred around the posts nearest to us.

'Is it always as wet as this?' I joked, feeling sorry for those who would be sprawling knee-deep in mud.

'Something wrong with the drainage,' Miss Dunne explained as we went down the steps. 'Would you believe we brought in fifty tons of topsoil to level it out again, two years ago. Volunteers, the students, spread it and rolled it – they worked through the night and were exhausted. But it made no difference, as you can see. Puddles galore.'

The doors were unlocked by a groundsman she had summoned to assist us, armed with two more lanterns.

I followed them into the black hole to find a cavernous labyrinth of supporting brick foundations rising to a magnificent vaulted ceiling. More stone steps led down even deeper, forming a space of some twenty feet between floor and ceiling, causing our voices to echo. After only a few steps we were prevented from going any further by mounds of old furniture and farm equipment piled precariously to the roof. Cobwebs as thick as muslin tied the furniture to the walls, the floor, and the ceiling. It was obvious that what was down there had not been moved for decades.

'Them ploughs was put in here when I first came,' our elderly groundsman assistant, Mr Atkins, declared. 'And I been here fifty years, ma'am.'

A small brick tunnel by the stone steps led off somewhere else. 'Any idea where that leads to, Mr Atkins?' I said.

'Dead end. Nought going on up there,' he replied.

Without waiting for permission, I stooped and scuttled through the tunnel, the kerchief over my head snatching cobwebs all the way through, thicker than I had ever seen before. The back of my throat was irritated by the dust.

'Don't go far, Miss Weston,' Miss Dunne called out behind me. 'If you don't mind I'd rather remain here.'

I didn't mind at all, finding the tunnel suddenly blocked by a rusting iron grille, a locked gate with a padlock and chain that appeared centuries old. Beyond, I could see that the tunnel widened into a larger, completely clear space with a flagstone floor and even more ornate vaulted ceiling. It was like a tiny cathedral in there. Remarkably, it was free of cobwebs and the floor was black. But there was something else about this wide-open void that I found odd, something strange, although I could not fathom quite what it was that puzzled me. Something looked out of place. And there were no cobwebs. Had I found it? The laboratory that never existed?

I kicked at the gate. To my complete surprise the whole grille creaked open with the padlock still attached; the old iron fixings into the wall had rotted away to nothing. The hinges barely held the gate upright as I edged by.

The faint noise of Miss Dunne calling wafted on a draught of fresh air, but she was now a long way behind me. I crossed the open space and followed more steps leading up, this time. These were also relatively cobweb free with what looked like candle holders set in hollowed-out sections of the ancient stone walls.

And then, the dead end. This must have been what Mr Atkins was referring to. But it was no ordinary dead end. It was entirely built from oak panelling. And light shone around the crack of what could only be a doorway.

I banged on the panelling. 'Is there anybody there?' I shouted. There was no answer. But I was determined to find out what was on the other side. I took a hatpin and wedged it high into the lighted crack in the frame.

Then I heard something behind me in the dark. I turned. All I remembered was his piercing eyes in the light from the lantern, his face covered in cobwebs. It was horrible. Frightening. I could taste bile in my mouth. My heart thumping. A chill on the back of my neck.

I screamed – and that was when I passed out.

I awoke spluttering in retaliation to smelling salts being waved under my nose. Attended by Mr Atkins and Miss Dunne, I was stretched out on the groundsman's jacket on the grass, near the rear entrance to the catacombs where we had first gone in.

'We were worried,' Miss Dunne said, 'I sent Atkins to get you.'

Still shaking, I began to cry, until I heard, 'I'm sorry I frightened you, Miss,' Mr Atkins said, wrenching his cloth cap in his fists. 'You screaming like that gave me quite a turn.' Miss Dunne pulled thick strands of cobwebs off his hair.

Then I began to laugh. 'I'm sorry, Mr Atkins' I said, 'I thought it was… Well, no harm done, then?' He helped me up onto my feet and dusted off his jacket. Miss Dunne took my arm and seemed to be pulling me to one side, for some reason. I looked down and realised I had been standing on a brass plaque, let into the grass.

So, that's where it had happened one dark Halloween, only five feet from the entrance to the catacombs. The polished plaque read:

In loving memory of Rene Beachamp ~ 31 October, 1879'

What, or who, had *he* seen to frighten him to death?

After assuring Miss Dunne in her office that I was completely recovered, I made excuses to leave. The way out, fortunately, led along the corridor of portraits I had seen earlier – the splendidly oak-panelled Corridor of Alumni. Using idle chit-chat to slow Miss Dunne down, I was able to examine closely the length of the corridor, from floor to ceiling. It wasn't until we reached the very last portrait, that of the college benefactor, that I found what I was searching for, high up, between the panels – the sharp point of my hatpin protruding only inches away from *Old Nick's* portrait.

For the first time, I took notice of his name, inscribed on a brass plate: *Nicolas Flamel.*

In the bottom corner of his portrait was a faded, and very long signature. The name meant nothing to me, but I wrote it down anyway. It was Italian.

Before I left Greenwold, conscious that it no longer mattered if Miss Dunne knew the *real* purpose of my visit or not, I enquired about another of their illusive characters: Betsy Pollock.

'She left, rather abruptly,' Miss Dunne advised. 'Didn't leave a forwarding address.'

'Would you happen to have a record of any other address for her?' I asked, hoping there would be something listed in her old employment records. 'A relative or next of kin, perhaps?'

Miss Dunne promised to search for me and we exchanged telephone numbers.

'And what was the name of the organisation you said were interested in making a donation?' I asked.

'Well, they haven't actually formed it yet, they're seeking other donors for a non-profit company that they'll call *The National Trust.* Sir Robert Hunter was the gentleman who came here. He was frightfully interested.'

On the train back to London, I excitedly summed up my discoveries.

Could there have been a laboratory in the catacombs? Absolutely yes. One area had been completely cleared and there hadn't been time for the spiders to reclaim possession.

Jacob had been telling the truth when he described to the police a panel by the professor's portrait giving access to the catacombs. I had stood on the other side of it.

As to any evidence of the professor's existence, or of his being seen by others, I had to admit defeat. But with ancient rumours of *Old Nick*, and a perfectly fit schoolmaster dying of fright only a few yards from the place Jacob supposedly worked with the professor, I had my suspicions that it was not the professor I should be searching for – but his ghost.

After a restless night I awoke with the realisation that the name Nicolas Flamel *did* mean an awful lot, something no one had mentioned during the trial. Then, they had only referred to the man in the portrait as *the benefactor* of Jacob's old college.

But Nicolas Flamel was also the name of the author of the *encyclopaedia of murder: Alchemy* – written hundreds of years earlier.

Obviously, I had to dig deeper into the background of Greenwold Hall and their mysterious Nicolas Flamel. And where better to start than with Sir Robert Hunter. I was particularly interested to hear what he had found so intriguing in the catacombs.

Chapter 25

Once I had reported to him with my findings, Papa was as eager as I to seek out further information on the professor at Greenwold College. After I had informed him that a Sir Robert Hunter had shown some curiosity with the place, he was delighted to be able to give me a personal introduction as he counted him as one of his few close friends. He telephoned him that evening and arranged an appointment for me the next morning.

'Elizabeth Weston,' I announced to the frock-coated butler in the reception hall, 'Sir Robert Hunter is expecting me.' His huge Georgian house sat in Grosvenor Street, off Park Lane, in the Mayfair district of London.

'So you're the grownup Lizzie,' Sir Robert said as he strode through the hall to greet me, taking both my hands firmly in his. 'You were a babe in arms when I last had the pleasure to meet you, your christening at Westminster.' He laughed loudly. 'Howled your head off!' He was a very tall, slender gentleman, with grey hair and long sideburns that reached almost to his chin. Still holding my hand, Sir Robert led me through the hall to a small library, filled floor-to-ceiling with books of every description on all four walls.

After telling Sir Robert how exciting I thought his new project was, preserving Britain's heritage, I got straight to the point. 'Sir Robert, you were interested in Greenwold Hall, the college.'

'Yes, remarkable place. Would make an ideal first candidate for our new company when it's formed. We've dug up loads of history,' Sir Robert claimed, cheering me up immensely. 'The roof's sagging. And they don't realise how serious the problem is.'

'Is it the rafters? Beetles or something?'

'Not at all,' my host obliged. 'It's the foundations. They're sinking.'

'I went down there,' I said. 'Deep down in the catacombs.'

'And did you notice?'

'Notice?' I asked, intrigued.

'A blank void right in the middle.'

'I did. I thought something was odd but couldn't quite place it.'

'The floor. The flagstone floor.'

'I saw that. But what about it is odd?'

'It's black, and it's dead level.'

'That's it! I remember the walls and columns being quite distorted through age, but the floor as smooth and level as a new stone floor. But not a problem, surely?'

'Well, hold on. Because it *is* a problem. It shouldn't *be* that flat, after five centuries of settling and wear and tear. So I lifted some of the stones and dug down around the steps. The steps go down another four steps, below that floor. The floor's three or four feet higher than originally. The undersides of the flagstones were all white and worn, well-trodden over the centuries – as it should be. The whole floor had been replaced face downwards.'

'Really?' Concealing something, I surmised.

'We found all sorts of acid burns and scars on the underside of some stones. Someone had excavated that whole area, I suspect some years ago. But they only back-filled it recently – very recently – with top soil instead of the old, stiff Northampton clay that held everything together.'

Was this the clue I so badly needed? I thought immediately of the puddled rugby pitch. *Students did the work, working through the night. They were exhausted* – Miss Dunne had said. Yes, exhausted because they were on a secret mission, no doubt, using the soil to cover up any evidence in the catacombs, raising it three feet or so. They had destroyed any evidence of a laboratory ever having been there. This heralded a tremendous breakthrough.

'Disturbing the old clay allowed the foundations to move, causing the roof to sag. They'll have to have the whole lot dug out again and underpin everything.'

'If you take it on, perhaps you'll find the ghosts,' I half joked.

'Ghosts they say? I'll tell you, Lizzie,' he said, 'with that roof sagging, and all the creaking and bumping going on through the night *that* would cause, it would take someone braver than I to sleep there.' He roared with laughter, slapping his knee.

To my pleasant surprise, Sir Robert retrieved his briefcase and pulled out a huge file of papers. 'This is all the history we dug up on the Greenwold estate and its former owner. One of my assistants extracted it all from historic manuscripts at the British Museum. It makes fascinating reading.'

'I'm frightfully interested,' I told him, clawing at the file, 'Would it be possible to borrow this for a day or two?'

'Help yourself. As long I get it back in a couple of weeks. We have a committee meeting. Need to decide if we're going to help them fix the roof. Make it our first official project soon as we get the money together. Tell you what,' he said, with a wide smile on his face, 'why don't you study all this and write a report on the salient points, something that I can use to persuade fellow donors? We'll pay you a fee, of course.'

After declining the fee but accepting an invitation to attend any works should they proceed, I agreed to write his report and took the file, making my excuses to leave.

During the carriage journey home, I was astounded by what I learned. Sir Robert's clerk had amassed a great deal of background information on Greenwold Hall, dating back to well before the seventeenth century and Oliver Cromwell. But, of course, I was only interested in one of its occupiers – Nicolas Flamel. Notes pencilled in the margins of the report proved to be of most interest to me.

Who was this man? – scribbled next to Flamel's name in a section of the report discussing the capture of King Charles I at the hall, caught my attention, and referred to his hand-written appendix where I read:

Flamel, Born in Paris. Little else known.

The item went on to say:

British Museum ~ August 1893:

A thorough search revealed nothing of any gentleman of that name throughout the whole of the seventeenth century. In a French Section we only found a Nicolas Flamel, Born in Paris, 1330, scribe and manuscript-seller, later known for his wealth and philanthropy. His house is still there, at No.52 rue de Montmorency.

He married Perenelle in 1368, said to have been an alchemist. She apparently made him immortal!

In contradiction, Paris manuscripts show he died on 22nd March, 1418, having designed his own tombstone. His remains are interred at the Musee de Cluny in Paris.

With two hundred years separating them, my first thoughts were that this *Parisian* bore little relationship to the Greenwold Hall owner – also thought to be Parisian, according to Miss Dunne – although he may well have been a distant ancestor.

Finding my extensive notes from the trial in my bag, I searched for pieces concerning *Alchemy* – the *encyclopaedia of murder*.

An ancient manuscript ascribed to Leonardo da Vinci, in 1507, referred to in the trial, confirmed *Alchemy* was the work of Perenelle Flamel, and added:

The science is dark – too dark for mere mortals. But alas, it works.

During the trial, like most others hearing this, I had assumed Da Vinci's affirmation was merely confirmation of medieval superstition and sorcery – and publication of such explosive statements did most probably help sell a lot of papers at a time when readers thirst for knowledge was unquenchable.

But here now, right in front of me, was another reason to question the superstition surrounding immortality. In the margin of his report, Sir Robert Hunter's clerk had scribbled:

What if Perenelle's formula worked?

Maybe this IS your man – 553 years old?!

I closed my eyes and, confident the professor was not a figment of Jacob's imagination, tried to reason further.

Was Greenwold's benefactor simply *masquerading* as a Flamel? And to what advantage? Is it just a coincidence that the professor closely resembled Flamel? And if he *were* one and the same, a five-hundred-and-fifty-three-year-old, wouldn't he have boasted to Jacob he was Flamel; proved the formula worked, shown him that he could turn lead into gold? Whoever he was, I was confident our missing nineteenth-century professor could answer a lot of questions. The last line of the clerk's notes on Flamel added further intrigue:

Perenelle Flamel died 29th September, 1397.

Michaelmas Day!

There it was again. That fateful day. Was it a coincidence that the elixir was completed on that same day – almost five hundred years later?

Was it a coincidence that the last ingredient was added, the last girl murdered for her soul – on that same day?

I doubted it. There *had* to be a connection. Most intriguing, indeed.

A disturbing scenario, following a night of nightmares, came to me the next morning before making my way to the British Library:

The alchemist, Perenelle Flamel, had instructed her husband that five essential ingredients, five souls, needed to be added:

Wench, widow and witch; wife and bitch.

I surmised that *she*, whom Da Vinci had said was in poor health, didn't want to be left behind – if her husband was to become immortal. Jacob had said that here was one way of her travelling into eternity with him – by donating her own soul. So, I concluded *hers* was the *wife's* soul referred to.

This meant that she had instructed her husband, Nicolas, to *murder* her – to purge her soul on Michaelmas Day. There was no other explanation.

And then other possible solutions struck me:

Either *Jacob*, in his madness, thought *he* was Nicolas Flamel, and the professor does not exist – the prosecution's case – or:

The professor *does* exist, and in *his* own madness, thought *he* was Nicolas Flamel – or, finally, God forbid:

The professor *does* exist – and *is* Nicolas Flamel. And *is* immortal.

The latter two would confirm Jacob's innocence – but how to prove it, was no easy task. And at that moment, the professor being hundreds of years old seemed absurd. I was determined to learn more about the illusive Monsieur Flamel but had no idea where to start. And with only two days remaining in which to save Jacob from hanging, I feared I would run out of time.

I needed hard evidence, something to convince the police, and arrived at the British Library, where Sir Robert Hunter's clerk had been, to try and locate anything else that may have been recorded about Nicolas Flamel. Fortunately, a great deal had been translated into English and deep within the archives in the French Section I found more interesting facts:

Fourteenth-century Monsieur and Madame Flamel had no issue, no children; and Nicolas, no kin. The name Flamel was therefore buried with them. This convinced me that the man whose portrait hung in Greenwold Hall was *unlikely* to be related to fourteenth-century Flamel – but still left the possibility, albeit impossible-to-believe, that he was one and the same man. And immortal.

I could not stop thinking about the clerk's note:-

Maybe this IS your man – 553 years old?!

At the trial, Dr Jensen from Apothecaries Hall spoke of the formulae in *Alchemy* as being viable. Admitting so, had caused him to faint. And he was a learned man. Had he fainted because he had disclosed an age-old secret? Was he afraid immortals would track him down, do him harm?

Maybe this IS your man – 553 years old?!

And then I found something startling: a copy of a drawing of Nicolas Flamel from 1400. It was held by a museum in Paris.

The resemblance and similarities were extraordinary.

The Victoria & Albert Museum in Kensington was my next port of call, where I had an appointment with a Mr Hardcastle, a curator and art expert.

'I have found a work signed: *Andrea di Michele di Francesco de' Cioni*,' I told him, reading the signature I had copied off the Nicolas Flamel portrait.

'*Really?*' Mr Hardcastle exclaimed.

'You've heard of him, then?'

'Well, who hasn't?' he laughed.

'But it's not a name like *Leonardo da Vinci*, is it? Everybody knows him.'

'Thanks to Andrea di Michele di Francesco de' Cioni,' he said.

'I'm sorry, I don't understand.'

'Signor de'Cioni *taught* da Vinci. If you have found such a work it would be priceless. He was born de'Cioni but when he became popular, and famous, he was known as *Andre del Verrocchio*, or simply: *Verrocchio*. It means: *of the true eye*. If your work bore his full name, it was painted well before he became famous. Worth an absolute fortune.'

'Enough to buy a new roof?' I asked him.

'A roof to cover half of London, I would think,' he laughed.

'So when might it have been painted?' I asked, intrigued.

'Before da Vinci. Verrocchio was born in 1435. Died in 1488.'

'He died in 1488?' I exclaimed. 'But the sitter is said to be seventeenth century.'

'Impossible, I'm afraid. If it *is* an early Verrocchio piece, take my word for it, second-half, fifteenth century. No later. Can I see it?'

'I'll make arrangements,' I promised him, and couldn't get out of there fast enough.

There was now no doubt in my mind.

Perenelle's formula in *Alchemy* had worked.

Five souls had been added to the elixir, including hers on Michaelmas Day, 1397, and Nicolas Flamel had consumed it.

The professor *was* Nicolas Flamel – and *IS* immortal.

The only question remaining was: *why* did he need more elixir?

'I'm onto something,' I told Mr Ecclestone on the telephone that evening, having explained what I had found. 'Can you force a recess, tell them you have found new evidence?'

'But we haven't found new evidence, have we – yet?' Mr Ecclestone replied on the crackling line. 'You may be onto something, but until you can stand the man in front of me, it all simply strengthens the prosecution's case; that Flamel was there in Jacob's head. Nowhere else. No one will accept your say-so that–'

'I know you'll think I'm a lunatic but I am convinced our professor *is immortal!*' I almost shouted. 'I just need more time to prove it. There's proof of his existence fifty years or so *after* his reported death in 1418, and over two hundred years later than that. Won't that be enough to convince the jury he may *still* be alive and well today? Cast a shadow of doubt? It all makes perfect sense.'

'Miss Weston, I shall finish what defence we have tomorrow afternoon. But they won't hang Mr Silver quite yet, even if he is found guilty. We might consider presenting any further evidence, if you obtain such, on appeal. But it needs to be something substantial, something solid. Find your professor. It's the only way.'

'Or someone to confirm his existence. Betsy Pollock,' I offered.

'Yes. She'll do. Whichever one, just get them here as quick as you can. We're running out of time.'

No sooner had I replaced the receiver, the telephone rang again. It was Miss Dunne, from Greenwold.

'I retrieved some old employment records and can tell you that Miss Elizabeth Pollock, whom we called *Betsy*, joined us in 1874, having been a nursing sister at the Small Pox and Vaccination Hospital in Islington.'

'Do you have her previous address, or next of kin, Miss Dunne?' I asked.

'Her next of kin were shown as her mother and a younger sister, Mary Pollock, from her given address: Haigh Lodge, Swain's Lane, Highgate, in London.'

The next morning, Papa being out until late, Giles and William, our tall and strong coachman and footman, drove me to Highgate, only five miles or so from my home. I was determined to get a confession from Betsy Pollock, one way or another.

Upon arrival, we found Swain's Lane had a high stone wall along its entire length, on one side, and modest houses with mature tree-lined gardens on the other. It would be a little while later when I would discover the purpose of that wall.

Dilapidated Haigh House sat in the shadow of the wall. From the grime and dirt hanging off the windows I feared it was empty. Giles knocked at the door. He was returning to the carriage when suddenly, behind him, the front door creaked open. A plumpish lady of about fifty or so, stood at the door in a dirty white pinafore.

Was this Betsy, I wondered?

'Milady would like a word, madam,' Giles told her as I made my way past overgrown shrubs up the garden path towards her.

'Would you happen to be Miss Pollock? Elizabeth Pollock?' I asked her. She eyed me suspiciously before shaking her head. 'You must be Mary. I'm Elizabeth Weston. I'm looking for Elizabeth.'

'She's gone.' A tear welled in her eye and she caught it with a corner of her pinafore.

'Gone?' I asked. 'Gone away, you mean?'

'She's over there,' the lady said, pointing across to the high wall. 'Can take you to her, if you like.'

Convinced Betsy Pollock existed, here was her sister offering me a personal introduction. My pulse quickened. We had just enough time to get her to the court. 'We can go in my carriage, if you prefer,' I told her as she slammed the door to the house behind her and took off her pinafore. Giles and William seemed eager to get started.

'No need,' she said, and strode off across the road. 'Follow me.'

I bade Giles and William wait with the carriage as I followed her on foot. A few yards from her house, an ornamental gatehouse appeared in the high wall. It was only then that I recognised what was protected behind the wall – 'Highgate Cemetery' a sign read. Mama was buried here recently. We had always arrived from the other end of that street.

I felt my heart falter.

Acknowledging the attendants at the gate, Mary Pollock led me along the pathways, between a plethora of headstones and mausoleums until we came to a less prestigious area where small plots lined the path. She stopped in front of a new headstone and bent down to adjust flowers in a vase.

'Elizabeth Pollock ~ Died 29th September, 1894. Sadly missed' – the stone revealed.

Betsy had died just over three months ago, on Michaelmas Day! And I felt every chance of saving Jacob had died with her. Looking over to where Mama was buried, I was heartbroken.

I had established that Betsy Pollock existed – but anything we might have learned from her had now turned to dust. Her sister, Mary, said she died suddenly on Michaelmas Day and the doctor attributed her death to heart failure – due to extreme overweight.

Mary had no knowledge of a Mr Jacob Silver, when I asked. Leaving her with my telephone number, in the hope that she might recall something later, however slight, I left that house certain that Jacob would hang.

The Trial: Day 10

I informed Mr Ecclestone of Betsy Pollock's demise the following morning before the court opened, and he in turn informed me that the art gallery owner, Mr St Clair, had still not shown up. He was still the only witness who could testify as to the professor's existence. I duly took my seat in the public gallery, hoping against all the odds that Jacob would be proved innocent by the end of the day.

Mr Ecclestone called his next witness.

'Sergeant Joseph Phillips, Metropolitan Police stationed at Charing Cross,' the uniformed officer announced after taking the oath. A mountain of a man, with a comically huge moustache, he towered above the witness box.

'Sergeant Phillips, were you involved with the accused, Jacob Silver, in the summer of 1888, when he was quarantined in his home at Victoria Embankment?'

'Yes, sir, I was a constable at the time. Jacob Silver had been in close proximity to an outbreak of plague.' The officer drew out an old notebook and referred to it. 'He was quarantined inside his home with a Miss Polly Daniels and a Nell Daniels, an eight-year-old child.'

It was commendable Mr Ecclestone had managed to trace him.

'And from your notes taken at the time, can you confirm the dates that Mr Silver was quarantined?'

He flicked through the pages. 'It began on the eighth of April and ended four months later, on the ninth of August, 1888.'

'Can you be sure the accused remained inside the premises?'

'Oh yes, sir. The doors to the front and rear, as well as the lower floor windows, were sealed by me, personally. Food and provisions were delivered by a small side window, too small for anyone to climb through.'

'Did the accused make any excuse to leave, during this four-month period?'

'No, sir.' The sergeant smiled. 'With Miss Daniels' company, I'm sure he was quite comfortable enough where he was.' A titter rose from the gallery.

'No further questions, m'lud,' announced Mr Ecclestone, taking a seat.

Mr Ponsonby leapt to his feet. 'Sergeant, were you aware of a third exit to those premises?'

The witness looked perplexed. 'Er, no, sir.'

'One to the river, via the basement?'

'To the Thames? No, sir, I was not.'

'So, unbeknownst to you, Mr Silver could have used this third exit at his leisure, is that correct?'

'Well, I suppose so, but he gave his word—'

'He could have used it, yes or no?'

'Yes, sir. He could.'

'No more questions, my lord.'

'The witness is excused,' said the judge, after checking with Mr Ecclestone.

The importance of the officer's evidence was obvious: if Jacob was in quarantine those four months, how could he have been responsible for desecrating Emily's grave? I thought the jury would rightly give Mr Ponsonby's suggestion of Jacob swimming in and out of the river access, presumably with a head in a bag, short shrift. Further, if Jacob did *not* take her head, then somebody else certainly did – and presented it to him, claiming Emily was still alive. That can only have been Betsy Pollock. But that lady was now dead.

Mr Ecclestone took out his silver pocket-watch, before calling his next witness. He was running out of time. I presumed Mr St Clair had yet to arrive.

'Mrs Agnes Levy, laundry assistant,' she announced, her hair wrapped in a drab kerchief.

'Mrs Levy you live in the Blackfriars district of London?'

'Yes.'

'And did you frequent the apothecary's shop at Number 72, Victoria Embankment from time to time over the last two years or so?'

'When it was open, yes.'

'And who would serve you there on those occasions?'

'The fat woman. Betsy she calls herself. She was usually the only one on duty. Occasionally the guv'nor, 'im over there, would be about, but it was mostly Betsy doin' the servin'.'

'Were you aware that Mr Silver, er, 'im over there, had a mistress living with him?'

'Betsy kept saying we would meet her one day, when she was

better. She was 'sposed to be poorly.'

'You are absolutely sure a lady named *Betsy* was employed in the shop and she spoke of a mistress in the house?'

'Certain of it. I was a customer for years. Of young Mr Silver and his father before him.'

'Do you recall the mistress' name, by any chance?'

'No, sorry,' she said, scratching her head under the kerchief. 'Wait a minute...' she looked skyward. 'No. It'll probably come to me, sooner or later.'

'Wait there, will you, Mrs Levy,' and to his lordship Mr Ecclestone said, 'No more questions, m'lud.'

Mr Ponsonby jumped to his feet like a hound after a hare. 'Mrs Levy, you only came forward a week ago, is that correct?'

'Yes, after a bloke came knocking on our doors.'

'A bloke?'

'Said he was a solicitor.'

'And you told him your story?'

'That's right.'

'Do you read the newspapers, madam?'

'Sometimes, yeah. Not the fancy ones, mind.'

'And have you been following this trial?'

'Hard not to, with all those headlines.'

'Were you paid for your splendid efforts?'

'Paid? What d'you mean by that?'

'Paid to tell a good story?'

'My lord!' yelled Mr Ecclestone, leaping to his feet. 'If the prosecution continue in this vein I will be obliged to reveal some of the more dubious facts about some of *his* witnesses' careers.'

'My lord,' interrupted Mr Ponsonby, 'it was a simple enough question? I'll settle for a yes or no.'

The judge addressed the witness. 'You were approached by a solicitor, madam. Did he offer any incentive for you to provide information?'

'No, your lordship, he didn't. And I resent that kind of remark coming from *him*,' Mrs Levy added, referring to Mr Ponsonby. 'Oh, an' it's just come to me. I remember now, your lordship, 'er name was Emily. The mistress? It was Emily.'

'No more questions, m'lud,' Mr Ponsonby offered, quietly sitting down, having failed entirely to discredit the witness.

It was approaching noon after Mr Ecclestone had called three more former customers of the shop who all swore that they were served there by a *rather large* woman they knew as *Betsy*. Although he tried, Mr Ponsonby was unable to find fault with any of their testimonies.

If Betsy *existed*, then the psychiatrist had been proved wrong; the jury could be persuaded he was wrong about the professor, too. And wrong about Jacob taking Emily's head. That was Mr Ecclestone's plan of attack. Further, a witness stated Betsy described Emily's condition, proving that Betsy was involved in the deception of Emily being alive. As I saw it, Mr Ecclestone was close to destroying all the prosecution's claims – with or without the help of the art gallery owner.

The evidence of the shop customers seemed to cheer Jacob. Overnight, I had written him a short letter explaining my recovery and that I was alive and well and thinking of him, sitting up in the public gallery. I got the note to Mr Ecclestone that morning. I continually stared over to the dock, hoping to catch Jacob's eye, but he was concentrating on the witness box.

'I call my next witness, Mr Jean-Louis St Clair, m'lud.'

An usher opened a door and called his name – and I saw Jacob smile. But the witness was nowhere to be seen. The judge looked down at Mr Ecclestone implying that he need do something.

'Er, could we try just once more, m'lud?'

'Mr Jean-Louis St Clair,' the usher called out again, but to no avail.

Mr Ecclestone appeared to panic, turning to his juniors behind him and causing one of them to rush outside, no doubt to find the illusive Mr St Clair and drag him into the courtroom.

'Might I suggest this is a good time for a recess, m'lud?' Mr Ecclestone enquired, but the judge had a different view.

'No. It is not. Find your witness or carry on with the next, Mr Ecclestone,' the judge insisted, twiddling his thumbs.

'Er, m'lud, his evidence is vital to my client's defence.' Turning over various papers and consulting those behind him, yet again, Mr Ecclestone knew he could delay no further. 'Might I ask that Mr St Clair's evidence, the statement he made to the police, be read to the court, m'lud?'

The judge turned to the prosecutor, 'Mr Ponsonby?'

Mr Ponsonby could barely contain his amusement at the defence's dilemma. 'Certainly not, m'lud. This is a witness I need to cross-examine. There is hardly a line in his statement I agree with.'

I was sure he was exaggerating, making the most of it. The usher returned from the corridor without the witness and closed the door behind him, shaking his head to the judge.

'If that is it, Mr Ecclestone, then so be it. Your witness has not bothered to turn up. What do you propose to do now?' the judge asked, leaning back in his chair.

Mr Ecclestone hesitated and looked over to Jacob, then up to me, his palms outstretched implying: *What more could I do?*

'That concludes the case for the defence, m'lud,' he said solemnly and sat down.

Mr Ponsonby had a wide grin on his face.

'Very well,' said the judge. 'We will adjourn until tomorrow morning at ten, when the prosecution will begin summing up.'

'All stand!' called an usher, and everybody bowed as the judge left the courtroom.

'Where is he?' Jacob shouted from the dock. 'Where is that scoundrel from the gallery?' he called over his shoulder, as two jailers fought to lead him away.

I almost collided with the enrobed Mr Ecclestone as he dashed from the courtroom.

'I'm sorry, Miss Weston. But there was nothing else I could do,' he pleaded.

'What if I can find Mr St Clair before ten tomorrow? Would they allow his evidence.'

'We could try. It would not be a precedent.'

'Then I'll go now and try to track him down,' I told him, making my way out to the street.

Giles, my footman, pushed his way through a small noisy crowd gathered around my carriage and we immediately set off to the Strand, only a short distance away.

When I arrived the front door to the art gallery was ajar. I asked Giles to accompany me inside, calling out for Mr St Clair. But there was no reply. No one was there. Hundreds of valuable paintings adorned the walls, the front door open and yet no one was in attendance. I found the office door and knocked. Not receiving any response, I turned the handle. It was locked.

Giles asked me to stand back and leapt at the door, kicking it open.

We entered and found a man, later identified as Mr St Clair, stretched out on the couch.

The fool must have dozed off, I decided, and went over to shake him. I moved his arm. That was when I realised he would not be coming to Jacob's rescue – he was dead.

I had no recollection of the next half hour until regaining

consciousness in my carriage. By this time the art gallery was swarming with police and a detective inspector came to speak to me.

I ensured that the inspector was fully aware of the importance of the gallery owner's death – the removal of an important witness in a murder trial. I begged that he urgently inform the court, hopefully to delay the trial.

But it was all of no use. Mr Ecclestone explained that the art gallery owner's death was a separate matter, a new investigation. Only if it could later be proved the professor had killed an important witness in Jacob's trial, could the two matters be connected – and an appeal could end in Jacob's release.

The summing up began the following morning in my absence, and the jury would have to rely on what they had heard thus far before making a decision.

Meanwhile, the police established that Mr St Clair had died through suffocation and, after a post mortem, the cause was found – a number of gold Spanish doubloons were stuck in his gullet.

The Trial: Verdict

Shaken and nervous after my discovery at the art gallery, I decided I was not ready to attend the court again and missed the next day's proceedings. I arrived the following day, later than I expected. I was advised by an usher that the judge's summing up had been completed a while before and the jury had just returned, having been out for two hours. I took my seat in the gallery just in time to hear:

'And are these the verdicts of you all?' the Clerk to the Court asked the jury foreman.

Clutching a folded cloth cap, the foreman looked nervously over to Jacob Silver. His croaking voice was barely audible as he nodded his head.

'Speak up,' demanded the clerk.

'Yes,' said the foreman, blinking rapidly and looking like he was eager to get the business over and done with.

'And do you find the accused, Jacob Silver, guilty or not guilty of the murder of Polly Daniels?'

The foreman hesitated. A deathly hush urged he say the words. He stared about him then back at Jacob, as if to plead for forgiveness before blurting out:

'Guilty.'

I gasped, along with all those around me. Prosecutor Mr Ponsonby turned to face everybody up in the public gallery, a broad smile on his face.

'As to the second charge, the murder of Letty Norton, how do you find – guilty or not guilty?'

'Guilty,' the foreman announced more confidently.

And so it was on counts three and four – the murders of poor Nora Perkins and Rebecca Muxlow. Four counts of murder. Guilty as charged.

I was sickened to the core.

Old Mrs Muxlow, seated in the back of the courtroom below me, alongside other witnesses, smiled a twisted smile before dabbing her eyes.

'*I'm innocent!*' screamed Jacob from the dock.

In response the gallery broke into loud cheers, laughter and applause. Mr Ponsonby stood and took a bow to everybody's amusement.

'We're not finished yet, Mr Ponsonby, if you please,' the judge said angrily.

'For the murder of Police Constable Albert Everett, how do you find? Guilty or not guilty?'

'Guilty,' said the foreman.

'And on the count of robbing the grave of Emily Muxlow, how do you find?' the clerk said.

'Not guilty.'

'Take the prisoner down,' ordered the judge. 'I will pronounce sentence tomorrow at noon.' Turning to the jury, he added, 'Members of the jury this has been a particularly horrendous case and in the circumstances I am ordering that you not be recalled for jury duty for at least another ten years. You are now free to go.'

The members of the jury congratulated themselves and stepped down from the jury box as Jacob made one final taunt:

'*You'll go to hell, the lot of you!*'

Although Papa had warned me to expect the worst, my belief in Jacob's innocence had me hoping the jury would believe his story to the very end, so sure was I of the professor's guilt.

And I was still as sure.

The professor had led this innocent scholar to find the solution to an ancient potion – the promise of eternal life. In wickedly manipulating his eager student into unwittingly bringing him these women to extract their souls, he had only to remove evidence of his own existence to have committed murder.

Perfect murder.

And he was free to go and do it again. I was sure he also had something to do with Miss Pollock's death on that fateful day – removing the only living witness to his crimes. Full of hope of winning an appeal, I had no idea then that these points would be impossible to prove.

As Jacob was dragged down and the public gallery cleared, I leaned over the rail and wept, vowing to prove his innocence.

The following day, although I arrived well before noon, my reserved seat in the gallery was occupied by a scruffy thug with whom I was in no state to argue. I summoned the attendant who had so graciously accepted my bribes for the duration of the trial but he said he could do nothing.

'Trial of the century,' he declared. 'First come, first served.'

The gallery was packed to capacity. The best view I could gain was from standing at the back and I was just in time to catch a glimpse of the judge with a black square of silk over his head, and hear those words that I dreaded most:

'. . . that you be taken hence to a place of lawful execution and you there be hanged by the neck . . .'

Chapter 26

'Now, remember. You promised you would be on your best behaviour,' Papa reminded me as the huge gates were opened and our carriage was waved through by the guardsmen in their crimson tunics and bearskin hats. 'None of this nonsense about innocence and perfect murders. Her Majesty will not hear of it. Leave all the talking to me. Your job is to just sit there looking pretty. You understand?'

'Yes, Papa.' But I knew that if Her Majesty would just listen for a moment or two, she would delay any execution before a full investigation of Nicolas Flamel had been undertaken – and perhaps demand a retrial. Whether she could or not, I had no idea. I decided to bide my time and take control of negotiations at the first opportunity. Unfortunately, I had uncovered no more evidence to support my assumption of the professor's immortality but with Papa's offer to help, and the Queen's unlimited resources, I imagined anything was possible.

A balding personal private secretary bowed and shook hands with Papa, like they were old friends. 'Robert, how nice to see you again. And this is…?' he queried, obviously not expecting other guests.

'My daughter, Lizzie.' I curtsied. He smiled. 'Her Majesty suggested bring her along, she hasn't seen her since she was a baby,' Papa said.

'Excellent, excellent. Now, I've managed to fit you in for seven minutes between the Prime Minister and an Indian Maharaja.'

'Seven minutes? But this is about a man's life. I would hope any life is worth more than seven minutes.'

'Her Majesty's schedule is extremely tight, Robert. If she likes what she's hearing you'll find time is of no object. She won't mind keeping anyone waiting provided she is being, shall I say, *entertained?*' Papa smiled at me. 'Excellent, excellent,' said the secretary as he led the way through the splendour that was Buckingham Palace. 'We're in the Green Room.'

Her Majesty was seated at an ornate writing bureau as we entered, wearing a wonderful black satin dress with a sparkling diamond necklace. She looked radiant and stood to greet us, the effort appearing to give the elderly monarch some pain.

'Bobby, oh do come in, it's been so long and...' after giving me a delightful smile, 'this is your dear Lizzie. My, how you have grown, my child.' I curtsied deeply but she was having none of that. She took my hand and led me over to a table laden with portraits of her extended family. 'Goodness, surely we can find someone here who would adore such a sweet gel?'

Papa laughed, bowing respectfully. 'An honour, Your Majesty.'

Pointing at various photographic portraits, Her Majesty commanded I stare at them until I was confident I had found the right man, after which she would order him back from wherever he was in the world to come and sweep me off my feet. I was flattered.

'But Bobby, what is it that is so urgent?' she said, as she took a place on the sofa, patting it for him to sit beside her.

I was so proud of Papa at that moment as he presented his case, knowing it was what I had desired.

'Ma'am, it's this boy...'

In Pentonville Prison, two legs in grey-flannel trousers dragged to the centre of a windowless room. A pair of polished boots either side ensured the legs shuffled onto a cross chalked onto the bare-boarded floor. A padre said prayers.

'They're going to hang him, any minute, Ma'am. We must stop it!' Papa explained.

I noticed a newspaper headline over on the bureau: '*Silver Hangs Today*'.

'Ah, the alchemist. Such imagination! Eternal life,' the Queen said. She threw her hands up to the ceiling, in praise, 'If only!'

'But I know so much more about him now. We really can't afford to lose the boy, Ma'am,' Papa urged, pulling out a sheath of letters. 'These pleas are from notable scientists begging your majesty to intervene. Monsieur Simond of the Pasteur Institute says: "The solution to plague is close, thanks to Jacob Silver"; Alexandre Yersin: "Jacob Silver saved us ten years in understanding diphtheria"; Marie Curie, Ma'am: "Mr Silver's knowledge of radioactivity and X-rays was far in advance of my own theories." '

He flicked through more letters. 'The list goes on and on, Ma'am. They beg you—'

'Enough!' the Queen commanded, raising her hand. 'I hear you.' She stood and went over to a portrait of Queen Elizabeth I, hanging on the green satin wall amid a dozen other portraits of her ancestors. Papa stood beside her, resplendent in his high collar and tails.

'*She* was rumoured to have had her own alchemist, you know. Turned lead into gold. Heaven knows what she did with it all.'

Papa followed her back to the sofa and offered her his hand as she sat down. 'I *could* stop it, Bobby. But there'd be a public outrage. Could do without a revolution this time in my life, thank you very much. Mind, if there were a solution...' A footman knocked, entered and bowed, then led in a maid with a silver tray. 'You'll stay for tea?'

' 'Fraid not, Ma'am,' Papa said, taking my hand and bowing quickly. 'I need to hurry. We may already be too late. If you'll excuse us, Your Majesty?'

'*No revolution, Bobby. I implore you!*' Her Majesty called out as we left.

A noose passed over Jacob's head, the knot slid tight to the back of his neck.

'*I'M INNOCENT, I TELL YOU! You'll rot in hell, the lot of you!*' he cried out before cotton wool was stuffed into his mouth.

A bag was pulled over his head. No more talk. No more delays. The job had to be done.

His whole body trembled.

A puddle of urine formed at his feet.

BANG!

The trapdoor.

Jacob's body plummeted ten feet.

The taught rope quivered.

The padre and hangman looked skyward and begged forgiveness for what they had done.

After some moments, the rope snaked down the hatch and lay on the body.

The trapdoor closed back up on a genius dispatched.

Outside the prison, an officer pinned a notice to a board. The deed was done.

A mob cheered. Family hugged aggrieved mothers.

Lizzie Weston watched the elderly Mrs Muxlow sitting alone in her carriage under her black veil, her face betraying just one emotion:

Vengeance at last.

As the sun set, a plain wooden box was lowered into a hole. A stick with a painted name appealed for some higher authority to come for the soul of one: *'Jacob Silver ~ Murderer'.*

Lizzie Weston arrived home that afternoon heartbroken. Her father had tried, tried harder than most would dare. But he had failed to save the man she loved, he told her.

'You must now forget this man, Lizzie. Live your own life to the full. He was not right for you, and now justice has been served you need to accept things the way they are. He has gone, and will never return. Don't waste away your life mourning someone who didn't deserve you. I beg you. Life is too short,' he said solemnly.

But Lizzie wanted to mourn – and mourn alone.

She shut herself in her room.

There was a knock at the door.

'Telephone call for you, ma'am,' Millie, her maid said, popping her head inside the door.

Lizzie went downstairs to take the call.

'Miss Weston? Lizzie Weston?' the caller asked.

'Yes,' she said, 'this is Miss Weston. Who is this, may I ask?'

'My name's Pollock, Elizabeth Pollock. They call me Betsy. You came and saw my sister, asking about my mother. I wondered what it was about.'

Chapter 27

'This one, m'lady,' said the ruffian carrying the lantern. 'The soil's packed down 'ard, I tell yer.'

'You brought shovels?' she asked. They had. 'Then please dig. We need to hurry.'

Lizzie Weston waited nervously as the three men shovelled away at her beloved's grave in the darkness. It would cost her dearly for their services, but she would pay eagerly.

While they dug she kept watch over her shoulder, anxious they be discovered, all the while her mind in turmoil over what Betsy had told her.

When Betsy telephoned and Lizzie explained that the purpose of her enquiry was Jacob Silver, Betsy became frightened and disconnected the call. Undeterred, Lizzie had travelled to Highgate, arriving late at night. Her coachman forced Betsy to let Lizzie in. Betsy confessed everything: how she had helped the professor in addicting Jacob to convince him Emily was alive; how she had cleared up the bloodied remains after the professor murdered Jacob's models.

Asked why she had left Jacob to be arrested and stand trial, Betsy replied: 'The professor threatened to kill me and my sister, if I didn't go along with it.'

'And now Jacob is dead. They've hung an innocent man,' Lizzie groaned. 'The professor got away with murder.'

'Yes, but no harm'll come to Jacob, the professor told me,' Betsy said, taking Lizzie's hand between her dimpled fingers, 'You see, the professor needed to prove the elixir worked. If it did, he would use it to resurrect someone special, he said.'

'And who was this *someone special*?' Lizzie asked her. 'Who was so important that had him murder all those poor women?'

'His wife,' she said. 'He missed her so. It'd been a long time, he said. So Master Jacob was fed the elixir. "His last examination," the professor said. "A test. If he got it right, no harm'll ever come to him." ' She squeezed Lizzie's hands and stared into her eyes. 'I tell you, duck, he wouldn't've suffered none. He'll be as right as rain. The professor said: "They might *think* they've killed him when they dangle him on the end of a rope, but he's immortal." He'll be back, don't you worry, deary.'

They had been digging for an hour when a cheap pine coffin lid was revealed in the glow from the lantern.

'Let me,' the fattest of the three cried, shocking them as he slithered down into the hole.

He smote the thin coffin lid with a shovel, splitting it from end to end. He struck again, splintering a gaping hole in the top. He reached through into the hole and yanked back half the lid at the head end, shuddering at the blackness revealed inside and averting his eyes. He reached for the lantern and crossed himself, his lips moving in quiet prayer. Squeezing his eyes shut, he raised his head and made no attempt to peer inside.

Lizzie gasped.

Her knees quivered at the edge of the grave.

The two diggers held onto her, lest she fall in.

'We're finished,' she said. 'Cover it back up.'

Opening his eyes again, the fat man quickly replaced the broken lid and the three of them shovelled earth back over the coffin.

Back at the hole in the fence, Lizzie thanked them, paid them handsomely, conditional on their silence, and bade them farewell.

'Nobody need know we were ever here, you understand?' They grunted happily and dissolved into the blackness.

'Did you look, Bert?' one of the diggers asked the fat man.

'What? And be struck by lightnin'?' Lizzie heard him reply.

She found her carriage and, after donating her muddied outer clothing to a passing beggar, began the journey home.

Lizzie considered how she might broach the subject with her father, having convinced him earlier that she had taken his advice and forgotten Jacob Silver. But regardless of his sentiments, she was adamant that what she had done this night had to be done – after Betsy Pollock had told her story.

Invading the prison graveyard would be difficult enough to explain, but what she discovered there would certainly prove harder.

But for some bags of sand, the coffin of *Jacob Silver ~ Murderer*, was empty.

The M'Naughten Rule – 1843

The *right-wrong* test

"Every man is to be presumed to be sane, and ... that to establish a defence on the ground of insanity, it must be clearly proved that, at the time of the committing of the act, the party accused was labouring under such a defect of reason, from disease of mind, and not to know the nature and quality of the act he was doing; or if he did know it, that he did not know he was doing what was wrong."

(Queen v. M'Naghten, 8 Eng. Rep. 718 [1843])

ABOUT THE AUTHOR

Chris James was a murder squad detective in the UK and has studied criminology most of his adult life.

He currently lives in Mallorca, in the Mediterranean where it is rumoured he is 297 years old.

Also by Chris James
ALCHEMY – turning Silver to Gold – the sequel

Screenplays:

CLASSIFIED: Viper
Miracle Cures
Honey
Doing Time
Tottenham Rules
Alchemy
Adolf's Queen of Queens
Find My Perfect Hag

If you enjoyed reading *Alchemy*, it would mean so much to the author if you left a short review. Simply go to the book's page on Amazon and you'll find a place to leave one, here:

http://www.amazon.com/Alchemy-historical-psychological-suspense-thriller-ebook/product-reviews/B00TOEHXK8

Follow the progress of Alchemy and message the author on Facebook at:

https://www.facebook.com/pages/Alchemy-a-story-of-perfect-murder/1549475088638310?fref=ts

Printed in Great Britain
by Amazon.co.uk, Ltd.,
Marston Gate.